For my wife and my children.

Without the support and inspiration of each of you,
I would never have been able to complete this.

Chapter 1

9th March 1527

An Invitation

The early morning dew hung still heavy in the air as a figure, cloaked against the dawn chill, moved silently through the streets of London. Only nodding to acknowledge the greetings of those few others who had business so early in the morning, the man pulled his cloak tighter as he turned the corner into the street that he sought to be met by a stiff gust of icy wind. Momentarily, he felt that some heavenly force warded him away from his destination. The unusual manner of his summoning and the time at which it had led him to be standing at this unfamiliar corner stirred a notion that the wind nudged him back to save him from what awaited a short distance down this dim road.

Shaking the thought from his sleepy mind, the man stole himself against the chill and moved towards the address to which he had been called regarding a very particular commission. Having made enquiries, it had not been difficult to discover that the gentleman who requested, very specifically, his attendance was not without means and held some favour at the court of King Henry VIII. It was the patronage that this work may carry that had led to his compliance with the somewhat odd request. Odd even by the standard of the odd requests to which he was used.

Checking the address that he clutched in his numbing fingers, the man confirmed that he was indeed in the correct place before knocking uncertainly at the large, intricately engraved front door. After a brief moment, just long enough for the thought of leaving to flash across his mind, the door was opened by a young man who was fully dressed and groomed, obviously in expectation of a visitor.

"I am come to an appointment with Sir Thomas More." The accent immediately marked him as continental, and the young man nodded, opened the door more fully and beckoned the visitor in. Grateful to get out of the cold, the cloaked figure stepped over the threshold and fumbled to loosen his thick cloak with his cold fingers, eventually passing it to the waiting doorman. He shuffled his feet slightly on the reeds covering the floor to dry the damp from his boots. The younger man took the cloak over his left arm, and gestured with his right towards a closed door.

Pointing at the door, the visitor received the silent confirmation he sought. For a reason he could not place, he felt too awkward to break the silence that had developed. Instead he moved to the door and gently pushed it open. As it slowly swung, the door revealed the contents of the room beyond. The first wall, to his left, marked the room as a library of sorts, being filled from floor to ceiling with row upon row of books. The far wall boasted a fine stained glass window from the ceiling half way down the wall, below which rested a large, dark wood desk, partially obscured by piles of papers and opened books. Finally, as the door opened to its full width, the wall to the right glowed with an immense fire that burned below an ornate mantel piece. In front of the fire stood three plain red armchairs, two with their backs to the door and one facing him. The room confirmed the rumours of the wealth of his newest patron.

"Master Holbein, I presume?" The voice was deep and full of authority and as the figure rose from the chair, the silhouette it cut before the fire matched the voice. The frame was broad, made broader by the fine clothes that increased the size of the man before him. The visitor was unable to make out the face of his host, shadowed as it was by the flames behind it. "Please, come and sit." The shape gestured to the chair that stood facing the guest.

"Thank you, sir." Moving as he spoke, somewhat nervously, Hans Holbein sat in the large armchair before the welcoming fire.

"Good, good." Sir Thomas commented, retaking his own seat. Only now could Hans make out the facial features of his host as he turned and met his gaze. The face was broad yet the features were soft and the stare held a forced sternness that hid deep compassion, Hans thought for a short moment as an uneasy silence threatened to settle between the two men.

"Is the fire not a beautiful mystery, Master Holbein?" Sir Thomas offered, apparently deep in thought, though actually he sought in his mind for a suitable beginning to the tale he wished to tell his visitor.

"Indeed it is," Hans consented, "and its warmth is most welcome this cold morn." Holbein was unsure as to the direction his host intended this conversation to take, but was convivial, particularly in light of the commission he was hoping to secure.

"Each morning a carefully constructed fire is laid upon this hearth. Each length of wood is perfectly laid to allow the movement of air around the fire and to support the structure that will be built upon it. The foundations are set and, layer by layer, it takes shape until deemed complete. Shortly after, another will come to this fireplace and set alight the work of the first. Then the flame consumes all." There was a long pause, but Thomas More did not remove his gaze from the grate.

"The outer layer of the fuel is removed almost immediately, seared away by the sudden, raging heat. It is over time, by persistence, though, that the wood is utterly destroyed to feed the hunger of the fire, which only wanes when all of the goodness, all of the life is burned from that which fed it. At the end, only a pile of ashes remain, lifeless and without any further use. Then, they are swept away and disposed of." Sir Thomas sighed deeply, almost as if in sympathy for the remnants of his study fire. He looked up at last from the spot that had held him mesmerised and was confronted by the unconcealed confusion on the face of his guest.

"My point, sir, is this," Sir Thomas continued, his tone suddenly becoming more stern, perhaps as a defensive reaction to the accusing gaze that fixed him, "how did the foundation of this fire begin? How were the first logs laid? How was the construction of each layer affected by that foundation, and the layer it was placed upon? What made it finished? Is the fire devouring dead, dried kindling wood, or my finest furniture?"

There was a moment of silence as Hans struggled to decide whether the question was a rhetorical one or whether his host awaited a reply. Searching the face of Sir Thomas for an indication, Holbein was eventually forced to shrug his shoulders.

"Exactly!" Sir Thomas exclaimed, obviously pleased that his point was progressing. "You and I shall never know. Shortly after the fire had been lit, perhaps we could have seen hints of what lay within, but the longer the flames eat the less we may discern. From the black pile of ashes, who may ever ascertain their previous form? The proud structure so carefully constructed is lost. It no longer matters. It can be discarded. I could tell you it was once anything I fancied." Sir Thomas appeared once again captured by the dancing flames and Hans Holbein sat in the uncomfortable silence until he shifted noisily in his chair and broke the spell of the fire.

"I apologise, Master Holbein. All this must seem to you as the vain wanderings of a man who has procured your presence. It is perhaps, a precursor to our business. But I have been rude in my ramblings. Would you care for any food or drink?"

"No thank you, sir." Hans was now utterly bewildered. "I must confess to great intrigue at the need for such a secret visit at this early hour, sir. I was led to believe that this would be a commission for a family portrait."

"And so it is, Master Holbein, so it is." Sir Thomas stood and strode to the large desk at the end of the room behind Hans. "I must apologise," he continued as he searched through the papers on the table, "for the lengths to which I have gone to keep our meeting free from the ears of others." Obviously finding what he wanted, Sir Thomas moved urgently back to his seat and, placing the paper on the floor between the chair he now sat back down in and the empty one that stood next to him, he fixed Hans in a stern stare which made the artist feel as though Sir Thomas sought to extract testimony from him in a court of law.

"Before I begin, I must have your solemn oath that what is said here today will never be repeated from your mouth."

A chill ran down Hans' back at the severity of the tone. For a moment he considered that he may not wish to become involved in something requiring such an oath as an induction, though his desire to hear so deep a secret soon ate away at his doubt.

"Sir," Holbein replied, "so long as knowledge of this bears no great danger to my person, you have my oath before God to ensure my discretion."

"This knowledge will not endanger your person, but rather it will give to you the power to destroy the lives of others." Sir Thomas held the gaze of the artist, searching within his eyes for a clue as to his intention and sincerity. Holbein was now unable to resist agreeing to the conditions set in order to learn more. He nodded his assent to his host.

"Good." Sir Thomas began, drawing his breath slowly. "This is a commission for two paintings. I have chosen you because of your reputation for a subtle touch and for hiding meaning within your paintings for those who know that there is meaning there. Your unusual summoning at this time was a necessary precaution, as you must be made aware of the full background of what you will be asked to create for us in order to do justice to the requirement." Sir Thomas stopped for a moment and moved forward in his seat, never releasing his gaze from Holbein's eyes. "What you will learn," he continued, "will alter your perception of the past and of the present, of humanity and of the art of history, and you must be ready."

"Sir," Holbein licked his lips with a burning anticipation, "I can assure you that I will hear all that you feel I must, and I do not doubt that I can create for you a picture that will meet with your approval. I pray you, then, to begin." Sir Thomas nodded in acceptance of Holbein's promise.

"Everything that I shall tell you is based upon fact. The parts that I may exclude are necessarily many, but are easily found should you wish to look closely enough." Glistening blue eyes bored into Hans as More spoke. "All that I have added is my best guess as to that which God alone may tell – the inner thoughts of men's minds." Sir Thomas shuffled in his chair as he made himself comfortable to begin his tale. "We begin," he said with no little drama, "on Easter Sunday, the 14th April in the year of our Lord 1471."

Chapter 2

14th April 1471 - Blooding

Mist clung to the glistening, dewy hilltops, refusing the warm draw of the sun that stood proudly at the rim of the clear spring sky. Though the sun was not shaded, a chill still cut through the air and tickled at the back of the neck of a rider who sat alone, looking almost like a ghost atop a dark demonic horse in the lingering haze. His mount stomped its front hoof in the damp grass with a dull thud, spraying moisture fully half the way up its own leg as the rider tugged at its reins to contain the horse's excitement. Clearly the beast knew what was to come, even if its rider could only wish that he did.

"How does it look, brother?" The voice made the man jump in his saddle, but the alarm was momentary as he well knew the sound of it.

"Cold, wet and foggy, sire." The reply was somewhat solemn and brought a deep frown to the brow of King Edward.

"You are nervous, Richard." It sounded more a command than an enquiry. Richard, Duke of Gloucester, shot a hard gaze over his shoulder at his brother, whose own horse was moving alongside him, and replied shortly.

"No, sire. I have come here to do my duty this day, to my country, to my king and to my brother." His gaze turned into the haze before them. "Today, here at Barnet, you will reclaim your throne and your exile will end." Richard kept his tone deep, thinking this to be the best way to mask the dread he truly felt in his very core.

"*Our* exile, Richard, shall end. It was ours together and we shall return to London together in triumph." Edward thought for a moment. He had forgotten that his brother was only eighteen years of age and that this was to be his first taste of the mud of a battlefield. "Do not think," he continued in a softened tone, "that your loyalty has gone unnoticed these long months. Your support has been the bedrock upon which I have built my return, and where our brother's blood has fuelled his own ambition, yours has thickened your loyalty." Perhaps Edward over-stated the measure of his brother's importance, but then perhaps not. Either way, he felt it would serve to stiffen Richard's resolve.

"Thank you, sire." Richard replied, his eyes darting back to his brother. "But I need no thanks for doing right, Edward. I would serve a thousand exiles with you and not falter." Richard smiled for the first time since his brother had startled him, allowing only a faint upturning of his thin lips. His slender nose sniffed at the cold air. He looked little like his brother, who was tall and broad as Richard was slender, and of a more normal height.

"By God, no!" Edward roared loudly. "I have had enough exile to last me a hundred lifetimes!" Rearing his horse, Edward laughed heartily and called down the hill behind him to where the mist concealed ranks of soldiers who stood like figurines on a child's playroom floor.

"Draw up the lines!" Edward bellowed. His command was echoed by a dozen lesser voices and a great clamour grew as each part of the assembled mass ground into motion, lurching like a wheel stiffened by a lack of use until it eventually moved smoothly up the hill to draw up around its leader.

"Do not ignore your fear, Richard." Edward spoke softly again as his army obeyed his words.

"I am not afraid, my king." Richard snapped defensively. He did not want his brother to know the dread that gnawed on his stomach like some disease ridden rat on an old rope. More than anything else he craved his brother's respect as a man and as a soldier. At ten years his elder, Richard had always been aware of his brother's stature, as king and as a man who stood a full foot taller than himself, though Richard was not particularly short, he had long since given up hope of matching his brother. He was lithe while his brother was broad and imposing. Edward was proven in battle and commanded respect, and Richard wanted desperately to be like the king who he served.

"If you are not afraid, then you are a fool, brother." Edward was blunt and Richard smarted at the jibe, though that had not been the effect that his brother had desired. The young man felt himself blush, and thanked the heavens for the cool air that hid the worst of it. He bit his lip hard in anger at the apparent disapproval of his brother and at his own inability to control his reaction. Unable to answer, Richard simply stared into his brother's eyes, but was surprised to see only a look of concern rather than ridicule within them.

"Your fear is your own spirit guarding you against harm. Ignore it, and you lose its protection. Listen to it and it will keep you safe. God has no desire to see any of us die, and so he gave us fear to protect us." The brothers looked at each other for a long moment, not as a king to his noble subject, but as men bound by a love that transcends a feudal relationship. Almost as one, they then nodded to each other as if an agreement had been reached in the silence.

"God be with you, Richard." The king turned his horse to assume his position at the head of this army that he hoped would help him to begin the reclaiming of his throne.

"And may He speed you to your rightful victory, sire." Watching his brother disappearing into the lingering fog to his left, Richard placed a hand upon the pommel of his sword, swallowed hard and asked God to deliver him safely from this field. It seemed an age that the wall of men and metal stood unmoving upon the hill. The only sound was the stamping of the hooves of excited horses as they sensed the mounting tension.

Somewhere ahead in the mist could be heard the ghostly clinking and thudding that signified the enemy's assembly not too far in front. Richard looked down from his mount onto the field where this battle would take place at any moment. He could not even see the grass as the fog thickened but sank low. Perhaps it lingered to see the outcome of this day. The horse fidgeted beneath him, puffing great plumes of hot breath that mingled with the surrounding cloak of mist and were gone. Whatever was to happen on this field today, Richard reflected that God must not want to see it. That worried him. Fear began to rise from his stomach and he felt it lodging in his throat as if it tried to escape and shout to the world that Richard of Gloucester was afraid for his life. He closed his lips tightly to prevent this release, looking around him at his retinue. He wondered what they all felt now. He also wondered whether they knew how he felt, whether his face betrayed the fears of his mind. Now, he felt physically sick as silence descended for a brief moment on both sides of the field.

"Charge!" The voice of King Edward IV broke through the fog like a rolling thunder through a quiet night sky. The sound of a thousand men running down the hill, noisily drawing swords, rang in Richard's ears as he momentarily forgot himself before digging his heels sharply into the sides of his mount. As the horse gathered speed to a gallop down the gentle slope of the hillside, the melee that awaited became unavoidable. The horse would carry him to the very thick of it, and Richard found that this notion calmed the acid in his throat a little. He drew his sword and spurred the horse on faster to meet the enemy.

Suddenly, everything around the young man seemed to slow down, like some strange theatre piece, and the clamour about him was drowned out by the pounding of his own heart like a beating drum, and the sound of blood rushing in a raging torrent through his head. Then, in a blink of his wind filled eyes, the din returned, enhanced by the now clearly approaching Lancastrian line. Richard squinted into the thinning mist as wraith-like warriors began to emerge, ethereal, as if floating toward him. Raising his sword to shoulder height, the rider allowed a smile to trace itself across his lips at the thought of all those shadows that had provided the only test of his swordsmanship to date. As these shadows began to form solid shapes Richard gritted his teeth hard and swung his sword downwards. The two lines met like a mighty wave crashing into the immovable cliffs of Dover and Richard's arm jarred painfully. Looking down, he saw an armoured figure falling backwards, livery and a chainmail vest cleaved open from naval to chest and framed in bright red blood which reached out and licked at the duke's forearm. Finally, Richard was tasting the nervous excitement of battle. And it felt good.

Raising his sword again, the duke spied his next target and again his weapon deftly met its mark with a reassuring thud and another jar that reached his shoulder. Either side of him, Richard heard the sound of steel upon steel and the howls of those who failed to avoid an oncoming weapon.

Unbeknownst to either commander, the mist had caused the opposing lines to form up off centre and whilst the Yorkist right found scant resistance, the left flank was routed and the battle pivoted uneasily around the clatter and clamour of the fierce melee at its centre. As the Lancastrian right regrouped to move left and engage the Yorkist centre, the fog all but blinded their charge until they were upon their target, only to realise that the livery of those that they raised their swords against matched their own. For a moment an eerie silence broke out as the front line of the Lancastrian right realised who stood before them and the Lancastrian centre was presented by a charge of its own right flank. Those behind the first line who could see no further failed to halt their charge and pushed through their own line with a blood curdling scream that was designed to inspire fear within the enemy but instead caused an immediate cry of treason from the Lancastrian ranks.

Richard, meanwhile, had ploughed a furrow through the Lancastrian lines, leaving behind him a dozen bloodied corpses. His retinue were struggling to keep up with the young duke and several had fallen. Hearing the cries of betrayal from his left, Richard halted and swung his horse around, unsure what he should do. Unsure even if the cries of treason came from within their own ranks or those of the enemy, he was suddenly lost, his confidence evaporating with the mist and deserting him.

The Lancastrian army loyal to King Henry began to peel away from the engagement from right to left and the Yorkist lines gave chase for a short while, with a few straggling Lancastrians being picked off as the retreat became complete. Richard sat astride his mount in the midst of the corpses and those struggling noisily to cling on to their lives, his sword gripped so tightly in his right hand that his knuckles were whitened and he could no longer feel his fingers. He gazed, mesmerised, at the sight of what had just occurred, as a passer-by may stumble upon the scene of a roadside ambush and stare at the murdered corpses with sorrow for their suffering and disgust for those who would perpetrate such a dire act. In short, he felt strangely detached from what surrounded him in spite of his own involvement in the scene.

Looking down, he could see the faces of those his own hand had slain. Previously they had been featureless targets but now he could see their vacant eyes peering into the clouding skies as if for a last glimpse of the spirit that had already vacated their mortal bodies. Closing his eyes, Richard tried to force down the guilt that he already felt rising in his stomach. Surely, this was not how a soldier was supposed to feel upon the field of victory. His brother must not feel this weakness, so nor would he. With his eyes shut tightly he drew upon the excitement that he had felt in the raw, searing heat of the battle and resolved to keep that as a cork to contain all of the other feelings. Opening his eyes, Richard turned and began to canter back along the distance that he had charged towards the encampment. He never once looked down again as he retreated to the moral sanctuary of his tent.

Pushing aside the canvas at the entrance, the young duke released the breath that pounded in his chest and, without willing his hand to do so, he released the grip that he had maintained on his red, stained weapon and it clattered as it hit the ground. Immediately, he plunged his hands into the bowl of icy water that stood beside the entrance, not noticing the cold biting his fingers. He stood motionless and watched, with a frown playing across his forehead, as thin tendrils of deep scarlet spread from his hands across the surface of the water as though taking it over. It made him feel sick. Quickly, before all of the clear water was lost, he cupped his hands and threw handfuls of the water into his face to remove the grime of battle, and perhaps the guilt he was beginning to feel too. He shivered at the cold. A strange trembling gripped at his limbs. As he moved to the large oak chair to the left of the tent, he stripped away the armour that was flecked with an awful mixture of mud and blood, along with the clothes beneath it which bore splatters of both too, and collapsed into the seat, instinctively reaching to the table on his right for the leather bound prayer book that was his constant companion. In spite of his will to feel no need for it, he opened the book and read for over two hours, alone.

When he emerged, Richard squinted as he pushed the heavy fabric of his tent door. The midday sun was warm on his cheeks as he strolled through the lush green grass to the king's opulent red and blue marquee. Stepping inside, the smell of roasting meat confronted him like another curtain to be pushed through. The air was thick and hung heavy in his nostrils and his mouth began to water as he tasted the sweet scent drawn over his taste buds. The noise died down as those gathered around the king realised that the duke had entered. Richard was becoming aware of a strange sensation in his legs as he stood still, when his brother called from the table with a natural authority that Richard had always felt truly befitted a king.

"Ah, brother!" Richard looked at the king and an uneasy smile passed fleetingly across his lips. "We began to fear that you had disappeared in the mist of this morning." Richard winced as the flattering, raucous laughs of the gathered lords at the king's table bellowed around the tent. About a dozen men, all of whom had now forgone their armour in favour of the lavish finery of court clothing, sat at a long table erected in the king's tent and were devouring several roasted boars.

"Come and sit at my side, Richard." Edward gestured grandiosely to the empty place setting at his right side. The young man shifted uncomfortably on his soles, brushed his damp palms down his thighs and strode around the table to the seat set by for him. The honour of the position saved for him was in no way lost on the duke, but he did not share his brother's taste for the more tangible trappings of power. Fawning old men and overconfident young lords irritated Richard. They served no real purpose other than to inflate the ego of whosoever could provide them with the warmest shelter today. At the first sign of a chill, they immediately sought warmer climates. Always sure not to leave the old shelter before the new was secured and proven safe. 'The hounds offer you better loyalty than these men.' Richard thought as he sat down, glancing at his brother's three large hunting hounds. 'And they have better table manners too.' A smile brushed his lips as he eyed the carnage along the table and the surrounding floor.

Richard suddenly became aware that his brother was staring at him, and almost jumped, as though the king may have read his thoughts and disapproved. He shifted under his brother's heavy gaze. Even sitting, Edward dwarfed Richard's lithe young frame. His abiding childhood memory of his brother had always been of his size and strength. Richard was convinced that Edward's stature alone was demonstration of his credentials as ruler of England. Disappointed to have more resembled their father, Richard knew he would never lose his respect for and dread fear of his brother and king.

"Sire?" he questioned his brother's intense stare softly. As much respect as he had for his king, his brother had never made him feel anything other than a beloved younger sibling. Perhaps, Richard always considered, the ten year gap between them increased the protective, nurturing feeling that he hoped his brother felt for him.

"I was getting worried about you, Richard." Edward spoke in a soft tone that mirrored his brother's, but which also prevented the others around the table from hearing. "Where did you get to?" he queried, his voice full of concern. Edward was fully aware that this had been Richard's first taste of battle and he well remembered the floods of opposing emotions that the experience could release.

"I needed a little time alone, your grace." Richard tried not to sound feeble but his head sank as he spoke, aware that his admission could easily be construed as weakness. There was a prolonged pause. Even in the clamour of the feasting, it felt to Richard like a hollow silence.

"You must be feeling raw." Edward's tone had not changed. The concern was a surprise to Richard. A pleasant one, though. Edward saw the frown fold itself into his brother's brow. He studied the fresh, young face before him. At eighteen, Richard was the king's most trusted subject, beyond even Lord Hastings at his other side. His brother was one of the few men whose loyalty he had never yet had cause to question. They had shared two long, harsh periods of exile and Richard had never shown any sign of wanting to be anywhere but at Edward's side. He had ascended to high office before the rebellion they now sought to quell by virtue of his birth but this was his first real chance to prove himself as a man. Edward had found Richard something of an enigma. Difficult to get close to, yet fiercely loyal to his family. When their cousin the Earl of Warwick had risen in rebellion the previous year, it was Richard who the king had most keenly awaited to declare his hand and when Richard had not hesitated, Edward had felt a deep guilt for doubting his brother. He comforted himself that blind faith was not a luxury that he could afford. Warwick had, after all, recruited their other brother, George, Duke of Clarence to his cause. Richard, however, had not hesitated to board the ship with Edward at Kings Lynn on that wet 2nd October last year. The date of their enforced flight had not been lost on Edward. As King of England, he had hoped to reward his brother with a far more enjoyable day to celebrate his eighteenth birthday. Richard had never even mentioned it.

"Battle," Edward leaned deliberately into his brother, "affects all men in different ways. I have seen men who boast of their prowess piss themselves as a charging enemy approaches." Edward leaned forward and raised his tankard to a broad, middle aged man further along the table who Richard vaguely recognised. He ceased his rolling laughter to raise his own goblet in the king's direction with a nod. Edward turned back to Richard with a cheeky smirk on his face. Clearly, that was one of the men he spoke of. Richard smiled too. "I have also seen the very opposite," Edward continued, suddenly serious, "and I saw it in you today, Richard." Edward smiled broadly again. "The quietest, most reserved man may become a wild animal on the battlefield. War can turn a man inside out and he may even surprise himself." Richard nodded, unsure how else to respond. Edward sat back into his chair and raised his voice now to address all around. "Today, we rise again, brother." The king beamed and all around were instantly silenced, focused upon him.

"Today is Easter Sunday, sire." Richard still spoke softly and only to his brother.

"True." Edward's voice boomed through the silence of the tent now. He rose from his chair to his full height. A magnificent sight that had served Edward well. He clumsily grabbed a goblet of wine from the table. "To God, and His England!" he called and his salute was echoed by all of the gathered lords. Richard mouthed the words with a silent reverence and looked up to see the towering figure of the king looking directly into his eyes. "To our risen Saviour." Edward toasted more soberly. The toast was again echoed, also somewhat soberly. Richard smiled at his brother, knowing that this toast had been made for his benefit. He noted, though, that the religious sentiment raised less passion amongst those gathered than the self-praising of patriotism. Richard already had a reputation as a pious man, which he wanted to be proud of, but he knew that to feel so would be considered a sin. He knew from recent history, though, that the temporal world required more from a man of his position than just pious devotion. That alone was what had led his own family to imprison King Henry within the Tower. Richard fully appreciated that a more rounded world view was necessary to retain power. Today, he had taken his first step towards this position.

A further hour passed with little eating and much drinking before many of the lords departed with varying degrees of drunken swaying, and only a few remained snoring loudly where they had slumped at the table.

"Richard." Edward spoke softly again as he noticed his brother rise from his chair. Although he had consumed as much as everyone else, the king's capacity was legendary, put down by most to the size of his frame, and by a few to long practise. Either way, his head was still clear. "Please, sit a moment longer." Richard sat without hesitation, though he was unsure what his brother might want with him. "There is something that I need to tell you." Edward told him slowly.

"Sire?" Richard held the king's powerful gaze without flinching.

"Amongst the slain today was the Earl of Warwick." Edward spoke deliberately, waiting for a reaction.

"Then the largest thorn is removed from your side, your grace." Richard did not hesitate nor blink.

"Richard, I know you were close. I would not blame you…"

"Sire," Richard interrupted. 'Too defensive?' he instantly wondered. He continued, though, without missing a beat.

"Warwick was like a father to me. This much is no secret. Much of what I am today I owe to him." Richard now felt Edward's gaze weighing more heavily upon him. Searching. Questioning. Silent. "That," Richard continued, "is why his betrayal cut so deeply, as did that of George. Yet in that instant, when he declared against you, he declared against your family. He declared against me, and severed all of those bonds." A sudden blaze of anger burned within the young duke's stomach. 'What must I do?' he wondered. 'How many times must I convince him?' As quickly as it had come, the blaze was quashed. Richard was well aware that Edward had been betrayed by those he held closest before and needed to remain suspicious. Richard, though, still had an uncomfortable feeling in his gut, as though the embers still smouldered there.

There was a long, heavy silence. Edward's eyes searched Richard's face for a sign. He wasn't sure what it would be. Shock? Grief? Sadness? Elation? No, not elation. Not even Edward could feel that. Richard had spent the majority of his formative years in Warwick's household, treated as one of his own family. That was the main reason that Edward had been unsure which side Richard would take when things began to go so badly, and why he had been moved when Clarence had joined Warwick. The politician in him remained suspicious, though. Was Richard planted at his side to spy on him? Did he still harbour some loyalty to Edward's most powerful adversary? Edward the brother berated his political caution. Edward the politician challenged his own fraternal desire to trust. Edward the king realised that he must satisfy his political misgivings in order to retain his crown. The question, therefore, had to be asked: How far could he really trust Richard?

"I simply thought that you should hear the news from me." Edward looked away finally. The duke felt his lungs re-inflate, only now realising that he had held his breath throughout the silence without willing it. Despite Edward's apparently genuine concern, Richard knew well that this had been orchestrated to gauge his reaction to the news. The pain returned in the pit of his stomach. His brother still did not trust him. As he rose and left, he refused to betray his sadness at the loss of a man he had thought of as a father. His brother would doubtless have misread this as a form of betrayal. The simple fact was that Richard had loved Warwick and felt every bit as betrayed by him as Edward did. Even that, though, did little to numb the pain of another loss.

"Richard." He was snapped from his thoughts by the return of his brother's powerful, regal tone. He turned slowly. Edward was smiling softly after him. "We ride tomorrow to pursue the rest of the Lancastrian rebels."

"Lancastrian rebels?" Richard mused. "No doubt they refer to us as the Yorkist rebels. Perspective is a powerful and distorting looking glass."

"When we meet them next, you shall lead out my forces, Richard." Edward spoke with the solid authority of a monarch bestowing a great honour. And a great honour it was indeed, Richard knew, but a continuation of the endless testing too.

"Thank you, sire," he conceded graciously, bowing as he stepped back from the tent doorway and took a long slow lungful of the crisp spring air. Whatever else he felt, he was glad to be home again.

Chapter 3

4th May 1471 - Judgement

It had been three weeks since Barnet, and Richard felt as though his feet had not touched the ground. After rallying additional troops, they had made a forced march to intercept the troops provided by the French to follow Edward, Prince of Wales, the son of Henry VI, and the reason for the former monarch's preservation. Richard had once questioned his brother several years ago as to why he had failed to do away with a living former monarch. Edward had clapped him firmly on the back.

"Politics is a difficult mistress, Richard." The boy reeled from the blow from his elder brother. At twelve, he still hoped to share that stature some day. He was also of an age to be deeply embarrassed by talk of mistresses.

"But he is locked in the Tower," Richard protested uncertainly, "and none would miss him."

"The Lord does not look kindly upon cold blooded murderers." The lad felt chastised. He knew his scriptures well, and enjoyed worship. He dropped his head. "Besides," Edward continued, a glint in his eye, "why hurry an enemy into God's gracious care?" he laughed loudly. Richard felt uncomfortable at the joke, and was beginning to regret his initial suggestion. Edward's laughter halted abruptly and he held Richard in a gaze that took his breath for several long seconds.

"Henry will be dealt with when the time is right." Edward's voice was deep and cool, like a draft from a chill dungeon that sent a shiver running up Richard's spine. "Henry is a weak fool. But he remains the Lancastrian claimant. While the head of their line is a weak minded, feeble, failed king who I hold under lock and key, I retain control." As Edward broke the stare, Richard tried to pull air into his aching chest without his brother noticing his discomfort. "Henry has a son." Edward continued. "A boy at present, under the control of Henry's formidable wife. He grows each day in his exile, out of my reach. If Henry were removed, the line would be revitalised in his son and I would lose my control." Edward looked again deeply into Richard's eyes. He fully intended to mould his brother into a political heavyweight upon whom he could rely in the years to come, and there were certain truths that need to be learned early if Richard was to help to tighten his eldest brother's grip on the crown. "If a flower's head is removed, in time it will grow another." Edward began again. "How do you ensure that the flower will never return, Richard?"

"Sire," Richard swallowed the knot in his throat, "by removing the root."

"Precisely!" Edward exclaimed. The response impressed him, more so since Richard's face displayed a dawning realisation of the meaning he was trying to convey. "Go on."

"If Henry were removed," Richard continued uncertainly, "his son would simply step into his place, but would be even more dangerous." Looking to his king for approval, Richard received an encouraging nod. "The line must be extinguished entirely. Henry's son must be removed to stop the line spreading further, and then Henry..." Richard hesitated.

"And then Henry will die." Edward finished bluntly.

Now, Richard blinked the chill air from his eyes as his mount shifted nervously below him. The Prince of Wales was here. This was the best chance that they had ever had to put an end to these troubles once and for all. So much of his family's future depended upon what would happen on this field outside of Tewkesbury. And Richard was to lead the king's forces into the battle. He felt the weight of the responsibility sit heavy on his shoulders. The fulfilment of his father's life works. The proving of himself as a man. Vindicating the trust that his brother had placed in him. Ensuring the future of his family. So much rested on today, but Richard was no longer a nervous, awe struck twelve year old boy and had, in the last few days, found himself daring to look forward to this moment. Even so, he felt the familiar surge of nervous excitement swelling in his thighs as they gripped the saddle.

Flanked by his retinue and followed by some five hundred men on foot, Richard raised his heavy mace high above his head. There was a moment of silence before he deliberately tilted the black head of his weapon forwards.

"For England and King Edward!" Richard roared and a clamour rose behind him. He spurred his horse on and drove the charge towards the Duke of Somerset at the head of the Prince's army. As Richard charged, Somerset called out his forces to meet them.

"Today," Somerset had told his men just before they had launched across the field, "God's anointed shall be restored in full, no longer opposed by greedy false kings." Now, as his large bay pounded the earth and shortened the distance between the two armies, he clenched his teeth and focused his sight firmly upon the usurper's own brother.

As the two forces clashed, Richard swung his mace from high above his head and sent a seated knight from his saddle to a crumpled heap of metal on the dirt behind the now riderless horse. He spied the Duke of Somerset to his left. Each swing of his mace clanked or thudded against sword, armour, shield, flesh or an uneasy combination of those things. The sharp metallic sound of intense, tight battle rang in his ears all around and he could not alter his course to meet Somerset. His shield jarred several times but he kept his seat and felt no significant pain. After a last look behind to his left, he gave up on the idea of pursuing Somerset.

Like the sharp point of an arrow through a straw target, Richard pushed into the enemy ranks and the wedge that followed him drove them further apart. As Gloucester's men pushed forward, Somerset's forces had to fall back. Richard drove his horse on, a throaty roar resonating unbidden from within his chest. Again and again his mace bore down onto the back of the heads of Somerset's now retreating forces. Richard could barely hear his own roar above the panicked clamour around him as men called out the fall back, sword ground against sword and those who found their position lost either shrieked in terror or fell in a frenzy of wild aggression. Still Richard's arm jarred on men's backs. All around him was the gurgling of throats filling with torrents of warm blood, the last feeling their owners would experience.

Finally, several hundred feet forward of the point at which the armies had clashed, Richard pulled up his horse. Quickly, he was surrounded by his retinue as the enemy fell back ever further. Richard looked down at his mace and felt slightly sick at the sight of the thick, dark blood running from its flanks like a ribbon of silk to the floor. He shook himself from the moment as his friend, Francis, Viscount Lovell, pulled his horse up alongside Richard's.

"What kept you?" Richard bellowed above the noise.

"Someone has to clear up the mess you leave behind, Richard!" The reply was accompanied by a broad smile that Lovell was rarely seen without. Lovell and Richard had grown up together at Warwick and the years had forged a close bond between them.

"Where is Percy?" Richard asked, suddenly a little concerned.

"Right here." Came the firm reply from his other side. Robert Percy was more wiry than Lovell and completed the trio brought together by the custom of farming young nobles out to the households of other nobles, but fused together by their experiences during that time.

Richard nodded to them both and stood up in his stirrups. Looking for his brother, behind them and to the left, he saw the huge figure of the king. Flicking the congealing streams of blood from his weapon, he raised it above his head and circled it. Almost instantly, the army flanking Edward charged at speed directly towards the position held by the Prince of Wales.

A huge cheer went up around Richard as he signalled the king to attack. He had led the assault and it had gone better than he could have hoped. Closing his eyes, he thanked God for blessing him and his cause this day. As he opened his eyes, he felt a new, foreign sensation. It was not, though, an unpleasant one. He looked at the advancing army thundering behind his brother and then let his gaze carry to the shortening distance to the mercenaries that surrounded the rebels. It was then that Richard was able to place the strange feeling. 'They must all be finished.' It was like a voice echoing in his head. 'They must pay for our exile. My family will be restored and we will bring peace to this kingdom.' The feeling became like a burning in his chest as he accepted it, embraced it and let it grow. He wanted more. He was good at this and it felt good to destroy those who had brought hardship to his life. He caught himself for a moment, realising his thoughts sounded like some crazed blood lust. 'No,' he thought, 'I have a greater purpose.'

He pointed his horse at the left flank of the enemy, his mace still raised. He pulled the reins sharply and his mount reared high on its hind legs and a deep rumbling sound bubbled up from his stomach and was instantly echoed from all around him.

"Chaaaaaaaaarge!!"

Two days later, Richard sat at a broad oak table in the dining hall of the tavern in the heart of Tewkesbury at which Edward had made for his Constable a makeshift court martial. The Prince of Wales had been slain during the battle, and all that remained of his lieutenants had been forcibly removed from sanctuary earlier today to face justice at Richard's hands. Although Richard did not exactly approve of removing persons from the sanctuary of the Lord's house, he recognised the need for it and felt assured that the Lord would understand his brother's instruction as being for the good of the nation. The young duke was also well aware that the convening of a court of chivalry under the Constable of England in these circumstances was a mere formality and the result a forgone conclusion.

There was a sharp pounding at the door at the far end of the room. Richard pulled himself straight in his chair and cleared his throat.

"Enter," he called. The heavy door swung open with a tired groan. Fourteen men were marched into the room, each flanked at either bound arm by the king's soldiers. As the men were lined up before Richard, he fixed Somerset in his gaze and held it in silence for a long moment.

"You all stand before this Court of Chivalry, on this, the sixth day of May in the year of our Lord 1471, charged with the crime of treason." Richard continued to bore into Somerset's eyes, as though he was the only accused man before him, and the Lancastrian stared back unflinchingly. "Your presence upon the battlefield two days ago is the evidence and testimony before God of your guilt. Res ipse loquitur. Do you wish to say anything in your defence prior to sentencing?"

Thirteen men looked to the ground. One held his head upright and still held the gaze of his accuser. There was sniffling and weeping from either side of him, but he remained unmoved.

"I am aware," the Duke of Somerset spoke in a calm, level tone, his voice resolute, "that there is nothing that I may say to alter the outcome of these illegal proceedings."

"You are in no position to question the legitimacy of this court." Richard attempted to match Somerset's calm authority.

"Perhaps, sir," the duke continued, his eyes creasing with the sign of his age as he smiled gently, apparently ignoring Richard's words, "but," he continued, "the Lord our God shall judge each one of us in full and with complete knowledge of our hearts. I go to Him at peace with my actions, for I defended God's anointed king on the field of battle, a king who would never remove God's sons from the house of their Father to execute them."

"Enough." Richard shouted. His face flushed as his anger swelled. Whether Somerset knew it or not, to question Richard's position before God was probably the one way to dismantle the young man's resolve to remain in control.

"My lord," Somerset's smile broadened slightly, "the blood in your cheeks bears witness to your own guilt in this matter." There was a long silence as the men stared at each other, locked in a battle of wills. There was the faint sound of the soldiers shuffling uneasily behind the accused men as the atmosphere within the room built.

"I will stand before the Lord," Richard's voice was raised, "with a clear conscience, sir. It is I who defend God's chosen king. My family will restore order where Lancastrian rule has sown division and malcontent." Richard paused and took a deep breath. The air burned in his tight chest and he released it slowly, allowing it to draw the tension from his body. "The Lord is punishing these lands for your king's failings and that must be righted for the good of all England. You will go now before God and see the truth of my words and the error of your mind." Again there was a long silence. Richard felt the blood pounding in his temples as he attempted to retain his authority.

"You may, my lord," Somerset spoke quietly, "murder me now, and I shall go gladly before God, for I die having been removed by force from prayer and sanctuary within His house." The pause that followed was deliberate to allow the words to meet their mark. "When I reach my place in Heaven,

I shall pray for forgiveness for you, my lord, that you may one day join me in the glory of His presence."

"My Lord Somerset," Richard burned with conviction and broiling anger at the old man's words, "it is I who shall pray for your soul during its torment in purgatory and I hope not to see you there, for that would mean that I had failed to continue God's work. There is one thing upon which we shall agree, sir." All in the room were now conscious of the tension and Richard was all too aware that to lose authority and the moral platform now would be disastrous, and would allow Somerset a final victory. As he held the other's gaze unblinkingly, he attempted to inject as much venom, sincerity and zeal as he could muster in the final words before his court. "You shall discover the truth of God's will before I shall." Immediately, Richard gestured the soldiers to remove the prisoners to prevent Somerset replying. His confidence was shaken, though his conviction remained unmoved, and his temper had almost got the better of him. Somerset glanced back over his shoulder as he was led from the court to see the young Duke of Gloucester staring into the centre of the room, deep in thought.

Chapter 4

A Request

Sir Thomas More rose from his seat and picked up the long iron poker that rested beside the fireplace. He began gently prodding at the burning pile of wood. After a moment, he turned to his guest.

"At the age of eighteen," he began softly, "Richard had proven his unswerving loyalty to his brother. At least he believed that he should have." Sir Thomas shot a glinting eye in Holbein's direction before returning to poking the fire. "He had shared the king's exile and played a pivotal role in his restoration to the throne. He had remained loyal to Edward in spite of their brother George's betrayal and the overwhelming odds against their cause when they fled these shores. The mighty Earl of Warwick, the Kingmaker, was dead, as was the childless Prince of Wales. It was upon the king's triumphant return to London some three weeks later that Henry was finally," Sir Thomas cleared his throat meaningfully, "disposed of, and the Lancastrian rebellion, headless and crushed of body, was over. Richard," he continued in a lilting tone, "had acquitted himself in battle better than his brother could have hoped. Edward must have been pleased to have one so close upon whom he could rely, and Richard was doubtless looking forward to reaping the rewards of his brother's restoration."

Holbein nodded in apparent agreement with his host. His concern was, however, that little of what he had heard so far was particularly unknown and seemed to have little to do with a painting commission. As if reading the artist's thoughts, More suddenly spoke again.

"Please have patience with my tale, Master Holbein. As I have stated to you previously, all will become clear to you in due course." Holbein was embarrassed at his host's perception, but said nothing as Sir Thomas moved his attention back to the fire and prodded it again with his poker so that it cracked loudly and danced more quickly. As he began to tell his story again, Sir Thomas stared a little wearily into the fire.

Richard sat in the gardens of the Palace of Westminster on a crisp March morning and stared at the blossom that was beginning to form on the rows of trees lining the path before him to the Palace. It had been almost a year since Edward's triumphal return to the throne and life had been very good for the duke. He found favour with the renewed and invigorated king, but still the picture was not complete. Two things had been playing upon Richard's mind for some months now, and he believed that he had the solution for both. All that he needed was the king's approval, and that was what he sought today. In spite of their closeness and Richard's surety that his brother would accede to his request, the Duke of Gloucester feared rousing his brother's suspicion by making it. Edward, he mused, had become inwardly more suspicious of all who surrounded him, though his flamboyance often covered his fears in public.

"My Lord of Gloucester." Richard was shaken from his day dreaming by the booming voice of his brother rumbling from behind him. He leapt from the bench and turned, a broad smile spreading across his thin face. The smile flickered slightly as the duke was confronted by both the king and his queen.

"Sire." Richard pushed the smile awkwardly back across his face. "My Lady," he bowed his head to the queen. He had hoped to speak to Edward alone. Queen Elizabeth rarely left Edward's side these days and Richard felt uneasy about the growing influence that her and her family enjoyed at court. The Woodvilles seemed to be jealously gathering the pickings from the king's table and, like hungry dogs, Richard feared that they would turn on anyone that they viewed as a rival. Elizabeth returned Richard's awkward smile with a deliberately awkward one of her own. Edward appeared oblivious to the silent undertow in the greetings.

"Richard." Edward smiled and wrapped his left arm around Gloucester's shoulder. As they all walked along the path, Richard must have appeared as a young boy beneath a father's arm, such was the difference in size between the brothers. "My dearest brother," the king continued exuberantly, "there need be no formality here between us."

"Are you happy with this, Elizabeth?" Richard queried, teasing the queen.

"Of course." Her face twisted and her voice was cold.

"Now," Edward carried on as though nothing had been said, "as bracing as this fine morning is, I have much to do, so let us get to business. What would you ask of me brother? If I may grant it you, it is yours, and as king," Edward beamed with pleasure at himself, "there is nothing I cannot grant but that which the Lord God reserves for himself."

Richard looked nervously at his feet. They were moving quickly to keep pace with the king. The duke forced himself to remember at all times that the queen walked silently, unseen beside Edward.

"I have been troubled for some months, Edward." Richard was halted as his brother strode in front of him. Elizabeth released the king's arm and moved to stand at Richard's side.

"Troubled, Richard?" Edward's brow was heavily furrowed. "Have the offices that you have gained not sufficed for you?" Concern was plain upon his face.

"Your grace," Richard spoke quickly with the realisation of his own words, "I did not mean to cause you such sudden alarm. My troubles are not great and barely affect the king. Forgive my choice of words." Edward exhaled with a deliberately heavy sigh and smiled his beaming grin again. Richard always found it both comforting and infectious and smiled, more to himself than to Edward. "My thoughts," Richard continued gravely, "have turned twofold to the subject of marriage. With your position more secure, I feel that the time is right for me to settle down and start a family of my own." Richard accidentally glanced sideways at the queen as he paused for thought.

"Well, well! Time to make a real man of you little brother" Edward winked behind his grin. "You said that your thoughts turned to it twofold, Richard? I believe that I understand the one count, but a second eludes me." Richard felt a little uneasy at Edward's innuendo, though he had expected it fully.

"I would like to ask your majesty's permission to marry..." Richard paused, met his brother's gaze and swallowed the lump swelling in his throat, suddenly conscious again of the queen's eyes upon him as he continued, "to marry Lady Anne Neville."

There was an uneasy silence, broken only by the gentle breeze brushing through the trees above. Edward was staring over Richard's head, his bottom lip sucked in over his teeth. Richard shot a glance at Elizabeth, who stood perfectly still, with no emotion visible on her face as she looked dutifully at her husband.

"The widow's whereabouts are not known to us, Richard, even if I were to agree." Edward spoke softly, thoughtfully, though he was clearly shaken by the request. It was not something that he had expected from his youngest brother.

"Sire, I have located her." Richard was pleased with his brother's response. It was not often that he was able to surprise Edward.

"Tell me one thing, brother." Edward's voice appeared distracted. "Do you seek marriage to Anne, or to her father's estates?" Elizabeth now moved her calm, icy gaze to Richard, clearly interested in the duke's response to the blunt and pointed question.

"Brother," Richard smiled dryly, "you are aware that I spent much of my youth in the custody of the Earl of Warwick,

Anne's father. During my time at Middleham, I came to know Lady Anne. I would not pretend," he quickly continued, "that we were ever particularly close, but Anne showed me only kindness then, before her marriage to the Prince of Wales."

"I am aware of the facts of this matter." Edward contemplated, growing visibly impatient. Richard knew this trait well in his brother and hoped to use it to eventually secure Edward's approval if he seemed to be unreceptive to the idea.

"Yes, forgive me." Richard replied slowly. "I knew the Lady Anne then. When she was widowed, she disappeared for a time. It has come to my attention that our brother George and his wife hold her under house arrest and have put her to work here in London to keep her from remarrying." Edward refocused instantly on his brother at this last sentence. Any mention of George acting with an ulterior motive made Edward most nervous. Having pardoned his brother for his part in the rebellion, he kept a close watch over his dealings, yet this was news that he had not yet heard. And it was most unwelcome.

The reason for George's organising of such a vanishing was immediately clear to Edward. George had married Isabel Neville, and through her stood to claim the substantial estate of the Earl of Warwick and, more directly, that of the late Earl's wife. Currently in sanctuary, her death would place her daughters, and their husbands, in line for a share of the Beauchamp and Despenser lands, which formed a substantial portion of the Warwick estates. His dealings with the Earl of Warwick had left Edward deeply shaken and suspicious. Government of the farthest reaches of the kingdom was delegated to a few of Edward's family and closest allies. Clarence held royal authority in the West Country and Edward was well aware of his avarice and ambition. Allowing Richard to marry into this picture had its benefits.

Since the summer of last year, Richard had been placed in power in the north, as part of which he had effectively occupied much of Warwick's northern estates. As one who had unswervingly displayed his loyalty to the king, Richard's installation in the north offered Edward the benefit of having arguably his strongest ally occupying the farthest and most unruly region of Edward's kingdom. There had been several of the queen's family considered for the same role, including her brother, Earl Rivers, who was held in great esteem by many, but Edward had always intended to reserve this richest and most responsible reward for his brother.

Allowing Richard to marry Anne would serve to strengthen the duke's position and authority in the north. The political advantage was obvious and immediate. It would clearly mark Richard as the king's man in the north. Edward's mind raced, trying to consider all of the sides of this puzzle, for something stung the back of his mind to remind him that there was probably more to this than was immediately clear.

The second advantage to Edward was also quite plain. His assent to this union would demonstrate his authority to Clarence. And that was something he was always keen to do. He found that his brother's ambition needed continual checking. To allow Richard a share of what George coveted would prevent him gathering more power to himself and remind him of precisely who was king. Edward could not help but smile thinly as he pictured George's face on hearing the news. The smile broadened as he imagined his brother wondering how Edward had known where to find Anne.

Richard looked sideways, trying to gauge his brother's reaction. He was in no doubt why Edward was grinning, but he wondered how far the king would look into his intentions whilst distracted by thoughts of irritating George.

"Sire?" Richard deliberately interrupted the king's thoughts while he still found pleasure in them.

"Patience, Richard." The king held his gaze forward. The duke thought he looked as though he was trying to make out something that was still too far away to be clear. "Much may rest upon this decision and I shall not take it lightly." Out of sight of the king, Richard rolled his eyes high into his eyelids. He liked to consider himself more learned than his brother and told himself that this was the reason Edward always took so long to ponder things that Richard saw straight and clear. However, his insecurity always reminded him that the king may be considering some side of the issue that Richard missed. Try as he may, Richard never managed to shake these echoes from his thoughts. Edward turned and they strolled on almost aimlessly, through the canopy of white and pink blossom. The streaming early day sun flicked at Richard's eyes through the branches and blossom flowers. He wondered how much of his motive Edward would discern.

So far, the king was happy with the advantages of Richard's request. His youngest brother's desire for the marriage was, at least upon the surface, plain to Edward. As Edward would gain stronger control of the north, so, by the same measure, Richard's power, authority and wealth would have to increase. As nervous as this made him, it was a Devil's choice. To control the north he must have a powerful representative there. But to have a powerful representative there may do more to unsettle the region. The Lord knows Warwick had done just that. Still, if a lord must become mighty, he could think of none he would rather it be. Edward was nagged by a single repeating question. Is there more to Richard's request than the obvious security? As much as he wished to put George in his place, Edward was wary of setting his two brothers on a collision course. He had learned the need for family unity well. 'Still,' he thought, 'if George wishes matters brought to a head, so be it.' He had arguably more to lose by disaffecting Richard.

Suddenly, Edward became aware that the trio were about to run out of path, and that Richard would expect an answer. He searched for any other motive. All he could lay his mind on was the chance that Richard actually loved Anne of old. It was not beyond the realms of possibility and Edward could fathom no subterfuge. The request was reasonable. Edward halted and turned to his brother. Elizabeth strode to his side. Her silence had been complete as they walked, and Richard had almost forgotten that she was present.

"Brother." Edward spoke sternly. He was amused by the frown that shot across Richard's brow. "Go, find your bride." The king smiled broadly and Richard grinned back, clearly relieved. He slapped the duke's upper arm, the two laughed aloud together and then Richard nodded, bowed an informal half-bow and turned to run back through the gardens. Edward could not help but smile as he watched the exuberant young duke run, jumping once to bat a low branch and showering himself with blossom.

"Are you sure that your decision is wise, Ned?" Elizabeth's voice was as cool as the spring breeze that gently lifted her hair from her shoulders. "A decision made in haste only leaves all the more time to regret it."

"Elizabeth," Edward spoke slowly, "I see the danger, but there is benefit in it for us too." He thought for a moment, turning to meet his wife's eyes. "And I would struggle to deny Richard anything he asked of me. I see no way to do so without risk."

There was a long pause. Just as Edward moved to walk on, he was pulled back by Elizabeth's soft voice, which seemed to brush his ear with the breeze.

"There is a way, my king." She paused, drawing Edward in. "There is always a way."

"Then you must tell me my love." The two turned and walked back towards the palace as Elizabeth spoke her hushed words.

Chapter 5

21st May 1472 - Rescue

In the weeks since securing the king's permission to marry, Richard had led a short campaign to quell the Scottish incursions into the north of England. The swift success had further hardened the respect and affection in which Richard was increasingly held by a region long tormented, often neglected and in long need of a champion. Although careful not to rush his progress south, Richard had been pre-occupied by his desire to return to London. Before he had left, his brother George had flatly refused to release Anne from his 'care'. When Richard had been barely able to contain his frustration, Edward had suggested that he vent his 'aggravated spirit' upon the Scots whilst the king dealt with Clarence's obstructions.

Following a triumphal return to London, Richard had been disheartened to learn that all Edward had for him was George's incredible assurance that he neither knew nor cared where the Lady Anne currently resided. In fact, Richard had grown somewhat more than disheartened by his brother's contribution to the affair since he had not even wanted to bring the matter to George's attention before Anne had been recovered. Still, if Edward had exhausted all of his routes, and if Richard really wanted to complete this matter, then he had his own means.

Fearing such resistance from George, and perhaps a lack of commitment from Edward, Richard had set men to work under the direction of Francis Lovell with a single task. They were to establish and monitor Anne's whereabouts until he returned. And they had not been idle. Having been moved twice, Anne was now within the household of one of Clarence's retainers. The unremarkable house on the unremarkable street upon which Richard now stood, watching, sheltering from the thin dark rain that reflected the last of the dying light of the day was where she had last been taken. Wrapped in a plain black cloak, only the white of Richard's burning eyes flashed to denote his presence.

With two steps backwards, the young duke checked around the corner behind him and found, as he expected to, that Lovell sat astride a large bay, holding another saddled to his left and Richard's own jet black steed to his right, invisible in the creeping shadows but for the glinting of the rain that coated the three shapes.

"We are still here, Richard." The hushed, gruff voice of Lovell cut clearly through the splashing all around. "Now, my lord, go get you a bride." There was a momentary flash of white teeth as Lovell smiled and then he slowly, silently began to turn the horses around. Richard stepped forward with a wide stride, lifted the hood of his cloak over his head and refocused his gaze upon the house opposite. His left hand slipped slowly to his hip and found the tightly wrapped leather it sought to confirm a final time that his mace hung there ready.

The duke's purposeful stride masked the tense trembling beginning to spread from the very pit of his stomach. Each time he planted his foot a pace further across the street the sodden earth seemed to suck at the soles of his boots and with each pace he felt that he had to pull harder to free his back foot, as though the mud below him tugged him back, pleading with him not to go on, sensing his growing nerves. Immediately, he forced the growing disquiet to the back of his mind. He knew this feeling well now. 'I am Richard, Duke of Gloucester' he recited to himself, drowning out all other thoughts, 'and I shall have my way'. Without outward falter, he quashed the tide of his concerns and stood before the oak door. Raising his right hand he pounded the door three times with the side of his clenched fist. He was about to beat the door again when it swung open sharply and his eyes were met by wide, bright grey eyes that struck the duke as wild as they darted about his face.

"Yes!" The crackling voice seemed to fit the eyes. Richard was slightly taken aback. The man before him was scruffily attired and of indefinite, but probably advanced, age. Lank grey hair lay across his shoulders and a curled upper lip exposed two blackened teeth that hung lonely in his mouth. As Richard drew up his frame to answer, he was abruptly cut short. "Well, whadaya want? Eh?" the man squawked, irritable and impatient.

"I would speak with the master of the house."

"You would, if I'd let ya!" the voice rasped back, its owner grinning in obvious pleasure at his witticism. Richard clenched his fist tightly at his side, but then forced his fingers open and tried to relax.

"I have come to collect the Lady Anne Neville from this household." He was pleased at how calm his voice was remaining. The face at the door now looked clearly startled, taken aback. That expression was followed closely by a puzzled furrow across the old man's brow. He leaned forward slightly, eyeing the young man with a new, confused suspicion. He shot glances left and right, up and down the dim street. The dusk was made fuzzier by his failing eyesight, but even so, he was fairly confident there was no militia queuing behind the rather slight figure in front of him. Something was not right. After a moment, he smiled broadly and his cracking cackle broke the peace that drifted on the evening's cool breeze. Richard's self imposed calmness began to seep from him, as if blown off softly by the same breeze.

"I have no intention of standing here any longer." Richard's teeth gritted tightly to add an air of menace. "Now," he grabbed the grinning figure by his tunic with both hands, "will you fetch the Lady, or should I?"

"Well, young sir," the rasping voice announced, the grin never wavering, "if you would like to try to collect her alone," he paused a moment, holding the piercing dark eyes housed under the shadow of the hood, "then I would very much like to see it." As he stepped back the visitor released his grip and the old man motioned him through the doorway into a candlelit hallway. Still he grinned, and Richard found it disconcerting. Clearly the man thought that he knew something that Richard did not.

The corridor in which Richard stood was flickering as the candles danced in the draught from the open door, which the old man was now closing. Richard kept his cloak drawn close around him and his hood over his head. The rain dripped from the tip of the hood above his nose and from the hem of his cloak that hung only a few inches above the floor. Quickly, a patch of sodden rushes marked the spot on the floor where the stranger to this house stood, waiting, as the door shut with a thud that made the flames of each candle leap. The corners of Richard's mouth turned down artificially as he watched the man drop a broad beam across the doorway. He wondered whether it was to keep him in or others out. Not that it mattered either way.

"You'll find your 'Lady'," the man quipped, turning to meet the other as he teased him, "in the kitchen, peelin' veggies." He nodded towards the door behind Richard's left shoulder. That grin was back. Without a moment's hesitation, Richard turned on his heels, the reeds swishing underfoot, and unlatched the door. If he had taken a minute, he might have felt that this was too easy, but Richard was now used to getting what he wanted. Immediately, the heat from the room thudded into Richard's torso. He inhaled a nose full of hot, rich, sweet smelling air, heavy with the scent of roasting pig. The heat dried Richard's eyes and he blinked furiously as he tried to focus on his surroundings.

The young man stood at the top of a short, steep flight of steps that led down into a large, square kitchen. The floor was layered with rushes, patchy where fat spattered from the large fireplace and water sloshed from the large pots of vegetables. A spit boy stood in breeches, his hair and skin sooty with rivers of pink cleaned by the sweat that matted his thick hair to his head. Two women sat at the far wall chopping a variety of vegetables into a row of large pots, and a third sat closer to the corner with a large pile of peelings to her right and an even larger stack of unpeeled vegetables to her left. As Richard's eyes reached her, she looked up to meet them. Even in those brown cloth servant rags, and through the dusting of soot that darkened her face, he recognised Anne, and her nobility, and found himself gripping the banister at the top of the stairs, suddenly nervous, and angry.

Lady Anne Neville had grown to be quite accustomed to unexpected situations. Betrothed to the Prince of Wales, widowed, her father killed as a traitor. She was barely surprised to be in her brother-in-law's kitchen, working under an undignified form of house arrest. And still she was only a teenager. Although she was not poorly treated, it was hardly befitting of her upbringing and position. With her father dead, she had no-one to protect her and held little hope of escaping her predicament whilst she still stood to inherit that which her sister and brother-in-law coveted with raging avarice.

This was the third London household into which she had been secreted, moved twice in the dead of night without warning or explanation. Having been here for a week, she felt another move would come soon. Each move brought with it a renewed, deepened sense of despair. The longer she remained in one place, the greater her chances of being found, she continued to tell herself, often against her better reason. Each time that she forced herself to believe that there may be hope, the night time brought with it thoughts as cold and dark as the stone floors upon which she slept. Even if she stayed in one place for a year, who would even be looking for her? And if her champion were to seek her out, arriving at the door in his shining plate mail astride his huge white charger, what chance would he have against George, Duke of Clarence? These were the thoughts that accompanied her into uncomfortable, fitful sleep. Her hope was always short lived, yet always she managed to keep a shallow breath of life in it. Her father had not raised her to give up and cower under a yoke. She would bear the weight with her head held high for as long as it took.

This evening, Anne felt at a real low. Her chores seemed never ending. The pile of vegetables seemed to grow each time she turned her back on it and the searing heat from the fire left her feeling drained and weak, and her hands ached and stung. She looked up to the table against the rear wall, opposite the fire, where five men always sat, whenever she was there. All wore leather breeches and grey-white blousons. Five heavy leather jerkins were piled behind the table and five swords stood against the wooden side of the staircase, within easy reach. A pitcher of mead sat half empty in the middle of the table. The drinking had started early today and the tiresome performance of innuendo directed at the young girls moving in and out of the kitchen had begun. The oldest, the sergeant, who looked around forty, though was probably a decade younger, was clearly emboldened by his fourth mug of mead. The other four men hushed as he leaned over towards Anne.

"Would my Lady care to peel herself a real man?" There was muffled, stifled giggling amongst the others. The man's lips curled as he grinned at Anne. She looked slowly up at him, held his gaze for long seconds, mustering within her all of her dignity. Without faltering, she reached down with her left hand.

"Some things," Anne replied calmly, fighting against the lump in her throat, "are simply not worth the effort of peeling." With that, she gently launched a tiny, thin runt of a carrot onto the table. It landed directly in front of the man, spinning to a halt. There was a moment of complete silence before one of the men snorted loudly and all four suddenly roared with laughter. The sergeant stood sharply, pounding his fists onto the table, and glaring at Anne. Her stomach twisted, but she forced herself to hold his stare with a blank expression.

"I'll show you something you'll not forget, woman!" the man bellowed as the fire cracked loudly. The man on the far side of the sergeant tugged at his arm, clearly suggesting that he sit back down before the matter went too far, but as the commotion grew, Anne's eyes drifted above the bustle to the figure at the top of the stairs. A long cloak hung just above the ground, dripping silently, and as her gaze lifted to the shoulders of the figure, the cloth was releasing its moisture in the heat of the fire so that a mist rose slowly from him, creating an eerie haze about his head through which she could make out no features clearly, but the man, as she supposed the figure was, appeared to be staring directly at her. He looked down at the table, where the friction between the men was continuing to build, and began to descend the staircase.

Richard's heart had thumped hard as he had caught Anne's gaze, almost lurching him forward down the stairs. He drew his eyes away to complete their circuit of the room and they rested finally upon the large wooden table between the stairs and the spot where Anne sat. He had been unsure of what to expect at this point. Nothing? A small army? That had always depended upon how confident his brother was that no-one would have the will or the resource to find his ward. Apparently, he was quite confident, but not complacent. About right, Richard mused, for George. And Richard liked it when people underestimated him, because he revelled in shocking them and watching them reel, off balance. He was certainly ready to see George's face when he lost the battle with his little brother. He shook himself back to the moment. The battle was still to be won.

He placed one foot before the other and descended the dozen creaky steps before him, his eyes never moving from the table of arguing men, his hand wandering unbidden to the mace at his side. With each step he found his bravado nibbled at by a familiar nervous feeling. Had he bitten off more than he was able to manage? As he gripped the bound handle, he was reassured by the skill that hours of practice had sown deep within his subconscious. He had never yet outstretched himself.

As he reached the bare flagstone floor at the base of the stairs, where the rushes had been brushed aside by continued traffic, his boots did not make their familiar click, but squelched slightly with the mud that they still held. By this point too, one of the men on the far side of the table who had been less interested in the growing commotion than in his mug of ale, had noticed the stranger moving down the staircase and was drawing the attention of the other men to his presence. The sergeant turned to face him, cheeks flushed and puffing, and motioned to the others, who cautiously reached for their swords. A sudden air of sobriety fell upon the room.

"And what might you want?" The sergeant's tone was full of a practised authority meant to intimidate. Usually, it worked.

"I have come," Richard began, not at all intimidated, "to collect the finest ware that this kitchen has to offer."

"What?" the sergeant frowned, as the man to his left passed over his sword.

"You have something here precious to me," Richard continued calmly, "something that belongs in finer surrounds." He cast his gaze slowly, deliberately, across the men as his palms parted his cloak and spread out to his sides. His eyes shot back to the man some fifteen feet in front of him, steam still rising in tendrils from his shoulders and head. "And which deserves to be in far better company."

Anne sat, paralysed, listening. Could it be? The sergeant shot a glance at her, guessing the stranger's meaning, but she did not even notice. Her eyes were fixed on the mysterious figure, and her stomach began to flutter.

"Well, well," the soldier's eyes darted back to the hooded figure, "at last!" he grinned, raising his broadsword up before himself. "Perhaps I'll send you back from whence you came with a message for yer master."

"Perhaps," Richard retorted, smiling uncontrollably, "you can deliver this message that you have yourself." With that, he threw back his head and the heavy, damp cloak slumped behind him in a heap. He threw his eyes to Anne for her reaction.

The sergeant stepped back, lowering his sword, obviously caught off guard by the gesture. Anne shot to her feet, her hands covering her open mouth. She had not recognised the voice. Well, it had been so many years that the voice had to have changed, but the face that had been unveiled was unmistakable. She had known the boy so well, growing up in her father's castle, and she knew the man by reputation, but she still saw the boy in the fire lit grin that she now looked upon. Truly, she was amazed to see him. Was she still trapped within one of her cruel daydreams? She immediately doubted this, since in her daydream she would have imagined more than one man to fight off five soldiers. She struggled to catch her breath. Her heart thumped so hard that she feared it would leap into her throat.

"Who's that then?" shouted the youngest of the five from the far side of the table.

"That's, erm," the sergeant's voice broke and trailed off.

"Richard," the visitor interrupted, "third Duke of Gloucester." He bowed with mock respect, bending low and spreading his arms, but keeping his head high to hold the stares of the men. After a moment, though, he could not prevent his eyes from straying over to meet the Lady Anne's. He smiled at the expression of shock on her face. The five men looked at each other, clearly unsure of the situation.

"Enough games now." Richard stood up straight. "I have come to remove the Lady Anne from this place. Now, will you step aside?" There was a moment's pause, with four figures awaiting a lead from their sergeant.

"Our orders stand." He raised himself to his full height and his sword resumed its ready position in front of him. "We give 'er to no-one," he nodded in Anne's direction, "whoever they may be." He swallowed nervously.

"Very well." Richard said lightly. "Then I shall take her. You may try to stop me if you wish. Whoever you may be." With that, he took a stride forward, towards the men rather than Anne. The sergeant immediately launched himself towards the young man, a reaction Richard was counting upon. As his sword swung down from high above the sergeant's right shoulder, Richard crouched and leaned his body to the left. As the sergeant's hulking torso lurched past him, Richard uncurled his legs and sprung upwards, forcing his right hand under the sergeant's right arm to continue his momentum and as the man began to stumble under the weight of his own motion, Richard swung his left leg up to push the sergeant's backside. He tripped forward, desperately trying to remain on his feet. His sword clattered to the floor as his arms flailed furiously. Finally, he was halted by his shoulders slamming, one each, into two of the spindles on the staircase. After the sharp pain that shot down his back, the sergeant grimaced. Now he was really annoyed, as much by the foolishness he felt as the pain in his shoulders. He pulled himself upright, but another sharp pain halted him and he finally realised. His head was stuck fast between the spindles. He tried to pull once more but the searing pain in his ears stopped him and his shoulders slumped. The room seemed very quiet behind him. 'Fools,' he thought. He drew a lung full of the hot, uncomfortable kitchen air.

"Get him!" he bellowed, motioning with his left arm from roughly where he knew the table was to the spot where the other man had stood. "Kill him!"

There was a clattering commotion as the remaining four lined up, positioning themselves between the duke and the lady. They eyed each other in turn, silently asking each other whether they really should attack the king's brother, or whether it would be worse to explain to the sergeant, and the duke's older brother, why they did not. Any indecision was soon banished.

"Now, you halfwits!" the sergeant bellowed again as he began again to try and free himself. The four men lurched forward towards Richard.

The first man reached him with his sword above his right shoulder, but was moving slower than the sergeant had. As he whipped his arm down, Richard took a pace forward, placing his right foot behind the man's right foot and leaning his body under the man's arm. The attacking right arm thudded painlessly onto Richard's left shoulder, and at the same moment he leaned his full weight into the man's torso and jolted his right hand into the other's chest, sending him toppling over Richard's foot. The man behind stumbled over the reeling soldier and crashed to the floor, cracking his head loudly on the flags. He remained still. The two others lunged at Richard together. In a fluid sliding movement, he slid his body sideways to miss both thrusts to his front, grabbed the wrist closest to him and pulled it to continue its motion. As the man fell forward, Richard clenched his fist and smashed it into the man's cheek, sending him crashing to the floor in front of the fire. The second recovered his wayward lunge and sliced his sword back from across his body towards Richard's midriff. The duke took a wide step backwards and the tip of the sword whistled past his stomach. Preparing for the returning stroke, Richard placed his right hand around the familiar hilt of his mace. As expected, his opponent reversed his swing. In one swift, liquid movement, Richard caught his wrist with his outstretched left hand and pulled his mace from his waist upwards, slamming it into the man's braced right elbow with a crack that told Richard the man would not use that arm to attack him again. The sword clanged on the floor and the man whimpered loudly, falling to his knees.

Richard relaxed his tense shoulders and rolled his neck, but a shiver shot down his spine and he turned to see his first attacker half upright, picking his sword up. The duke stamped on the blade high, near the hilt, and trapped the man's hand, pinching it on the floor so that the man's face screwed up in pain. Making eye contact, Richard shook his head slowly. The other blinked, and then Richard felt him try to pull the sword from under his foot. He tilted his head sideways in exaggerated disapproval, tossed his mace in the air, flipping it so that he caught the top of the shaft. He waited for a moment while the pain of realisation fell over the soldier's face, and then crashed the handle of his mace across the side of the man's head. As he crumpled to the ground, Richard slid his mace back into his belt and kicked the sword so that it slid under the table. He looked around, and apart from the sergeant still fidgeting at the stairs and the two kitchen maids holding each other in the corner, all was quiet.

Finally, Richard looked slowly over to the Lady Anne. She was still standing in the corner, frozen. As Richard stretched out his arm to her Anne's legs grew unsteady. Overcome by a combination of the heat and her emotions, she tried to move towards him. Richard saw her instability and the light of the fire danced across the tears streaming down her red cheeks and he stepped towards her, sliding his left arm around her back and sweeping her legs up with his right arm. He pulled her tight to his chest and, closing his eyes, he lay his head on top of hers for a moment.

For her part, Anne surrendered into Richard's arms, defeated by the moment. As she hovered on the very edges of consciousness she could hear nothing, not even the roar of the fire, over the soft, rhythmic beating of her saviour's heart. She thought it sounded unrushed by the exertion, but she thought nothing more.

The young duke stood for a moment savouring both his complete success and the sweet, heavy scent of roasting meat. Though he would not allow it to show, the heat of the room was stifling and each breath he drew felt more uncomfortable than the last. Anne was limp in his arms now and felt heavier than he knew she was. He felt an achy trembling in the back of his thighs as the adrenalin of the fight began to wear off. In a moment, another wave washed upwards from his calves and he knew it was time to leave before the heat got the better of his limbs. He sucked a deep lung full of the searing dry air through his nose and turned, pulling Anne closer to his chest in spite of the uncomfortable heat in order to balance himself better as he moved. As he rounded the base of the stairs, the red cheeks of the sergeant greeted him, still wedged between two spindles. He began to writhe anew as he caught sight of Richard carrying Anne. Only one man was going to have to take the blame for the loss of Clarence's ward.

"Oi!" he squeaked with a voice that cracked on the dry air. "You can't take 'er from 'ere." Richard stopped at the base of the stairs, holding the man's gaze for a moment and then began to climb, deliberately shaking his head at the other.

"You'll pay," the trapped man continued, "when your brother hears of this."

"I should hold your tongue," Richard retorted without stopping his ascent, "for you find yourself somewhat prone for one who would make threats." Richard continued past the man's trapped head. As he tried to pull up his right foot, he found it would not move. And it was not as a result of his increasing tiredness. He felt thick fingers around the boot leather at his ankle. He grew weary of this nuisance.

"Release your grip now." Richard demanded. He had no intention of repeating the warning. The hand squeezed tighter still and Richard felt his blood heat up like a dry branch thrown on a raging pyre. He lifted his left foot and planted his heel heavily onto the man's wrist. At once, there was a yelp like that of a scalded pup and the fingers about Richard's boot instinctively released their grip in response to the shock. Instantly Richard moved his left foot back up a step and shuffled his feet around to turn on the narrow step whilst retaining his balance, holding Anne's body. The pained face of the soldier looked up at his but he did not hesitate as he swung his right boot quickly and heavily. There was an unpleasant crunch as Richard's foot met the man's jaw and he followed his swing all the way through. As his foot came back to rest on the step, the soldier's head flopped and hung limp over the stair below. Turning slowly, Richard summoned all of his strength and mounted the remaining steps.

As he stepped back into the hall the door opposite slammed shut. The passageway was empty. Moving slowly along it, Richard's shoulders dropped, aching as he saw the narrow knotted beam that barred the door. He felt sure that if he were to stop and set Anne down now he would not be able to raise her up again. When he got close enough to the door he swung his right foot up again, twisting at the ankle so that the outside of his foot met the underside of the bar and raised it from its cradle. Fortunately the beam was not a heavy one, though Richard still winced at the pain in his foot. He lifted the latch and the door swung open, letting in the cool evening air from the street outside. Feeling his legs buckle, Richard drew in the refreshing air and it stung his lungs with the cold. He gave two high pitched whistles.

Instantly, Lovell appeared at a gallop around the corner holding the two other horses. He drew Richard's horse up before the duke and as Richard lifted Anne up, Lovell reached to help. He watched as Richard wearily pulled himself onto the saddle behind Anne and positioned her across his lap. She stirred and muttered something onto the breeze, then sunk once more into Richard's chest.

"My lord," Lovell spoke with a tone Richard knew well, "you seem a little short of breath." The duke could not help but smile and looked over to see Lovell beaming back.

"A fair evening's exercise," he panted back, "but now the horses shall do their part." Both men spurred their horses on, the empty third running alongside Lovell who retained its reins.

"You have the letter?" Richard called as they raced against the wind through the drizzle and darkness.

"Richard," Lovell shouted back abruptly, "you have done your part, I will do mine when we reach the carriage. Now, shut up and ride!"

There were few people in the kingdom able to speak to the Duke of Gloucester in such a manner. Fortunately for Lovell, he was one. So they rode on into the night towards their destination.

Chapter 6

22nd May 1472 - The Letter

Anne blinked fiercely as the sharp morning rays pierced her eyes. They filled with soothing tears as they fought to adjust. The haze created by the tears only served to increase her sense of disorientation. Where was she? What had happened last night? Richard. Was it a dream? Her mind raced. She expected to snap out of it and find herself still trapped by George and Isabel. She forced herself to think. She was in a bed, and wherever she was it didn't smell like the place she had awoken in yesterday morning, if that even was yesterday, for she had no sense of time, other than that it was clearly day. Still, there was no longer the heavy, hanging, musty odour. Slowly, as her eyes grew accustomed to the light and her tears began to subside, she found that her bed lay against a wall of broad, bare stone. She pushed back the rough blanket and sat up, her back aching, though she did not know why. The chamber was narrow, barely leaving room to stand beside the bed, and there was only a small cabinet between the end of the bed and the dark oak door that rose to a point. The blinding light shone through a tall, narrow window in the wall opposite the bed, to her right. She was clothed in a plain white gown. As plain as it was, it was also comfortable. She frowned as she ran her fingers across her chest. She did not remember how she got into this gown and that made her feel even more uneasy. She wanted to get out of the bed and find out where she was, but a part of her dreaded learning that she was captive in a new prison.

She stood slowly, stretching her back, and tugged the blanket from the bed, swinging it around her shoulders to act as a cloak, thus protecting her modesty against whoever may be on the other side of the door. She listened a moment, but could hear nothing. Stepping forward, she placed her right hand on the latch of the door, but found herself hesitating to open it. In that instant, she felt the latch rise, but it was not her lifting it. Her stomach knotted and she lurched backward with surprise, holding her breath as the door slowly creaked open. Anne had no idea what she would do. She was clearly trapped in this small, enclosed room. Pulling the blanket close around her neck she resolved at all costs to retain her dignity. Even drawn up to her full height, she was completely unprepared for the figure that stepped through the doorway.

A large body pushed the door wide open and stood, all but filling the frame. The direction of the light meant that Anne's eyes took a moment to adapt and focus through the shade created by the form. The blanket around her neck had been pulled so tight in her tension that as she finally relaxed her grip she gasped and gulped in the cool dawn air. A nun. She could hardly have been more relieved. The figure wore the unmistakable habit of a nun, framing a broad, instantly comforting smile. She held before her a small tray with a wooden bowl and a pile of broken up bread.

"Good morning." The voice was soft, yet seemed to fill the room. "I apologise if I startled you." The stranger moved over to the cabinet at the end of the bed and set the tray down gently. "You should eat something." The tone was comfortable in the harsh, bare surroundings. Anne felt a little easier. "I'm sure you have many questions."

"Yes." Anne managed only a single word. She had not thought beyond the door of the room yet, but now uneasiness began to fill her stomach again, leaving little space for breakfast. Where was she? How had she come to be here? Had she exchanged one jailer for another? She had felt relief at the sight of the nun, but it was not unknown to be an effective prisoner in the Lord's house, particularly when hiding someone you did not want found easily. Her stomach tightened uncomfortably again and an acid taste stung her throat. She was unsure which question to ask first, or whether she truly wished to hear the answers, or even whether the person before her would have any of the answers she needed. The seemingly unending moment was broken as the nun turned from the cabinet, still smiling.

"There is a letter upon the tray." She began, and Anne's eyes shot across to it. She had not seen the sealed note beside the bread. Why had she failed to notice it? "It may answer your questions. You are free to treat this place as your own home."

Anne watched in silence as the nun nodded slowly and wafted from the room, pulling the door shut behind her. Suddenly conscious of herself, Anne closed her lips tightly, raising her gaping jaw. She stepped hesitantly to the tray and eyed the letter cautiously. Her hand hovered, not quite touching the surface of the envelope. The wax seal was clearly Plantagenet. Richard? A haze of events in a London kitchen suddenly flooded her thoughts. Even if it was him, Anne was unsure still as to his motives. She knew well that the dowry for anyone marrying her was appealing. The Neville and Beauchamp fortune remained immense, and, for her part at least, available. The prevention of her marriage had been the reason her sister and brother-in-law had hidden her away. The obtaining of her inheritance was the most likely motive that she could think of for Richard's removal of her to this place. As she thought, her hand came to rest tentatively on the note. Nibbling on her bottom lip, she resolved that she must have answers, whatever they may be.

She lifted the letter. The paper felt so heavy as she ran her finger under the lip of the envelope to break the clump of wax from the body of the letter. Slowly, knowing that the rest of her life may depend upon its contents, Anne opened the letter and began to read. As she read, a tear rolled slowly down her left cheek.

Richard sat in a high backed chair gazing into the dancing morning flames in the wide hearth. Edward sat at a broad oak table in the centre of the room moving papers from side to side. Richard could hear the movements, though he was sure Edward would not really be working so early in the morning. He glanced to his right and caught his brother gazing out of the leaded window on the far side of the room from the fire. The duke guessed why the king had summoned him so early. He knew that they awaited their brother George, who had received the same summons but was slow to obey, as was George's wont with Edward's commands. Sure that the Duke of Clarence would by now know the events of the previous evening, Richard hoped he retained the support of the king for his actions. Though he disapproved of George's treachery, Richard maintained a reasonable relationship with George and had yet to be upon the receiving end of one of Clarence's infamous temper tantrums, though he was more than prepared to face one today for his cause. As Edward looked back and caught his brother's gaze, the young duke's stomach tightened. Holding the king's stare for a moment, Richard was unsure whether it was because of what may happen in this room in moments, or because of what may be happening right now, far away in the church of St Martin le Grande.

In that instant, the door behind Richard's chair crashed open and heavy footfalls thudded into the room, announcing George's arrival. Hidden by the chair back the young duke placed his fingertips together and his lips thinned into a dry smile of anticipation.

Edward despised moments like this. He found his role as king came naturally to him. His physical presence was always enough the get him through any situation in which his natural charm and likeability did not win through. Elizabeth often quipped with her family that every man in the kingdom wanted to be Edward, and every woman wanted to be with him. Although he was aware that it was always said within earshot, he could not help but be flattered, and he was well aware that he was generally liked amongst the men at court and was never short of female attention. Yet as easy as he found managing the country, it always proved equally difficult to manage his own family. George had always been a firebrand, jealous of Edward's position, continually plotting and positioning himself with one eye on the throne. To date, Edward had stayed one step ahead, especially since Warwick's rebellion had publically exposed Clarence's intentions. Once suppressed, this had worked in Edward's favour, but not solved his problem.

There was only one reason why Edward was in a quandary today. Even now he was utterly unsure how to resolve this matter. He was used to dealing with George. If the dependable right arm of his rule, whom he had not really thought he need worry about and upon whom he intended to lean more heavily, was to become erratic and unpredictable, he may find his position in real danger. He could not afford for Richard to turn on him too. Elizabeth's suggestion echoed in his mind. It could restrain Richard, or push him into rebellion.

The thundering pound of a fist on the thick wood of the desk pulled Edward rudely back into the moment.

"I will have justice, Edward!" George shrieked, his voice heightened as it always did when he was excited or annoyed. "You cannot allow Gloucester to act with such disregard for my property and your law." His harsh tone and stare was met squarely by his brother's bright blue eyes.

"I will remind you," Edward said calmly and without blinking, "that I may allow anything that I wish to allow, George." Richard chose his moment, rising silently from the chair and standing squarely between the roaring fire and his raging brother.

"And I do not believe," he tried to lower his tone, in contrast to George's and to sound authoritative, conscious that he was the youngest protagonist, "that Lady Anne is your property, nor that there is any law that would prolong her time as your prisoner."

George had been startled by the sudden sound of his younger brother's voice, but had not broken the locked gaze of the elder. He felt his blood begin to boil, first at the cheek of Gloucester, but secondly, and to a greater extent, by the knowing smile of victory that was growing on Edward's face. How George despised that smile. Closing his eyes slowly, he turned. As he opened them, he saw Richard, silhouetted by the dancing flames so that he appeared to shimmer at the edges. 'The golden boy.' George thought to himself and smiled, curling his top lip.

"Ah, brother, I did not realise that you had arrived." George opened his arms in greeting, but neither brother moved forward to the other. "The door still hangs true," George smiled and waved his outstretched arm in its direction, "so I thought we were still awaiting your arrival." Without turning, George addressed the king. "Have you checked that everything is still here, my lord?"

"George," Richard chuckled, mimicking his brother's amiable tone, "the king holds nothing here the he should not." They held each other in a cold stare.

"Sir," George's tone hardened, "your tongue runs away with you. You imply some theft or," George waved his arms elaborately, "or misappropriation on my part."

"My tongue follows where my mind leads it, and reports that which my eyes have seen." The intensity in the two men's stares grew fiercer still.

"Your mind will lead you into great trouble, little brother."

"I fear no harm while I have right, and God, on my side."

"You have no idea of what is happening, do you?" George drew breath but was prevented from continuing.

"Enough!" Edward's booming voice echoed off the stone wall, competing with the thud of his fist on the table. George turned his head slowly, holding eye contact with Richard for as long as possible, trying to measure his reaction to the exchange. "Both of you sit." Edward had risen from his chair and was leaning his imposing frame across the desk. Richard sat again in the chair before the fire, and George strode over to the chair opposing. As he passed Richard, he muttered to the young duke.

"Sit. Good boy." Standing a moment at the chair to force his point home, George smiled and sat slowly. He saw the red flush across his brother's cheeks, obvious even in the red glow of the fire. Edward sank back into his chair and it creaked under his weight.

"We all know why we are here." Edward stated.

"Because the Duke of Gloucester has something of mine that I would have returned." Clarence interrupted. Richard stared into the fire and said nothing.

"You are well aware," Edward retorted, his patience clearly straining, "that I have assented to Richard and Lady Anne's union. You will not stand in the way of this." Clarence's eyes remained fixed upon Richard, who in turn did not look away from the hearth.

"Sire," George simpered, "Gloucester's act was nothing less than thievery of a title to an estate. The act of a desperate lack-land." At last, Clarence drew the reaction he sought. Richard slammed his palms onto the arms of the chair, not without some pain to himself.

"If my lord seeks only to nip at my toes like an attention starved puppy, then we are done."

"Richard," Edward intervened, "please be calmed." He waited a moment before addressing Clarence. "George, if you wish to reach agreement, we shall. If you do not, agreement shall be pressed upon you." George knew his baiting was ended now, but hoped that it had unsettled Richard enough to tilt negotiations in his favour. There was an uneasy silence, broken only by the cracking of the fire splitting its fuel as it greedily devoured another log. Eventually, George broke the tension.

"Then let us cut to the chase. The matter is simple. How will the Warwick inheritance be split?"

"Evenly seems the clear answer." Edward spoke thoughtfully, though felt sure that George would not agree.

"Would my lord trample so roughly over tradition and precedent?" George spoke with a forced calmness, still eyeing the side of Richard's face that he could see. "I am the elder brother, and my Lady Isabel the eldest daughter of Warwick. Surely, then, the inheritance is rightfully mine."

"Take it then." All eyes shot to Richard. "I wish only the hand of the Lady Anne in this." Here, Richard knew he made his greatest gamble. He had known George would want all, and would expect a bitter fight. Failing to rise to it would unsettle him. More unsettled, Richard hoped, would be the king. Gloucester was gambling his political future on the king's fear of Clarence replacing Warwick as his mightiest subject. He felt confident that the prospect of this would force the king to impose a fairer settlement, with Gloucester emerging as the selfless, love struck figure of chivalry pressed to accept the gifts of the king. It was not a gamble he would take if he were anything but sure of his brother's reaction in light of his older brother's ambition. To lose would be to lose everything that he wanted to build. He stared unflinchingly into the flames. There was no outward sign of the wrenching that gripped his stomach.

"That decision," Edward snapped, with a faint hint of confusion in his voice, "is not yours to make, Richard." There was a protracted silence again and Richard fought to suppress the grin that pulled on the corners of his mouth. He was suddenly very conscious of George's eyes burning into his right cheek.

"Well, sire," George spoke to the king whilst looking directly at Richard, "we shall submit to your will, but I must press both mine and my wife's legitimately greater claim." Richard suspected that George had realised what had just occurred.

"My patience grows thin with you Clarence." Edward gritted his teeth. He was unsure what Richard's scheme was.

Perhaps he really didn't have one. Whatever George hoped, all knew that passing the entire estate to either brother was unlikely, with George by far the less likely of the two to receive the bulk. No, whether for reasons of good form or for his own, as yet unclear, device, Richard did not mean what he said. Edward remained calm though, sure of his own intentions in this matter. "Warwick's estate," he continued, "will divide neatly between the West Marches and the northern estates. The Marches shall go to Clarence, the north to Gloucester. The details shall be finalised in due course, but this is my decision."

"Sire," George rose to his feet, "I must protest."

"Clarence," Edward stood from his own chair and leaned forward, "I assure you that you shall not protest any further. You have my decision."

Richard looked up to Clarence and only now allowed the smile to escape. The scowl across George's pointed features displayed all too clearly his fury. He knew George was aware of his precarious position and would not risk an open opposition to the king unless he was prepared for a rebellion, and Richard hoped his swift action had not given George this luxury. His smile clearly forced his brother beyond the bounds of his composure. He leaned aggressively over Richard.

"You," he hissed quietly but with venom, "have no idea of what you are involved in."

"Clarence!" Edward boomed quickly, and Richard felt the king's voice shake the very bones of his body. For the first time, the king rounded his desk and strode across the room. He squared his frame before Clarence, towering above him and fixing his eyes with a burning stare. "Enough. Get you gone." The heat of their intense gaze burned a moment longer before Clarence lowered his head, sank into a shallow bow, glanced sideways at Richard's shocked face, then swiftly spun on his heels and left the room, slamming the heavy door behind him. Edward loosened his shoulders, heaved a heavy sigh and lowered himself into the chair opposite his youngest brother.

"I shall never know why I allow him to remain at court." Edward gazed into the fire, making an effort not to meet his brother's eyes. There was no response and Edward felt the weight of a thousand confused questions upon his left cheek. Still there was silence. "Still," Edward broke the impasse uneasily, "he is of no more matter. What of your bride, brother?" Edward looked over now and smiled at Richard.

"She is secure, sire." Richard wondered if he dare pursue a line that the king had so clearly closed. "She awaits the resolution of matters just now settled." He found himself unable to prevent the question. "What did George speak of, your grace, that I know not?" His breath left him as he awaited the king's response.

"He seeks only to excite your passion, Richard, to heat your blood." Leaning forward in his chair, Edward now spoke sternly. "Do not allow him the satisfaction." Rising from his seat, the king turned back towards his desk. "I will hear no more of this today. You have all the answers you need." There was a creak of straining wood as the man's large body settled once more behind the table. The look of concern so familiar to Richard washed over Edward's face, but was quickly replaced with a soft smile. "And you, young lad, have arrangements to make."

Taking that as his leave, Richard rose from his seat, stroked his right hand over his left cheek, which suddenly felt warm from the flames and made for the door. As his hand met the latch, he paused. As he opened the door, he looked back into the room and saw his brother gazing to a far window. Richard was uneasy at the thought that George may be plotting something. He was more uneasy still that Edward appeared to know something of what was happening and was unwilling to include his loyal brother. And that look of concern sat heavily on the king's face again.

Chapter 7

24th May 1472 - The Wave

It had been two full days now since her arrival at St Martin Le Grande, and after a flurry of questions, Anne had learned that she had been delivered into sanctuary at the Dover church in the early morning and, though restlessly, she had slept the whole journey, the move to her chamber in the cloister and most of the morning. There had been preparations made for her arrival the day before, the news of which she found both comforting and unnerving. Still, if nothing else, she had been enjoying the freedom of roaming the grounds at will. The letter that had been delivered with her had barely left her hand since its first reading, and she had read it now so many times that she knew each word without looking, yet almost every hour, she looked again, scared that the words may have changed. Each time she read it felt like the first, she got the same excited knot in her stomach and she was bursting to tell someone of its contents and the promise they held, yet in the regimented surroundings of the church her agitation felt out of place. She was a stranger to these people and so she had spent much of her time in silent prayer with the now precious letter pressed between her palms. She searched for the answer to one question. Should she trust the contents?

In contrast to her previous solitude, the last two days had been a happy quiet and Anne had been grateful for the peace and rest that had been afforded her. Yet this had been tinged with a sense of urgency stoked by the contents of that note. As weary as her limbs had been, for they were now regaining their strength, her mind remained full of spirit and vigour and she wanted answers, she wanted to understand. Although she remained relieved to have been freed from her sister's grasp, she was uncertain what the future held for her. The letter kindled hope, but she had known hope before and seen it snatched from her. All of her prayers for the last two days had been focussed upon the hope those faceless words gave her.

Now, sitting on her bed, Anne was gazing upwards to the small window that had so harshly greeted her on her first morning there. The deep orange that seeped upwards from below the window to warm the grey, cloudy sky spoke of the promise of what tomorrow may bring, and also signalled that it was time for the evening meal that would precede the evening worship. Turning the letter in her hand, she stood and pressed it to her heart. A tap at the door echoed softly around the room and startled Anne from her daydreaming.

"Enter." She called in response. The door was opened with a slow sigh from its hinges to reveal the figure of a slim, narrow man. Barely more than a boy in fact. Clad in worn leather and a mud splattered pale brown tunic. Anne recognised that the figure was a messenger. But from where? Her heart skipped into her throat a moment. At least he was not a soldier. The figure offered a low bow and then rose quickly to stand rigid as the stones of the four walls surrounding Anne.

"My Lady." The accent was unmistakeable to Anne. She knew well that this young but throaty voice hailed from Yorkshire. Curiously, she found some solace in that, whether through familiarity alone or the hope that the familiarity translated to friendship. "I bring word that my Lord of Gloucester approaches with all haste and requests a measure of my Lady's time if she would see him from her sanctuary." Anne's heart soared as she had never known it to before. She turned, to appear in thought, but in reality to prevent the man at her door from seeing the smile that she could not wrest from her lips.

"My Lady?" the voice pressed, pulling her back from her runaway thoughts.

"Yes, yes." She set her face straight and turned again to face the doorway. "You may tell your Lord of Gloucester," she spoke slowly and deepened her voice, "that I shall receive him." She was still a Lady, and had no intention of betraying her mind, especially to a message carrier come from a man whose intentions she remained more than a little suspicious of. The man nodded his head and began to turn. "And," Anne ceased a moment. She felt the need to add a polite sentiment, alongside the desire to make a passionate one known, but her mind begged for caution. She continued in spite of her doubt. "And please offer the duke my thanks for his recent intervention on my behalf, kind, and personal, as it was." She nodded at the man, who shot her an excited grin.

"Yes, my Lady." The man bowed in confirmation and pulled the door shut. Anne heard his footsteps in a hurried walk along the corridor outside and smiled. Then a horrifying thought struck her. What would she wear?

The sun was setting as Richard neared the abbey. He could taste the salty tang of the cool sea air at the back of his throat and the world was turning an odd shade of pale red as the burning orb of the sun, looking twice its normal size, sank reluctantly into the ocean on the distant horizon. That scent was one that Richard rarely encountered. Although he didn't actively avoid the coast, it had never held happy memories for him. The taste in his mouth sent a nervous twisting to his stomach. He was reminded of flights to the coast, the last the most desperate ever, and of rough, swirling voyages into a black sea, and of years spent in comfortable, but unhappy, exile. He was surprised to find himself reminded now of that last night of fear, the embers of a memory kindled by the combination of his current nerves and the scent of the ocean.

Half an hour out to sea, with a thick blackness pressing in about the ship, Richard had stood, leaning over the port bow, unsure whether he was more nervous of what awaited the next time he touched land or the thought that he may never touch land again. He could feel the swells below the hull rising higher and broader by the minute and the fine drizzle that had persisted all day was becoming thicker and no longer fell straight down but was being driven into his cheeks by the pulsing wind. He had been at sea before but had managed to avoid bad weather. It appeared that a bad day was to end even worse than it had begun. What felt like seconds later, white tentacles of foam spray leaped at the ship like some vast oceanic beast trying to drag it down to the crushing depths below. He gripped the bow's railing more tightly, unsure whether he should let go and move below or hold tight for fear of falling. He willed his fingers to release their grip but they were numbing in the biting cold and refused to do his bidding. His stomach knotted tightly with a sudden uncontrollable fear, not for his safety, but at his inability to control his own actions. Just then he lurched forward as something slammed into his left shoulder. His body reacted by releasing instinctively and he span on his heels to see what had been launched at him, only to be startled by the broad outline of a man encased in a sea-soaked, heavy overcoat. The ruddy cheeks flashing in the white spray and flitting moonlight were unmistakably those of the ship's captain.

"Ye should get below, sir," he boomed in a broad Norfolk accent. "We be battonin' down fer the storm." Richard didn't speak, still gathering his wits. The man stood before him gently swaying with the rhythmic rise and fall of the ship. "Alright are ya?" the captain continued, placing a broad firm hand on the smaller man's shoulder, something that Richard was unused to but actually welcomed now. He squeezed a nod. The other man held his stare. "Scary thing," he began again, leaning in to call over the growing roar, "a storm at sea, no land in reach."

Richard found himself unable to do anything but nod another shallow nod. The man had reached the very heart of his fears. In an instant, the other's hard, stern visage softened and a broad, warm smile spread over his face.

"I remember," the older man's voice echoed, drowning out the swirl about them, "the first time I was caught in a storm at sea. Barely twelve year old I were, staring slack jawed at waves higher 'en anything I'd imagined could be." The captain moved beside Richard, seeming at ease in the squall and jerk of the deck. A result, Richard felt sure, of long experience. His ease was in stark contrast to the raging disquiet in the young man's stomach. "Petrified I were. I'll never forget when the cap'n stood over me. Fierce man, he were! Everyone were afeared of 'im." The older man gazed into the dark, as if something held his attention in the blackness that surrounded them. Suddenly his attention was back on the deck. "All he said," the voice continued, distantly, "was "Can you see it?". Well, I tell ye, I froze. Not a clue what I was meant to answer and terrified of answering wrong."

"Well what did you answer?" Richard tried to draw himself up, but could not prevent his hand seeking out the sturdy rail again. He hated not being in control of the situation and forced his eyes to hold those of the seaman.

"Nothing. The cold bit me tongue too tight. I'm not sure I were meant to answer, truth be told, 'cos the cap'n carried on anyways. "Can you see the wave that'll carry off your soul?" he said. I still didn't know what to say. I looked hard into the dark and saw nothing so all I could say was the truth, an' 'ope it didn't earn me a clout! "Good," he answered." The man leaned his bulk over Richard and spoke more quietly. "Then 'e told me somethin' I have taken with me on every voyage since."

"Yes." Richard tried to exert some authority but it seemed ridiculous in the circumstances.

"When your time comes, you will see the wave rise up and you will know that it is your moment. Until you see that wave, know that you are invincible and that no other wave can harm you." As the captain finished, the two stood in silence. Richard pondered the words, and how the moment made them all the more poignant. He felt a shiver run down his spine. It was the other man that broke the silence first.

"Ha, ha!" he boomed, amused by the look that had crept slowly over the lad's face. "These words have served me well on many a stormy night, but I'll tell you the question I cannot answer." The man paused for effect, enjoying the young nobleman hanging on to his words. The duke looked into his eyes like a fish on a hook hauled on deck and begging to be rushed to its fate. His jaw opened slightly. The older man could not suppress a faint smile of triumph at the landing of such a big catch. "Well, is it the wave that was meant for ye, or is it the fear of a situation you can't escape that causes ye to see the wave? Maybe ye just comes to a point when ye see so clearly in the midst of the rage that ye just knows yer time is come. Until then, though, naught can harm thee."

The words hung between the two men as the wind buffeted them. Their eyes met and the larger man grabbed a fistful of the duke's tunic to steady him as they went below deck. The younger shifted his shoulder, breaking the captain's hold and fixed him with a hard stare. He widened his stance and steadied himself.

"I see no wave, sir," he spoke as steadily as he now stood, but allowed a smile to slip across his lips. "Now," he stepped forward assuredly, "let us get out of this wind." The captain laughed loudly as he turned and the two men walked side by side across the deck, both unmoved by the raging storm.

Richard jerked back to the cold evening as his horse stumbled slightly. He shook the cobwebs of that memory from his mind and sucked in a deep lungful of the salty, cold air that chilled his lungs. That night seemed a lifetime ago now as the duke rode with his retinue to seek a union with the Lady Anne.

"My lord," the deep voice drifted softly on the dusk breeze, as though the speaker knew he interrupted some deep, far away daydream, "we near the abbey. Should we stop here?"

"Ah." Richard refocused his thoughts. "Yes. Here will do." He recalled his request to be told when they neared the church. "Pitch camp, and fetch my clothes." The other man nodded to acknowledge the instruction. Richard looked at himself and brushed the dust from his right thigh absently. "I can scarce woo my lady while wearing half of the road!" Richard smiled, and the soldier gave a gentle laugh in courtesy, though he thought he spied a little nervousness in the duke's eyes now. He supposed that was only to be expected, even of one so lordly as the Duke of Gloucester, and he spurred his horse as he barked the orders to the rest of the train.

Chapter 8

25th May 1472 - Decision Time

Lady Anne Neville sat in the front pew, gazing at the altar as the last fading glow of the day pressed through the stained glass windows around her. She had come to pray, to place the events of the evening into the hands of the Lord and to ask for his guidance in this matter. However, she now found herself lost in a swirling waking dream of questions that may be asked, answers that may be given, what may depend upon this evening. For all of her wandering thoughts, she could not escape the feeling that her entire future was to be decided before the sun would rise again.

Grasping her hands more tightly, she silently recited the Lord's Prayer, her eyes closed so that she did not notice the man who had moved softly down the aisle. She jumped and opened her eyes as she sensed someone sit to her left.

"I am sorry, my Lady." The voice echoed faintly around the church. "I did not mean to disturb you." Without looking up, Anne felt a shiver run down her spine.

"My Lord." Anne mustered all of her composure. "I thank you." Anne crossed herself and looked slowly at Richard, who frowned. Anne smiled. "Not you, my lord."

"Of course." Richard flushed, and cursed himself for it. He couldn't believe that he was so tense. He had ensured that they would remain alone here for as long as was required, yet he felt the weight of a thousand eyes in Anne's gaze. "I trust that your stay here has given you a little peace in which to gather yourself, my lady."

"It has," Anne replied, "and I am in your debt for all time for the improved condition of my detainment." Anne smiled coyly. There was a heavy silence and the duke clenched his teeth hard. Then he could not help a broad smile from spreading over his face.

"It has been a long time, Anne." Richard spoke loudly now, and relaxed instantly. "But your tongue remains quick."

"And you," Anne returned with a smile of her own, "still like playing the hero, Richard."

"You are no prisoner here." Richard turned his eyes to the cross atop the altar as he spoke. He drew a deep breath. "Though I confess I have my reasons for acting now, you are free to follow the path you desire from this day, and in fact have been for two days."

Anne wondered whether Richard truly believed what he said. For years, Anne had accepted that she would be expected to follow the path of whichever man she was presently bound to, though she would not say as much to Richard. She had brushed down the dress she had arrived in, as it remained preferable to other options here, but had wrapped herself in a heavy black cloak to hide the plain dress. She placed her hand on the envelope that lay on her lap, concealed by the over cloak.

"Richard, you wrote many kind words in your letter. Now, I need to know whether you meant them." Anne searched Richard's eyes for a hint of his true intentions as she pushed a lock of her long dark hair from over her left eye.

"Each and every one, Anne." Richard slid himself off the pew and knelt before Anne, whose jaw opened in anticipation. "Lady Anne Neville, I have come to ask for your hand in marriage, that I may bring you and those you love under the protection of my roof and my sword for all time." Richard held Anne's gaze and his own urge to run. "If you do not wish to be my wife," he blurted uneasily, "you are free to stay here, or leave for wherever you would go, still under my protection if you desire it. I say this," he added swiftly, "only so that you know that this decision is yours alone and I would have you make it without pressure or coercion, for it is yours to make freely."

"My Lord of Gloucester, it seems your chivalry knows no bounds." Anne allowed the moment to hang heavily in the air between them. "It would be my honour to become your wife, my lord. And," she continued, "it would be my pleasure to be your wife, Richard, particularly if the contents of your letter prove true."

A broad smile exploded across Richard's face. A thousand thoughts flooded his mind and he could hardly decipher them or tell which one he wanted to let out first.

"Anne," Richard spoke quickly and excitedly, "I will spend my lifetime proving the truth of those words to you." He pulled Anne to her feet, grasping both of her hands. "Arrangements have begun for the marriage, it will be spectacular. I have a dressmaker awaiting your instruction, and..." Richard caught himself and paused. "Is this acceptable, Anne? As I speak it sounds presumptuous. Have I overstepped the mark?"

"No, Richard." Anne spoke calmly, with amusement on her face. "It sounds beautiful."

"Good." Richard nodded, gathering to him as much dignity as he could muster. "Then perhaps we should retire for the evening. The road here has left me exhausted and the thought of the return leg does little to ease the feeling." He smiled again broadly. "Though I am awash with an excitement that I doubt will submit to sleep." Releasing Anne's hands slowly, his fingertips deliberately lingering on hers, Richard stepped sideways into the aisle, bowed his head to the altar in respect and then lowered his head with a soft smile to Anne. She watched, unable to suppress another grin, as Richard stepped backwards between the pews, sweeping lower and spreading his arms. As he neared the rear of the church, he halted suddenly and rose bolt upright, his right forefinger raised high into the air.

"I had almost forgotten, Lady Anne. There is a small gift in your chamber for our return to London," he smiled, paused a moment as if to say something else, then spun on his heel and bounded from the chapel, his footsteps echoing around the vaulted ceiling. Anne turned to face the altar, nibbling on her thumb nail, and mouthed a silent thank you to the large shimmering gold cross that hung behind the draped table. She was suddenly overcome with a desire to return to her small, sparse bed chamber.

Moments later, the heavy door of the small room swung slowly open. Anne stepped hesitantly into the chamber. Her eye was drawn to the small table where a tall candle flickered, casting a soft glow over the bed, upon which a large dark square was visible. She moved nervously to the side of the bed, wondering whether she dared to believe that it wouldn't be some cruel twist to ruin what she hoped for. She reached her hand out and exhaled her anxiety as a deep softness engulfed her fingers. Holding the top edge of the package she slowly lifted it and, unfurling before her, she watched a beautiful crimson dress with exquisite cream lacework fall slowly to caress the hard stone of the floor. As she pulled it to herself, immersing her body in the plush fabric, her eye drifted down her front and was drawn to another shape on her pillow. Grasping the sumptuous dress to her chest with her right hand, she reached down and wrapped her left hand around a thin stem. She lifted the flower to her chin, the soft touch of the petals on her cool skin sending a shiver of pleasure down her spine and spreading goose bumps over the surface of her arms. Inhaling the light rose scent deep into her being, she smiled the first smile of contentment she could remember enjoying for so many years.

Chapter 9

5th June 1472 - Conditional Love

Ten days after leaving the south coast, Richard stood in the now familiar long, tapestry lined hallway. The mid afternoon sun soaked through the high windows, gently warming the cool air that drifted through the shadowy hallway. The duke's mind began to wander. This, he mused, was the first moment that he had had to stop and think in two weeks. His return from Scotland had faded in his memory behind the securing of Anne into sanctuary, his confrontation with his brothers, the dash to the coast, this time through choice, he smiled to himself. Having successfully obtained Anne's agreement to a union, things had moved apace. Their return to London had left little time to prepare for the ceremony, but still it had been everything that they had hoped for. The day had been bright but cool. The Abbey had rumbled with the murmurs and shuffles from the amassed gentry. No seat remained empty, and Richard's heart had jumped as Anne had glided down the aisle to him, stepping through the rainbow of the light cast across the church by the stained glass windows. The scent of roses and incense filled Richard's nostrils as they exchanged vows and a tender kiss on Anne's soft lips had seemed the perfect end to the perfect day.

The last few days had been spent making further arrangements for Richard and Anne to move their household to Middleham Castle, where they intended to make their home. This, Richard pondered, was the final formality before they left.

The door at the end of the corridor slowly opened and warm air reached out in tendrils, pushing at Richard's legs. The young man beyond the door called softly, his voice echoing slightly around the stone walls.

"The king will see you now, my lord." The man bowed low and stepped back as he spoke to allow Richard to pass.

"Thank you." Richard said as he passed the figure. A frown folded into the duke's brow as the man failed to make eye contact with him, then, as he left the room, shot a nervous glance to the far wall. When the door closed with a soft thud, Richard followed the man's gaze to the opposite side of the room. A pair of tapestries framed a plain door. Nothing stood out from the area. Richard shook it from his mind. There was business to be resolved. Edward was sitting behind his broad desk, gazing from the window, just as Richard had seen him so many times before. He turned as the duke strode across the bare floorboards and Richard's frown returned as he noticed the thin, strained smile on his brother's lips. Sitting down in the chair before the king's desk, Richard began to feel uneasy.

"Well, Richard." Edward shifted in his seat and Richard thought he seemed nervous, not something that he was used to seeing in his older brother. "The last weeks have been eventful."

"In all of the right ways, sire." The duke smiled, searching his brother's face for some clue as to what vexed him.

"Indeed!" Edward boomed, his mood seemingly lightened suddenly. "Who would have thought it? My little brother all grown up and almost respectable!" Edward winked to Richard as he laughed. The younger joined in to humour the king. He was growing more uncertain and a tinge of nervousness emerged at the back of his mind.

"Edward," Richard sought to regain a handle on the meeting, "I have many arrangements to make before we leave and am honoured that you have made the time to discuss these matters." He let the comment hang between them.

"Quite, Richard." Edward was subdued again. "As you are aware, I have been deciding the detail of the settlement of the Warwick inheritance as it affects both you and George." The two men held each other's gaze for a long moment.

"I thought that we had settled this matter, Edward." Richard narrowed his eyes. He did not like the direction that this meeting was taking.

"There is one matter we have not discussed." The king pulled a heavy wedge of papers from beside his chair and dropped them in the centre of the desk between them. "I have your deeds of land and title which are, in content, precisely as we agreed." Edward placed his broad hand on top of the papers. "However, there is a clause within these documents which I would not wish another to inform you of, though I am wont to tell you myself."

"Edward?" Richard was growing agitated now.

"My brother," Edward began heavily, "you know that I count you amongst my most trusted and faithful subjects, that I love you dearly as a brother, and consider you a good friend too."

"Your grace, you are making me nervous." Richard laid his feelings out before his brother in the hope of reaching the point of the conversation more quickly, since Edward seemed determined to evade it.

"Richard," Edward drew himself up in his chair, "I have placed a clause within your title which in essence ties your and your Lady's inheritance to the line of male heirs of the body of John Neville. Should that line fail, your title will revert to a life interest only."

A thick, dense silence filled the air and hung between the two men. Richard felt his cheeks flush and begin to burn with an uncomfortable mixture of rage and embarrassment swelling from the pit of his stomach as his head began to swim, the implications of what his brother was saying beginning to spread from his mind in a dozen different directions like the surface of a frozen pool as a stone cracks the ice in uncertain, indirect lines. Edward watched the reaction on his brother's face that he had expected to see. He was prepared for his younger brother's wrath, but he saw something in the young duke's eyes that he had not anticipated. Eventually, Edward could stand the silence no longer.

"As John Neville left only one living male heir, this means that your inheritance is effectively dependent upon the body and issue of George Neville."

"I am aware of this, sire." Richard swallowed the bitter pain in his throat, fearing that he would lose control of his welling tears of frustration. "How have I so offended my king as to deserve this?" he asked with gentle vehemence.

"Richard, you have not. I said…"

"You said," Richard snapped angrily, "that you trusted me."

"And so I do." Edward frowned as if struggling to find a way to convince his brother.

"Then why, sire?" Richard jumped to his feet and pounded a whitened fist onto the desk. "Why?"

"It is complicated Richard."

"How?" Richard leaned in shouting. "How?" The duke struggled to repress his anger. He took a deep breath and sat back down in the chair. "I presume that George's title contains some similar caveat." There was no hint of a question in Richard's tone but Edward's face betrayed him instantly.

"George is irrelevant…" Edward was again unable to complete his sentence as Richard rose slowly to his feet and leaned over the stack of papers towards his brother.

"How dare you, Edward." Richard's voice was quiet, almost calm but for the shaking that lay beneath it.

"Richard, sit down."

"How dare you repay my service by tying my hands in this way."

"Sit down Gloucester." Edward's firm tone rose above his brother's growing anger.

"I shall not accept this easily." The desk rocked as Richard thumped it again. Edward rose slowly to his feet and leaned toward the duke, towering over him. Richard's face remained as hard as granite, not intimidated by the size of the king's broad frame.

"I care not how you accept it," Edward said calmly but with unmistakable force in his voice, "but accept it you will. Do not forget yourself, Gloucester."

Richard knew that he could not afford to forget himself now, nor could he allow his temper to cause him some further embarrassment. He clenched his teeth together, knowing that he must acquiesce and consoling himself that this game would be long and that this was only another part of the whole, in which he still stood well.

"So, I shall take my leave, your grace, and depart to Middleham to see that your will is done in the north." He offered a shallow bow and spun around, marching across the room with his fists still tightly clenched at his side. As he opened the door, Richard drew himself up and turned back to his brother. "Perhaps," he said softly, "perhaps there I shall be able to earn your trust, my king." He bowed again and stepped through the door, pulling it closed behind him.

Inside the chamber, Edward collapsed into his chair. He pushed both of his palms into his face and rubbed the feeling of having betrayed his brother from himself.

"You already have, my dear brother," he muttered to the departed man before turning back to his window.

Richard leaned his back onto the door and finally allowed an escaping tear to roll down his cheek. Wiping it away before someone should see, he stood up straight. "So be it." He spoke to himself in a determined tone as he started along the cool corridor.

Behind him, within the study, Edward spoke to no-one in particular.

"I hope that you are right in this." At that moment, Queen Elizabeth entered from the side door, moved silently over to her husband's chair and placed a hand on his shoulder. Edward reached up and gently squeezed her hand, still gazing out of the window.

Chapter 10

Interlude

Sir Thomas More gazed into the fire, silent, as though lost again in the flames. Holbein was about to clear his throat to break the lengthy silence when a knock at the door saved him.

"Erm." Sir Thomas seemed to take a moment to work out where he was, as if slowly waking from a too-short slumber. "Er, yes, yes. Enter." The door squeaked a little as it swung open to reveal an elderly man at the door, this time holding a silver tray upon which rested two silver tankards, a large, ornately engraved pitcher and a platter of cooked meats, with a thick wedge of bread beside it.

"Sir," the man breathed heavily as he entered, "I have taken the liberty of preparing some refreshments for you and your guest." He slowly set the tray on a small table between the two men's seats. The smell of the warm meat was quickly followed by the sweet scent of the ale which swam within the pitcher.

"Thank you, John." Sir Thomas returned his focus to his visitor. "Master Holbein, please, eat and drink if you wish. The morning grows late."

"It does, sir." Holbein's accent, he hoped, masked the lack of enthusiasm that he had allowed to slip into his tone. He smiled and reached for a piece of pork as the old man left the room silently.

"I fear that I may be taking too long in the telling of my tale, Master Holbein." Sir Thomas narrowed his eyes. Hans grimaced as he chewed the strip of roasted meat. He knew his shrewd host had seen his waning interest. "Perhaps we should move our story ahead a little." Sir Thomas raised an eyebrow questioningly.

"Sir," Holbein was suddenly a little unsure of himself and sought to make good any offence that he had caused, "I am here to listen to your story as you wish."

"Yes." Sir Thomas's response was a thoughtful statement. He poured a tankard of ale for himself and nodded to Holbein enquiringly, who in turn felt obliged by good manners to accept his host's offer, though he rarely drank at this time of day himself. "Well," More continued as he filled the other tankard, "suffice it to say that in general, Richard began to establish himself in the north as a just lord, often defending the rights of commoners against the nobility, petitioning for the financial causes of the region and representing the Crown in its most troublesome area. There are many individual tales that I could tell you." Sir Thomas looked at Holbein for a reaction and was pleased to see that the young man did not offer one. "However, all of these are still well documented should one wish to discover them." The older man allowed a smile to crease the corners of his eyes as a thought passed through his mind. "The painting of my picture in full," he leaned forward to emphasise what he was about to say, "will aid the fuller painting of your picture." He poked a chubby finger at Hans with obvious pleasure at his own analogy. Hans, for his part, smiled uncomfortably.

Chapter 11

12th July 1473 - Eternal Commitment

The mid July sun streamed through the narrow window and pounded at Richard's face as he sat in the alcove, his knees drawn up to his chin. In his first year at Middleham, he had initiated so much change that it was becoming a challenge to manage, and had so many plans, not just for the structure and physical surroundings of the castle, which he was determined to create as a rival for anything in the south, the pride of northern estates. No, his plans extended to the reformation and galvanising of the economy of the northern counties, its political structure and the justice system that he had discovered there. Having spent countless evenings recounting his ideas to Anne and listening to hers, they had both grown convinced that not only was there much scope for work to be done, but that the position in which they now stood provided the perfect foundation upon which to establish a powerful northern region, with them and their dynasty as its figurehead, representing the Crown.

All of their plans seemed so far away now, as Richard struggled to find the farthest point on the horizon that he was able to see clearly. The rolling fields surrounding Middleham stretched out like gently rippling waves until they met the sky at some inestimable distance.

A piercing scream yanked Richard from that horizon back into his room. Another scream followed, the unmistakable shriek of agony. He shifted on the cool stone of the alcove. The largest part of him wanted to leap down and respond, but he fought the urge and sat, heated by the unrelenting sun. He sunk his face into his knees and clenched his teeth.

Another scream split the air. Longer and louder.

Richard wondered how much longer it would go on. So much depended upon today that Richard felt uneasy at his own helplessness in the situation. He despised being out of control. He struggled intensely with the feeling that he could not trust others to deal with such important matters.

There was a prolonged scream, gurgling as it waned, that caused Richard to finally look over at the door on the opposite side of the room. There was silence. He felt himself lean towards the door as if being drawn to it. The urge to get up was consuming him. Silence. Then, as he held his breath, the faint sound of footsteps swelled as they drew closer to the door. They seemed to pause directly behind the door. That was the final straw. Richard slid from his perch and planted his feet firmly on the dark oak floorboards. At that moment, the door that held Richard so transfixed flung open to reveal one of Anne's ladies in waiting. She held a large, tubular heap of blankets in her arms that caused Richard's jaw to widen slowly. He snapped his eyes back to the face of the woman before him, which was round and flushed but sported a broad smile.

"My lord," she spoke softly and in a hushed tone, but with a suppressed excitement in her voice, "you have a perfect baby boy."

The duke stood rooted to the spot. All impetus to move deserted him instantaneously and he found himself frozen, searching for a reaction. He barely even noticed the woman's face betray a growing concern, unsure what she should do. Then, suddenly, so many emotions came in such a rush that he felt like a blade of grass on a river being inexorably pulled towards a crushing waterfall. He leapt in the air and yelped, bounding across the room towards the open door like a puppy. The woman shrieked in shock as Richard planted a kiss on her rosy cheek. As suddenly as he had erupted he was still again. He stood directly in front of the woman with his arms making a cradle in front of him. He nodded to the lady silently, seemingly unable to vocalise his desire to hold his baby son.

Without needing the words, the bundle of blankets was slowly, gently lowered into the arms of the waiting duke.

Richard's face beamed as he looked down at the screwed up eyes of his son. He shot an excited glance at the lady, who moved back from the doorway. As he stepped into the room beyond, Richard saw the large four poster bed with what appeared to be a small army of pinafore wearing women surrounding it. One of the figures looked up to see who had entered and immediately shuffled over to the doorway.

"My lord," she spoke breathlessly, "everything is well. Lady Anne is resting."

"But she is well, safe?" Richard enquired.

"She is, my lord." The lady replied, nervously rubbing her hands on her apron, which was streaked with dark red. "She is very well, but exhausted by the exertion."

"Um," Richard acknowledged, "of course." He was sure that Anne would not want him to see her in her current state but he could not resist craning his neck over the nurse. The bed was still shielded from view, but he called in a kind of hushed shouting that was more of a loud whisper to protect the delicate ears in the crook of his right elbow.

"He is perfect, my lady," he called, struggling to contain his excitement and restrain his voice. "I love you, Anne." He turned to walk back out of the room, then turned carefully. "And thank you." Crossing the threshold back into the other room, he turned again, calling a little louder. "And I love you." The door was pushed shut behind him and he knew now that it was time for the moment for which he had waited for months. He moved with a careful, nervous urgency.

The chapel at Middleham Castle was not far from the duke and duchess's apartments. Richard had insisted upon that on their arrival and had spent much of his spare time, such as it was, in there with his prayer book seeking help and guidance for his plans. He also found the peace there that allowed him to think more clearly than in the verbal melee that dominated the many meetings that he held to obtain the views of the local magnates. Each rarely shared a single opinion with any other and so the proceedings often became lost in petty squabbling. On more than one occasion, Richard had left the meetings part way through and, by all accounts that reached him later, his departure had gone completely unnoticed.

Nudging the chapel's heavy oak door open with his shoulder, Richard was greeted by a gentle warmth washing over him as dozens of candles danced and flickered at the disturbance of the air as if rejoicing at their arrival. Richard was pleased at the effect. The chapel had been prepared earlier that day when Anne had gone into labour, and it was precisely how Richard had wanted it to be. Striding to the altar, Richard shifted the baby into one arm and crossed himself, lowering his head to the altar table in respect. His prayer book was laid on the first pew beside the spot where he always sat. 'Perfect' he thought to himself. Now, though, he stood before the altar, holding his son closely. He looked down to see the wrinkles fading as the pink face tried to push its eyelids apart.

"Lord," Richard spoke to the altar, "I ask for your eternal blessings upon my son, Edward." A warm shiver soaked down his back as he used his son's name aloud for the first time. "I pray that Your strength will protect him when mine fails, that the love of our Lord Jesus Christ shall surround him when mine will not suffice and that the wisdom of the Holy Spirit will guide him where I can offer no lead. Father God, I place my son into your hands and ask that you bless him with a very long and very, very happy life to the glory of Your name. Amen." Richard crossed himself again.

"And for my part, Edward," he continued softly to the piercing blue eyes that seemed to be transfixed upon his face, his mother's eyes, "I have a promise that I would make to you now." He sat down in his pew, feeling that he held his entire world cradled in his arms. He gently pulled the blanket down so that he could see the whole of Edward's soft, innocent face. He fumbled in the pocket of his tunic and slid out a circle of hard, cold gold. Turning it in his fingers, he pulled it closer to his eyes and it flashed in the light of the dancing candles. He stopped it as the flicking flames picked out the light and shade of an image standing proud on the face of the token. After gazing at the image a moment, as if lost, he held it before the baby's eyes, just to one side so that he could maintain eye contact with his son as he spoke to him.

"This," he said in a hushed voice, "is my coat of arms." He thought a moment. "Our coat of arms." Richard felt a warm wave of emotion wash over him at those words. He swallowed it back down. "I chose the boar for our symbol for a reason, my son. During my time here as a boy I did much hunting as part of my tutelage. One spring morning we were hunting deer in the forest and tracked a female with her foal. I thought that I could get closer than was needed for my bow. Between you and I," he grinned, "I just enjoyed being sneaky. Anyway, I stepped on a dry twig and the snap echoed through the trees. The deer bolted through the damp heather and disappeared. It took a moment for the foal to look up, realise what was happening and bound off after its mother. I remember thinking that I could probably have shot the young thing in the time its mother left it alone amongst the trees." Richard lowered the medallion and repositioned the baby in his arm.

"It was then that I heard a rustling to my left. I turned and by instinct notched the arrow in my hand. As my eyes scanned the forest floor, they picked out the hunched form of a boar, its tusks glinting with moisture and its front foot pawing slowly at the earth. We stared at each other for a long moment before my eye was caught again by two small mounds shuffling around some six feet behind the beast. This," he paused for dramatic effect, enjoying his own tale, "was another mother, with two babies. But she was not about to run. I lost my nerve before she did and backed slowly through the trees, counting myself lucky to have escaped unscathed. My heart pounded as I made my way back to the castle." Richard smiled at the eyes that gazed up at him with a look of unquestioning awe. He felt so proud and this moment was all that he had wanted it to be, all that he had planned.

"When I told my guardian," he said that word with a strange pang of loss, "what had happened, he too thought me fortunate and he immediately set me to reading the story of St Anthony, who was protected by a wild boar as he lived in a cave. It was then that I made the decision to adopt the boar as my personal symbol and to make it a true representation of my philosophy. To protect my family, my king and my country with all of my being, with my life if it must be so." He smiled again gently to his son. "I liked the notion of modelling myself upon a ferocious wild animal, willing to take on adversaries that seem indomitable without fear, driven by a fierce sense of duty and an overwhelming need to protect that which it loves. The greatest friend and ally anyone could wish for, but the worst enemy a man could ever have." Richard looked up at the large crucifix that hung as if held by some invisible force above the altar.

"Today, Edward," he continued, speaking slowly and deliberately as though he truly believed that his son understood him, "I make you this promise: I swear to you before almighty God that I shall not allow you to suffer my life as you grow to be a man as long as I am alive to prevent it. You shall not live an uncertain life in the household of others, nor shall you suffer one day of exile as I did, separated from your home and family. I shall build for you a secure and safe future as the king's greatest subject." Richard gently stroked his baby son's cheek and the shining blue eyes flickered and slowly sank until they were closed.

The two remained in the soft warmth and dancing light of the chapel for almost two hours before the younger decided that feeding time had arrived, announcing as much to his father with no ceremony whatsoever. It was a sound to which Richard became pleasantly used over the months that followed.

Chapter 12

9th March 1475 - Family Business

Edward of Middleham was almost two years old when he, along with his father and mother arrived in London on a warm, bright spring morning. Sitting at the window of the carriage, he blinked as the low ball of the sun flicked between the tall buildings. He was absorbed by the strange surroundings. The houses here were like the trees at home and the youngster had seen nothing like it before. He bobbed about in the carriage craning his neck out of the window to look ahead. Suddenly, he was lifted up and away from the curtain at the window and the fascinating scene disappeared behind the rich red velvet.

"Come away from there, Edward." His mother spoke softly but with unmistakable firmness in his tone. "You will tumble from that window." Anne pulled the wriggling body of her adventurous son away onto her lap and began to gently tickle his stomach to pull his attention away from what lay beyond the window. The tickle drew the kind of giggle that always made both Anne and Richard smile broadly to each other. It was closely followed by the kind of rumbling belch that always shocked Anne but caused Richard to laugh out loud.

"How long do we have before you depart?" Anne enquired without meeting Richard's eyes.

"There are a few more days to make preparations." Richard looked at his son, who was now chewing on his own sleeve. This was to be the first significant time that he would spend away from his new family, and he was not truly looking forward to it. In almost three years at Middleham things had moved so quickly. Richard had become patron of churches and colleges, he was finding ways to improve the economic situation of the whole region, using his influence on his brother to affect taxes and levies. The benefit was beginning to become apparent already and was winning Richard wide spread support and admiration. He had also spent long hours in the assize courts around the north and had found himself uncomfortable at the kind of justice that he continually witnessed there. It was based on the division between high and low, rich and poor rather than right and wrong. This was not entirely surprising to the duke. He was not naive enough to ignore political and social realities and had been at the epicentre of power wrangles for as long as he could remember, but to actually sit and listen to the gross inequity handed out to those with a genuine cause had affected Richard deeply and had left him resolved to add the correction of these matters to those issues he had already committed himself to tackle.

"We shall miss daddy, shall we not, Eddie?" Anne cooed in a high pitched voice at Edward, who gazed up at her as though she spoke some foreign language.

"It will leave you plenty of time to catch up at court and to visit some family." Richard smiled at both Anne and his son. He knew that Anne did not really want to stay in London but had come, along with Edward, only to save prolonging their separation. Although Richard knew that his family could expect to be welcomed and well cared for at court, he was also aware that it would be out of duty rather than pleasure, particularly with both Richard and the king away.

The carriage slowed and teetered to a halt to signal to those within that they had arrived at the palace. Richard heaved a preparatory sigh as the door was opened onto a set of steps that led almost directly to the foot of the state entrance to the Palace of Westminster. As they disembarked Richard was surprised to see the huge frame of his brother, arms spread wide, almost filling the doorway. He smiled, finding himself pleased to look upon Edward's beaming face once again.

"Richard!" the familiar voice boomed across the flagstone courtyard. "My Richard, it has been far too long!"

"And yet it feels as though I have never left, your grace." Richard lowered his head as a demonstration of his respect. He did frequently visit London when matters of state required him to do so, or when his brother needed his unswerving support at Council in a generally unpopular matter. Richard never failed to perform his duty, often finding himself in a position to mediate forcibly between the king and those who offered resistance to policy. Gloucester was often successful in this, and revelled in the faith his eldest brother placed in him to resolve such matters. The duke always used his visits to raise the concerns of the northern region before the king and was usually able to manoeuvre his issues into a moment when the king required some favour of him and thus he was able to return to Middleham bearing good news of his achievements at court.

"Where is my little nephew?" King Edward bounded down the steps, speaking in a tone not dissimilar to that which Anne had just used, causing Richard to suppress an amused smirk. "Ah, the Lady Anne." Edward stopped and lowered his head slightly. "It is good to see you in London once more. The climate in the north must suit you my lady. You look very well."

"Thank you your grace." Anne curtsied expertly with her son in her arms. "You are too kind."

"Nonsense!" Edward roared. "I hold dear the lady who keeps my brother so very happy," he patted Richard's flat stomach playfully, as though it were larger, "and who gives us such handsome additions to the Plantagenet family." Now, he tweaked his namesake's knee, causing him to wriggle and burst into laughter.

"Your Royal Highness." Richard spoke loudly toward the door where the slender figure of Queen Elizabeth had appeared as they were talking. He bowed an exaggerated greeting. Richard always used this most formal of addresses when speaking to his sister-in-law and it always drew a frown from his brother. Whenever the two spoke of it, Richard insisted that it was only proper to address the queen in such a fashion and that he did not know Elizabeth well enough to feel comfortable being more informal. The truth, however, was that Richard found Elizabeth aloof when he considered her far from above him. He had begun to believe that Edward was ignorant of the harm that he was causing by the promotion of the queen's family to some of the highest positions in the land to the exclusion of older, more established families. If Edward had ever managed to get the truth out of Richard, he would have learned that in fact the duke felt that the queen and her family threatened his political position as the king's greatest subject and his prized status as brother, friend and confidant of Edward. He always felt that Elizabeth disapproved of him at court. He always felt it, but had no evidence that it was the case. Elizabeth simply nodded her head slowly and remained, unmoving, in the doorway.

"Let us get inside." Edward broke the tension that he had failed to notice. He waved a hand and a young man jogged over stiffly. "Take the duchess and my nephew to their apartments." Edward instructed the man without looking at him and did not see the low bow that made up the acknowledgement of the order. "The duke and I," he turned to Richard wearing his broadest smile, "have business before morning." Richard beamed back, aware that this would mean plenty of wine and merriment and little of business. He could not help shooting a cold glance at Elizabeth whose face betrayed no reaction.

Hours later, Richard sat before a wide stone hearth in which a gentle fire cracked and spat. It was not cold, but as the evening fell deeper over London a chill seeped slowly into the room. More than the fire, the red wine was beginning to warm the duke from his very core. He and the king, who had wandered to the circular table in the centre of the square room to refill his goblet from the large golden pitcher that sat there, had passed the time until now exchanging stories of their growing families. Edward had a daughter and two sons, the youngest close enough to Richard's own son in age that they were lost for almost an hour swapping tales of sleepless nights, teething, first steps and words. It was not very often that the brothers were able to share these moments since Richard had left Edward's court to manage his northern territories. Richard held such times dear, as all too often the pressures of state prevented meetings such as this.

Richard suspected, though, that the moment had passed now. Edward's face had betrayed him as he had risen from his chair on the other side of the fireplace. Richard knew his brother had something that he wanted to discuss now, though he was not sure he would want to hear it.

"Richard," the voice drifted thoughtfully across the warm air just as the duke had expected, "do you know why I count you my chief advisor?"

"Because I am not often here to give you advise?" Richard called back playfully.

"Very funny." Edward gently nudged the side of his brother's head as he passed on his way back to his chair. "Truly, Richard, why do you think it so?" Edward's tone was unusually subdued, causing Richard to frown.

"I am loyal," he replied, "and you trust me to do my duty to my king." There was a moment of quiet, broken only by a log splitting on the fire.

"No." The reply was sharp and took Richard aback. He felt suddenly defensive, on edge. Was Edward accusing him of something?

"Edward?" he queried. There was no response for some time and Richard felt a surge of heat rush through him. An uncomfortable pressure was building behind his nose. He knew he was losing his temper. "Edward!" he snapped, demanding an answer.

"No, that is not the reason, though it is true and I am thankful for it. You may be the greatest amongst them, Richard, but I have loyal subjects all around me." Richard felt a little hurt in spite of the compliment. His dedication to Edward in the execution of his duties was something he prided himself on, all the more so because of what he saw as the inequity of his current settlement. He continued to hope to improve matters by his diligence. He held his tongue for a moment though.

"The reason I hold your counsel so dear, my brother, is because it is honest." Edward leaned in from the seat he had retaken. "I am surrounded by those who seem to think that loyalty is agreeing with everything that I say, that I am kept secure by over-loud laughter at my every quip. There is but one person who offers me their steadfast honesty, who sees no fear in disagreement, nor danger in not finding me funny. I am not quite so vain as to believe I am right all of the time and only you, Richard, will tell me without fear that I am wrong." A warm smile spread across the king's face. "To any king, such service is more precious than gold, even if he knows it not."

Richard was stunned. His jaw sank slightly ajar. He had not expected that, and not only because such an outpouring was so unlike Edward. Suddenly, the king sat back in his chair and his massive frame rocked as he roared with laughter. Richard leapt to his feet.

"Do you mock me, Edward?"

"By God I do not." Edward rose also, towering over his younger brother. "It was just the look on your face!" He threw his arms around Richard, still shaking with laughter. After a second, Richard released his own tension in a roar to rival his brother's before Edward pulled back, clasping Richard's shoulders tightly and fixing him with eyes that suddenly burned with a familiar passion. The dancing light could have been from the fire, though Richard thought not.

"Never," Edward began softly, "never, ever stop doing what it is right and true to do and begin doing what you think I want." The king wrapped his large palm around the back of the duke's head. "Swear it to me, Richard."

"I swear it, Edward." Richard held his brother's gaze. "I shall tell you that you are wrong at every opportunity." There was a moment's silence and the two burst into fresh laughter, picked up their goblets, clanked them together loudly and threw the contents down their throats.

Not too much later the evening became a blur of wine and laughter and Richard awoke the next morning unsure how he had got to his room, into his bed, or, as he looked under his blanket, undressed. A sure sign of a good night, and that he was less used to such sessions than his brother.

When the morning of their departure arrived, the royal household arose early in a clamour of activity as chests were carried along halls, trunks were hauled down staircases, maids scurried from door to door in dull dresses that hissed along the floors, footmen in bright uniform thudded across rooms purposefully and squires tacked ill-tempered, whinnying horses. Richard meandered through the chaos of dashing forms, stretching his arms and ruffling his hair, amused at all of the frantic commotion. Having risen early, the duke was satisfied that his preparations were going smoothly and he wanted to make the most of what time remained with his wife and son before leaving.

He had grabbed moments of the last few days with them but had found himself swept up by the performance of his brother's court. He had been trapped between Council meetings in warm stuffy rooms with warm stuffy men, all of whom disagreed with each other and yet all managed to agree with the king, and heavy meals with copious amounts of wine and ale at which the same matters were trawled over again and even less was resolved as the gathered gentry simpered before Edward and whispered, Richard had no doubt, against him behind his back. For his part, the king drank and ate furiously, as though his life were at stake. Even for his immense frame, Richard was shocked at the volumes Edward consumed in his revelry, and by the way in which some of the queen's family and others, like Lord Hastings, joined in and encouraged him. Enjoying a night of drinking with his brother was one matter, but Richard could not imagine wanting to do it every night as Edward clearly did. It was precisely this kind of endless, childish and petty squabbling that ensured nothing was actually done and which Richard was determined to stamp out in the north. Only one group of people benefitted from the maintenance of the status quo and that was the smallest one, the one that fought hardest to maintain the status quo. It infuriated him.

Now, though, he was set to depart. As much as he hid it from all around him for fear of appearing weakened, he was dreading leaving Anne and Edward for foreign soil. He had left them for brief times since Edward's birth when duty had forced it, but he had never been more than a day or so hard ride from home should he need to return. Now, he was heading to the coast, over the channel and into hostile territory and there was every chance that the more success they achieved, the longer he would be kept away. This thought left him uneasy, though there was little choice, for he had no intention of failure.

As he entered their apartments, Richard saw Edward lying on a deep fur rug a few paces from a softly crackling fire. His arms and legs sprawled from his body, his face tilted slightly toward the hearth. With eyes pressed tightly shut and his mouth hung open, the child was a vision that drew up a choking lump in Richard's throat. Just then, Anne stepped through the door from the bed chamber wearing a long, deep red dress that flowed behind her like a gently rippling stream. She was concentrating on the book that lay open in her palms.

Richard instantly recognised her prayer book. The moment seemed to hang for an age, as though time slowed to allow the duke to bathe in his contentment at the scene. As a satisfied smile grew across his lips, he sighed deeply.

Anne jumped at the disturbance, almost dropping her book.

"Aah!" she gasped, gathering herself. "You startled me, my lord."

"I am sorry." Richard's gaze turned to his sleeping son.

"He awoke just after you left." Anne whispered, stepping slowly across the room toward Richard. "I think he realised that you had gone and decided to take a little more sleep." She was well aware that her husband loved to hear such things, and she was happy to flatter him.

"I would think myself the most fortunate man in all of God's creation," Richard looked deep into his wife's eyes, placing a palm gently on her cheek, "but for the fact that I must leave you this morning."

"I know," Anne replied softly, "that the Lord's breathe shall blow you back to me as soon as the time is right." She raised her hand and squeezed the back of Richard's at her cheek. "You have no need to hide your feelings from me Richard." She smiled a gentle, encouraging smile. "They are part of what I love in you."

"May a man have nothing to himself once he marries?" Richard frowned. "Not even his thoughts?" He could not suppress a brief smile.

"In a man's world, the Lord must afford a woman some advantage." She smiled back at Richard, who wrapped his arms around her and pulled her close. As they held each other in the warm glow of the fire, Richard gazed over Anne's shoulder at their son and tried to draw back up the tear that was escaping down his cheek.

After a moment, he slipped from Anne's arms and crept to the rug before the fire. Kneeling slowly, careful not to awake his sleeping son, he was struck by the beautiful innocence of his face, untouched yet by the rough world. Anne watched her husband's movements with a warm contentment even his impending departure could not cool. Leaning down, he gently kissed the soft forehead and whispered, as though telling the boy some secret for long preservation. "This is to keep you safe until we meet again. I am never far away from you, Edward."

The morning had passed in something of a blur. They had left London for the coast early and made excellent time. The plan had been to leave on the early tide the following day and arrive at Calais in plenty of time to fix camp before light faded. They had barely finished loading Edward's ships in time to catch the tide and at the last moment Edward had sent word that he wished Richard to sail with him. All of the confusion and rush unsettled Richard. His ships had been loaded and ready ahead of time and last minute alterations did not, he thought, bode well. He had been pacing Edward's cabin alone since they set sail. It could only be around half an hour before they would land at Calais and in spite of the hurried summons he had not yet seen the king and his temper grew frayed. Edward had pulled him from pillar to post since he had got to London and though he did his utmost not to show it, this drove him wild and this morning was approaching the limit of that which Richard was prepared to tolerate. He found his fists were clenched tight without him willing it when the clunk of the door latch behind him caused him to spin on his heels. Edward was crouched at the doorway, being nearly a foot and a half taller than the frame. There were few places below deck where Edward could stand comfortably and so he always spent most of his time onboard a ship on deck, but on this occasion at least, the cramped conditions did nothing to suppress his beaming smile. Edward had always been blessed with the kind of infectious personality that filled a room.

When he laughed uncontrollably, those around him erupted and when he smiled the broad grin that covered his face now, and his bright blues eyes glinted as though stars passed into view from behind clouds somewhere deep within them, even Richard's sharp temper was quelled. His fingers relaxed and he allowed himself to smile back at his brother.

"Richard!" Edward's voice filled the small cabin. "I'm sorry to have kept you so long." He strode across the room, tilting his head to avoid the beams across the ceiling. "Who would have ever thought that invading France could take so much work!" he laughed as he sank into the chair in the corner and stretched his neck, rolling the stiffness from it.

"Sire," Richard began.

"Oh dear!" Edward interrupted. Richard started at the loud interjection and Edward revelled in the reaction he had drawn. "I must have really upset you if it begins with 'Sire', little brother." Richard's fist clenched tighter than before, but he forced himself this time to unfurl his fingers.

"What do you want of me, Edward?" Richard spoke deliberately through clenched teeth to demonstrate his irritation to his brother.

"It is not often that we are able to speak alone anymore, Richard." Edward fixed his brother's eyes in a piercing stare that gripped the duke instantly. The younger frowned deeply, wondering, suddenly concerned, where this conversation may lead. He hated Edward's ability to manipulate a situation to ensure that he had no foothold, no firm ground below his feet. The king allowed the moment to hang between them a while. Richard played the game and maintained the silence.

"Please, Richard, sit." Edward spoke softly. The duke looked to one side, suppressing his annoyance. Then, as calmly as he could manage, he strode to the seat beside his brother.

"Edward," Richard leaned forward in his chair, clasping his hands in his lap and squeezing them tightly, "we have spoken a good deal in the past few days, so I am unclear what you would say now that could not have been said before and why you felt that you must haul me over hear the very moment before our setting sail." Now, Richard looked up from his lap and stared at Edward. He was pleased to see a brief flash of shock pass over his brother's face as Richard sought his solid ground. As quickly as it appeared, the expression was gone again. Edward was a master of masking his true thoughts and intentions in a negotiation. And this was beginning to feel to Richard like a negotiation. One who knew Edward less well may have missed the fleeting lapse, but Richard was determined to ensure that his brother knew that he was more than ready for anything that Edward may have planned. There was a pause.

"How is your family?" Edward enquired coolly.

"I believe I have told you all of our baby tales." Richard sat back in his chair, relaxing a little. He thought his brother was losing whatever high ground he had held. Now it was Edward who leaned forward, looking at the boarded cabin floor between them.

"Perhaps I should be clearer." Edward raised his eyes slowly. He wanted to see Richard's face now, to judge his reaction. Having fought his conscience until the last moment, he had surrendered to the festering doubt that had grown from something Elizabeth had said in passing. It had nipped and then gnawed at the back of his mind for weeks now. Although he had hoped that spending some time with Richard over the past few days would put his concerns to rest, he had decided that it was something that needed the light of day to cause it to shrivel and die. At least he had prayed that it would slay this demon. The alternative barely stood thinking to a conclusion. That was why he had only called for Richard at the last moment. His stomach knotted tightly now as he poised himself for the reaction that would follow next. "When I said 'family'," Edward emphasised the word with some force and fixed his pale blue eyes onto the dark brown orbs of his brother's, "I was referring to your wife's family, Richard." He was amazed at how tense and nervous he felt as he spoke. He struggled to shake it off. It made him uncomfortable and threatened his hold on the moment. "I meant Warwick's family." He added to breach a moment of awkward silence. The timber around them groaned and creaked as if feeling the weight of the moment. The gentle sway of the vessel on the swelling waters was the only thing that caused Richard's ice cold stare to move at all.

Richard took a moment to measure his response. He felt sure that Edward would not raise this matter lightly given the history. He had fully expected the matter to have been raised long before today. He wondered what Edward was expecting from him. He had spied the passing unease on the king's face as he had spoken and guessed he awaited some degree of indignant rage from the duke. This time, though, Richard was prepared and was allowing himself to drink in the discomfort he knew that Edward felt and probably expected him to be feeling right now. He allowed the moment to hang a little longer, holding his brother's gaze and waiting for just the right point to spring his answer. When it presented itself, when he judged that the silence had been held long enough, he spoke slowly and softly, but barely blinked to break his brother's stare.

"I have made no secret of my actions, nor of my intentions where they concern Anne's family and I have done so to ensure that my king's fears were at each turn allayed in full." As he said these words, Richard was pleased that they sounded even better than he had hoped, for he had indeed kept the court informed of each step he had taken and was sure that his calm reassurance would kindle the sense of guilt within the king that he hoped was, at least in some small measure, present before they had even spoken.

Edward was taken aback. He was prepared for shouting, arguing and slamming of cabin doors, but not for this. It was most unlike his brother to remain so composed under what he would undoubtedly view as a direct attack upon his honour.

"Indeed," Edward drew himself up in his chair as he attempted to regain himself, "I am aware of the grace and favour that you have shown to Anne's family in providing homes and incomes for them." In that moment, Edward decided to throw caution to the tide and to speak plainly to his younger brother. Elizabeth would never approve. But then Elizabeth was not here. "My dear Richard," he shifted forward in his chair and allowed his shoulders to relax a little, "let me speak openly with you now." The duke's face betrayed a sense of disbelief at the sentiment that Edward actually found quite hurtful and which hardened his determination to proceed. "I am," he sought for the correct word, "unnerved by your rapidly progressing programme of restoring Warwick's family to security, if not yet power."

Richard found himself now utterly unable to restrain himself and could not prevent himself from erupting into a roaring laugh that soon filled and infected the cabin, as Edward smiled and began to giggle nervously. "Aaah, Edward," Richard fought to keep air in his lungs enough to speak as he recovered from his amusement, "welcome back!" Leaning forward he reached a hand around the back of his brother's head. "I've missed you," he smiled softly, "truly I have." Edward, suddenly uncomfortable, was lost for words. Fortunately, his brother spoke again. "For so long now you have seemed lost to some indefinite night of politics and court." He paused, not yet feeling that they spoke plainly enough for him to voice a concern that he held, not dissimilar to Edward's own, though he sensed that it may be given air before their discussion was over. "Somewhere beyond the king," he continued almost at a whisper, "I have lost the man. My brother. My friend." He gazed hard into Edward's eyes.

"I am forever your friend and brother, Richard," the elder spoke as though to someone he had wronged, "never doubt it." Edward was growing strangely at ease with the situation now. He could think of no other whom he would tolerate speaking to him in this way, at least not since the days had been good with Warwick. It had been some time since he had been challenged by anyone other than George, whose motive always overshadowed any of his words. The greatest part of him felt it inappropriate, yet he found it refreshing.

"You asked me the very evening that I arrived in London," Richard continued as though Edward had not said anything, "to be honest with you and to tell you when I felt that you were wrong." Edward nodded slowly. "Well," Richard continued, a note of building excitement ringing through his voice now, "the reverse has to be true also." His eyes began to dart across Edward's obviously thoughtful face. "I cannot be honest with my advice to you if you are not honest with me about all things." Edward nodded again blankly. "If you were to be honest with me, Edward," Richard stood as he spoke, a kind of nervous excitement preventing him from sitting still any longer, "if you asked me that which you really want answered, you would be telling me that however much you would like to trust me, you find it all but impossible. That your fingers still bear the painful scars where they have been burnt before by friend and family alike and that you fear that I shall next betray you, that my steps to restore Warwick's family may be the beginnings of a rebellion, that I may play upon some residual support for Warwick and the feeling his adherents held that he was wronged by you." Richard stopped a moment to gather his breath and tried to measure Edward's reaction. The king looked pale, his face strangely hollow, as though he had suffered a great fright. "If there is something you wish to ask me then please ask me now." Richard pleaded.

"If," Edward struggled to get his words out, unsure of himself. "If I were to be concerned about all that you have said and if I were to ask you now whether I have anything to fear, how would you answer?"

"Arrgghh!" Richard let out a long rumbling growl of frustration. "Still you will not just ask me openly!"

"Well then." Edward said sharply, rising now from his own seat to resume his favoured position above all others, though he was forced to stoop below the eaves of the cabin. Colour returned to his cheeks immediately. "Richard, should I be concerned about your care for Warwick's family?"

"At last!" Richard sighed and smiled. He could not help feeling an excited sense of achievement at having made the king ask the question. "We have been through too much together to take petty offence at reasonable questions." The duke turned his back on his king now, for what he was about to say still caused him pain and he did not wish Edward to see it. "I know my place and station, Edward. You have seen to that, and I do not blame you for it." Richard was uncomfortable lying so completely whilst insisting Edward be honest with him.

"Is that what this is all about?" Edward roared. Though without anger, his voice was that of one having uncovered a conspiracy. "Revenge? Strength?"

"No, no, no." It was true Richard still harboured a deep resentment at the way in which his title had been bound up in the fortunes of another, but it was also true that this was not what drove him now. "You know that I was close to Warwick, much as you were, though I was somewhat younger." He was facing Edward again now, his eyes imploring the other to listen. "He was my guardian, and when you and he came to blows, he offered me the choice of siding with him for the good of England. I begged him not to take up arms against you but he made it plain that his conscience left him no option. Before returning me to your custody, he asked one thing of me. That if he should fail and if it should be within my power to do so, that I ensure his family be taken care of. For his part, he swore that if he were successful, he would see to it that I was not harmed."

This revelation hung between the two men a long while. Richard began to wonder if he would regret telling Edward this. He knew that the events surrounding Warwick's rebellion would remain raw for some time still, but he also knew that his own relationship with Warwick was something that had always made the king uneasy, especially in light of their other brother, George's, decision to side with Warwick through those days. Richard hoped that his honesty might finally put to rest his brother's doubts. He also thought that it might bring him closer to the matter he wished to voice.

"Richard," Edward spoke thoughtfully after a prolonged pause with only the sound of the beating waves upon the hull of the ship disturbing the silence. "You more than any other have never given me reason to doubt your loyalty to me and perhaps that causes me to think that I am not seeing something. I am afraid that you suffer for the hurt others do me, but I have no real fear of you betraying me. You have passed up opportunity after opportunity to do that very thing." Edward thought for a moment, eyeing Richard. "Perhaps I was just concerned that your wife may be exercising an unhealthy influence over you. I apologise if it seems that I doubt you."

That was the moment that Richard had been waiting for. He mustered all of his courage for a sentence that could radically change his relationship with the king forever.

"Perhaps, your grace, that is a concern we share in common." He tried his utmost to make this sound like a throw away comment, but hoped that his brother had heeded his words. The glance that Edward shot his way informed him that the sentiment had registered. Richard held his breath.

"What?" Edward's tone had transformed, it was suddenly stern, the booming voice that he used to fill palace halls when he wished to ensure that he was heard. Richard tried to look startled at Edward's response, which was in truth precisely what he had expected. "It seems it is your turn to raise a matter honestly with me, Richard." Edward moderated his tone slightly, but still clear within it was displeasure that his brother had chosen to bring this matter to the table.

"As you raise the issue of spousal influence," Richard reminded the king, "I am sure that you are aware of the feeling at court about the queen's family." Even Richard was unsure whether this was a statement or a question.

"Be very careful, Gloucester." Edward warned, his eyes narrowing. He was indeed aware of the feeling at court that the queen's family were undeserving of the positions into which he had promoted them, but it was precisely those whisperers that Edward felt a need to protect himself from and it was by forwarding those over whom he had the most control that he sought to build that protection. Since the queen's family held their positions not by hereditary right but by Edward's patronage, he felt confident in the control that he was able to exercise over them.

Richard was unsurprised by Edward's warning, nor by the hint at formality that was clearly intended to remind him exactly who it was that he spoke to. Yet he felt that this opportunity had presented itself to him and that he should not let it pass. He was unlikely to have Edward's ear alone again for some time, particularly if the campaign in France should go well. Elizabeth guarded the king jealously and vigilantly at court. Here, at sea, she could not. As Richard looked at his brother's face he watched a flash of fury burn across his narrowed eyes that also urged him to caution in the way he continued.

"Sire," Richard put an air of concerned surprise into his voice, "your mood seems to have darkened somewhat." Now, he frowned in mock confusion. "Perhaps we should resume this discussion when your humour is better." Rising from his chair as if to leave, Richard knew that Edward would not be able to allow this to pass. He looked into the king's eyes and saw that they had ignited into a blaze of rage.

"Sit down, Richard." Edward's voice boomed around the cabin. He now suspected that Richard was trying either to manipulate him or was mocking him. Anyone else would likely have found themselves on the sharp end of Edward's temper, but he found himself instead concerned that Richard was resorting to such tactics. "We will finish this now." His tone was moderated, in the hope of letting Richard know that he was not getting irritated by his games. Richard sat slowly back down, trying not to allow his deflation to show. Still, at the least he was able to continue his point.

"Edward," Richard began, still searching his mind for the best way to proceed, "you rightly raised your concern at the circumstances currently surrounding Anne's family." It came to him just in time. "All I sought to do was to give voice to a growing concern I have about the current circumstances of the queen's family." The duke hoped to avoid the king's wrath by mirroring the concern the king had expressed whilst carefully avoiding directing any criticism of the queen herself. It appeared to have the desired effect, as Edward's eyes grew less narrow and the fire was quenched by the pale, watery blue that Richard knew so well. Edward recognised that Richard had stepped back from the edge of the precipice over which he had waved a foot. This pleased him. Richard still knew his boundaries.

"My dearest brother," Edward relaxed his shoulders, which had begun to ache as a swelling anger had tightened his muscles. "I am, of course, grateful for your concern. It means the world to me to know that you worry so genuinely that it overtakes the fear most would have to speak to me the way that you do."

"A younger brother should fear the elder?" Richard's tone was playful. It was met by a broad smile from Edward's face.

"I am sure, young duke, you know precisely what I mean." Edward's tone was now the match for Richard's. "I acknowledge your concern as you have acknowledged mine." Edward continued, his face softened in the candlelight and still smiling. "I would make this accord with you; I shall henceforth trust that you shall not betray me in your dealings with Warwick's family, if you will trust that I am able to manage my patronage at court." Leaning forward, Edward's eyes fixed again on Richard's and narrowed faintly. "I am no fool, Richard, trust me." There was a hint of imploring in Edward's eyes that Richard had not seen before.

There was silence between them again. Richard forced his mind to process this moment faster. Should he agree? Think faster. It would offer him the freedom to pursue what he was trying to do without challenge, safe under the protection of the king himself. Think. Think. He would also be giving up the ability to speak against the queen's family. Which option offered him the best outcome? He did not trust that Edward could control his wife, whose influence was spreading and cascading throughout her family. Nor did he truly believe that Edward would simply cease to be concerned about what he did at a word from Richard. However, he had managed to make Edward aware of his concerns and reach this point with the king still in good humour. He knew that would be the best that he could hope for from today.

"I," Richard began slowly and had bought just enough time for himself, for it came to him like a clap of thunder. "I shall agree to your wishes," he nodded in deference to the king, "notwithstanding my prior agreement to always advise you when you are wrong." Although this sounded entirely reasonable, it offered Richard a perfect caveat, since he would only want to raise the issue when he felt the king was in the wrong. Effectively, he was promising Edward nothing. To his delight, Edward threw his head back and roared with laughter.

"Then we are done, little brother." Edward's voice boomed. "We shall soon be landed and in two weeks time you and I shall be seated in the throne room of France accepting Louis' surrender and planning how we divide the spoils."

"I look forward to it, Edward." Richard smiled, rising from his seat. "Your victory shall bring glory not seen since Agincourt." A shiver of anticipation ran from the base of his spine to the nape of his neck, causing his skin to pimple under his hair. This was what he had come for and he was looking forward to what promised to be a more glorious campaign than Edward's recapture of the throne. It was to be another opportunity to prove his valour in battle and his value to the king. He would return to England, and to his family, a hero. "I will take my leave, sire, to return to my ship before we land and ensure all there is ready." Richard bowed low and turned for the door. As he opened it, he looked back to see Edward smiling.

"Our destiny lies in this campaign, Richard." Another shiver prickled the duke's back and he nodded his agreement. He pulled the cabin door shut and felt the nervous excitement propel his legs along the corridor and back up on deck.

In his cabin, Edward turned his chair to face out to sea. He leaned forward, watching the wake of the ship as it scythed through the water. Dark shapes of other ships dotted the blue water like stars in the shadowed night sky. A frown passed over his brow as he spoke to the wind. "I am not the fool you seem to think me, brother. I shall have an eye upon you." He sighed and buried his face in his hands, swaying rhythmically with the motion of the ship.

Chapter 13

29th August 1475 - Where Angels Fear To Tread

It was only one week after landing that Richard found himself seated in a vast hall, lined with broad tables and laid for a feast more lavish than he could ever have imagined. Gold seemed to ooze from the walls, drip from the ceiling and seep up from the ground. Richard was finding it difficult not to be numbed by his awe at the sight before him, but he was determined to keep his wits about him for what was to follow, for what the French king had to say to them. He mused about what was about to happen and how he would feel. What, if anything, he should say. His gaze was fixed upon a vast tapestry that hung to his right, though he did not even register the subject spread across its surface. His eyes sunk slowly to the table before him, barely visible beneath the gold and fire red rubies glinting in the candlelight that flooded the hall more brightly than the sun. Each bowl and platter was piled with the largest selection and variety of food that Richard had ever seen, yet he wanted none of it. His stomach was tight and it twisted uncomfortably as he tried to remain still in his chair.

Edward's voice soaked into his consciousness, echoing around the hall as he sat to Richard's left talking loudly to the English nobles that filled the other chairs at their table and stretched to Edward's left and Richard's right, all chattering loudly so that a dull noise rang around the hall. Edward sat in the centre of the table, directly opposite the centre of the long table, similarly adorned, that ran the length of the far side of the hall.

French gentleman had begun to file into the chairs, each directly opposite an English counterpart. They all wore solemn expressions and Richard could not help but raise a smile at their ridiculously extravagant clothes. None of them spoke a single word and the men either side of Richard began to hush as the French took their seats until only Edward's voice remained, though it still filled the room with an echoing boom. It was only when the last of the positions opposite were filled that Edward finished his tale about a large stag that had failed to evade him on his last hunt.

Richard ran his eyes along the table opposite with distain. One seat was still empty, in the very centre, opposite Edward. Louis's seat, twice the size of any other, remained empty as an eerie hush descended upon the room which none now seemed willing to break. The silence persisted a long moment. Eventually, Richard cleared his throat loudly in deliberate irreverence. He then clanked his goblet loudly off the table and took a swig of the potent, heavy red wine that sloshed around within it. In unison, every French nose was turned up in his direction.

A moment later the large double doors at the end of the hall to Richard's right rumbled open like a lingering, far off growl of thunder and a trumpet blast announced, finally, the arrival of King Louis of France, who strode across the hall purposefully, spinning on his heels in an exaggerated turn at the end of the French table and marching to his seat, which was pulled back for him by two young serving boys who seemed to appear from nowhere. He stepped deliberately around and in front of the chair. Standing, stony faced, he eyed each of the English faces opposite coldly. His gaze eventually came to rest upon the English king, to whom he nodded slowly and proffered a thin, obviously false smile before sitting. Richard shot a glance at his brother, who was smiling in return. Lord Hastings, at Edward's other shoulder, tilted his head toward the king and whispered something short that caused Edward to jerk his head sharply in acknowledgement. Hastings was a portly man, some years older than Edward and greying around the extremes of his thick hair. He was known to be very close to Edward at court and though court matters did not greatly concern Richard, Hastings had now been party to something that did irritate the duke. Slowly, Louis sank into his chair. During another long silence, Richard fidgeted in his chair with a growing irritation.

"King Edward," Louis spoke in slow French, although he must have known that each of the men opposite both spoke and understood his language perfectly, "and your lords and advisors." The king's voice was shrill, particularly in comparison to Edward's. He was barely taller than Richard and so would be dwarfed by Edward's frame at close quarters, and his features were thin and pointed, not unlike Richard's own. His lips barely moved as he spoke and Richard found himself powerless to do other than despise him. "We are together now," Louis continued, "to conclude matters of your invasion of France." There were disapproving mutters from the French side of the room and it was Edward's turn to shift in his seat.

Louis waved his right arm absently and the doors at the end of the hall reopened to reveal a line of footmen, all dressed in dark blue, each carrying a silver platter above their right shoulder. At a further gesture from Louis, the line moved silently along the centre of the hall and then each man turned to face a place setting at the English table. Stepping forward they set down each platter before an Englishman, retreated to the centre of the room, turned smartly to face the French table, bowed low to Louis and marched from the room, their heels clicking harshly in the hollow space. The doors closed gently behind the last man. Throughout this display, Richard had stared with a fierce, burning, bubbling rage at Louis, trying with all of his might to force the weight of his gaze upon the French king. Louis, however, remained motionless, his eyes not moving from Edward's face.

"Before each of you is your agreed gift from the French nation. Before King Edward is also our Treaty. Louis gestured to the covered platter before the English king. "As soon as your signature is upon this document," Louis continued sternly, "you may each take your gift."

Edward leaned forward and removed the ornate silver cloche. Beneath it was a thick stack of parchment, bound by a white lace cord, a quill resting atop it. To the right of the document sat a large, plain leather purse, obviously full of coin and in front of that was a small pot of ink in which to dip the pen. Only now did Richard break his stare to look intensely at the contents of the platter before his brother, then to his brother's face. He saw Edward's eyes fixed upon the papers, clearly thinking, though Richard knew his mind was made. He watched Edward look to his left, at Lord Hastings, who nodded gently at Edward's enquiring look. He then moved his head round to his right to meet Richard's smouldering hazel brown eyes. The duke held the king, trying hard to betray no emotion. After a moment, he gave a single, slow shake of his head and returned his stare to the French king. Edward knew well Richard's thoughts on the matter and Richard knew the king had taken the advice of other lords over his. Edward paused a brief moment before following his brother's eyes back to the French king. Reaching for the quill, he dipped it lightly into the dark liquid within the silver rimmed glass pot.

"King Louis," Edward's deep voice echoed imposingly around the grand hall as he spoke deliberately, as if scripted, "I thank you for your hospitality and am pleased to accept the terms of your Treaty." Edward's French accent was good in spite of little practice. "England accepts France's tribute and shall remove himself from French soil for so long as it is maintained." With that, Edward pulled the delicate lace so that the parchment unfurled with a gentle rustle. With a scratch of the quill, Edward marked his approval at the base of the document. Louis looked less than amused at Edward's words, but said nothing as Edward signed the Treaty, put down the quill and lifted the heavy purse, shaking it to hear the gold jangle.

"Now," Louis spoke a little louder, "let us eat." He raised his arms to the English lords. "And please enjoy the gifts you each have from France." Each man at the French table, taking Louis' signal, began to reach for the food that covered the table and to sip gently from the golden goblets of wine that stood before them. In response, the Englishmen began to grab food and each took a mouthful of the rich wine before loudly lifting the lids from their platters, weighing and shaking the purses upon them. A loud variety of voices erupted around the room, both French and English, until the hall was filled with talking, laughing and the clinking and clanking of plates and goblets. Only one man remained silent. Only one plate remained empty. Only one platter still had its lid in place. And this fact had not escaped the attention of the French king.

Some five minutes passed before Edward noticed that his brother had failed to join in the celebrations.

"Richard." Edward whispered loudly at his brother, but Richard's eyes remained unmoved. Edward followed his burning gaze across the room to King Louis, who, to Edward's horror, appeared to have caught the stare and was holding it. "Richard!" Edward hissed louder, but still at a whisper. When the duke still failed to respond, the king grabbed his shoulder and wrenched it around until Richard faced him. Edward searched his brother's face with a sense of shock and concern. His teeth were clenched so that his jaw bulged, his lips were thin, pressed tightly together and his nostrils flared widely with each breath. In his dark eyes, a burning rage was plain to see, the flames of the candles around the hall reflected and magnified like stars shooting across the night sky of the young man's eyes. Edward fought to gather himself. He had never seen such hatred and unconcealed rage on his brother's face, even when his thin temper snapped.

"Richard," Edward started again, clearly now, though still in a low, hushed tone, betraying his desire to keep that which disturbed Richard quiet, "I know your feelings on this matter.

You have made them clear enough." The duke looked away, but Edward tugged his attention back using the grip he still held on his brother's shoulder. "You forget yourself, Richard." Edward spoke bluntly and seemed to have forgotten to moderate his tone, which was hardened and becoming audible to those around him.

Gloucester thought hard. His simmering anger was fogging his mind and he was fighting with his own temper. He knew in his heart that he must keep his tongue, as Edward had reminded him, for the sake of all England, but it was proving a more difficult task than he had envisaged. He kept his jaw locked firmly to prevent the escape of any unwise words.

"You had your say last night and I listened." Edward's eyes seared into Richard's as he pleaded him to remain calm, but Richard could hold his tongue no longer.

"But you did not listen, your highness." Richard spat through clenched teeth. He saw the king draw breath but refused him the time to interrupt. "You asked me, made me promise, to always tell you when you were wrong." Richard's voice grew louder and Edward dug his fingers into the duke's shoulder to remind him where he was. "And I still say that you are wrong now."

"We have been through this, brother." Edward stretched a smile across his lips, trying to take the sting from Richard's mood, and spoke softly. He could deal with his brother's irreverence later, but needed to save face now. So, he would go over it one more time. Quietly. "Our allies abandoned us even before we landed. We are on foreign soil, outnumbered and out financed. We had no hope from the moment we set foot on French sand, so we have no option but to limit the damage." Edward took a deep breath. He could make out no softening of his brother's face. "By signing this Treaty, England receives an annual pension from France." No reaction. "It is just as the Roman Empire imposed upon its provinces, and England will see it as such. A tribute from the King of France, paying us to preserve his throne." Searching his brother's eyes, Edward still saw unquenched fire there. "Richard," he sighed, "it is a victory. It is the best result that we could have hoped for."

"So," Richard snapped, almost snarling, his upper lip curling, "if our destiny is to be made here, then you would have it that our destiny is to seek victory in dismal defeat, to strain honour from shame, to submit to those who should kneel at our feet?" Spitting with rage, Richard's eyes bore into Edward's and the king sensed an almost tangible force pushing against him. He knew his brother to be possessed of an immensely strong will and the exercise of it was becoming an ever increasing concern to the king. It suited Edward at the Scottish border when it held back any attempt to pillage border villages. It suited him less well before his face at the court of the king of France.

"You will hold your tongue until later, Richard." Edward held the uncomfortably heavy stare of his brother. "We shall conclude this in private." His soft tone masked his concern and annoyance. There was a silence between them as Edward fought to resist breaking his brother's eye contact and the other struggled not to release the contents of his mind upon the king. Finally, Richard gave a nod of acquiescence and sharply turned his resolute gaze back to the French king. Slowly, with a sense of withering tiredness, Edward followed Richard's eyes and was horror struck to see that Louis was meeting Richard's stare and had clearly been watching their exchange. Edward could not help himself. He rolled his eyes and buried his forehead in his left palm in despair. Now, he truly feared that the situation could be lost. He searched his mind frantically for some way to defuse the impending debacle, but he had not thought that Louis would need no more encouragement than seeing Edward's reaction, and in that moment, it was too late.

"Is our food not to the liking of the Duke of Gloucester?" Louis enquired, his tone betraying that he knew this was not the issue.

"I fear, sir," Edward spoke, his French becoming shaky as he answered Louis' question before Richard had the chance, "that my young brother is wearied by our exertions this past week and that his humour suffers somewhat."

Louis had not moved his eyes from Richard's while Edward spoke, but now a thin malevolent smirk was unveiled across his lips. Edward shot a glance at his brother, who now sat forward in his chair, a clenched fist twitching on the table beside his plate. Louis wondered whether he would need to say any more. His answer arrived swiftly.

"My humour," Richard stood and pounded his fist on the surface of the table so that plates, bowls and goblets three settings either side of him jumped from the table and clattered back down again, "suffers not from weariness." Richard spoke in a loud, clear voice. The shock on the faces of those around him was only increased by the fact that Richard was speaking in English. He almost broke into a smile at the sight of those around Louis whispering frantically in his ear. "My humour suffers from witnessing the sale of English honour."

"In France," Louis spoke in French, slowly with a furrowed brow, moving his head to face Edward, "we do not suffer such impertinence from our lesser. I would remind you also, King Edward, that for the time being you remain a guest of France." The sickening smile seemed fixed fast in place. Edward opened his mouth, unsure what to say now, but he was interrupted before even a word came to him.

"I am perfectly able to speak for myself." Richard leaned over the table, both fists planted firmly. "In England, we do not suffer our lesser to speak out of place either," the duke called across the hall, still retorting the French king's jibes in English, "but the day shall never come when an Englishman finds his better at the court of France." There was an audible intake of breath throughout the hall and sniggers could be heard from the farther ends of Richard's side. This was all that Richard needed to spur him on. "Not Frenchman, Spaniard nor Italian have I found yet that I consider the equal of the Englishman who tends my farthest fields," he leaned forward a little more for effect, "and I include present company," he hissed as muttering broke out either side of the duke and there was again furtive whispering at Louis' ear, which he waved away. The French king firmly burned his eyes into his English counterpart as Edward's jaw sank.

"King Edward," Louis spoke sternly, deliberately ignoring the huffing duke, "I suggest that you control your subordinates before I withdraw my generosity."

Again, Edward had no time to reply.

"I will show you what I think of your 'generosity'." Richard sneered, straightening and lifting the cloche from his platter noisily, tossing it to the side. He dangled the heavy leather purse before his eyes for a moment, absently, as if transfixed, but it did not postpone the matter for long. Pushing his right leg back for balance with a grinding of wooden chair leg on marble floor, he raised the purse high above his head and slammed it into the floor in the very centre of the hall. Upon contact the seams of the purse burst and large, shining gold coins exploded from it in all directions. They danced around the polished floor, glinting in the flickering candlelight as the room echoed to the tapping, clinking and clanging of the French king's gift to the Duke of Gloucester spraying out before all those present. As the final coin slowed its spin, Richard watched Louis' face appear and disappear on its one side. It settled noisily on the floor, and then there was no sound to be heard. Silence. A silence louder by far than either Richard's shouting or the ringing of the coin filled the room. Only now did Edward manage to seize the initiative. He rose to his feet, knowing that his greatest asset in any situation was his huge, imposing frame. He towered menacingly over Richard.

"Enough!" Edward boomed in English. "You shall leave now and wait for me in my apartments." Edward's wide stance and deep tone assured Richard that this really was the end and that there was no more room for his temper in this situation. Richard pushed back his chair further and strode from the table along the hall without another word. At the end of the hall he pushed the double doors open wide with a crash and was gone. Edward now turned his attention to King Louis and the salvaging of this evening. To offend the French king could condemn the remainder of Edward's reign to fighting for survival against not only the French but also a French-sponsored Scotland and Ireland. Richard could have just ruined in a fit of temper any hope of peace for the duration of the Yorkist rule.

"King Louis," Edward returned to his near perfect French accent, "I offer my apologies for the Duke of Gloucester. His youthful temperament was heated by the thought of battle." He looked to his counterpart for some indication of how much damage his younger brother had caused, but the wily French king betrayed nothing. Was he waiting to see how far Edward would go in his apology? Did he intend to see if Edward would grovel? If so, he would be disappointed.

"England," Edward continued calmly, "accepts France's offer of peace as agreed in the Treaty we have just concluded." Hoping to remind the French king that matters were already finalised, Edward let these words hang between them. There was a heavy silence. Edward smiled softly and nodded his head at Louis. Eventually, Louis raised his goblet, tilted it to Edward and drank deeply. Edward returned the toast and a moment later a clamour of talk and merriment grew up nervously around the two monarchs until it seemed that Richard's outburst had been forgotten. Edward knew though that Louis would not take the insult lightly.

Edward both ate and drank heavily all evening. He was unsure whether he hoped the night would last an eternity or end in a forgotten, fleeting moment. There was still Richard to deal with and although Edward boiled with anger at his brother's rash outburst, he was hardly looking forward to confronting the duke and his conviction that the king was in the wrong. Edward drank deeply and all around saw that he appeared distracted and was not, as was his usual wont, the very heart of the celebrations.

It was almost three o'clock in the morning when Edward stood before the doors of the sumptuous apartments in which Louis had installed him for the duration of his stay. That stay was due to end in a few more days but Edward had determined to leave the following day now, not least to remove Richard from the French court before further outbursts saw them in mortal danger on foreign soil. His head swimming from uncounted goblets of the heady red wine and a warm tiredness hanging from his limbs heavily, Edward inhaled deeply and pushed the floral engraved gold leafed door open.

The room beyond was dimly lit by a handful of shallow candles and a fire in the hearth that, at this hour, was no more than a softly glowing red heap on the left hand wall of the opulent room. It had been over six hours since Edward had instructed Richard to await him here. Had it been anyone but the Duke of Gloucester, Edward would suspect that the person would have retired and would report in the late morning when the king was rested and, they would hope, his mood soothed. Indeed Edward would have secretly welcomed the chance to take to his bed now. Richard, though, would still be there, both because that was the instruction his king had given him and because he obviously still had plenty to say on the subject of the Treaty.

There was only one place that Richard would be if he were still there. Straightening himself with a tired stiffness, Edward strode across the room to the chairs before the fireplace. Sure enough, Richard's pointed features came into view as Edward rounded the chairs. Sinking into the seat beside Richard, he gazed at the duke's right cheek, all that was visible to him as he still stared directly into the glowing embers. The red light made Richard's cheek appear flushed, though Edward could not tell if it was a flush of anger renewed by his arrival or just the fire's reflection on his pale skin. His eyes danced with red flicks of light that at least seemed to Edward far brighter than the dying hearth's glow.

"You have drowned your wits I trust." The words seemed to escape from Richard like a lazy exhaling. There was no response from Edward, not least because it was in essence true. A long moment passed in silence. "Did you apologise for me?" Richard asked slowly and without looking across from the fire.

"You know that I had to." Edward replied, blinking his drying eyes. Richard's eyes did not move and the silence seemed eternal to Edward as he tried to stop his dizzying head from spinning. He began to wonder whether his brother awaited an apology.

"Maybe." Richard blinked and tilted his head toward Edward. "I meant every word though, Edward, and remain adamant." Now the young duke turned to look into Edward's eyes. Suddenly, a broad smile spread across his face and his eyes danced with a different, more mischievous light. "But did you see that French peacock's face?" Both brothers burst into uncontrollable laughter. Edward had arrived determined to deal forcefully with the duke for the incident that he had created. Whether because he was tired, warm or intoxicated, or because Louis face and those at his sides had been a picture of suppressed outrage and shock that now seemed amusing, the king's determination ebbed from him as he sniggered until his sides ached and his breath was short.

Edward awoke the next morning still slumped in that same chair. The throbbing in his sides had been replaced by one in his head, reminding him of at least part of last night, and a night in the chair had left his neck and shoulders stiff. He shifted uncomfortably. Immediately he thought that he should have been harder on Gloucester. The moment was gone, though, and had ended in a choice between Louis and Richard. Edward had no doubt that he needed and wanted his brother's good will far more than that of the French king. After all, he had arrived here a week earlier with his brother and the express intention of taking Louis' throne. More importantly, it was breakfast time.

Richard had arisen around six in the morning and was beginning preparations to leave France. As he stood at the tall narrow window of his room in the pale dawn light, he reflected that his actions of the previous evening had been rash and that he owed his brother and king an apology. He was, however, satisfied that his conscience remained clear having given voice to his convictions. He had spent much of yesterday in prayer on the matter. Having managed to divert his brother's mind, hardly a difficult feat given his state, he was satisfied with the past day, though could not shake the sense of having let Edward down.

Chapter 14

Lunch

The morning was all but passed and Hans Holbein was becoming aware that the study in which he sat was becoming stuffy as the still air was warmed by the fire without refreshment in the room without opening window and with the door tightly shut. The oppressive atmosphere began to stifle the artist as he sat silently listening to Sir Thomas More's tale. His host seemed unaffected, but Holbein was becoming increasingly uncomfortable.

After what felt like an age of quiet, More finally looked up from the hearth at his guest. A frown folded across his forehead as he noticed that his guest was flushed in the cheek and was at the moment mopping is brow.

"Master Holbein," Sir Thomas began, fearing he had lost his guest's attention, "would you care for some refreshment?"

"That would be most welcome, sir." Holbein replied, assured that the bringing of refreshments would necessarily require the door to be opened and that some fresher air might invade the stale room. Sir Thomas rang a small bell that rested at his side and within moments the heavy door glided inwards and an elderly man shuffled into the room and gave a shallow bow.

"I believe we are ready for lunch." More gave a short smile with his instruction and received a further nod of acknowledgement. For the moment, Holbein was more than content to drink in the cool air that seeped in behind the old man, though his stomach was beginning to complain at the passing of the morning and he suddenly realised that he was growing hungry.

"I trust," Sir Thomas interrupted his thoughts, "that your attention has been maintained through my story to this point." Holbein sensed a hint of menace in his host's voice. In spite of his discomfort, the artist had, as he had been instructed, paid close attention to Sir Thomas's story, though he was shocked by some of what he was hearing.

"Sir Thomas," Hans spoke in a reassuring tone, "I have absorbed your every word, though I confess to being a little surprised at some of the…" Holbein searched for a polite phrase, but was rescued from stretching his command of English by his host.

"Unfashionable content?" More suggested, having fully expected such a comment at some point.

"Yes, Sir Thomas." Holbein smiled appreciatively. "Unfashionable content," he repeated. Sir Thomas looked suddenly a little pensive, as if sizing up his guest afresh to determine how far he could be trusted. Clearly deciding he had come too far to cease trusting in Holbein's discretion now, Sir Thomas inhaled deeply.

"The tale I am relating may sound unfashionable at present," More said in a hushed tone, as though he suddenly feared someone was listening, "but it will become dangerous before it ends." Sir Thomas fixed Hans Holbein with a cold stare. "The Tudors have worked hard to fashion a collective memory of their predecessor. I confess that their work has been so well executed that I believed I had the truth for the telling." More turned to the hearth again and fell silent.

"You now believe differently?" Hans enquired nervously, unsure of how far he was able to push his host on this matter. There was a long pause before Sir Thomas replied.

"It took surprisingly little research," More began, still gazing absently into the dancing flames, "to unearth facts that so radically contradict the accepted truth that I could do no other than look further. The extent of my findings I shall make clear as we progress, but suffice it to say that we shall move from 'unfashionable' to dangerous before the day is over." He looked once more deep into Holbein's eyes, searching them for a sign of something. He was not sure what. Concern? Fear? Whatever he was looking for, he was satisfied that it was not there. He seemed to have grasped Holbein's attention again too as his lips hung apart in anticipation.

"My concern," Sir Thomas began anew, "is that a combination of Tudor storytelling and the passage of time without its contradiction will lead to the loss of the truth of our history."

Holbein was taken aback by the fire that sprung up in Sir Thomas's eyes as he spoke now, though he questioned whether it was borne of a passion of conviction or of a nervous timidity about the sentiment of what he said. The painter felt certain the former was the more likely.

"When we miss-tell our history we lie to our forebears and our children to our own dishonour. Lawyers and artists," Sir Thomas smiled as if to himself, "make a profession of finding the truth, only to disguise it again." Holbein returned the smile and shifted uncomfortably.

As lunch arrived, Sir Thomas buzzed about the room shuffling papers, reading and signing documents. He took several draughts of ale but barely ate, much as Holbein did as he observed the near frantic comings and goings. He surmised that Sir Thomas had allowed this window to deal with the day's business and intended to seal Hans and himself in the room after lunch for the remainder of whatever there may be to conclude. Holbein remained a little confused by what the morning had brought and what may be to come, but he was finding himself tugged into Sir Thomas's story by the very nature of its lack of 'fashion'.

Almost an hour passed of their break before the food was cleared away, though the drinks were left. Sir Thomas seemed to have signed the last of the papers and instructed everyone to leave. Holbein drew a deep breath of the cool air before the door was shut again and although he dreaded the warming and drying of the air, he was surprised by how keen he was for his host to continue his tale.

"Well," Sir Thomas sank back into his chair with a contented weariness, "back to the meat of today's business if you will permit me Master Holbein."

"At your pleasure." Holbein nodded.

"Then we shall move to the events of January in 1478, another episode whose detail is sinking into the cloud of myth."

Chapter 15

11th February 1478- Justice

Richard sat in a daze. The House of Parliament felt even more cavernous and he felt lost among the silence of its members. Only one voice resonated around the room, but the words had long since been lost in the mist that Richard felt surrounded him. Visits to London had been few in the years since Edward's Treaty of Picquigny. To the twenty five year old duke, the events of his 22nd year seemed far away, yet they poured back through his mind now like a rushing, swollen river. The king had not seemed to begrudge the duke the rapturous welcome afforded to him on his return to London by its people. Word of his outburst before King Louis and of his refusal to accept French money as a bribe to leave France had arrived in London before the party's return, no doubt so that the king could gauge the general mood following his obtaining of the French tribute. To Edward's dismay, the consensus view appeared to be that he and his nobles had elected to capitulate to the French king and had accepted a bribe rather than enforcing the English king's right to the French throne.

In contradiction, news of Richard's steadfast refusal to take the French money and of his patriotic stance before King Louis himself had been greeted by the people of London with glee and before the king and his nobility returned Richard was being openly hailed as the hero of the expedition, basking in chivalric honour. When this news had reached the king he had allowed Richard pride of place at his side during the procession through the streets of London. The duke had been loudly cheered along each road with his brother the king at his side. Clearly, Edward had hoped to shine in the reflected glory of his younger brother's popularity whilst allowing it to cast a broad, dark shadow over what was obviously an unpopular decision. As long as the crowds had something to cheer, they would forget any bad news from the venture. Richard, lost in the adulation, cared little for his brother's motives at the time. Since then, the duke had been absorbed in matters of the north and the securing of the Scottish border so that his journeys to London had become fewer.

A loud thud like a low clap of thunder punched through the cloud surrounding Richard's thoughts and he shook himself back to the moment. The sight that he was fighting so hard to comprehend was that of his eldest brother, King Edward IV of England, presenting the case for high treason to the gathering of all of Parliament, against his other brother, George, Duke of Clarence. All of those present were in no doubt that the presentation was merely a formality, the king paying lip service to the due process of the law, but Richard was finding it deeply disturbing. George had spent almost eight months in the Tower to date but Richard had not dared to believe that this day would arrive. Edward was requesting a guilty verdict and a sentence of death for his own brother, and could be assured that Parliament would grant it.

Richard was well aware of the case that his brother laid out and was equally aware that Edward was entitled to the verdict he requested. George was a lot of things, but throughout his erratic, irreverent and treacherous behaviour, he was, and remained always, Richard's brother. And Edward's brother. Suddenly, Richard became aware that his eyes had settled on Clarence's face as Edward's voice continued, as if from another room. George sat stiffly upright in his chair, his chin held high, making no secret of his contempt for these proceedings whilst maintaining a proud and, Richard contemplated, dignified manner, obviously silently resigned to the outcome.

"It is by virtue of this evidence," Edward's voice rang clear in Richard's ears now, "that I now ask this full gathering of our

Parliament to approve the case before you for the greater weal of all of the kingdom and all of its population."

As if sensing the eyes burning into him, Clarence now turned his head for the first time since taking his seat to meet his younger brother's stare. A soft smile flickered on his lips as their eyes met and Richard mirrored the smile, making no effort to disguise it. Edward moved from the centre of the chamber to his seat at its head. As he did so, the Speaker rose to call for a vote of those assembled.

"May I have the 'ayes'." The Speaker's voice called with a tone of assured authority. It was a moment before the silence was broken, but like the first raindrop of a coming storm, the chamber soon rang out the sounds of many voices concurring. Clarence's eyes remained on Richard, but a frown rippled on his forehead briefly as the voices died down and Richard's lips failed to move.

"And the 'nays'." There was quiet again, this time longer lasted. Richard held George's eyes and Clarence could see a struggle darkening his brother's face. Slowly he saw Richard's lips part and a wave of nervous knotting passed through his stomach. He could not allow Richard to do this. So much would depend upon him now.

Having wrestled with his conscience and his sense of duty, both to his king and to his kin, the duke had been unable to bring himself to join the chorus of 'ayes', knowing that his voice would not be missed. The more burning question as the noise died down was whether he should oppose one brother to support another. Again. For all of George's faults, he had equal strengths and Richard still held him dear. He had refused more than once to support George in open rebellion against Edward and was not wont to agree to Edward's demand to have George executed now, though he saw clearly the case, if not the need, for it. He had always maintained that the Plantagenets had enough enemies without turning on each other. Having lost his father and one brother before he was old enough to know them well, the thought of participating in the killing of another tied knots in his gut. He accepted, though, that the king often lacked the luxury of sentiment in the protection of the realm.

Richard had just resolved to speak out against the sentence when he saw George, at whom he still stared, slightly, almost imperceptibly, yet definitely shake his head, as if he knew of his younger brother's turmoil and offered him a way out. Richard frowned deliberately at George, enquiring as to his meaning. Again, Clarence shook his head, this time more obviously telling Richard not to say what he had clearly opened his mouth to say. When Richard's mouth closed, the frown still creasing his forehead, George returned his eyes to his front and it was too late for Richard to object as both verdict and sentence were confirmed. Shooting a glance at the king, Richard was at least satisfied that Edward also did not look happy as the matter was concluded. Watching Clarence being escorted from the chamber, Richard sank his head into his right palm and allowed that fog to descend numbingly over him again.

Later that same day, Richard sat before his brother the king in his chamber at the Palace of Westminster and gazed into the desk between them as if lost.

"Richard!" Edward called, as though his brother had not answered a previous call. He looked up to his brother slowly now. "Richard," he continued softly, "pray tell me you understand what I have done." There was a pleading look in the king's eyes. Richard searched them deeply, as if expecting to see some sign of his brother's true feelings there.

"I know," Richard replied, sounding a little distracted, "that George's greatest crime lies in betraying your trust and that his greatest mistake was in leaving you no choice but to deal with him once and for all." Edward sat back in his chair and grinned his child-like smile at Richard. "But," Richard snapped before his brother had time to relax any further, "do not believe for one moment that I am anything else than disgusted by your decision to condemn my brother to death today."

"Do not presume," Edward retorted leaning into the desk again, and then he paused as if deciding to say something else than he intended, "that I am pleased by what I have done." Edward seemed a little nervous and it was true he was concerned about how his youngest brother would react. Having just dealt with Clarence the last thing he wanted was to have to deal with another brother, particularly when it would be his last, most loved, most trusted and most powerful brother."

"Is there any chance of clemency, sire?" Richard asked as though he knew the answer but felt compelled to enquire anyway.

"I have shown George nothing but leniency for many years and can allow him to continue no longer."

"If I could secure his promise to cause you no more injury, would your grace reconsider?" Richard spoke calmly, but was growing tense. Edward was surprised and a little alarmed at the duke's persistence in the matter, though it also touched his heart painfully.

"I have had his word, Richard, and watched it vanish into smoke when it suits him. This course pains me and though Edward the man may not wish his brother killed, Edward the king must see a traitor executed."

"So be it." Richard sighed, an audible shake in his voice. "I have but one request to make of your highness."

"If I can grant it," Edward smiled softly, "you know well that I will, Richard." There was a pause. Richard shifted in his chair.

"I," the duke's voice cracked as soon as he began, a wave of emotion overcoming him. He coughed to cover the lump that pushed up into his throat. "I bring a request from our mother that if, as she greatly regrets, the sentence imposed is to be carried out, George be afforded the honour of selecting the manner of his own end." Richard fixed Edward in a hard stare but felt an unquenchable welling in his eyes that he feared would betray him. Comforting his mother through the afternoon had done little to aid his own humour.

"Of course." Edward was a little taken aback by the request, but if it would appease his brother and his mother, then it would be worth his agreement.

"Mother also requests that the sentence be carried out in private."

"So it shall be." Edward acquiesced, wondering whether there would be still more to come.

"My thanks to you, sire." Richard lowered his head, his voice bolstered by formal sincerity. There was a moment of silence as the king eyed his brother.

"Enough of this dissembling." Edward's tone was changed and he seemed suddenly angry or impatient with Richard. "I know your feelings and would not wish to upset you, nor to lose our close bond, over George's treason had I a choice."

"Very well." Richard stared hard back into Edward's eyes. He was satisfied both that his brother understood his position and that he was not going to change the king's mind. "I shall inform George." Richard moved to stand.

"No!" Edward snapped, startling his brother. "Ah," the king thought quickly, "not yet, Richard." He made an effort to look relaxed, recovering from his outburst. "We have much business to catch up with." Edward smiled a forced smile. "Since your last triumphal entry into London, your visits have grown rare. I would hear your news of the north and of the situation at the Scottish border."

"Edward," the duke ceased his formality, suspicious of the king's eruption and swift rebottling, "you receive my regular reports on all such affairs, which surely makes plain that it is the weight of business there that prevents my regular attendance at court."

"Ay." Edward smiled broadly. "I hear much that is not contained within your reports also."

"Enlighten me." Richard resisted the concerned frown that sought to furrow his brow and returned his brother's smile. Edward was obviously trying to worry the duke and Richard would not give in to his games so easily.

"I hear almost continual complaint," Edward exaggerated, with an accompanying gesture, "from those against whom you rule in the assizes."

"Some people," Richard relaxed into his chair a little, "cannot accept fair judgement unless 'fair' be in their favour."

"Some people's definition of 'fair judgement'," Edward replied, also sliding down in his chair a little, "is not related to equitable principals, but social ones." He watched as the corners of Richard's mouth turned downwards to signify his nonchalance. "You seem determined to offend all such views, and people."

"God's justice is not based upon social rank but upon the heart of a man." Richard stated, folding his arms. "Such things are an artificial construct of the few for the control of the many."

"Are you not one of those few, brother?" Edward laughed to Richard's annoyance. "I fear that the world is not ready for your 'enlightened' viewpoint."

"Then perhaps it needs to be awakened!" Richard retorted.

"I think," Edward chuckled, "that it is a good job that I, and not you, are king of this England."

"Perhaps," Richard replied, lifting his demeanour and smiling back, "the Lord placed you there to control my more enlightened tendencies."

"And perhaps it is only a lack of courage that stops me from following your lead."

"It is political reality, Edward." Richard leaned forward, surprised by his brother's candour. "Something I have the luxury of not worrying about, for I have the power to enforce my will yet someone to tell me when to cease exercising that power."

"Sometimes I envy you that, Richard."

"It is how you get your work done. I envy you that!" Richard replied. "But enough philosophy, I must away to my business."

"Must you?" Edward implored. "We could spend this evening comparing our views on my wine collection if you prefer it to politics." Richard stood.

"No, I must visit George." He leaned across the desk between them and patted Edward's ever broadening stomach. "And methinks your grace has sampled more than enough of his wine collection recently." Richard smiled and turned to leave. As he crossed the chamber he was even keener to leave and discover why Edward was so clearly trying to detain him.

The sun was setting into a rosy haze as Richard entered the Tower to climb to George's lodging. The air outside was cool and clean but as soon as he passed the Tower threshold it became musty and oppressive. He watched his own feet climb the stairs and with each step, the returning lump grew higher and more uncomfortable in his throat. It suddenly hit him like a punch to the stomach that he was here to visit his condemned brother, possibly for the last time, having had to explain what was happening to their distraught mother earlier today.

As he reached the first floor, he was about to set foot toward the second when he stalled and froze where he stood. He listened more closely. Convinced his ears were playing tricks on him, he turned to face the first floor corridor and strained to listen. There it was again. It was unmistakeable. The voice was raised, though Richard could not make out the angry words. The voice, though, was definitely that of Queen

Elizabeth. The talking ceased and almost immediately Richard heard the sound of a bolt being withdrawn and a door creaking open. Unsure why, Richard instinctively wanted to hide and rounded a few steps on the staircase towards the second floor, relying on the fact that the queen was likely to descend and leave rather than climb the Tower further. As footsteps drew nearer he felt a sudden panic rise. What if she did go upward, to see Clarence perhaps? He shifted on the step, unsure whether to stay still, go up or even start down as though leaving an upper level. He heard steps, masked by the sound of a long trailing gown scuffing the stone floor as the queen moved. Richard felt his hands begin to tremble. Why was he so nervous? Even if the queen found him, what would, or could, she do? The echo of the steps grew louder and rang in his ears as the scratching of the dress forced his teeth to clench as it grated on the very ends of his nerves. There was no time left. He had nowhere to hide if he went up and standing still would only amplify suspicion. The duke prepared, with one foot hovering off the step, to begin a false descent if needed.

The footfalls clearly reached the staircase and stopped. Each second that they remained soundless felt like an age to Richard. He felt his whole body begin to rock and thud with the beat of his own heart. His head span. Why was he so shaken? A footstep. But which way? His foot began to sink and he felt as though he was off balance, about to fall forward. Another step. He bent his knee and sank slightly down, his foot meeting the stone, cold and solid against his own burning weakness. Another step. Softer. He froze again between steps. Another, and another, softer still. He held his breath, straining to hear. The footfalls were definitely moving away. Richard released the air from his fired lungs silently, puffing out his cheeks. With the footsteps now faded, the duke turned and climbed a step. Then he stopped. Overwhelmed by curiosity, he looked back over his shoulder, down the staircase. Why was the queen in the Tower? Who was she visiting if not George? If this was the reason that Edward had tried to delay him, then he was missing something. He now had to know who it was that Elizabeth had been to see that Edward did not want him to know about. He turned and jogged down the few steps to the landing and along the corridor. As he rounded a corner he saw a guard leaning against a wall next to a large oak door. That had to be the one. The sentry suddenly noticed Richard's approach and stood bolt upright and to attention, looking directly at the opposite wall.

Not wanting to draw attention to his presence, Richard did not acknowledge the guard but left him standing rigid. He drew up beside the door and put his hand onto the latch to open the viewing window at eye level that covered the grill used to check on residents before opening the door. As his hand hung on the catch he was haunted again by a sense of fear that bordered upon terror. What was happening to him? He took a deep breath and lifted the cool iron latch, pulling the window open.

It took a moment for his eyes to search the grey twilight of the room beyond. It was small and there was a little of the fading day's light straining into the room from some high window that Richard could not see. The shape of a low bed began to form out of the gloom. As Richard's eyes adjusted, he could make out a figure seated on the bed. The shape was hunched over with its head buried in its hands and elbows balanced on knees, making it all the more difficult to pick out any detail.

As if sensing Richard's frustration, the figure slowly, stiffly began to sit upright and turn to face the chink of light that sliced through the small gap between the door and the shadowed face that peered through at him. The two undistinguishable shapes stared at each other for a long moment, sizing each other. The duke tried to force his eyes to cut through the gloom, desperate to know upon whom he gazed. The man in the cell, for Richard had discerned that much, looked at the door only vaguely wondering who this next visitor might be. He was still pre-occupied by the content of his last meeting and even the thought that this may be some physical reinforcement of its content did little to move his mind.

Richard screwed his eyes tightly shut for a few seconds to try and make more of what little light soaked the dank cell. A wave of tiredness washed through him from his head, along his back, down his heavy legs and into his leaden feet. He had not slept well these last few nights and closing his eyes allowed exhaustion to overtake him momentarily. In that instant, he wanted to surrender to it, but as quickly as it came, he chased the notion from his mind, called upon his body to respond and opened his eyes as a wave of fresh energy washed away the aching weariness.

His eyes struggled now with the comparative influx of light but after a moment of adjustment and refocusing he saw the shape on the bed more clearly. The face was still hazy but Richard could make out what he first thought to be a portly figure but then he thought again that it was a thin, elderly man wearing robes that made him look more bulky in his seated position. A thought shot through the back of his mind. Were those the robes of a nobleman or of a clergyman? He wondered because he had thought that he was abreast of those nobles currently languishing in his brother's disfavour. Perhaps Edward had arrested a bishop or priest. That only intensified his curiosity at the queen's visit. As he closed the viewing window, Richard was left with more questions than answers.

Almost surprised, the duke found himself stood before George's door waiting for it to be opened. He had drifted up the staircase and along the hall lost within his own thoughts. Who was the priest in the cell? Why did Elizabeth visit him in the Tower? Was it anything to do with George? Perhaps most perplexing of all, why had he felt that welling of terror at the prospect of being caught on the stairs by the queen? If there was one place that he felt he could get answers to these questions, it would surely be in his brother's room.

As the door was opened by the guard, Richard strode into George's apartment to find his brother seated at a small bureau below a thin window, using the dying light of the day and the jumping, flickering of two candles to write at the desk. Clarence did not flinch nor raise his head to see who had entered. Richard knew that George would pay him no heed until he had finished what he was writing. As a matter of principle, the Duke of Clarence would not interrupt what he was doing, since he found no-one more important than himself, not even his brother the king. That was the largest part of the reason that he found himself in his current circumstance. Gloucester noisily dragged a chair across the flagstones and sat immediately to George's right, his chair facing George's side, right at the edge of his peripheral vision. He sat and waited for his brother. Perhaps for the last time. He saw a faint, restrained grin tug at George's cheek, obviously amused by Richard's unsubtle attendance, and he could not help but smile softly himself.

After a few moments, George laid down his quill and rubbed his palms up and down his face before exhaling loudly and turning his chair, also noisily, to face his visitor.

"Richard," George smiled a tired yet sincere greeting, "forgive me. A few last matters to conclude. What, pray tell, brings you to my illustrious residence at this hour?" Clarence gestured in his own flamboyant manner around the dimming room.

"News, an offer." Richard paused. "Concern, love, confusion." He bit his lip, unsure as to how George would react.

"Tell me of the first portion." George still smiled and remained as difficult to read as ever. Clearly, he had not allowed fear of what was to come to cloud his spirit yet. "There will be time for the rest later."

"Our mother sends her love." Richard dropped his head, suddenly saddened and somewhat ashamed of the conversation that he was about to have with a brother condemned to death by another brother. Clarence nodded as Richard lifted his chin back up, drawing a deep breath. "She shall visit you tomorrow but found herself unable to bear the proceedings today." He saw no particular need to tell his brother that their mother had broken down in tears when he had told her of Parliament's decision. "At her request, I petitioned the king to allow you the dignity of selecting your own method of execution," he flinched a little at the word, "and the honour of a private ceremony out of the public eye."

"Good old mother!" George chuckled. "And how did Edward take the request?"

"He acquiesced with surprising ease." Richard felt his mood lift a little, hauled up by George's apparent good humour.

"I bet that he did," George grinned distantly, "and not because mother asked it of him."

"George?" Richard questioned, but the elder waved the comment away.

"I have it!" George called as if in answer to some unasked riddle.

"I beg your pardon?" Richard frowned.

"If I am to be executed, tell Edward that I wish to be shut up, head first, in the largest butt of his finest malmsey." George burst into a roar of laughter which Richard found himself joining in with a little uncomfortably. "At least I shall depart this earth a happy man and shall take as much of his precious wine with me as I am able!" Richard relaxed further and the brothers laughed together freely. George wiped his eyes, which streamed with tears brought on by their laughter. Both men breathed deeply to regain their composure.

"I shall tell him of your demands." Richard spluttered, fighting to control himself. "Ah," he sighed away the last of the jollity. "Is there anything else that I can do for you?"

"Erm," George turned back to his desk and stared at the papers as though considering something, and then he turned back sharply. "No, no. I think all is in hand." George fixed his piercing grey eyes on his brother. "Thank you, though."

"We may not always have seen eye to eye on all matters, George, but you retain my love." It was true that in spite of their arguments and George's disloyalty to Edward, Richard still cared deeply for his brother. George had always been able to make him laugh, even now, and, until this point, seemed to be able to apply sufficient charm to any situation as to seem untouchable. Richard, on the other hand, cared little for what others thought of him and lacked George's natural charisma.

"Edward should be more grateful for your loyalty. Your badge of the boar and your motto both suit you well, Richard. If I didn't know you better, I'd say you had gone to great lengths to create your image."

"I have created nothing!" Richard snapped. "I am who I am and I make no excuse for that to you, Edward or anyone else."

"Richard!" Clarence leapt back in his seat and threw up his arms. "I meant no offence. In fact, I meant the opposite." He leaned forward now, as if to reinforce a point. "There are princes and nobles across Europe who have worked to sculpt an image for years, yet fall short even of your shadow. There is no wealth in all of England to equate to the value of your standing." George spread his palms in mock amazement. "Yet you have gained all of this by simply being you, using the gifts the Lord blessed you with without even realising that you do so." George sat back again. "You amaze me, Richard. Never stop. Never compromise. Never cease to be what you are."

Richard sat dumbstruck, bemused by his brother's words. George had always been so self-obsessed that Richard thought he barely even saw anyone around him and his constant opposition to Edward had, by extension, left him often at odds with Richard. Gloucester sniffed loudly.

"Is there something in the air up here that affects your senses, George?"

"If there is, it serves only to bring me to them." Clarence sounded distant, as if he spoke through a heavy veil that muffled his voice. "Now," he said suddenly and clearly, "you said that you bring with you concerns and confusion. Tell me more of these."

"Er," Richard stuttered, still a little off balance at his brother's words. "I remain unsure firstly why you have persisted in opposing Edward to this point. More than once you have been excused, yet you have brought yourself to this and I cannot understand why."

"Tell me why you think it *might* be." George reclined in his chair and eyed Richard, a smile passing over his lips again.

"I refuse to see in you greed so blind that your reason is made a slave to it, yet I can see no other explanation that I do accept for you to drive so hard and so fast along this road."

"And yet I am greedy, Richard, and vain and disloyal. The facts speak for themselves, yet you refuse to see what stands in plain light before you."

"Perhaps we should add pride to the list of traits that shall keep you out of Heaven." Richard was scornful of his brother's light hearted admissions.

"Perhaps so," George laughed, "I had forgotten that one." He stopped laughing suddenly. "For proud I am, brother, as proud a Plantagenet as you. Born of the most royal of blood, we have a divine right to pride."

"No." Richard snapped. "The things you talk of are each a sin in the eyes if the Almighty and you should be repenting such failings now, given your circumstance." Richard felt a rush of blood surge around his body as his fervour grew. "The royal blood that we share gives us a privileged position from which to help the people of England to a better life, not to further our own selfish ends."

"You should have grown out of such naivety by now Richard. It does not become one of your years and it grows in the shade of Edward's shadow." George spoke with a hissing spite. "God shall judge me when the time is right and I do not fear that, for He alone holds all of the facts and shall decide upon them fairly. He cares not for petty failings and character flaws, but for the contents of our hearts, for our actions undertaken in good faith and for the way in which we treat others during the life He gives us."

"Then I shall leave your repentance between you and your conscience." Richard conceded, not wishing to move into a confrontation, for he had other matters to tackle before he left.

"At least you hold your temper a little better with age." George smiled.

"Only a little." Richard replied darkly.

"So," George continued regardless, "is my past conduct your only cause for concern?"

Richard hesitated for a long moment. As usual, his enigmatic older brother had frustrated him within moments of amusing him and had seemed either oblivious to Richard's concern for his immortal soul, or was taunting him for his convictions. Either way, Richard had made his point and had not visited his brother tonight for an argument. The question that burned in Richard's mind was whether to pursue his other line of questioning given his brother's mood. The answer, though, was simple and clear. This would be his last opportunity to quiz his brother further.

"Why would the queen be downstairs visiting one of the cells?" Richard watched George closely for a reaction to his snap question. He saw his brother's eyes dart to his, clearly a little shocked at the news, before he blinked and regained his composure.

"Why should I know of such things?" George enquired coldly.

"Because there is a prisoner downstairs who I do not recognise by visage nor by virtue of his imprisonment."

"Yet you would have it that I know this man and the queen's business with him from my apartment?" George gestured around the room, his tone obviously indignant.

"I know that there are things that you do not tell me, George." Richard was sure of it, but also knew that his stubborn, arrogant brother would not surrender to badgering, but rather would enjoy watching Richard grow more irate at his evasions. "I am no child any longer. Why do you not trust me?" Perhaps a change of direction would loosen George's tongue. The question was met by a piercing stare.

"Perhaps," George began slowly, thoughtfully, "you are not asking the right questions." Richard flushed as he felt the blood begin to pound uncomfortably in his nose. He was losing his temper fast, but fought to suppress it.

"Why must you be so cryptic?" Richard asked as calmly as he could manage, leaning in with the question.

"Why," George tipped forward to meet him, "do you not ask the right question?"

Richard's head fell into his hands. He wanted to walk out and not give in to George's games, but at the same time he was determined not to leave without finding out what George knew. Another option flashed through his mind. He wondered whether George would be willing to talk from the flat of his back with a bloodied nose. He took a deep breath and sat upright as he blew it out again. He had not come to beat his brother to within a hair's breadth of a fate that would come to meet him in a few days time anyway. He could not shake the feeling that George wanted to tell him something behind all of the teasing.

"Why have you done all of this?" Richard asked, almost pleading.

"We have already discussed this." George reclined, dismissing the question with a wave of his hand.

"Who is the man downstairs?"

"I have answered that too."

"Why was Elizabeth here?"

"I told you, I do not know."

"Why did I feel such fear at the notion of being discovered here by her?" Silence. Richard had barely meant to speak the words yet they had escaped him in the exchange. The question hung between them. George's face twisted as though he agreed with some thought he had shared only with himself.

"You, Richard, the finest pillar of chivalric honour in the kingdom are in fear of our washerwoman queen?"

"You mock me, George." Richard flushed.

"I do not." George replied calmly. "I am your eldest brother,"

"Elder brother." Richard corrected him instinctively.

"Yes." George said absently, looking down at his own palms. "Of course."

"Just tell me the truth, George." Clarence seemed to consider something momentarily again.

"The truth is all about timing, my dear Richard. A wrongly timed truth is raped of its truest meaning." George's voice was forceful but Richard winced a little at the distasteful wording. "That is a coin that you must learn both sides of in politics, brother, for it will serve you well as both shield and sword."

"What do I have to do?" Richard called as if to the walls.

"Ah!" George yelped in delight. "At last."

"At last what?" Richard frowned, lost.

"At last you get close to the right question."

Richard's frown deepened, but then lifted quickly as it dawned upon him. There was only one question that would be the right one to George. There was only one thing, only one person, the pre-occupied George. George. If he were in Richard's position, there is only one question that he would ask.

"What about me?" Richard ventured.

"That is the question." George spread his arms to meet it. A heavy silence lingered as Richard awaited an answer.

"Well?" Richard demanded impatiently.

"I cannot give you that truth now." George sighed. Richard rose sharply from his seat and turned to leave. The choice that faced him now was to leave, or to violently assault his brother. "But," George continued quickly, thoroughly enjoying toying with his little brother, "I can tell you that when the time is right, all of your questions will be answered and then you will have need to ask yourself that last question again."

Richard turned to face his brother again, though he gazed thoughtfully at the floor to his side rather than at George. This was hardly the answer that Richard wanted.

"George," Richard spoke to that spot on the floor for he felt the emotion of the moment threatening to overtake him, "I had hoped that we could end all things between us on good terms, with honesty," he shook his head slowly as he continued, "but it is clear that it cannot happen if it does not suit your designs, even now." Looking up to his brother, Richard was met by a blank stare. "You," Richard said tiredly, "would stand in the middle of a drought ravaged land and wonder only why God deprived you of water. Then you would demand to remain dry in a rainstorm."

"Have you quite finished?" George bellowed, cutting Richard off mid sentence and causing him to jump a little. "Your self-righteous pomposity sickens me every bit as much as my selfishness defies your belief." George rose to his feet to look down upon his little brother, to establish some dominance of the situation. "Has it never occurred to you that we are not so dissimilar, you and I?" Richard sneered at the suggestion, making no effort to disguise his distaste. "Duty is to you as self is to me. We both are driven by that which we hold dearest. One day, you shall find that put to the ultimate test. You will be forced to decide between your duty, your family, your God, your conscience, your ambition." George paused. "And it will be your sense of duty that will cloud matters. That which drives you will touch each arm of your confusion and weave them together until you can no longer focus on that which you originally thought was so clear."

"You grow more cryptic, George." Richard frowned deeply. "Am I destined to leave you with more questions than I shall have answers?" Richard did not expect an answer even to this, but was resigned to it.

"Perhaps," George smiled his wry grin, "but remember all that I have said to you."

"I shall." Richard paused a moment, as if considering his next words. "I shall miss you also. More than I think I realise even now."

"'Tis true." George concurred sincerely. "You shall miss me, little brother!" Both laughed aloud. "Be well," George eventually continued more seriously, "and be true, Richard." George spoke now through a pearling tear, though Richard was not quite sure whether it was born of laughter or sadness.

"I will see Edward in the morning with your request."

"Then you will leave London?" George asked. Richard thought for a moment.

"I had intended it, though I shall stay if you wish it." The young duke felt a heavy cloak of sorrow suddenly weigh upon his shoulders and some invisible fingers tugged at his stomach. He found himself unable to believe that this moment had come.

"No," George replied, almost solemn, "I think that I should rather we parted as we are." Richard nodded his agreement. The two stood for a moment, locked in an awkward silence that neither really wanted to end, for it would be the last they would share. Eventually Richard stepped forward and pulled George into a strong embrace. George placed a hand on Richards back and squeezed gently. When the two parted, Richard nodded his head low, spun on his heels and left the room, and his brother, behind. He descended the staircase in a hazy blur of tears he hoped no other would see and ambled home.

Chapter 16

9th March 1480 - The Wisdom Of Solomon

    Time had passed swiftly since his last visit to London and Richard would gladly confess that he had not missed the city, nor its politics. It was a little over two years since George had been executed, in accordance with his wishes. As much as he understood its need, the fact of it still disturbed him. In quiet moments, often in the chapel, his brother's face would appear and their last exchange be replayed in his mind as if pushed before him. Always it was accompanied by that nervous knotting in his stomach that he had felt that day and always George's prophetic promise that one day all would become clear echoed through his mind with a growing frustration. He missed his brother, though he would not admit as much freely.
    A heavy haze of white morning light still hung over the city as Francis Lovell and William Catesby drew their horses along either side of Richard's own. He blinked away his daydreaming as he heard Catesby's deep voice above the rhythmic clacking of horseshoes on cobble stones.
    "Strange to be back?" William questioned.
    "Not really." Richard replied with a smile. "Why do you ask?"
    "Just making conversation." Catesby shrugged.
    "What he means," Lovell returned, "is that you seem to make an effort to avoid visiting London wherever possible and he wonders if there is a reason." Lovell winked as Richard looked at him and the duke tried to keep the smile from his face.
    "Is this so, William?" Richard demanded.
    "No, my lord." Catesby replied apologetically.

"My affairs are my own," Richard told him, his tone firm, "and I should thank you to refrain from gossip concerning them." He scowled deliberately at the lawyer, whose face drained of colour and betrayed concern.

"I, I." William stammered, looking at Richard, who could no longer keep his face straight. "You arse, Francis!" he called across Richard.

"Every time, William." Lovell called back. "Your humour is a slave to your ambition."

"I am hurt that you think me so fickle in my favour, William." Richard teased.

"Royal blood has a curious tendency to heat and cool of its own accord, my lord," Catesby teased back, "and one can never presume that it does not boil, for once burned, the wound can be deep."

"Ooohh!" Richard and Lovell cooed together.

"Well," Richard laughed, "I hereby grant you both protection from any heat of my blood. We have been through too much together for me to take offence at any of your words."

"Then, my lord," Catesby spoke haughtily, "you too are an arse."

"William!" Richard snapped. "Do not overstep the boundary!"

"Very funny." Catesby drawled. He and Lovell fell back and Richard heard them laughing behind him, but all he could feel now was a growing sense foreboding with each step that brought him closer to the king.

Richard was so distracted by his own thoughts that he passed into the palace and found himself strolling through a long corridor passing between the chill dimness of the walls and the sudden drenching warmth of the high windows which sent a shiver down his spine. He barely noticed the woman who passed him, except that her presence meant that she had come from Edward's offices. Hardly unusual, except that she was a little older than his brother's usual taste. He only managed a glance at her face as she hurried away, her presence intriguing Richard, not least as a distraction from his daydreaming.

Almost at the king's door, he found a quickening of his step as he drew closer. He had only really come to London for one reason and that reason was currently within Edward's office. He knocked on the door and pushed it open without awaiting an answer. The king looked up from his desk, about to chastise one who would dare to enter unbidden, but his face brightened when he saw who the visitor was. Richard, for his part, was immediately struck by the change in his brother's visage, which had become broader and ruddy. The light that always shone from his bright eyes was still there, but it was framed now by dispersing wrinkles. He stood to greet Richard slowly and uncomfortably. The rest of his frame had not been left behind. Having always been tall and broad, Edward was now spreading at the waist and had become a truly immense sight. He moved uneasily across the room and threw his arms around Richard joyfully. The younger man stretched his arms but could not encompass him, so patted his back firmly.

When they separated, Richard's eyes were already on the silent figure sat in front of Edward's desk. He clapped his hand again on the king's back and sprang over to the chair.

"Margaret!" he called with obvious, unbridled delight.

"Richard." The soft voice acknowledged and a narrow face smiled thinly up at him. "It is good to see you." The voice carried a slight accent born of many years spent on the continent.

"Burgundy must suit you my lady, for you look very well on your time there." The grin on his lips faltered a little as he now saw the concerned look on her face. "But I see that something vexes our sister upon her return." He glanced at Edward but smiled again. "And I have come all this way to see you."

"I wish that I had been able to visit on a more pleasant occasion," Margaret reflected sombrely, "but it is necessity rather than desire that has brought me here." She looked up into her brother's deep brown eyes, filled with concern. "Yet," she spoke clearly, pushing her lips into a smile, "it is refreshing indeed to see you here, Richard." She rose from her chair and wrapped her arms around her brother, who noted how firmly she squeezed him. "News of your success," she continued softly, as if privately, in his ear, "both military and otherwise, reaches our ears in Burgundy regularly and we hear it with great interest." She pulled back, releasing her grip on him and fixed him with a deliberate, piercing stare. "You do well for your brother," she said, a little louder, "and father would be proud."

Richard flushed a little, fighting to hide the colour in his cheeks. His father had died when Richard was only eight, along with Edmund, his brother who had been between Edward and George in age. Both had been drawn by Lancastrian taunts into a battle that they were never going to win. Their father's pride, temper and impatience had cost dear. Edward was raising reinforcements that could have swung the battle and the Duke of York and Edmund had been securely ensconced within the resilient walls of Sandal Castle, but Queen Margaret drew them out. The duke and his son were captured at the ensuing Battle of Wakefield. The news had left Richard, the eleven year old George and their sisters distraught and their mother had struggled with little success to hide her own devastation at the loss of her beloved husband and son on the same day. This turn of events had led to Richard's time in exile with George at Utrecht while Edward had fought to seize the throne.

It had been a few years after the event that Richard had learned, from George, the terrible truth of the fate shared by his father and brother. None had seen fit to tell the eight year old boy the details until some petty squabble with the teenage George had caused him to reveal all. Richard had, to George's amusement, run in tears to their mother, retelling George's tale to her. He had then been struck dumb as large, shining tears budded in his mother's sad eyes and rolled slowly down her cheek. She held him close a moment and then sat him down and recounted the details as she knew them. She spoke softly, was very matter of fact, yet the rolling tear on her cheek was followed by another, and another, and they continued all of the time she talked. Richard listened, jaw ajar, as he learned of the capture of his father and brother after the battle was lost. Edmund had pleaded for his life, but the proud duke would not give his enemy the satisfaction. He had been beaten, sat atop an anthill as a mock throne with a tattered paper crown to be ridiculed by the Lancastrian soldiers. Still he had not surrendered the dignity they tried to rob him of. Finally, Queen Margaret had ordered father and son executed. They had been beheaded and their pale, bruised, grotesque heads skewered high on spikes at either side of the gates of the city of York.

Richard had not known what to say to his mother, and had simply moved forward to hug her. In the silence, he had felt his mother jerking and shaking as she tried to suppress the tears that soaked through his shirt until she stole back her composure and straightened herself up. From that day forward, Richard had lowered his head each time he passed through the city gates, partly in solemn respect for his father and brother and partly because their bloodstained faces impaled high on spikes had so haunted his dreams in the months that followed that he could not bear to look at that place, however dear the city remained to him and his family.

"Perhaps," Margaret continued, "we shall have our time to exchange news at tonight's banquet." She looked deliberately at Edward, who stood where Richard had left him. "Some good news from this visit would be most welcome."

Richard followed her gaze and watched Edward shift uncomfortably. He frowned. Something had already passed between his siblings. He had no real desire to put either on the spot in front of the other and he knew that he stood a far better chance of learning the truth of it from Edward when they were alone. So he tried to lighten the mood.

"Edward," he called to his brother, "a banquet?" He strode across and placed a hand on the king's substantial stomach. "How very unlike you!" he grinned.

"Well," Edward said smiling, putting on a formal tone and glad of the distraction, "one is required to put one's country before oneself on occasion." He winked and the men laughed together. Edward's whole frame juddered and Richard hid his shock at the change in his brother. Virtually all military matters had been left to Richard during the past year, not only because they were all but exclusive to the Scottish borders, but increasingly the king was losing his taste for battle. It was rumoured that he could barely take to the saddle any longer for the hunt, let alone to ride into battle. Whilst Richard revelled in the autonomy that this gave him in his affairs, his concern at his brother's decadent lifestyle played constantly on his mind. The only reason that he said nothing was that he knew doing otherwise would bring him into confrontation with the queen, who he felt sure prospered in terms of wealth and influence with Edward distracted. He found it easier to simply stay away from London.

"I shall retire a while," Margaret's solemn voice interrupted Richard's thoughts and the two men turned back to her, "and prepare for this evening."

"Prepare?" Richard questioned loudly. "My lady would barely need a minute. You look wonderful, Margaret." The lie sat heavy with him, for she looked tired and forlorn. "Anne is here and is keen to see you. She claims it is interest in continental fashion, but I suspect she will seek yet more embarrassing childhood stories with which to tease me."

"I know little of fashion," Margaret smiled at him again, though he was sure there was little feeling behind it, "but will have plenty to tell Anne on the other count." Richard turned up his nose in mock disapproval but winked at her, a cheeky glint flashing from his eye in the growing sunlight. "Edward."

She curtsied slowly, taking her leave of the king with a rustle of her skirts. The men both bowed as she left the room, pulling the door closed behind her. There was a moment in which they stood, frozen, in silence, waiting for their sister to reach a distance from the door beyond which she could not hear them. After a suitable amount of time, Richard turned a fierce scowl upon his brother.

"What upsets Margaret?" Richard demanded with all the force of a brother defending his sister. Edward waved his hand in dismissal as he moved back to his chair. He sat heavily, then jumped as Richard's fist pounded on his desk and he looked up to see his brother's angry glare. He looked absently back to some papers spread out on his desk.

"I shall ask only once today, Richard," Edward spoke coolly without looking up, "that you remember yourself."

"I shall, Edward," the duke replied through clenched teeth, "if you shall remember me also."

"Sit." Edward waved to the chair that Margaret had vacated and Richard, after a short pause during which he considered refusing, took the seat. Edward spent a moment shuffling papers, as if to make his point, for he seemed to pay little attention to anything in particular, before he spoke to the duke again. "Margaret has come from Burgundy to request our aid against a fresh threat of French aggression." The statement was met with a blank stare from Richard. "I have said no."

"May I ask why?" Richard moderated the shock and immediate, burning anger that sought to accompany the question.

"Political reality." Edward stated shortly.

"Aside from the fact that Burgundy's Duchess is our sister," Richard frowned, "is the reality not that we have more to gain from a strong, independent Burgundy joined with us in opposition to France than from a France free from the distraction of threat and confrontation at her own border?"

"Perhaps, at first glance." Edward mused slowly, looking at his brother as though disappointed by the superficial nature of his argument, though Edward had himself wrestled with the same considerations in these last hours.

"We have strong trade links with Burgundy, too." Richard stated plainly, pursuing his point. "If it is lost to France we face economic as well as military and political uncertainty. We could do without any one, Edward. All at once would be disastrous."

"True." Edward conceded. "Yet there is a longer game to be played out here."

"A game that involves risking the life of your sister and the security of your throne?" Richard was dismayed and his tone did not disguise it.

"If I were to side with Margaret and promise the troops which Burgundy has requested," Edward smiled, "I know that with you at its head, our army would be formidable indeed. Please be assured that this is not the issue at hand."

"Sire," Richard offered with deference, "I know well the trust that you place in me in matters of war. It is the lack of trust that you appear to have in me in matters of politics that concerns me. Do I not administer the north as well as I defend it?"

"Indeed, brother, you do." Edward smiled. "As difficult as it may be for you to comprehend, this is not about you. I have made my decision."

"I shall respect it, your grace." Richard lied, his temper rising at the king's jibes. "My interest is in why it was made so when it appears so contrary to my perception of the matter." Happy that he had restrained himself suitably, Richard smiled awkwardly.

"I am sure," Edward began slowly, "that you remember Picquigny?"

"Of course." Richard's gaze fell to his side at the memory of both his anger and the shame he had felt at letting his king down on the occasion.

"Well," Edward continued, somewhat pleased by the obvious embarrassment the mention of this still caused Richard, "one of the provisions of my Treaty with Louis was that his son, Le Dauphine, should wed my daughter, Elizabeth, when he is of age."

"This is well known." Richard replied flatly.

"Do you believe that Louis would honour that agreement if I were to treat with Burgundy against him?" Edward leaned in a little, curious to see how Richard would assess the matter.

"Do you believe that he will honour the agreement if in one swoop the threat from Burgundy is removed, he sees that you will not even defend your own sister against his aggression and he considers that perhaps he could turn the situation around and lay claim to your throne?" Richard spoke quickly and sharply. Edward sat slowly back in his chair again, his face showing no sign of his thoughts. He and the queen had discussed this matter and agreed that the union with the French throne was the surest route to peace, and power. Yet Richard had cast dark shadows of doubt amongst his clarity with an insight that had eluded him and the queen during their long deliberations since Burgundy's request had first arrived. Perhaps the wine had not aided the process of his thought, and once settled, he had given the matter no further consideration. He found himself unwilling to change his mind now, as if at his younger brother's behest.

"You asked," Edward began, his mind still a little distracted, but seeking to regain his authority, "why it is that I seem to doubt your advice in matters of policy." The king knew that this was a line Richard would pursue to the utter exclusion of his more uncomfortable line of questioning. The duke's eyes flashed, his attention clearly engaged. "I am afraid," Edward continued forcefully, having taken the initiative again, "that you have, very kindly, just approved my thinking." He allowed the cryptic pronouncement to hang between them until Richard was forced to take the bait.

"How is it so, Edward?" The younger man was clearly bemused. His face flushed with a mixture of embarrassment and anger that caused him to shuffle in his seat, his right knee bouncing unbidden in a nervous reflex. Edward had always spoken to him as though he was still the eight year old boy he had been when Edward became head of the family and it had always made Richard feel like that little boy again. He liked to believe that it was born of a sense of protection, yet as he grew older he had begun to fear that it may be a tool Edward used to suppress his growing understanding of the world around him.

"Your suggestion was the first thing that entered your mind." Edward explained like a tutor whose pupil failed to grasp some mathematical principle. "It was born of the impetuous passion that defines you, Richard." The king's eyes pierced Richard as he spoke. Richard's face betrayed confusion. "That is no criticism." Edward continued calmly. "It is what makes you who you are and I would have you no other way. It lies at the very heart of your success in battle, because your decisions are made and you have acted whilst all around you are still thinking what they should do." Edward moved his eyes to the desk in front of him. "Perhaps," he reflected, "I procrastinate too much these days." He looked up again to judge his brother's response. Richard tried to hide his agreement with the sentiment, but the king spotted the momentary raising of Richard's eyebrows. "It is a curse of kingship that would ruin all that makes you so indomitable." Edward's voice did now hold an unmistakable admiration for the duke. "Every decision that I make, however small, can have so deep an impact that a superficial glance simply cannot be enough."

"I see that, Edward," Richard told him with conviction, "but..."

"But," the king interrupted, "once I have made a decision, it must remain made, set from that moment forward in the hardest stone, even if it should prove to be wrong, for the only thing more dangerous to a king than rashness in decision making is a shifting of a mind once made up." Edward looked hard at his brother now as if willing his point across in his stare. "We should look to our history and learn from the mistakes of our predecessors. Henry was weak and indecisive and it cost him his throne. I seek a balance by considering my decisions and then having the conviction to see them through."

"Why, then, do you not at least hear my counsel before making your mind up, for it may assist in finding a balance?" Richard persisted, clearly hurt.

"I think I know it in most cases, brother, and weigh it with the counsel of others evenly." Edward smiled softly at him. "I have an hundred advisors, each with an hundred opinions as to what they think I might wish to hear, yet yours is constant in my mind, though you are here so rarely now, and though that alone does not make it the right opinion." Richard sat in silence, unsure of how to feel.

"Your decision in this instance, then," Richard began slowly, "is to rely upon the French alliance to the exclusion of all other considerations?"

"Ha!" Edward laughed. "Even in seeing my point your wit is sharper than your sword. But yes, it is so. Le Dauphane is almost of age and my emissaries press Louis for a date for the union even as we speak. If he were to renege, then I shall reassess the situation, but the greatest gain remains in the French alliance at present.

"Then so be it." Richard stated loudly, clapping his hands together and smiling broadly. The time had come to stop arguing with the king.

"Good." Edward smiled back. "I note your objections, but expect your full support outside of this office."

"Of course." Richard puffed out his chest. "As always."

"As always." Edward repeated, nodding his approval. "Until this evening."

"I shall see you there, Edward." Richard smiled as he took his leave. Edward watched him go thoughtfully. Since George had been executed, Richard had grown more distant, from the capital and from Edward. Though he performed his duty impeccably, and every fibre of Edward's being believed in his brother's oft proven and unwavering loyalty to him, hard earned experience and the urging of his closest counsellors for caution nurtured a faint, nagging, gnawing doubt at the back of his mind. Did he have Richard under control?

Anne was startled from the sewing that she had been engrossed in for the past hour by the clattering slam of the apartment door. It was far too loud to signal the return of her son, who had been playing with his cousins all morning, and there was only one other who would enter unbidden.

"Richard." She called to the unseen door around the corner. There was no reply. She rose from her chair by the glinting light of the window where she had been working and moved towards the corner that led to the source of the noise, a growing sense of apprehension gripping her stomach.

"Richard, is that you?" she called a little nervously. The lack of a response was now making her uneasy. There were very few places that Anne felt truly safe and even in those places she only ever relaxed completely when Richard was with her. She did not enjoy her own weakness, but her experiences in the years before her marriage to Richard had left their mark and she found herself all but surrendered to her husband, though willingly and without regret. Cautiously, and moving away from the point of the corner in case someone there should try and grab her. She held her breath and stepped squarely to face the door.

She released her breath as she saw the unmistakable frame of her husband standing with his back to her, his hands raised high and wide, pushed flat on the door as though trying to prevent some intruder from barging into the room. His head was hanging between his shoulders, his dark hair covering the sides of his face.

"Richard?" she said softly, only a little above a whisper. "What has happened?"

"Nothing." The reply came after a brief pause, a musical note forced through it as Richard pushed himself from the door and turned to face into the room, the exhausted smile of masked defeat spread upon his face.

"You are either drunk," Anne smiled, "or frustrated. With your brother, it could be either, but I think it a little early for you to be so intoxicated as to need the support of the door." She smiled affectionately, hoping that Richard would take the invitation to share with her whatever had annoyed him. He smiled back at her. Of course he saw the invitation.

"My brother," he began, striding across to her, "is an arrogant, blinkered, wife ruled ass." He reached his wife and kissed her lightly on the forehead.

"He is the king." Anne said frankly in an attempt to explain. She placed the side of her head onto his chest and he wrapped his arms around her.

"Perhaps," Richard conceded, the embrace drawing his frustration from him. "Yet he would abandon his own family to build his policy upon a single pillar that stands on the shifting sands of French favour."

"I am certain," Anne spoke softly, "that he has the best interests of the kingdom at heart."

"I do not doubt it." Richard gently stroked his fingers through Anne's long dark hair. "I am concerned that it is the queen who drives these things, though, and she will only ever have the best interests of her parasitic family at heart. She drowns my brother in wine and gorges him on rich food so that he is easier to mould to her will. Doubtless the French alliance is her primary concern.

"Such matters are the reason that we stay in the north and serve your brother at a distance." Anne said coolly.

"True." Richard's voice was thoughtful. "But what would happen if it were ever a choice between me and what his queen thinks is right for the kingdom?" There was obvious concern in his voice. Anne pushed away from him, her palms on his chest and she looked him directly in the eye, resolve burning from deep within.

"We shall never place him in such a position, shall we?" Her firm tone told Richard that this was not really a question, but a statement of definite fact. Richard admired the undercurrent of strength that he always saw in his wife's face when she was determined. They stood in silence for a moment, engrossed in each other.

"Forgive me," he asked eventually, pushing a stray lock of mahogany hair from his wife's face. He ran his fingers gently down the side of her face and she smiled softly. "I fear that all things balance so delicately on Edward's favour, which is fine," he added quickly, "since I do not intend to jeopardise our relationship, but it balances also upon the male line of some other family, and this grows less likely to be rectified as Edward falls farther under the spell of his wife." Richard spat the last word venomously. "I have promised our son that he will not endure the uncertainty and insecurity of my childhood, yet what security we have feels beyond my control. I feel," Richard thought for a long moment and watched a faint frown of concern fold across Anne's pale forehead, "helpless."

"Richard," Anne's tone was powerful and took her husband aback, "do not dare to say such things! You are the rock upon which the future of your son, your wife and your region are flourishing and none need you to begin to feel sorrow for yourself now."

"You are right, of course." Richard responded with a smile, much to his wife's relief. "Frustration is a cunning beast that hides behind and feeds so many other afflictions." He frowned, as if a sudden notion had confused him.

"What is it, Richard?" Anne asked, seeing the expression.

"Nothing." Richard wrestled with himself. "I," he paused.

"Go on, Richard." Anne's sapphire blue eyes pleaded to know what was troubling him.

"I was about to say something I had never believed that I would even think."

"You know that you can tell me anything."

"I do." Richard confirmed without delay. "I was about to say," he continued with an uncharacteristic nervous edge, "that I could do better service to this nation than Edward. I can't believe," he continued quickly, "that I would think such a thing."

"Thinking such a thing is not your damnation, Richard, but rather your disbelief is your salvation." Anne told her husband in a sombre tone, though a gentle smile caressed her lips as she paused. "Your brother," she looked away a moment, "my father," she paused with obvious sadness and longing, "both lacked that disbelief. They were possessed of a conviction that they could do better." Anne looked deeply into Richard's eyes. "To think such a thing is human, it is to act upon it that would defy all that you are."

"How is it that you are always so right? Such wisdom would shame Solomon." Richard grinned.

"Solomon was only a man. His wife probably whispered all of the wisdom in his ear." Anne smiled and her eyes lit up like candles out of the pitch black night.

"Ha!" Richard laughed. "I believe you may even be right!" He tickled his wife's waist and she wriggled from his arms and turned to run into the room, but Richard caught her arm and spun her back around into his embrace and pressed his lips to hers. Anne slowly closed her eyes and softly kissed him back.

Chapter 17

1483

Sir Thomas More's study was once again growing stuffy and oppressive as the bright, leaping flames licked at the drying air. Hans reached for his tankard to sooth his prickling throat. Sir Thomas had stopped speaking for a while and was gazing, lost, into the flames as though deep in thought upon his own words.

"So," Hans broke the silence uncomfortably and jumped as the fire cracked loudly, as if chastising him for distracting the man it held mesmerised. Sir Thomas looked sideways at his guest, his eyes like those of someone awakening from a too-short and shallow sleep. "You believe," he continued, his eyes flashing to the fire as if awaiting another snap, "that this could have been the point at which the Duke of Gloucester began to covet the throne?" Hans frowned, unsure of his own question.

"Maybe," Sir Thomas replied absently, "and maybe not. That is a judgement for each to make for himself, since we will never truly know what lay in the hearts and minds of those we cannot interrogate." His gaze fell back to the fireplace. "I had believed," Sir Thomas continued, as if to the flames, a faint smile highlighted by the glow from the hearth, "that it was the profession of lawyers to disguise the truth."

"I am not sure that I understand you, Sir Thomas." Hans ventured.

"I am not sure that you are meant to just yet, Master Holbein." More flashed a broad smile at his guest. "Forgive me. My mind quakes with that which I must tell you." He shifted in his armchair. "We may even begin the telling of a new kind of history, you and I." Sir Thomas's face glowed with undisguised excitement at the notion. Hans was finding himself more and more engrossed in the tale and in the promise of what was still to be told. More's storytelling was drawing him in and he found himself daring to like the persona being described of a man known throughout Europe only as a usurping child murderer. It was hard to believe that the two could be the same man.

"We shall move now," Sir Thomas began again, "to those most infamous events of the year 1483 and I shall tell the facts as I know them to be, for there is much to tell and to describe it without passion or prejudice becomes more difficult as it unfurls."

Chapter 18

17th April 1483 - A Fork In The Road

The warmth of the April sun that streamed into Richard's study warmed his back, causing him to shudder with a long, satisfied shiver. He sat up from his desk and gazed absent-mindedly from the window before him, which offered a view over unfurling fields and hilltops, the faces of which shone bright green in the early sun beyond the long shadow of the castle wall and tower that had already begun to creep back toward him since he had taken his seat an hour earlier.

Although he had started writing almost an hour ago, the letter before him bore the greeting 'My Dearest Edward', but nothing more, for he was struggling to find the words with which to fill his latest letter. Little of consequence had happened in the past few weeks. Little, at least, to rival the events of the past twelve months. The small shadow of a cloud drifted across a hilltop before him as his mind wandered back.

There had been almost continual and open war with Scotland from 1480, when both Richard and his counterpart the Duke of Albany, had become unable to stand the forced, uncomfortable peace any longer. Edward had left the matter almost completely to Richard and at the head of a motivated, loyal army, Richard had prevented any Scottish incursion into England and had led several very profitable and well celebrated raids into Scotland. Last year, in the summer of 1482, Richard had left the siege of Berwick with a portion of his force, deciding to end the matter conclusively. Within a month, he and his army stood in Edinburgh castle unopposed and before a desperate Duke of Albany suing frantically for peace. He smiled as he recalled drawing a lung full of cool air and savouring the experience. His men had hailed him in the streets of Edinburgh for days, not only for the historic victory against the bane of all of northern England, but also because not a single English soldier had been killed during the journey from Berwick to the taking of Edinburgh. Unheard of in such a campaign, his men had announced Richard's military skill as a legend of the future, predicting that he would one day rival the achievements of Alexander the Great himself. Although abashed, Richard had relished the praise, though he suspected that much of it had been propagated by Lovell and Richard Ratcliffe, who had both accompanied him on the campaign.

The English force had left Edinburgh after the agreement of terms and Richard had returned to the siege at Berwick, the city falling not long after. The victory was completed by the retaking of that symbolic fortress that had been surrendered to the Scots by the Lancastrians and had provided a platform for almost all of their attacks across the border since. These events had seen Richard's reputation across the country solidified and had endeared him even more greatly to those northern towns and cities terrorised by Scottish raids. The celebrations in York upon his return had lasted for several days.

Shortly after, he had visited London and had been received there almost as rapturously as he had in York, with the king at the head of the welcome. The feast that evening had been epic in its proportion, even by the standards attested to by Edward's still increasing girth. Richard had eaten, and taken his fair share of drink, but found himself uncomfortable in the decedent, hedonistic court that now revelled endlessly around Edward. Although concerned that the worst influences of the Woodville dominated court were taking a serious toll on his brother, Richard had long since ceased giving voice to this concern since it always led to deriding fury from the king. Edward, he had concluded, could look after himself.

Richard had noted, though, that more than ever before, Elizabeth seemed to stalk her husband's footsteps. One was never seen without the other. Was it, Richard had wondered, a symptom of jealousy? After all, it was no secret at court that Edward kept for himself a string of mistresses. No. This had always been common knowledge and never seemed to have been a cause for concern to Elizabeth before. Rather, Richard believed, she was using Edward's growing frailties to increase her own influence over him. Although he had never had a direct confrontation with the queen, he had always felt uneasy around her, as though there was always something that she kept hidden from him. Or perhaps he was merely suspicious. The only pleasant distraction had been a light hearted argument with Earl Rivers. The queen's brother, whom Edward had placed in charge of the Prince of Wales' household at Ludlow castle, was the only member of the Woodville family that Richard genuinely liked and, indeed, respected. It was often noted how similar they were in academic and theological fields and in their religious fervour and piety. Richard had, somewhat grudgingly, congratulated Rivers on the publication of his translation from the French of Sayings of the Philosophers, which William Caxton had made one of his first printed books. Secretly, Richard had hoped to achieve the same and to be amongst the first to benefit from the revolution that Caxton was offering. Rivers had graciously accepted the acknowledgement and then teased Richard.

"They say," Rivers had told him with a mischievous smile lighting his face, "that you and I are so alike that you are called 'the Rivers of the north', throughout the south." This had been greeted with general laughter and cooing which had subsided quickly as all around awaited a response. Richard had to suppress a smile of his own.

"That is strange indeed," Richard had replied slowly, an exaggerated frown crumpling his brow as he tried not to grin, "for I hear talk in the north that Earl Rivers could almost be the Gloucester of the south." There were sharp intakes of breath from all sides. "If only," Richard continued, calling above the murmurs, "he had possessed a northern set of balls to swing on the battlefield." The room erupted with raucous laughter, interspersed with voices from farther away trying to discover the cause of the commotion. Even Rivers had burst into laughter at the attack upon his military prowess, since it did clearly separate the two men. The two had traded put downs for almost an hour, drinking to each one until both were left helpless by a combination of laughter and unsteady legs. It had been the one moment in which Richard had relaxed and enjoyed himself.

Richard leaned forward over his desk, gazing out of the window as the shadows crept ever closer to him. His eyes watered as he tried to make out the farthest point on the horizon upon which he could focus as his mind continued to wander through the past months.

Earlier this year, in February, Richard had received word from his brother that a county palatine was to be created for him covering Cumberland and south west Scotland, and that he was to be made hereditary warden of the west Marches. Richard had written back to Edward excitedly thanking him for his generosity and enthusiastically declaring his intention to permanently conquer that region of Scotland in Edward's name and to his glory. Since that day, Richard's head had been filled with little else than his plans, which he had run through time and again with Anne until he was sure that she must have been tired of hearing them. The making of an hereditary sub kingdom covering a swathe of the country from the midlands, through the north and into Scotland, which he would rule in Edward's name, was recognition and reward indeed. More than this, though, it created something that he could pass to his beloved son, and in doing so could secure the position of his descendants at the very heart of power for all of time. Richard smiled as he recalled the end of one such conversation with Anne.

"The real heart of the matter," Richard had explained pensively after reciting his ideas once again, "is that this is the greatest opportunity we shall have to create this inheritance.

As the king's brother I am in a position to establish that which we want for our son. You see," Richard continued fervently as if trying to convince Anne, "when Edward is gone, and we are gone, our son shall be cousin to the new king and distanced from power, for there shall be a new brother of the new king at his right hand. So, the family shall diverge and with each generation the bond to the throne is diluted. Just as our cousins hold little influence, so shall our children and our children's children, so this, right here and right now, is our chance to build a security that our family will otherwise not enjoy."

"You are right." Anne had replied simply, smiling softly.

"I am concerned," Richard had continued chewing his bottom lip nervously, "that it may seem vanity or a challenge to my king." Richard looked down as if in shame. "It is not as though Edward will not be wary, given the betrayals he has suffered, not least at George's hands." He glanced up at Anne, trying to discern her reaction.

"You think too much." Anne rebuked him. "If you have not yet earned Edward's trust, then you never shall and should cease trying. It is he who is offering you this honour in sure recognition of all that you have done for him." Anne smiled. "It would be rude to refuse such an offer."

"Now," Richard conceded, "it is you who are right. I fear what others may think too much at times. Perhaps we do deserve this."

"Not perhaps." Anne had told him forcefully in conclusion as the young Edward had bounded into his father's arms pleading that they should go riding before dark. At ten years of age he was growing fast and Richard hoped that, having resisted the tradition of sending young boys into the household of other nobles for their tuition, he remained contented in the safety Richard provided for him that had been so absent from his own childhood. Now, the final piece of his son's security was about to fall into place.

Richard was shaken from his thoughts by a loud rapping at the door that echoed around the stone walls with urgency. He looked at the letter before him, which still contained the line of greeting. It was simply not taking form this morning. Only a few moments after the first a second, louder, longer and more urgent knocking snapped Richard out of his thoughts altogether.

"Enter," he called, a little irritated by the impatience of whoever stood on the other side of the door. The door was flung open by a red faced, panting figure. Richard opened his mouth to chastise the over-eager intruder when he saw the consternation plain on the young man's face, his road worn clothes dusty, his legs caked in crusting mud and a large envelope wavering in his trembling right hand. Instantly, his irritation evaporated, replaced with a quivering in his stomach that he had felt before. Something was wrong. War perhaps?

"What is it?" Richard asked, springing to his feet and striding to the man, his hand outstretched for the letter, his eyes fixed upon it.

"My lord," the man panted, a broad London accent clear through his heavy breath, "I have been sent from London to deliver this message from my master." The man nervously thrust the envelope toward Richard's reaching fingers.

"And who is your master?" Richard demanded, snatching the letter urgently and beginning to open the unfamiliar seal.

"Lord Hastings, sir." The man spluttered, still fighting to regain his breath. Richard paused a moment, obviously taken aback by the name, then returned to noisily removing the letter from its envelope, a deep frown folding into his brow. He unfurled the letter, read it quickly, re-read it, then shot a glance at the man in the doorway. The lowering of his head told Richard that he knew at least the content of the beginnings of the letter.

"Anne!" Richard bellowed in a deep voice that reverberated through the west wing of Middleham Castle.

"Er," he returned to the messenger, clearly distracted, "to the kitchens. You will be fed and given clean clothes."

"Thank you, my lord." The man blurted, only too happy to be given leave to remove himself.

"Anne!" Richard called again, louder, pacing the room in a large circle. Finally he heard footsteps approaching along the hall at a jogging pace. He stood still, fixed on the doorway some ten paces in front of him. He fought the swimming sensation of numbness that was seeping into his mind. A nervous trembling that he had not felt in years gripped his legs. Anne arrived in the room in a flurry of crimson skirts.

"What is it?" she asked with obvious concern at the sight that greeted her.

"It..." Richard stalled. He swallowed hard and looked fleetingly at the paper that hung in his fingers. Anne stepped toward him. Richard stood still, almost looking through her. The letter in his hand fell slowly to the floor and when Anne looked back up from where it came to rest, she saw a glinting bead rolling down her husband's left cheek.

"The king," he spoke slowly. "Edward is dead." He tried furiously to mask the crackling emotion in his voice.

"Oh, Richard." Anne took the final few steps towards him and threw her arms around his shoulders, pulling his head onto hers. She felt him shaking as they stood in silence for what felt like an age. Eventually, Richard inhaled deeply and drew himself up. His eyes were reddened and his cheeks damp, but he made no effort to dry them.

"Are you alright?" Anne asked, unsure what else to say.

"We shall be." Richard smiled softly, ignoring the personal question to reassure his wife. He placed his hands on her upper arms. "We have a new King Edward to serve, my darling, and the opportunity to help to mould that new king."

"Richard," Anne said cautiously, "you should not bury your feelings. You love your brother."

"There are more pressing matters to attend to than my own grief." He bent down to the letter that had slipped from his hand.

"More pressing?" Anne repeated, confused.

"This letter," Richard explained as he rose again, "is come from Lord Hastings. Aside," he paused, as if his next words had suddenly deserted him. "Aside from the news of the king's death, this letter tells a concerning tale."

"What is happening?" Anne asked, almost demanding to know. Her concern for Richard grew. If there was news more than the death of his brother, this would be a test indeed of the strength she had always seen in him.

"Hastings writes," Richard began, turning away and moving to his desk, where he laid the letter carefully, his fingers lingering on the uppermost portion of the writing, "that on his deathbed, Edward made and signed a new will that..." Richard turned from the desk and fixed Anne with a firm stare, his eyes locked in hers. "It named me as Protector of the Realm during his son's minority rather than the queen."

Anne was stunned. Her jaw swung open at Richard's revelation. She tried to decide whether she believed this to be a good thing for them or a curse with the potential to ruin their lives. There was no question that Richard would make a truly great Protector, bringing firm leadership, equitable justice and delivering a well prepared monarch to a nation that would thank him for all of time. In fact, Richard's own father had been nominated Protector during the sickness of Henry VI and had been generally acclaimed as a good leader, eventually being asked to act as Henry's heir. Yet, as her mind leaped about she could not escape the knowledge that the last Protector of a monarch during his minority had met an untimely and suspicious end shortly after the end of his Protectorate.

"How do you feel about this?" Anne asked hesitantly, trying to read her husband's expression.

"Uncertain." Richard confessed, tilting his head. "Though you know that my sense of duty leads me and that I shall do what is required of me irrespective of my feelings." This was unequivocally true to Richard. He was proud that his motto, his life and his faith bore witness to this. "It will," he continued frankly, "mean leaving behind all that we have built, and planned, here. It will mean returning to London, to that puss filled whirlpool of immorality that passes for a court. That will have to change for a start." Richard smiled. "Oh, Anne, the challenge though." He seemed lifted from the man that had greeted Anne on her arrival, as though he had forgotten the cause of the challenge.

"What of the county palatine?" Anne asked suddenly reminded of all Richard's hopes that hung from it.

"Indeed," Richard's face darkened, "we have so far not talked of the real issue. My brother," Richard spoke through a tensed jaw and was pointing at the floor between himself and his wife, "the king of England, died six full days ago and not only has news of it just now reached my ear, but I must learn of it from Lord Hastings, not from the queen, not from my family. Furthermore," he continued with growing venom, as if suddenly realising just how angry he really was, "Hastings advises me to make all haste to collect the new king and to reach London, since, he informs me, the queen has seized the Great Seal, begins to issue decrees and openly plans, not only to ignore my brother's final wishes, but to completely exclude me from court, power and any access to her son." Richard's chest was heaving and his flushed cheeks were puffing as he blew out a frustrated breath.

Anne's heart skipped. This news seemed to get worse by the moment. If the queen and her family were allowed to pursue this course it would inevitably lead to the devastation of all of their plans. Elizabeth would not be likely to want a remnant of Plantagenet authority controlling so large a part of the country, and such wealthy lands, when there were so many members of her own family shouldering their way to power who would want what Richard had built. Their only hope would be that no other had contained and controlled that region as Richard had and this fact could make him indispensible to the new regime, at least until they felt secure enough to challenge him. It was something that Richard had discussed with Anne, Ratcliffe, Catesby and Lovell previously, though he could not have dreamed that the moment would prove so close at hand. Catesby had contested that Richard's success would only cause the greed-blinded Woodvilles to think it easy. Richard had joked that the 'Gloucester of the South' may then fancy himself as the 'Gloucester of all England', but Anne could see through the facade that he showed his friends. The thing that Richard feared most in the world was a fall from power that would jeopardise the security he had worked so hard to build for their son. Now, such a threat presented itself plainly. It seemed direct confrontation with the queen was coming sooner or later. Anne had no doubt which Richard would opt for.

"What will we do, Richard?" Anne asked nervously.

"I know not, yet." Richard confessed, turning toward his desk. His mind was a swirling blur of grief mingling with burning anger and more than a hint of cold, piercing fear. He planted his hands on either side of the letter that rested before him, as if searching it for some instruction that he knew was not there. He closed his eyes and began to pray silently for guidance. He allowed the words he thought to soothe his soul and warm calmness began to seep back to him. It was all too easy to forget at such times the power of a prayer. He felt assured that the Lord would see him through the storm as long as his course remained true.

"Richard, are you alright?" Anne asked, realising that amongst all else, her husband had just learned of the death of his beloved brother, to whose service he had devoted his life.

"I shall be," he replied, returning from his thoughts. He looked out of the window at the shadows that seemed now to stand still. "We shall be," he stated solidly, turning to face

Anne. He smiled and moved to her, taking her in a reassuring embrace. After a moment, he leaned back and placed his fingers under her chin, raising her eyes to meet his. "Forgive me, Anne," he said softly. "Are you well?"

"Of course." Anne lied. "I am just worried for you."

"Do not be." Richard gazed into her eyes. "I am not about to surrender my reason, nor all that we have worked for, to the Woodvilles now." He smiled a shallow smile that radiated determination. "Would you please send for Lovell and Catesby? We shall resolve our next move in the Great Hall in one hour." After a moment, Anne nodded and left to make the arrangements.

Chapter 19

20th April 1483 - The Third Letter

The trio of figures, lost at the immense table of the Great Hall, turned in unison as the Duke of Gloucester entered. Anne smiled at the sight of her husband restored from the man that she had left alone in his study an hour earlier. His stride was wide, his chest broad and he held under his arm a stack of papers. He clearly had business that he intended to resolve. Lovell and Catesby rose to greet him.

"My lord." William Catesby murmured solemnly.

"Richard." Lovell lowered his head slowly. "You have our deepest sympathy."

"I thank you both." Richard spoke in a buoyant tone that took the two men aback, though only broadened Anne's smile. "Though I have less need of your sympathy now than of your support." He reached the head of the table and slammed down his paperwork. He drew back the chair and paused, staring at the pair.

"You have it, Richard." Catesby lurched, suddenly realising what was awaited.

"Unquestioningly." Lovell qualified.

"You may yet live to regret such enthusiasm." Richard sat as he spoke, smiling at them as he rearranged the papers into three distinct piles. Lovell and Catesby exchanged uncertain glances.

"You appear to have made some decisions, Richard." Anne nodded to the three stacks.

"Subject to your approval," Richard said to all three, "I have prepared a reply to Hastings." Richard placed a hand on the left most papers. "It informs him of our deep regret at all of his news, though thanks him for his loyalty to my brother evident in its sending. It advices him that I shall make all haste to attend the new king." Richard looked intently across the three faces before him, his eyes burning. "I have instructed that he keep the closest possible watch upon the queen and her family for fear of some devised treachery that I hope I only imagine." The duke paused long enough to allow the triumvirate to ponderously motion their approval.

"The second?" Anne enquired when Richard did not begin to speak again. She knew all too well that he must not be allowed to dwell on his loss and sink deeper into a well of drowning self pity. Her husband was at his best when clear and decisive, and more than any other in their life together so far, this moment required such strength of him.

"The second," Richard smiled up at her again, his palm moving lightly to the centre stack of paper, "will be despatched immediately to Earl Rivers at Ludlow. As master of the Prince of Wales' household, he will doubtless have begun arrangements to move to London." Richard's eyes passed to the two men. "I have suggested that we meet at Northampton en route so that we may arrive in London together."

"You do not trust Rivers with the king." Lovell's tone was more stating the matter than questioning it.

"I cannot afford to trust any man in whom I have the slightest reason for doubt, but I shall offer Earl Rivers the opportunity to do his duty." Richard fixed Lovell with a hard stare. "In a time such as this, reputation means nothing and trust is for the earning, not the taking."

"Good answer." Lovell smiled cheekily against the duke's gaze, forcing the other to smile in return.

"Whilst it is proper that the Protector should accompany the king in any case," Richard's eyes softened as he spoke, "I think it will be better that he is wrest from Woodville control sooner rather than later, and certainly before he reaches his mother in London." Again, there were nods of agreement from the others.

"What of the third despatch?" Catesby interjected, frowning a little. The two parts had been obvious requirements to all around the table, but none could guess with any certainty at a third. As all eyes returned to Richard, he chewed gently on the left side of his bottom lip, making him appear a little nervous.

"My final letter." He drew his hand from the centre stack, hovered a moment over the final set of papers as if fearful that they may burn his palm, and then pulled his hand back to grasp the other at the edge of the table. "On this matter," he began hesitantly, "I must keep my own council alone."

"Richard?" Anne questioned instantly, disliking such sudden secrecy in her husband, for they always shared all such matters and it was rare too that Lovell and Catesby be omitted from his thoughts.

"I understand your concern," Richard raised his hands, "but I am less than certain of this matter and my own indecision unnerves me and councils me against this course, yet necessity seeks to bind me to it."

"Can we not discuss the matter?" Lovell queried uneasily. "Perhaps we can aid you in settling your mind with more surety." Lovell and Catesby, along with the currently absent Ratcliffe, had always enjoyed a privileged position alongside Anne in helping Richard to decide upon policy and direction in ruling the north. He always heard their opinions and often changed his own in the searching light of fresh eyes upon a subject. Keeping something from them did not sit well with any of the three gathered.

"I fear not." Richard replied sombrely. "I will ask you to respect my decision. Such is my uncertainty that I am not even able to settle upon what each of you may think of it. I am resolved to send the letter but fear that any one of you, no mind all three, would be able to talk me out of doing so. I shall accept the consequences if I act errantly, but would have those consequences on my head alone. Whether the mistake would lie in the sending or in the failure to send shall only become clear as we step on through these misty times, but if an error is made, it will be mine alone and attributable to no other." He looked directly into Anne's bright eyes as he spoke to all of them. "I ask that you accept my explanation and that I act only to protect you from what may happen." There was a heavy silence. Catesby shifted in his chair. Lovell tapped his fingertips together in front of his mouth before drawing in his breath sharply.

"We shall," Anne interrupted, sensing some new protest from the men, "of course, respect your decision." Lovell still made to object, so Anne snapped quickly to close the matter. "We all know that your decision will have been reached in good faith and we trust in that." Lovell exhaled and his gaze drifted distantly to the far end of the hall, admitting defeat.

"Thank you, my lady." Richard nodded, recognising the shield that his wife had provided for him. "If only the world were ruled by women," Richard smiled, "we should surely avoid so much unnecessary conflict."

"The world is ruled by women, Richard." Lovell winked at the duke. "Their true skill is in not letting us know." The three men chuckled.

"All men may know it," Anne replied, her tone remaining even, "as soon as they are mature enough to learn it." She turned to look Lovell squarely in the face. "You can hardly hold us responsible if no man ever attains such maturity." Instantly, Richard roared with laughter and Catesby smirked, unsure whether to be offended by Anne's comments. Lovell flushed with embarrassment but conceded with a deferent smile before joining in the laughter.

After a moment, Richard rose and gathered the three sets of letters from the table. The others respectfully stood for his departure. As he turned, he stopped a moment, his face suddenly darkened again by a remembered sorrow.

"I have also sent word that all of the lords, gentry and aldermen of this region should gather at York Minster in six days time. Before leaving, we shall hold mass for the soul of our lost king, and all shall swear loyalty to our new King Edward."

"Very well, my lord." Catesby called after Richard as he left. "We shall all be ready." Richard felt the emotion welling within his throat, drying it so that his voice would crack, and so he did not respond. The three left at the table eyed each other silently.

As he left the room, Richard was met by three men, all dressed for the road in worn riding clothes. He handed the first package, for Lord Hastings, to the man on his left, who nodded and turned, leaving in the direction of the stables. The second messenger, the next man in line, soon followed with the envelope meant for Rivers. As the third man held out his hand to receive his package, Richard moved to pass it over, then hesitated. Still he fought his own uncertainty. Even now, he could find no clear guidance in his thoughts, his soul nor his prayers. He closed his eyes, hoping for a moment of calm clarity, but it would not come, perhaps because he tried so hard to find it. The third man shifted his weight uncomfortably. Richard re-opened his eyes and smiled gently to mask the conflict that raged inside him. He was, however, still resolved.

"John," he said softly, "you are aware of what is required of you in this task?" Richard knew that there was no real need to check. The lithe man before him was both older, by some five years, and taller by a few inches than Richard. John Fletcher was also no mere messenger, but a squire in Richard's household who had served him since he first arrived at Middleham nearly ten years before. An accomplished swordsman, John was a favourite sparring partner of Richard's and seemed to always be more aware than most outside the upper classes of the more subtle areas of northern politics. This was something that Richard made frequent use of, with John always more than happy to add to Richard's understanding of the issues affecting the common man and how the duke's policies impacted them. Richard had built a trust in this man forged in the heat of the battlefield and tempered by cool reflection. There was no other man in whom he would place his trust to complete this commission.

"I shall deliver it in person and bring you news upon the road as early as possible." The accent was broad but the tone was soft as the man delivered a much abridged version of his orders. His hand was still outstretched.

"Of course." Richard smiled. "I should not have questioned it." He hesitated a moment longer, an uncertain smile on his lips, before laying the papers into John's hand. The other grasped them and spun on his heels, almost running along the hallway as though each second now bore the utmost importance. Richard twisted the wedding band on his left hand as he nervously wondered if he was doing the right thing.

He started as he realised that Anne had appeared from the Hall at his right arm. She slipped her left hand through the crook of his arm.

"What will happen to us?" Richard asked quietly without looking at his wife.

"Whatever it is," Anne replied squeezing his arm, "we shall face it together." She looked at the side of his face as he gazed distantly along the corridor. "You are unsure who to trust?"

"Of course I am!" Richard exclaimed, suddenly focussing on his wife. "I trust you, Lovell, Catesby, Ratcliffe and maybe John," he nodded to where the squire had just left his sight, "but no others. Even Hastings will have his own agenda driving his actions, for he has much to fear from a Woodville government no longer tempered by Edward." He paused for a moment, looking deeply into Anne's eyes, where he could see no hint of fear or doubt.

"In the coming weeks," he continued, pushing her hair from her cheek, "more than ever before, there will be no dark and light, no right and wrong, no good and evil. We must deal in shades of each, for the path shall wind through both sides and shall not be easy, but we must march that path to its righteous destination." The two stood before each other in silence as the candles along the hallway flickered. As they embraced, their shadows swayed gently together on the wall.

Chapter 20

21st April 1483 - Oaths Made

As Richard stepped solemnly along the central aisle of York Minster, he looked around at the hundreds of mourners, all dressed in black cloth, silk and fur, broken only by a variety of gold chains that glinted in the flames of the thousand candles placed on high staves that lined the walls and each side of the walkway. The minster was silent apart from the soft, slow footfalls of the procession that followed the Duke of Gloucester. He saw many familiar faces which solemnly nodded their deferent condolences to the deceased king's brother. None were conspicuous by their absence from the ceremony and that quietly pleased Richard. It had taken several days to prepare and move to York and Richard was conscious that time was a luxury that he could not afford to squander at the moment. Rivers and the young king would leave Ludlow soon and it was only eight days until Richard had asked to meet them at Northampton. The longer he delayed his arrival in London the worse the situation was bound to grow as opposing factions positioned themselves in the absence of either the new king or his Protector.

Shooting a glance over his shoulder, Richard smiled as he saw Anne holding their son's hand. Edward grinned back nervously, his ten year old face betraying how uncomfortable he felt dressed up tight in jet black breeches and doublet, a black fur cloak flowing down his back. He filled Richard with pride at his studies and had begun martial training, but the sight of his boy braving so public an engagement in spite of obvious unease impressed the duke still more, whilst making him wish he could whisk him out of the situation to safety. As they reached the front of the pews before the altar, Richard crossed himself and sat on the front pew in the centre. The procession behind him did as he had and filed into the rows of ornate oak benches. Anne sat beside Richard with their son on her other side.

Once all were seated, the Archbishop of York took the pulpit and began the mass. The service was long, sombre and full of prayers for the old king and blessings for his heir. To his own disgust, Richard found his mind wandering through long, mostly happy, memories of times spent with his brother. He had become so wrapped in those warm thoughts that he almost missed the Archbishop calling for the eulogy that Richard had asked to make following the mass. Just as the Archbishop frowned, Richard stood sharply and marched to the pulpit. His memories had stirred a pang of longing for those lost days that forced its way into his throat and threatened to choke his voice with grief. As he stood facing the congregation, he drew a long breath to swallow the knot down and began to speak in a deep, commanding tone.

"I spent a long time searching for the words with which to tell you all today of the respect in which I held my brother, our king. Finally," he continued, his voice filling the minster, "as I sat in my saddle atop a hill outside Middleham before leaving for this great city, I ran my eye across that horizon that I know so well and the words came to me." He paused a long moment as he scanned the audience. All were dutifully hanging upon his words. "There are those for all of us who are our guides in this foreign place that is life as we climb its unknown mountain. As we find our way, others may pass us by, stopping to point out something of interest that can be seen, some landmark, hidden coppice or the beautiful sunset. Such people may linger a while to share the view before they move on along their own path. Such experiences are exciting, if fleeting. It is our guides who wait by as we enjoy those moments and are ready to continue the ascent with us. It is they who lead us along the sure path, who spur us onward when the road is rocky and we may wish to take an easier path. When we need it, they will pull us up the steepest steps.

Often, we will resent their pushing and pulling, else we take their guidance for granted. It is only when their firm hand is lifted, is gone," he paused as he feared that his voice would falter. "It is only then that we are able to appreciate all that they have done for us. Only then can we see clearly how far we have climbed with their help. Those passers-by who we so enjoyed were gone when the way grew hard. Our guides enjoyed the good times with us, but endured the difficult also, often in spite of our abuse of them. They are the people without whom we could not have travelled so far nor reached so high. They make us the people we are without our even knowing it." Now his voice began to crack. He paused once more to compose himself and wrung his hands below the pulpit.

"I am privileged to have been able to call King Edward IV of England such a guiding influence in my life. He has shaped the man you see before you, though I often did not see it. Now," he drew himself up as if to steady his voice by firming his stature, "a new era is beginning and our new king, King Edward V, is now in need of a guide of his own. I," he thumped his clenched fist to his chest, "shall be proud to return the kindness that his father showed to me to see him safely though any danger and darkness that he may encounter. As Protector, I shall provide firm leadership that will shape a great, mighty and wise king for this, God's England. I stand before you today to pay my respects to the achievements of an old king, and to a new one full of exciting promise for a bright future. I pledge myself before you all and before God Almighty to the faithful service of King Edward V and ask nothing less from each of you." Slowly, deliberately, he allowed his gaze to fall over each face in the congregation before he called in a voice that reverberated around the great church. "God, and King Edward!" Instantly the ringing call was echoed by everyone within the minster as one. Richard stepped down from the pulpit, pleased with his speech and the response of those gathered. As he retook his seat, Anne smiled and gently squeezed his hand. He could not hide from her how upset he really was.

When the service had concluded, Richard led the procession from the minster and stood on the steps, blinking in the bright sunlight and gathering his thoughts. Slowly, almost uncertainly, the familiar figure of the mayor of York rounded his right shoulder and offered a bow of greeting. He was an elderly, rotund man with a narrow band of hair that was now silver with darker specks where it had once been the other way around. The mayor had provided staunch support for Richard's plans and reforms over the years, but was something of a sycophant, a trait that Richard did not value in those around him.

"My lord," the mayor simpered in an oily tone, "may I offer my personal condolences and those of this great city," he smiled, his lips thinning. "York grieves for the loss of our king and for your lordship's sadness." He bowed again extravagantly.

"My thanks." Richard replied, straining to be civil and to force back an inappropriate smile at the man's obsequiousness. "York's support for the new king is greatly appreciated."

"York is loyal, my lord." The mayor's eyes narrowed. "York is loyal to you." He paused to allow the comment to settle. Looking around nervously, he hushed his tone as he continued. "York is loyal to the king because it is loyal to you and will support you throughout what is to come." The man straightened but his face betrayed unease as he awaited a reaction. Richard frowned, working his way quickly through the man's words to seek out the root of his meaning, for he felt a little concern at the sentiment. The old mayor was a wily politician and perhaps saw something that Richard did not.

"I am grateful." Richard replied, unwilling to embroil himself deeper in the conversation now. "We are to depart to meet the king at Northampton in but one hour, and so I must take my leave." The mayor bowed again and stepped aside, allowing Richard, Anne and young Edward to descend the steps. As they started up the street to the waiting carriage Richard looked over his shoulder, still a little perplexed, to see the mayor now surrounded by knot of aldermen shrugging his shoulders and shaking his head.

Chapter 21

29th April 1483 – The Missing King

Eight days after leaving York, Richard sat at a large table in the inn set aside for the meeting that had been arranged for today. After settling in, the duke had taken his place early to allow himself time to reflect on the events of the past two weeks. His world had altered so radically and so quickly. He had begun to try to clarify in his own mind what it was that he thought his brother had done well as king so that he may emulate it in his guidance of the new king, and also what he believed his brother had got wrong, the mistakes that he had made, in order to not only warn Edward's son from similar mistakes, but also to help measure his own role as Protector. The conclusion that he and Anne had reached was that Edward's prime fault was in delaying his actions until it was too late for them to have any benefit. Richard had, in turn, resolved that whatever turmoil they walked into on their arrival in London, he would act swiftly and decisively and deal with any consequences as they arose. He had decided that it would be better to suffer for the making of a wrong decision than for a failure to act. Besides, such an approach may take the stagnant court enough by surprise to offer him some at least temporary advantage. Inaction had cost his brother dearly on many occasions, not least losing him the crown for a time, and Richard would not jeopardise the new king's position whilst he was Protector.

A message had reached him on the road yesterday informing him that Rivers and Edward had left Ludlow on 24th and would be in Northampton on 29th. Rivers had sent word that the new king was well, if understandably melancholic, and was looking forward to seeing his uncle and making the rest of his journey in his company. Richard felt sure that Rivers flattered him for some reason or other, but a part of him longed for it to be true, that he would be some comfort to his nephew in his time of need. First, though, he would need to get to know the young king, for they had seen little of each other in the years since Edward's infancy and Richard feared that it would be an uncomfortable meeting of strangers. He was also unsure of the extent of the influence that the Woodvilles would undoubtedly have already begun to exert over the boy. Given Hastings' warning, this had caused Richard growing concern over the past few days.

Two days earlier, John had also caught up with them and Richard had been keen to hear his news. The two had ridden behind the rest for a while so that the duke could glean all that he was able from the squire's report. The letter had been delivered and, according to John, its recipient had read it slowly, glanced sharply at John and re-read the letter even more slowly. He had then leapt from his seat and shouted for half a dozen different people to whom he had begun excitedly yelping instructions to make preparations to leave. When John, forgotten in the melee, had asked for a response to take back to his master, he had been feverishly told that the meeting in Northampton was acceptable, there had been some almost unintelligible babbling about what an honour it was to be asked and that it was about time, which Richard had forced John to recite verbatim with a full description of tone, manner and facial expressions. Once satisfied, Richard had thanked John and the two had passed the time discussing their respective journeys thus far before Richard had ridden back ahead to rejoin his family's carriage. He enjoyed John's company and his news had been welcome, though Richard still remained uncertain whether the whole idea was a good one or not. Either way, it seemed that there was to be a trio meeting at Northampton this day.

A pitcher of wine and a goblet were clanked noisily onto the table before Richard by a young barmaid whose round face flushed behind long dark locks that poured from her head over her shoulders as she offered the duke an embarrassed but respectful courtesy before shuffling hurriedly from the room. Richard tapped the table absently. There was no sign yet of either other party and Richard had sent men around the town to establish where Rivers and Edward were lodged. He grew impatient, unwilling to be left to his own thoughts again. Eyeing the pitcher for a long moment, he surrendered and poured the goblet half full, immediately draining it again.

Looking into the few droplets that gathered together in its centre as he straightened the goblet, he considered refilling it. A sensation of calm relaxation began to meander through his arms and legs. Perhaps more wine, enough to carry him beyond drunkenness, would numb the ever present pang of grief and put an end to his continuous over-thinking of what was yet to happen. Against this he weighed the thought of meeting his nephew, the new king, to whom he would be Protector, incapable of standing steady and speaking lucidly. That notion led him to consider his brother and the lifestyle into which he had descended. Richard despised the reported debauchery of Edward's court and had begun to blame it for his untimely death. At that thought, his mind was set and he slammed the goblet onto the table. Still gripping it tightly, he watched the pitcher rock as it threatened to tip over. His concentration was abruptly shattered as the door crashed open. How rude of the maid to burst in. Richard shot a scowl at the door, only for it to melt away at the plump, red cheeks that framed a broad smile. The figure, no taller than Richard but carrying significantly more weight, filled the doorway with arms spread wide.

"Started without me cousin?" the squeaky voice trilled. The man almost skipped across the room, arms still flung apart and Richard could not help himself, breaking into a deep laugh at the site that soaked away his tension in a moment.

"Henry." Richard sounded relieved to see him and rounded the table to meet the other's embrace. They clapped each other solidly on the back before Richard pushed Henry lightly from him and looked into his bright, hazel eyes. His round face was set in a mound of short, tufted brown hair and he wore the kind of clothes that would not have been out of place at a formal occasion of state. He was enrobed in velvet, fur and gold that must have doubled his apparent size. But all of this was nothing new, nor remarkable, to Richard. He searched Henry's eyes, looking for something else. For either some vindication or some warning. He saw only glee, but knew that Henry was shrewd enough not to betray anything. He would have to wait to be sure that his third letter had been well placed.

"Well, Richard," Henry began, pulling up a chair and filling Richard's goblet from the pitcher of wine, "I am sorry that it takes such times as these to bring us together. It has been a long time since Picquigny." He grinned broadly, then emptied the goblet even more swiftly than Richard had and the smile returned to his face. "Yet together we are." He paused. "And perhaps at the beginning of something incredible." Henry's brow rose as he spoke.

"Do not get carried away, cousin." Gloucester warned. "I have much to do." Seeing his chance for a first test, Richard fixed his eyes on the other man's, searching for a clue. "You do know the reason that I have sought your assistance?"

"Of course." Suddenly Henry was uncharacteristically serious. "I understand fully your need for one such as me." He leaned forward, his elbow propped up by the table. "Someone like me will prove very useful to you, I know."

"Oh yes?" Richard enquired uncertainly.

"Yes." Henry confirmed. "You need someone good looking, charismatic, intelligent and politically aware in order to compensate for yourself." There was a long silence during which the two men stared intensely at each other. Suddenly, Richard erupted, bursting into the kind of hearty laugh that he had not felt roll though his body for weeks. Almost immediately, Henry followed suit and the two filled the room with bellowing laughter.

"You do not change, Henry." Richard finally said through tears of laughter. He had found an emotional release in their joke that wanted to overtake him and he dared to begin to believe that he had made the right decision.

"I never shall, either!" Henry's shrill voice rang around the room. "But to a little business. Where is this new king of ours?"

"A fair question, one upon which I have myself been pondering." Richard admitted. "I had understood that they were due to arrive today but have heard no word of them."

"It grows late for an arrival." Henry frowned, a hint of concern in his voice.

"Yes." Richard agreed. "I await the return of my men who are as we speak seeking out word of them." He felt a sudden pang, not liking the appearance that he was not in control of matters. Earl Rivers would require the best of reasons for his failure to make their rendezvous.

"No mind." Henry waved a dismissive hand. "Their tardiness allows us time to exchange news, cousin." Richard smiled, knowing that this would mean that he was about to hear all of Henry's news whilst being afforded no time whatsoever to impart any of his own, though this seemed quite welcome at the moment.

True to form, Henry had barely taken a breath for half an hour. Not only had he given the fullest of details of his journey, but had now begun to recount tales of his tailors and shoemakers. Richard had stopped listening with any conviction after only a few minutes. Henry seemed to pour and drink wine without breaking a sentence, but Richard's attention was being absorbed more and more by the doorway on the far side of the room. His eyes kept flicking to it more frequently and for longer each time as he grew more uneasy at the lack of some news of Rivers and Edward.

"Do my stories bore the mighty Protector?" Henry asked quietly. The sudden silence wrung Richard's attention away from the door, but he had not heard what Henry had said last. He opened his jaw to speak, not sure what to say, but a sudden rapping at the door saved him from embarrassment. Instantly, he called for the visitor to enter.

"My lord," called the man who burst breathlessly through the door, "we could find no sign of the king's party." He seemed almost frantic. "There was word at one inn that they were due to stay there, but only watered their horses before," he stopped and swallowed.

"Before what?" Richard said darkly.

"Before riding on through the town." The man finished, remaining at the far side of the room and looking desperate to leave it. Richard shot a glance at Henry, who looked disturbed at the news.

"Where are they now?" Richard demanded, unable to prevent the annoyed tone that rumbled through the question.

"My lord," the man's tone was one of someone pleading for their life, "no one knows, but," he added sharply, "there is word that Earl Rivers is at the edge of town with a small retinue heading this way." There was silence at this news. The man wanted so desperately to be dismissed.

"Very well." Richard said eventually, lightening his tone. "Send more wine and three goblets." He waved a hand and the messenger stepped back through the door. As he pulled it shut before him, the man puffed out his cheeks and released the breath that he had been holding.

"What is this game that Rivers plays?" Henry asked darkly.

"I do not know," Richard was forced to admit, "but we shall soon uncover it." He smiled thinly from below a frown. "Whatever surprise he intends for me, I have a larger one for him."

"Less of the large, if you please!" Henry grinned, and both laughed again as the maid returned with two fresh pitchers of wine and three clean goblets. Barely a minute after her departure, there was a firm, confident knock at the door and immediately, Earl Rivers opened it and strode into the room. He smiled softly, sheepishly almost, at Richard, but then stopped in his tracks, his face dropping, as the man sitting with his back to the door turned his chair to face the earl, a round face grinning broadly at him. There was a moment of stunned silence as Rivers' eyes shot from one man to the other and back again before he regained his famous composure.

"Good evening, Richard," he offered respectfully. Gloucester stood, smiled and nodded, revelling in the earl's reaction and trying furiously not to show it. Rivers turned to the other man who sat reclined in his chair, clearly waiting and still beaming at him. "Buckingham." Rivers sneered dismissively. Immediately, Henry jumped to his feet.

"My dear Rivers," he shouted, his shrill voice almost causing Richard to erupt with laughter, "is that any way," Henry continued with unconcealed sarcasm, "to greet your beloved brother in law after so long a time?" He threw his arms open and strode across to meet the statuesque figure of Rivers. The Duke of Buckingham wrapped his arms around the taller man's waist, nuzzling his cheek into Rivers' chest like a tired infant seeking comfort in its mother's bosom. Richard's body shook with contained mirth as Rivers' face moved slowly from amazed shock to a disgusted sneer. He uncomfortably wriggled from Buckingham's embrace.

"Of course," the earl said stiffly, straightening his doublet, "it is always a pleasure Henry." Trying to ignore the still grinning Duke of Buckingham, Rivers stepped past him and marched on towards Richard's table. Gloucester could not prevent himself from smiling as he looked beyond Rivers to see Buckingham winking and mimicking the earl's uncomfortably deliberate walk. Gloucester passed the smile off as one meant to greet Rivers.

"Please, be seated Anthony." Richard gestured to the chair that Buckingham had vacated and the earl lowered himself into it. Swiftly, Henry swung another chair from the table to his right and slid it into the side of Rivers' seat, causing him to jolt, and planted himself roughly onto it, leaning in uncomfortably close to the earl.

"Where is the king?" Buckingham asked bluntly, though he still smiled. "Good Gloucester is keen to see his nephew." He stared closely at Rivers' face. The other shuffled uneasily, clearly unnerved by Buckingham's presence and his demeanour.

"I had hoped that we could discuss these matters," Anthony said slowly, fixing his eyes on Richard's, "in a more suitable manner."

"It appears that neither of us is getting that which we had thought to today." Richard's tone was solidly defiant. He had no intention of affording Rivers the comfort of doing this on his own terms. Rivers tilted his head, acknowledging Richard's stance and accepting the situation with all of the grace that he could muster.

"Edward and the remainder of his retinue are lodged at Stony Stratford." Rivers straightened his back. "He also is keen to see you."

"Yet he has been taken some ten miles beyond our appointed meeting place to a Woodville manor." Richard pointed out, sounding genuinely puzzled. "Why would that be, Earl Rivers?" He noted the shifting of Rivers' eyes.

"We arrived in Northampton early today," Rivers explained, "to find little available accommodation. Since your party was yet to reach the town, we feared that there would not be room enough for all of us." He smiled as Richard stared, listening, and he felt Buckingham's eyes burning into him too. "Given our early arrival," he continued, his throat drying, "I felt it best that we move on a little further to find our lodgings and that I then ride back to meet you." All eyes remained upon him and Rivers felt compelled to continue speaking. "Edward is tired from his journey and recent tragic events and had retired before I left."

"Very well." Richard said eventually. "I trust that you will join us for our meal this evening. I shall arrange a room here for you and send my men to arrange an inn for the rest of your party." There was a pause, but Richard had not meant it to be a question. Rivers simply smiled his acceptance despite his original intention to return to Stony Stratford immediately after speaking to Richard.

Over the two hours that followed, the three ate and drank. The conversation grew more and more cordial and light hearted, led in the main by Buckingham's elaborate tales of his dubious adventuring. These, combined with the warm food and heavy wine, seemed to relax the three and the weight of the moment was forgotten for a time.

Finally, it was Rivers who excused himself first, complaining of his achy road-weariness. As he made his polite farewells, Buckingham refilled his own goblet and the two dukes bid the earl a good night's sleep in preparation for the next day's journey. Leaving the room, Rivers stopped a little down the corridor, outside the room appointed as his, and looked back at the closed door of the room that he had just left. He did not like this course that had been imposed upon him. It offended against much that he held dear, yet he had accepted its necessity after much persuading. Shaking his head, he was taken by a further wave of exhaustion and entered his bedroom. He remembered little else of the evening and fell freely into a fitful sleep.

Beyond the door that had momentarily held the earl's attention, the other two men sat staring at the closed door that Rivers had just passed through. It was Buckingham who broke the silence when he was certain that the earl would be far enough away.

"Do you believe him?" Henry asked without taking his eyes from the oak door.

"Of course not." Richard snapped back sharply. He began to stab his fork onto his empty platter with a ringing clank. "The question is," he continued, "why is he lying?" The Duke of Gloucester had been deeply disturbed by the events of this evening. He had fully expected some Woodville resistance upon reaching London but this early play was most unexpected and led him to wonder as to its meaning. He had been sure that Rivers would be honest in this part of proceedings, but he had clearly underestimated the earl's family loyalty. For his part, though, Rivers had underestimated the Protector's commitment to his decision to act decisively.

"Whatever they have in mind," Buckingham seethed, "you may be sure that it will benefit only them." His clenched fist was on the table top and all semblance of joviality had left his face. His cheeks quivered as he clenched his teeth tightly.

"Your hatred of the Woodvilles remains undiminished, I see." Richard said, finding some amusement in the sight.

"Of course it is!" Henry spat, his face flushing. "That witch who your brother called wife had me wed to her twenty four year old sister when I was eleven so that their lowly family might get their grimy hands onto my lands and wealth." The duke's blood was clearly roused.

"Henry, Henry." Richard tried to soothe him. "I know well your hatred for them. It is a part of the reason that I have called upon you now. I shall need a man of your ability who shares a common cause. But listen carefully, Henry." Richard paused to ensure that Buckingham was focusing and listening to him. He held his gaze. "You are not here to exact instantaneous revenge for your own enjoyment. There is a bigger game at hand." The two men stared at each other.

"Can we still..." Buckingham began excitedly.

"No." Richard cut him off.

"Then could we just..."

"No!" Richard shouted, amused.

"Oh. But we can surely still..." Henry's face sank.

"No!" Gloucester suppressed a smile.

"And to think that I had some special boots made in the perfect shape just for the occasion!" His voice was sombre, but he winked at Richard, who shook his head and smiled at his cousin.

"We have plans to make before we retire, Henry, and a long day ahead of us tomorrow."

It was over an hour before they left the room, and another thirty minutes were taken to make the arrangements upon which they had settled.

Chapter 22

30th April 1483 – Stony Stratford

Rivers awoke early the next morning. He had not slept soundly and felt as weary as when he had gone to bed, such had been his concern that he should rise as early as possible. Sliding from the mattress, he sat and stretched his aching back. The room was sparse and lit by the dim dawning of a far off sunrise straining around ill fitting shutters so that it appeared hazy and misty.

Standing, the earl stepped gingerly to the shutters at the window opposite his bed and gently pushed them apart. The gentle creak of the hinges sounded like a deafening crash in the echoing silence because he was so keen not to awaken anyone else before he left. As the shutters parted, only a little more light entered the room, for the street outside was just as gloomy. No one appeared to be roaming around. Moving back to the plain chair beside the bed upon which he had rested his neatly folded clothes last night he began to dress as quickly and quietly as he could. His need to rise early had not been the only reason for his splintered sleep. His conscience had not allowed him the peace he needed for sound sleep.

"Reduced to skulking from an inn in the early hours of the morning," he mumbled grumpily to himself as he hauled on his boots. "I hope that you have this right." He straightened himself and pulled down his jacket. Ruffling his hair in the absence of a brush and mirror, he muttered to the wall. "Sisters."

Taking a deep breath, he strode to the door and placed a hand upon the cold, black iron latch. Biting his lip, he lifted the metal with an unavoidable click. Puffing out his cheeks, he softly exhaled and slowly pulled the door open. As a crack appeared, he paused, but there was no sound beyond. As the corridor was slowly revealed, he could see that it was empty. Carefully stepping out of the room, each floorboard seemed to creak angrily to give him away, but he could make out no other sound. Gripping the handrail, he tried to descend the stairs as lightly as possible but each groan of the wood seemed to shout along the corridor to summon Gloucester. Still, as his foot settled on the flagstone floor of the tavern, there was no sound other than the thudding of his own heart.

His horse was in the stables at the rear of the inn and Rivers knew that his greatest problem now was disturbing the animals there. Creeping in would probably unnerve the horses more than entering openly. He therefore resolved to stride in there and tack his horse as quickly as possible and leave as soon as he was ready. So, reaching the rear door that led to the stables, he calmly opened it and stepped in. There was some scuffling and whinnying but he continued regardless and it quickly subsided.

A few doors down, he spied his mount, its saddle hanging on the rear wall of the stable. Opening the door he patted the horse's neck and whispered a greeting to calm her. Lifting the heavy leather down from its support, he began to saddle the horse quickly. Glancing over his shoulder as a horse neighed, he paused part way through tightening a strap. His heart skipped and he forgot to breathe for a moment, but nothing else stirred. Contented that the horse was simply fidgety, he continued, though his heart pounded now and his fingers seemed to swell so that he could not work so swiftly any more. Finally finished, he grabbed the reins, pushed the stable door open and shot a glance left, toward the inn door. All was still silent. Turning right, toward his exit, the earl's breath was taken by fright as he saw a face almost directly in front of him. Blinking, he focused on the black head of the horse in the stable beside him poking out to investigate the commotion. Shaking his head, Rivers led his own horse along the stables.

The thin crack between the stable's double doors showed that the light of day was swelling. Pausing to press his ear to the strip of light, the earl heard no sound beyond, so lifted the beam that sealed the doors, swinging it high over its rest and pushing the door open with his shoulder. He was forced to raise his arm against the bright, rising ball of the sun.

"Going somewhere, Rivers?" The booming voice shattered the silence and the earl jumped visibly. Looking to his left, he saw Gloucester leaning on the wall beside the door casually, his arms folded. Knowing that he was undone, Rivers smiled a resigned smile and handed the reins to one of the soldiers that immediately rounded the corner of the building noisily.

"Apparently not," he conceded.

"Take him back to his room." Richard nodded to the remainder of the soldiers. "And see to it that he stays there until you hear otherwise from me." Two soldiers moved to flank Rivers, who smiled, defeated, at Richard. "Ensure that he is well provided for." Richard added. "Otherwise, you shall answer to me directly for it." The men nodded to show that they understood. As he turned to walk back through the stable block, Rivers spied the round form of Buckingham standing behind Richard. His face was screwed up, his shoulders raised and he was waving a short, childish wave with his fingers as he grinned the smuggest of smiles. Looking down, Rivers knew that he had failed his sister and perhaps his nephew as he marched, as if to the executioners block, back along the stables.

Richard turned to Buckingham to see him leaning his rotund form against the wall, a smile spread so broadly across his face that it almost joined his ears together. He looked like a wolf come home to find a lamb asleep in his den. They had no time though to enjoy the moment.

"Now," Richard growled, "we ride." With smooth athleticism he propelled himself into the saddle of his mount while Buckingham tried desperately to spring high enough, his right foot hooked by the stirrup as he pivoted precariously on his left heel. Richard's steed writhed and reared with excited impatience as he waited for his companion. Finally, a nervous soldier stepped forward and cupped his hands under Buckingham's left foot, lifting him toward the saddle. Finally ready, the two horses thundered out of the town in a cloud of dust with two columns of Richard's mounted retinue following close behind.

Two hours later, a dusty pillar rumbled toward the outskirts of Stoney Stratford. It was approaching eight o'clock and the townsfolk were beginning to emerge, drawn out by the news of the column of riders. The sun began to warm Richard's face as his gaze focussed to the east. He had intended to fan his men out through the town toward Edward's lodgings, but as they approached the disparate collection of buildings, it became clear that there was a large camp to the east near the manor house, and that there was some considerable activity there. The entire company peeled away to the left, the ground trembling at its passing as their pace quickened.

Minutes later, the front of the party passed into the rows of dark tents, some of which were laying flat on the ground. It was clear that the camp was being packed away. On the southern edge, a group of horsemen were forming ranks. Spurring his mount on faster still, Richard charged toward the congregation. Ploughing straight through the centre of the blocks of horses, Richard parted the soldiers with ease as they were startled by the line of armed men scything through their ranks. Emerging from the front line with only three of his guard, Richard saw a small group, turning their mounts to face the commotion. Behind three mounted men sitting in a row, the duke spied his nephew, craning his neck over those arranged to guard him. Halting his own horse, Richard eyed the men with a smouldering mistrust.

"Sire." Richard bowed his head to his nephew from his saddle. "It appears," he continued in an even tone, "that we have arrived just in time to join you for the remainder of your journey." There was silence. Edward looked away, his young face betraying his unease. Richard held his ground. He had made his greeting and would not chase a response. Clenching his jaw tightly, he deliberately stared through the three riders at the young boy behind them, who in turn avoided the burning gaze. After a long moment, the figure to Richard's right of the three nudged his horse forward a few paces to draw alongside the duke. Turning to him, the thin faced man whispered smoothly.

"Where is Earl Rivers?"

"Delayed." Richard replied loudly without shifting his gaze. "He suggested that we ride ahead to join our nephew for the remainder of the journey."

"Do not play games with me." The man hissed angrily. "Where is my uncle?"

"Do not forget yourself, Grey." Richard quietened his voice now. Though shocked by the nerve of Sir Richard Grey, the duke would not yet take his eyes from Edward. "You do not have your mother's skirts to hide behind here." The young man to his side was the queen's son by her first marriage, stepson to Richard's brother and one of the power hungry Woodvilles at the very centre of the court that Richard despised. "Sire," Richard called, speaking clearly again, "may we speak in private before departing?"

"You are not required here, Gloucester." Grey whispered, leaning toward the duke. "You shall not speak to his highness." Now, Richard slowly turned his head to face Grey. His dark brown eyes burned so intensely that Grey started as they reached him. The duke's blood boiled with fury at the whelp's disrespect, but it raged even more hotly at the confirmation that something was indeed afoot. He stared silently at the younger man's narrow face and watched as his startled expression passed. He waited a moment longer until it was replaced by the thin smile of one who had just remembered that they were still winning the game in spite of a momentary setback. Grey leaned in close again.

"Your time is at an end," he said with affected sympathy. Instantly, a look of shocked agony twisted the smirk from his face as Richard's right fist shot upwards to meet Grey's conveniently protruding chin, thrusting him backward and toppling him awkwardly from his saddle like a heavy sack might bounce from the back of a cart on a bumpy lane. Even before the thud and shriek that marked his landing, Richard's horse was striding forward, parting the other two stunned men with a fiery glare. Pulling his horse to a halt beside that of the twelve year old boy, whose face was obscured by rolling locks of golden blond hair that glistened in the sun, Richard took a deep, calming breath and composed himself with an unnerving immediacy.

"Your highness." Richard tried softly to gather the new king's attention. The boy shifted in his saddle uneasily. Richard leaned a little closer, speaking more firmly. "Edward!" The youngster started and looked nervously at his uncle as though fearing he was about to receive the same treatment that had been meted out to Grey. Seeing this fear, Richard tried to smile as warmly as his pointed features would allow. "My dear Edward," he said gently, "we must talk. If you would wish it, we can speak as we travel." The young king nodded sharply but his face betrayed his confusion at the situation.

There was a commotion behind as Sir Richard Grey scrambled to his feet only to be grabbed under both arms by two of Richard's men. He kicked and shrieked his protestations as they lifted him from the ground.

"Take him away." Richard snapped, irritated by the distraction.

"Richard?" Edward said, concerned. Turning, the duke was dismayed to see his nephew's distressed face gazing pleadingly at Sir Richard Grey.

"Do not worry," the man shrieked as his legs flailed below him, "your family shall save you from…"

"Take him away!" Richard interrupted furiously. The two men dragged Grey back through the narrow corridor that still remained in the ranks toward the rest of Richard's retinue. Staring at his young nephew, Richard feared that the situation was turning against him. A glance at the remaining member of his own guard, who held the reins to his own and two other, now empty horses, made it clear that this man was growing nervous too. The bulk of River's retinue still stood between him and his own men and he suddenly became aware that his situation had become most precarious should there be an order to seize him. He would not make it through the narrow corridor with Edward in tow unopposed. Enough nervous glances had shot around as Grey had passed for it to be obvious that these men grew uncertain, and that would make them unpredictable. They outnumbered his force two to one and an open conflict was hardly likely to help matters, but some decisive action was required quickly. He turned away from them all and chewed his bottom lip in a moment of thought before steering his horse back to face the ranks of perplexed faces. He cast his eye over them slowly.

"Men!" he called, his voice deep and filled with the resounding authority that he poured into his orders upon the field of battle. "I thank each of you with all of my heart for your assistance in bringing our king to this meeting point in safety." He slowly passed his gaze back over them. "Now that you have delivered him to his Protector," he continued, pausing to allow the fact of the title he had used to permeate the crowd, "you are all free to return home." There was some confused muttering, but no-one moved. Richard's stare kept the other two horsemen before the king from issuing any counter order. Forcing the issue, Richard spoke again. "You are all dismissed." There was a long moment of hollow silence as each man wondered to himself whether he should leave, or draw his sword, whether they had protected the king, or were supposed to now. Each without an answer, they all began to look to those around them for some confirmation of something. Finally, as Richard's grip on his reins tightened in preparation for what may come, a soft Welsh accent called from somewhere in the crowd.

"Let's be off then!"

"Ay!" another voice seconded.

Slowly, more murmurs of agreement seeped through the crowd and at each side, men began to break their ranks and disperse until eventually, Richard caught a reassuring glimpse of his own men. The knot in his stomach loosened a little as the danger passed. Buckingham's horse trotted gently to his side, passing the other two riders that had accompanied Grey, who had clearly decided to make a tactical withdrawal also.

"Nice accent." Richard whispered, suppressing a smile. Henry winked at him with the sparkling eyes of a mischievous lad and had to look away to avoid spluttering with laughter.

There was almost half an hour of strained silence as the party got underway, riding in a long, serpentine column away from sleepy Stony Stratford. Richard was eager to open a dialogue with his nephew but found himself strangely awkward in the boy's presence. Although he had expected a little unease by virtue of their unfamiliarity, the feeling had been magnified by the manner of their meeting. Once the procession had settled into a steady pace, Richard trotted to the young king's right shoulder. His black cloak enveloped him, his long curls of yellow hair falling in sharp contrast over the top of the heavy material, bouncing as he cantered along the dry, dusty road. Could this boy measure up, in so many ways, to his father? 'That,' thought Richard 'is now up to me.'

The twelve year old boy looked sideways as the rider pulled alongside him and then slowly returned his sombre eyes to staring at his hands on his reins. The duke shot a glance over his own right shoulder, where Buckingham had positioned himself just behind them, and fixed his eyes on his young nephew with resolute determination.

"Edward," he began, his voice calm and his tone even, "you have my deepest sympathies for your loss." He waited for a moment, but there was no response. "Your father was a great man," he continued, "and you have my love and my loyalty as he did. Together we shall continue his good work and I shall strive to make you a man, and a king, of whom he would be most proud." Richard's sentiments hung in the air between them for a moment. As he searched for something else to say without losing his temper, Edward finally spoke, quietly and without looking up.

"Where is my uncle?" His solemn tone, mixed with his own raw feelings for his brother, caused a swell of pity for the boy to rise in Richard's throat, though it was knotted with a wounded rage at his question. He clenched his teeth and inhaled deeply.

"Sire," Richard began, but the young king still did not raise his head. "Edward!" the Protector barked, his anger threatening to overtake him. The desired effect was achieved though as Edward's eyes snapped up to meet his. Richard's broiling temper was immediately quelled by the look of panicked fear on his nephew's face and a sense of self-conscious shame washed over him as he saw the glistening track of a single tear marking his left cheek. "Oh, Edward." Richard was suddenly filled with sympathy. "I am concerned that those who surround you do not hold in their hearts the best interests of either you or your subjects."

"They are the same people who advised my father, my lord." Edward spoke with a forced authority that gave his voice a sharp, abrupt tone.

"And you would wish to become as he was in these last years?" Richard snapped, immediately regretting his words.

"I would that I may become half the man that my father was." Edward straightened his back, but his cheeks flushed to betray his nerves.

"You shall become so much more, Edward. So very much more." Richard smiled awkwardly, but no reply came and the group rode on the remainder of that day's light in a thick, heavy silence.

Chapter 23

4th May 1483 - Turmoil

During the days since they had left Stony Stratford, Edward had softened a great deal toward his uncle, much to Richard's delight and relief. Buckingham's continual high spirits and childish jesting had taken the sting from Edward's harsh stares and by the morning of their arrival in London, the three were laughing and joking together at Richard and Henry's tales of misadventure. A particularly long fit of laughter had followed Buckingham's expertly reported story of a time when he had been forced to dress as a serving maid to escape a uniquely large and irate husband in a tavern where his face was unknown and therefore could not have saved him.

As they neared the city, all but a hundred of their retinue peeled away to establish a camp well outside of the city. The Protector wished to take great care not to march into London at the head of an army and risk misinterpretation of his arrival. He instructed Edward to ride at the head of the procession, wearing a deep blue velvet doublet and breeches, a matching cloak pushed behind his shoulders and flowing down his back. Behind him, on either side, rode Richard, the Protector, and Henry, Duke of Buckingham, both dressed in black mourning wear. Several feet behind them rode the one hundred of Richard's liveried and mounted guard.

The streets were lined with cheering and clapping Londoners, children darting between the legs of their elders, women leaned from high windows for a glimpse of the new young king and his company. Through each street, Richard's voice could be heard bellowing above the cacophony of the crowd.

"Behold," he called out, "your prince and sovereign." Each recitation sparked a fresh wave of cheering and clapping from those at the roadside, and with each passing street toward Westminster, the duke saw the young king's shoulders rise and his back straighten as his confidence grew in the rapture of his reception. Edward led the way to the Abbey where all of the nobility currently in London were gathered to welcome their new monarch. After brief greetings, all entered the Abbey to attend a mass for the deceased king, after which Richard led the congregation in an oath of loyalty to the new king as he had done in York. Once completed, Richard moved to his mother's residence at Baynards Castle by the Thames while Edward was installed at the Tower of London. Lord Hastings accompanied Richard and Buckingham to Baynards where the three had much to discuss. Anne and their son would also be at Baynards now and Richard was eager to see them.

As soon as they arrived at the Castle, Richard barely had a moment in which to offer his condolences to his mother before Hastings pleaded desperately to speak with him. Although eying him with undisguised suspicion, Hastings did not protest when the Protector gestured for Buckingham to accompany them. Settling around a large oak table, Hastings began to speak with an anguished furrowing of his brow.

"You are come just in time, my lord."

"Your face betrays your distress with little need for words, Hastings." Richard said with a smile. "Tell us all, that all may now be put right."

"I hope that it shall prove so simple." Hastings did not return Gloucester's smile. "News arrived before you of the arrest of Rivers and Grey and the Woodvilles have been swift in their reaction." Hastings spoke more quickly, as if gripped by a swelling panic. "The queen and her son Dorset," Richard marked the venom with which he said the name, for the two were far from friends, "are in sanctuary at Westminster along with your other nephew, young Richard." Hastings paused and fixed his eyes on Gloucester's. Now in his fifties, he was usually a lively figure at court, one of Edward's closest friends with whom he had shared many trials and many more drunken nights. Today, his face was creased and his eyes greyed by a lack of sleep. "And," he continued, "they have taken possession of the Great Seal. The queen has already begun issuing proclamations in her son's name with it."

"Is there anything more?" Richard asked with a calmness that instantly deflated the tension that Hastings had built.

"Erm." Hastings stammered, struggling to muster some composure. "The queen's brother, Sir Edward Woodville, has taken twenty ships of the fleet and a large portion of the royal treasury and fled to the continent." There was a long silence during which Hastings shifted uncomfortably, his eyes fixed on Richard.

"Very well." Richard's tone was deliberately measured. "The queen is of little concern. She has strengthened our position with her guilty retreat into sanctuary. With or without the Great Seal, she can have no authority now. Our only concern in this matter is to secure Richard and remove him from his mother's influence, since he is now next in line to the throne. Richard looked first at Buckingham, who slowly nodded his agreement, and then to Hastings, who was smiling a strange, almost grateful smile. He puffed out his cheeks as Richard's calm, instant command of the situation absorbed his tension.

"As for Sir Edward," Richard continued with a thin smile, "he shall find no rest whilst he holds the king's property from me. Fear not, Lord Hastings," said Richard, his tone deepened as he fixed his piercing eyes upon Hastings, "I shall see it returned."

"My mind is greatly eased, my lord." Hastings breathed deeply and rested his elbows upon the table.

"We should arrange a Council meeting as soon as possible to begin our arrangements." Buckingham interjected, as if he were feeling left out.

"Of course." Richard concurred.

"If I may," Hastings burst across the table excitedly, "please allow me to arrange the meeting."

"Certainly." Richard smiled at the ease with which Hastings had been pacified. "Allow a few days for matters to settle a little."

The atmosphere around the table lifted tangibly as Hastings asked for news of the dukes' journey and of the events at Stoney Stratford. Here, Buckingham was in his element and soon had both of the others roaring with laughter as he retold their arrest of Rivers and the disbanding of his men, and of those special boots. It was over half an hour before they were interrupted by a sharp rapping at the door. All turned toward the noise.

"Enter." Richard called. The door swung open to reveal a short figure, a flowing gown filling the door frame and dark hair falling over the shoulders. "Anne!" Richard jumped to his feet and strode to the doorway, taking his wife in a warm embrace. Buckingham and Hastings rose to their feet and bowed their heads.

"Please forgive my interruption, gentlemen." Anne spoke to the two men as Richard stepped back.

"It is good to see you." Gloucester smiled, wanting to say so much more but preserving some decorum.

"I am afraid that it may not be so." Anne replied quietly. "May I speak to you in private?" Richard frowned.

"There can be no secrets here." He turned into the room and moved to pull up a chair for Anne.

"Richard," Anne protested, but was cut short.

"Come and sit down, my dear." Richard insisted. "Join us." Uncomfortable, Anne walked to the seat and sat down. The three men returned to their seats and all looked to Anne in anticipation.

"A message has arrived this afternoon that I felt required your urgent attention." She hesitated, her eyes flashing to the other two men, though Richard missed the unease with which she glanced at them. He simply smiled and nodded expectantly. "George Neville passed away following a brief illness." Suddenly, it was as though all of the air had been sucked from the room and Richard's stomach twisted. Conscious of the moment, he fought to maintain his expression. Deliberately, he turned down the corners of his mouth to demonstrate sorrow, but his mind raced through the implications of the news that his wife had delivered. He wanted desperately to see the faces of Buckingham and Hastings, to try and read their reaction, but he was sure that they would be far more intent upon measuring his and that a rash glance now would give away his rising panic. These tidings could hardly have come at a worse time. Just as he needed a secure foundation from which to fend off the Woodvilles, establish his position at court and begin to take control of the new king, a large portion of what he had worked so hard for over the last ten years was being ripped from under him. Trying not to clench his jaw, he drew a deep breath to steady himself and slowly turned his eyes to the two men opposite him, both of whom had their gaze locked upon the Protector.

"Terrible news." He said solemnly. "Poor young George. We should ensure," he continued, returning his focus to his wife, "that suitable provision is made for his funeral." Anne nodded in response. The knotting in his stomach was not passing. It was time to excuse himself. "Gentlemen," he said with a shallow smile, "we have much work to do. Lord Hastings, I shall await news of the Council meeting."

"Of course, my lord." Hastings was shaken from his obviously distant thoughts and rose slowly. With a flourishing bow, he left the room. As the door closed behind him, Buckingham also stood.

"How do you wish to rid yourself of me?" the duke asked with a wry smile. Richard returned the expression. Nothing escaped Henry's astute mind.

"Arrange to have Hastings discretely followed." Richard's voice was suddenly weary, that of an aging man after a long day of labour. "I would know where he goes and who he confides in."

"Consider it done." Henry strode to Richard's side and placed a hand upon his shoulder. "Do not worry, Richard. You are ideally placed to correct this unfairness." With a pat of the shoulder upon which his hand rested, the Duke of Buckingham took his leave.

Anne and Richard sat in silence for a long while as Anne watched her husband wringing his hands on the table top. She knew what was going to happen next, and sure enough, once Buckingham was likely to be well out of earshot, Richard roared and slammed his whitened fists onto the table. Although Anne hated his rages, she had never feared Richard's temper for it was never directed at her and she never felt threatened by him.

"How could this happen to us now?" he bellowed to the ceiling. Anne had no reply for him.

"I was trying to avoid telling you in front of others." Anne sounded as though she was apologising.

"I know." Richard said, moderating his tone as he realised through his broiling frustration that his outburst may have made his wife feel guilty. "My poor judgement may still work in our favour."

"It was not poor judgement, Richard." Anne consoled her husband, warmed as she always was by his unfailing reference to things happening to both of them, a couple, a team, never allowing self pity to absorb him. "How do you believe that they will react?"

"I have no doubt," Richard rose as he spoke and began to pace to and fro across the room, the sound of his footfalls filling the room, "that Hastings will make much of this, and I would know who he sees fit to divulge the news to. What concerns me more, though, is that I am unsure as to what Henry is thinking." He began to chew on the skin at the side of his thumb nail as he sank into silent thought.

"How can this work in our favour, Richard?" Anne broke the rhythmic clicking of Richard's heels on the wooden floor. He stopped and wrapped his hands around the back of the chair in which he had been seated.

"I am merely trying to see the best in this circumstance." Richard smiled. "News of George's death could not have been kept secret for long. Everyone is well aware of the consequences for us and to have attempted, or even have been perceived to have attempted to keep it from the Council would only have served to make matters worse when the truth was finally, inevitably revealed. The last thing that we need right now is to appear to have something to hide. At least now they were here to witness the news and to measure my reaction to it."

"Which was indeed well mastered." Anne smiled.

"I hope so, my dear. Much now relies upon establishing my authority and I can afford no chink for my enemies to exploit, for I fear that the number of my foes may increase many fold as matters progress."

The couple spent over an hour shut away discussing the news and its potential impacts and Anne was left in no doubt that this added complication had caused Richard much distraction. She was only too aware of how highly he valued the security that he had worked hard to build for them and their son.

Chapter 24

10th May 1483 – Council Called

Richard sat at the head of the broad, long table in the Council Chambers at the Palace of Westminster. At his right hand sat Henry, Duke of Buckingham. To his left was Lord Hastings. Along the table beyond them were a variety of Richard's brother's former councillors. Try as he may, Richard could not view these men as anything other than a necessary evil. Although he recognised that they were needed to maintain the smooth running of government, that their collective skill and experience was invaluable to him as he tried to establish himself, he despised their kind of fickle, shallow loyalty, simpering self interest and lack of conviction in the advice that they gave. Yet these were the men that Edward had surrounded himself with and who, unavoidably, would seek to force themselves into the inner circle of the new king. And so, today, Richard knew that he must exert all of his authority in these proceedings. He also had something in mind with which to test the temperature of the Council's waters.

"Gentlemen." Richard's voice cut through the muttering of those now settled around the table and all of their faces turned to him. "We have much to conclude this day." There was a general grumbling of agreement from around the table. He shot a glance at Buckingham, who smiled back at him to show his support for the first matter that Richard was to raise.

"It would seem sense," he said calmly though his stomach fluttered as he began and he clasped his hands on the table to avoid showing the trembling that he felt within him, "to begin with the issue of the Protectorate." His eyes scanned the room before settling on Hastings, who spoke instantly as planned.

"The provision within the late king's will was clear." Lord Hastings' tone was even and calm. He was firmly on his own territory and oozed confidence. "There can be little to discuss. I move that the Council recognise Richard, Duke of Gloucester as Protector during the minority of King Edward." There was an empty silence for a moment in which a wild fear gripped Richard. If the Council would not install him, he would have a real struggle on his hands. If the Council were to side with the Woodvilles, then Richard's position would become most precarious, particularly following the loss of George Neville and a large portion of Richard's security. Slowly, Richard's eyes scanned the stony faces around him.

"Seconded." Buckingham finally offered loudly. Richard had hoped that some other member would second the motion to avoid reliance upon those known to be his closest allies. Henry had been briefed to wait and only to speak if it appeared that no other would.

"Then we shall take a vote." Hastings said. "Those in favour." Slowly, each voice in turn around the table uttered 'Aye' until all, without exception, had assented. Richard noted that the longest delays in answering came from Lord Stanley and Bishop Morton, who looked at each other before voting. "Those against." Hastings called. Silence.

"Good." Richard said, trying to contain his relief. "Now we can get to our real business." He relaxed a little, the weight of his primary concern now lifted. "A date must be set for King Edward's coronation. I propose that we arrange the ceremony for 22nd June."

"Why wait so long, my lord?" The tone was enquiring but Richard felt the accusatory sting of Bishop Morton's voice. Murmuring arose as all eyes turned to Morton, who smiled up the table at Richard.

"Six weeks shall provide just enough time to make all of the necessary arrangements." Richard waved his hand dismissively. "There are clothes to be made, decorations and food to be prepared. Much is needed of us all to make this the occasion that it deserves to be, Bishop Morton." Richard mirrored the other's smile. "I simply do not wish to rush the affair and see no requirement to do so."

"Very well." The Bishop opened his hands in acceptance and cast his eyes around the room. All faces were still firmly upon the Protector. Richard's face remained even, a gentle smile sitting on his lips. If they were awaiting an eruption or sign of weakness, he was determined that they would be disappointed.

"Then we are all agreed." Hastings stated firmly. "The date for the coronation shall be 22nd June." There were grumbled mutterings of agreement from those gathered and so the second matter of the Council's business was settled with little difficulty. Richard felt his confidence swelling as he began to feel a degree of control over the proceedings. He chose this moment for his planned test of the Council's will.

"Before we move on to the remainder of the matters before the Council, I have," he paused a moment, searching for and checking in his own mind the words that he would use next, "a request, gentlemen." Now, the slightly startled faces of both Hastings and Buckingham joined the intrigued expressions of the others. He had not told even them about this. "Following the events of our journey, the details of which I am sure that you are all familiar with, and the actions of the remainder of the family, the Woodvilles should be a source of grave concern to this Council." There was no reply from any member, though Richard had not expected any. He knew that there was little love for the Woodvilles at this table. But he also had no doubt that he was surrounded by political realists who were as uncertain of him as they were distrustful of the Queen's family. Each of them had been to some extent forced aside by the Woodville's avaricious pursuit of power and influence. Yet none knew enough about this northern lord to abandon that which they know. One of the first things that Richard was keen to do was to draw a line in the political sand beneath them and see who would choose which side. Perhaps more importantly, he was interested in who would attempt to take no side, for those were the men who he would need to watch most closely. The rest would expose themselves as against him or as keen allies of the emerging new power. A foot in each camp would mark them as dangerous political players waiting to see what would suit their needs most. In truth, there was no correct answer to be had. This was simply an opportunity for Richard to judge those with whom he was forced to surround himself for now. He relished for a long moment the tension around the table as all hung upon the coming words.

"Whilst I shall collect evidence of what has been happening here since my brother's death, I can bear witness to the treachery of Earl Rivers in attempting to prevent my contact with the young king. I therefore ask that the Council issue a warrant for the formal arrest and trial of Anthony Earl Rivers on a charge of treason." The hush in the room grew heavier. Eyes darted across the table to other eyes, each pair searching for an indication of the other's views and trying to decipher who was going to speak first. Richard leaned forward, pressing his hands together in front of his lips in anticipation.

"My lord," it was Bishop Rotherham who first broke the silence, "I would suggest that the timing of your request is somewhat inappropriate." There was some nodding and murmurings of agreement.

"How so, my lord?" Richard asked with a forced frown. The group would not escape his test so easily. "I should have thought that such a delicate moment was not a time to tolerate any such dangerous behaviour."

"Whilst I do not suggest that Earl Rivers' action be condoned, I merely make the point that to criminalise those with whom our new king is closest and most comfortable, and who, like yourself, are his closest family, at a time when he has just lost his father and is entering the highest office in the land may prove," the Bishop paused, eyeing Richard's interested face while searching for the right words, "counter productive."

The Protector glanced to either side. The Duke of Buckingham sat looking into his own lap and as he glanced across at Hastings, the other snapped his gaping jaw closed. His eyes darted over Richard's face, a look of puzzled irritation marking his own visage.

"Lord Hastings," Richard began with an amused smile, "perhaps we may put this matter directly to the vote?"

"Of course." Hastings replied absently, his eyes still fixed upon Richard's. "All those in favour?" A moment passed and a frown filled Hastings forehead. Richard slowly, casually raised his right hand, holding Hastings' stare. With a nod from the Protector, Hastings broke the lock and looked at Buckingham, who also silently held his right arm in the air, his gaze still lowered. A quick survey of the rest of the table revealed no more assenting hands. "Those against." This call brought a clattering around the table as every other member of the Council raised a hand, some more quickly than others. Turning his gaze back to Richard, Hastings himself now lifted his right hand level with his shoulder.

"Very well." Richard dismissed the matter with a wave of his arm. He had learned all that he wished to from this moment. Earl Rivers would keep until another day. "Now to the remainder of our business, gentlemen."

They spent a further two hours within the Council chamber covering many small details that required attention, though throughout Richard was a little distracted. He was, after all, now officially recognised as the Protector of the Realm.

Chapter 25

8th June 1483 – More Than A Memory

A month in London had passed swiftly for Richard. He had been busy building a relationship with his often obtuse and distant nephew and attempting to lay a firm foundation for their government. He had also been kept busy by the seemingly infinite minutia of government, which, although endlessly frustrating, Richard insisted on personally overseeing. He had taken these weeks to immerse himself in the machinery of each department, conscious of his own inexperience. It had quickly become clear how much of his work his brother had allowed his minsters to undertake with only minimal supervision.

In spite of several requests from himself and his nephew, Elizabeth Woodville and her youngest son still remained in sanctuary at Westminster Abbey, pleading at every opportunity that they were in fear for their lives. To Richard's great pleasure the queen's protestations had found no support, either at court or among the people.

Sitting within his mother's study at Baynards Castle, Richard's eyes wandered around the tapestries hanging from the walls, past several paintings and a large window, the clear blue morning sky briefly flooding his eyes with intense light and causing him to blink uncomfortably. When his vision sharpened again, he found himself staring at the huge portrait that hung above the fireplace. The face of his father met his eyes, appearing to look down directly at him, stern, as though passing judgment. The Protector felt a stiffening ache in his throat as he wondered whether his father would approve of his actions. Richard found himself feeling strangely attached to the man he had barely known, yet who had himself been Protector of the Realm in his time. A great part of him wanted to release the knot in his throat as a tear as he accepted that what he was really asking the inanimate painting was whether or not his father would be proud of him. He looked away from the weight of the stare as he recalled the end that his father had met. Had being Protector sealed his fate, or was it ambition for the throne? Perhaps one had led to the other. Perhaps Richard may be following too closely in his father's footsteps. But no, he would learn from the past, not relive it.

A loud rap at the door shook Richard from his musings and he straightened himself in his chair. His visitor was expected but had caught him off guard.

"Enter." He deepened his voice and gathered himself. The door swung open and a tall, slender man strode into the room, full of purpose and brimming with an obvious confidence. His skin was a deep bronze colour and a jet black, immaculately trimmed goatee beard framed thin, smiling lips. He wore breeches and a jerkin of black, trimmed with red and fitted tightly around his waist. As he approached the desk, he offered a flourishing bow and rose, standing bolt upright, still smiling.

"My lord." The man spoke softly, a gentle accent betraying his Portuguese roots.

"Sir Edward!" Richard stood and offered a hand to his guest, who shook it firmly, the long narrow blade that hung at his side rattling within its scabbard. "It is good to see you have returned. Please," he gestured to the chair beside his visitor, "be seated." The two men sat down opposite each other.

"I hope that you are well, my lord." Sir Edward said politely.

"There is much done and even more still to be done." Richard replied. "But all is well." Another, more gentle knock at the door disturbed the conversation, though Sir Edward did not turn around at the noise. Richard frowned at the interruption. "Come."

"Forgive me." The quiet, soft voice drifted into the room as the door cracked open. "I did not wish to disturb you." Anne stepped into the room, causing both Richard and his visitor to rise to their feet to greet the lady.

"Please, join us, Anne." Richard gestured to a second chair that stood beside that of the guest. Anne nodded and, her thick black skirts flowing, glided gracefully across toward the desk. Her long dark hair was scraped tightly behind her head into a bun allowing Richard to see the concern evident upon her brow.

"My lady." The deep, accented voice rolled from the tall man before Anne as he bowed low.

"Anne, may I introduce Sir Edward Brampton." Richard smiled as he spoke. "Sir Edward, my wife, the Lady Anne."

"Your beauty surpasses even its reputation, my lady." Sir Edward lowered his head, taking Anne's right hand and raising it to his lips.

"Your own reputation precedes you, Sir Edward." Anne replied, not flattered, but with some admiration. "A converted Portuguese Jew, the first Jew to be knighted, a loyal and skilled subject of the late king."

"And of our new king," Sir Edward continued Anne's sentence, "as well as his Protector." Brampton turned to Richard with a respectful tilting of his head. "But I wonder, my lady," he continued, "whether you refer to my conversion from Judaism or from being Portuguese?" He smiled broadly.

"To accept our Lord Jesus Christ as your saviour is the single most important thing that you may ever do in your life." Anne told him sternly, as if chastising a child. Sir Edward's face sank into an embarrassed apology as he was gripped by the fear that he had gone too far. Anne held his stare forcefully. "But being an Englishman comes a very close second." Anne smiled gently now. "The Lord will love you for converting to Christianity, but he will respect you for becoming an Englishman." Sir Edward burst into laughter as his nerves broke and Richard joined in as Anne moved around the third chair and sat down. The two men followed suit.

"Sir Edward was about to tell me of his mission." Richard told Anne, flashing her an enquiring glance that none other would have noticed.

"Then I am just in time to hear your tale." Anne replied, her expression almost invisibly telling Richard that she had interrupted with urgent news that he needed to hear.

"I am afraid that we may have to be satisfied with the brief account for the moment, my dear. I am left with little time and would enjoy the fuller details when there is the time to take pleasure in them."

"Very well." Sir Edward understood the Protector and inhaled deeply, gathering his thoughts. "We managed to catch up with Sir Edward Woodville and the fleet at the French coast." Brampton relaxed slightly into his chair. "I was able, without confrontation, to persuade all but two ships of the fleet to return with me."

"This is great news indeed!" Richard spread his hands, clearly pleased and impressed at the tidings.

"Does your charm know no bounds, Sir Edward?" Anne asked.

"Alas, my lady, it does." Brampton conceded, though he clearly revelled in the praise. "Sir Edward Woodville, the remaining two vessels and the bulk of the treasure eluded me."

"I am not concerned about the money." Richard said nonchalantly with a dismissive wave of his hand. He was slightly concerned. The royal finances were far from secure, apparently suffering from his brother's extravagance and lack of attention, but that could wait to be resolved. "Do you know where Woodville is now?"

"My sources tell me that he is in Brittany." Sir Edward replied.

"Good." Richard said absently. "So do mine." He fixed Brampton with a cold stare. "He can be dealt with later. It will suffice for now that he did not entirely succeed in his cowardly flight. Now," Richard was suddenly warmer again, "I am afraid that I must ask you to excuse me, Sir Edward."

"Of course, my lord." Brampton rose sharply. "My lady." He bowed to Anne, who acknowledged his farewell with a slow nod of her head. He turned and stepped across the room.

"Sir Edward," Richard called as he reached the door. Brampton stopped and turned. "Thank you for your assistance in this matter. You have done very well."

"Always a pleasure, my lord Protector." Sir Edward replied with a broad smile and low sweeping bow before leaving the room. In the instant that the door closed, Richard turned sharply to Anne, frowning deeply.

"What is it, Anne?" he asked quickly. "Is everything well?" He swallowed. "Is Edward well?"

"He is fine." Anne reassured her husband quickly. "I did not mean to concern you so."

"I know," Richard said, exhaling, "I know that you would not have waited if it were so serious, but you look so concerned and I find it impossible not to fear the worst."

"What I have come to tell you," Anne said slowly, her voice steady and deliberate, "is of such concern because it is so out of the ordinary, even by the standards of this year."

"My worry grows again, Anne." Richard frowned. "Tell me what the matter is."

"A visitor arrived directly after Sir Edward," Anne began, fixing her eyes tightly upon Richard's. "He begged an audience with you. I happened across the hall as he argued with your mother's doorman. The man insisted most frantically that he must see you immediately." Anne stopped talking, as though waiting for something.

"This is not so great an occurrence." Richard was puzzled.

"No." Anne agreed. "Yet when he saw me, he knew my name. He wears the robes of a bishop and he pleaded so desperately with me that he had news of which you must be made aware that he almost frightened me." She furrowed her brow, as if puzzled by her own words. "I know not why, but his pleading touched me so that I asked his name and his news."

"And?" Richard was unsure now whether he grew concerned, impatient or irritated.

"And he said that his name and his news were for you and you alone, that he could not tell even me. He said that even if he gave his name it would mean nothing to you." She narrowed her eyes, still staring intensely at Richard for some sign that any of this had meaning to him. "He told me that you visited him once, but would not know it." She paused. "He claims to have come to complete a task entrusted to him by your brother."

"Why," Richard laughed, "would some obscure bishop I do not know, that I have met without remembering it, arrive now with an errand from Edward?" There was a pause.

"Not Edward." Anne said slowly. Richard's face froze and he stared disbelievingly at his wife. "He claims to be here in fulfilment of the final wish of your brother George." The two stared in silence at each other. Both bewildered, both uncertain. Amongst everything else that had happened over the past months, this was proving the most shocking. How did a message from George fit into these events? Its arrival now could hardly be a coincidence. The silence persisted painfully until Richard's frown broke and he smiled a crooked, unconvincing grin.

"Well," he said loudly, "we shall not find out why he has come unless we get him in here."

"Very well." Anne agreed, moving to the door. Pulling it open, she beckoned into the corridor and shuffling footsteps approached instantly. A moment later, an aging man appeared in the doorway. A heavy, thick cassock added to a frame that would otherwise have been slight. His face was old and lined, yet soft, his white hair framing his pale visage. He smiled nervously and bowed.

"My lord," the man's voice quivered a little, betraying his unease, "I thank you for receiving me."

"Your beseeching of my wife left me with little option." Richard said tartly. "If you would claim to bear a message from my brother George, I would first have your name."

"Bishop Stillington, my lord." The man shifted in the frame of the door and, Richard noted, wrung his hands in front of himself. As Anne had promised, the name indeed meant nothing to the Protector.

"Well, Bishop Stillington," Richard caught himself snapping impatiently and moderated his tone a little, "please come and sit down."

"Thank you." Stillington nodded and swiftly strode across to the chair in which Brampton had sat only five minutes earlier. Anne sat next to him.

"Before you begin," Richard raised a finger and leaned forward onto the table, "I would know from you on what authority you bring this news. Why should I place any store in what you may say?" Richard's eyes narrowed a little as he awaited a response.

"You do not know my face, my lord?" the man queried, his eyes flashing between Richard and Anne, a soft smile across his lips.

"No." Richard retorted sharply. "Should I?" He was in no mood for this visitor to begin playing games.

"Probably not, my lord." Stillington shook his head. "I had not thought that you would. It was dark, and under very different circumstances that we last laid eyes upon each other."

"I meet many people that I cannot recall." Richard said irritably.

"Oh, we have not met," the bishop corrected the duke, "at least not properly. I should not have known that it was you had your brother not told me so that day," he paused, "in the Tower. When you visited the Duke of Clarence." He coaxed Richard a little further but there was no sign yet of recognition. "My cell was dark and for my part I saw only a pair of eyes at the door."

Realisation slammed into Richard like a towering wave crashing over him and washed through him sending a cold chill down his spine as it seemed to melt away any strength from his limbs. This was the man who sat in the dim cell that had so intrigued Richard because of the queen's visit to him. A nervous knot grew in his stomach as he realised that perhaps this man did have some news for him. It would mean that George had lied to him that day, but that would be no surprise. Richard had known there was something amiss just as he had known that George had no intention of telling him the truth. Now, at last, perhaps he would find out what it was and why the queen had been so interested in the occupant of that cell.

"I remember the encounter well." Richard reflected, unable to disguise his intrigue.

"The reason for my imprisonment, the true reason for your brother's imprisonment and execution, the reason for Queen Elizabeth's visit that so interested you and the reason that I am here today are all the very same matter." The Bishop glanced at Anne again, then back to Richard as he continued. "Your brother bid me hold this news until the time was right for you to hear it. I had not known when that time would be, but the events of these past months have, I think, brought about the moment he intended."

"Well," Richard said in a tone as even as he could manage, "you have us hooked, Bishop Stillington. Now, pray, enlighten us."

"Your brother was clear that I should pass this news to you," he looked at Anne again, smiling embarrassedly, "and only you."

"We shall hear your news together," Richard replied calmly, "or we shall not hear it. There are no secrets here." There was a silence as Richard fixed the Bishop with a weighty stare. The Bishop again moved his gaze between the Protector and his wife as if measuring the situation.

"Very well," he said eventually, "then prepare yourselves."

Barely a mile away from Baynards Castle in the upper room of a tavern, candlelight licked at dark oak beams and illuminated pale walls. Four men sat at each side of a small, square table. The fine attire of each man seemed completely out of place in this humble room in this humble inn, yet it was the chosen location for a concerned gathering, days in the planning, since secrecy was paramount for all of the men. Each had before him a large goblet of blood red wine, but nothing else remained in the room. The door was barred from the inside and each man was now as comfortable as such a situation would allow. They were alone and could not be overheard.

Lord Hastings drew a slow breath, passing his gaze from Lord Stanley on his left, over Bishop Morton opposite him and to Bishop Rotherham at his right.

"Gentlemen," Hastings began in a hushed undertone, "we are all aware of why we are here. To be agreed is our way forward." The other three nodded soberly.

"We find ourselves," Bishop Morton began slowly, "with a Protector dangerously unknown to us who is attempting to sweep away the very foundations of the structure that he finds here."

"And yet," Hastings interjected, "none of us would bemoan the deposition of the Woodvilles."

"No," Lord Stanley grumbled, "but to step into that which is unknown simply to escape an unfavourable status quo may not be wise. At least we know from long experience where we stand with the queen."

"True," Bishop Morton nodded, "yet there is more reason for concern than just this."

"I am led to believe," Bishop Rotherham said, wrapping his fingers around his expansive stomach and twisting up his nose, "that he has somewhat novel views on policy and justice in the north, favouring the common folk even over their betters." The Bishop spluttered the end of his sentence as if unable to believe his own words.

"He could not implement such a policy on a national scale." Lord Stanley waved a hand dismissively.

"Do not underestimate Richard's tenacity and skill." Hastings warned.

"Admiration, my lord?" Morton queried with a thin smile.

"And a little realism." Hastings smiled back. "We are foolish to pretend that Richard is not a powerful, competent and experienced governor."

"There is still more for us to worry about." Bishop Rotherham cut short the tension. "If Gloucester's circumstance has become strained, he could grow dangerous."

"Indeed." Morton agreed, his eyes still fixed on Hastings. "If the duke's interest in a large portion of his estates has been weakened, he will doubtless try to," Morton tilted his head as he sought the right phrase, "correct this."

"It will also unnerve him," Lord Stanley continued Morton's thought, "and that may make him erratic. We are all aware of his penchant for making war." There was a long pause as an unspoken question hung between the men, waiting for someone to give it voice. Eventually, an ever so slightly uncertain tone broke the silence.

"Do we really feel that there is a threat of Richard making an attempt on the throne?" Hastings spoke quietly, his eyes darting around the table. No answer came for many seconds that threatened to become minutes.

"He is," Lord Stanley's gravelly voice was not quietened, "a Plantagenet."

"Indeed." Bishop Morton agreed. "I would put nothing past our royal family. They have made war upon each other for decades at lesser opportunity and cause than now presents itself to our Protector."

"Yet Richard has always been nothing but loyal to his brother and at the very least has set out the same way with his nephew." Hastings countered.

"There is also the consideration of his position as Protector of the Realm." Bishop Rotherham seemed not to have heard Lord Hastings. "He cannot be ignorant of the fate of the last Duke of Gloucester to act as Protector to Henry VI."

"There was no evidence of foul play in Humphrey's death." Lord Hastings reminded the men.

"Precisely what would make this Duke of Gloucester so nervous." Retorted Lord Stanley. "When Edward is old enough to reign in his own right, and the Woodvilles will push for this to happen sooner rather than later," he added quickly, "Richard may find himself more a threat than an aid, particularly should the king revert to the influence of his mother."

"Without the question of Richard's willingness to simply hand over all of the power in the kingdom and retire into some less prestigious role." Rotherham said absently, as if more to himself than his audience.

"All of this amounts to a problem for us." Bishop Morton concluded darkly, his voice loaded with sombre severity. "We have a man with a war lust, weakened position, uncertain future and at conflict with the rest of the king's family about to assume the most powerful position in all the land. We also cannot discount the possibility of him attempting to seize power for himself." There were nods of agreement, though Hastings seemed less certain than the other three.

"The question, then, is what we are to do." Rotherham offered.

"We must be cautious," Morton replied immediately, "and consider these matters in all of our dealings."

"Richard must not be permitted to use his position to make a bid for power, if that is his intention." Lord Hastings added hurriedly. "Our concern remains for the young King Edward primarily."

"And for ourselves." Stanley mused, still distant. "Richard has eyes and ears in even the darkest corners."

Richard's heart thudded in anticipation at his visitor's words. He found himself holding his breath without meaning to as he waited for Bishop Stillington to begin. He felt the tension radiating from Anne beside Stillington too, though he could not move his eyes from the bishop's face. For his part, Bishop Stillington was swaying between a sense of powerful control at the secret that he was about to impart, the grip in which he held this great magnate, and a nervous unease at bearing the responsibility of this news, of risking the wrath of Richard Plantagenet.

"Your brother George first came to me many years ago." Bishop Stillington began, running his tongue across his lips as he paused. "He had parts of a story that he was attempting to piece together. From what he told me, shortly after your eldest brother's marriage to Elizabeth Woodville, the Earl of Warwick burned so hotly with rage that accusations and charges of betrayal erupted from him like Vesuvius over Pompey, showering George with shocking insights."

"That the earl was enraged," Richard said glancing at Anne, keen not to upset her with talk of her father, "is no news. He was finalising arrangements for Edward's marriage to the French princess when my brother cheerfully announced that he had already wed a widowed commoner in a secret ceremony. The earl lost much respect and was most displeased." Richard's right hand rubbed his right cheek as he continued. "George always sought a cause against Edward."

"That is not actually the case." Stillington said slowly, cautiously. Richard's frown demanded that he continue. "George only began to piece a story together at this point, and it was, from that moment onwards, the completion of that tale that fuelled the fire of his opposition to the king. The

Earl of Warwick created a monster in his rage." He turned to Anne, lowering his head. "Forgive me, my lady."

"I know well what my father did, my lord." Anne replied calmly, though Richard knew that the faint smile upon her lips betrayed the pain of the memory.

"One of the charges laid by the Earl of Warwick particularly caught George's ear, and it was this that he pursued. It was a matter known to very few." Stillington continued, beginning now to tell the story with his hands too. "The earl knew of it as a party to the matter and as, at the time, the closest friend and advisor to the king. Once calmed, the earl was unwilling to tell George more, fearing that he had already said too much. But," the Bishop smiled, "I am sure that you know how persistent George could be." Richard nodded, a fond smile passing across his face. "I certainly found out how ruthlessly driven he was when all that the earl would tell him was my name and that he should seek me out. Seek me out he did, and your brother had many ways in which to obtain what he wanted from me."

"He harmed you?" Richard asked, sitting upright. If George had resorted to torture, it may have tainted the information that he had obtained. To have resorted to such tactics against a man of the cloth would also further darken his memory of George.

"No, no." Stillington was quick to deny the suggestion. "He made several visits, growing more irate each time I declined to tell him what he wanted to know."

"I can imagine." Richard smiled again.

"Your brother was a bully and had his ways. Eventually, I could resist no longer and confirmed what he already knew, filling in more detail as I was able. From that day, George took me into his protection, though I was in no doubt that it was to protect what I knew rather than my person. That which George learned was the seed that grew at the root of all of his later actions."

"Then indeed I must hear this information, sir." Richard said with a mixture of concern and excitement. "You may now provide me with a reason that has eluded me for all of my adult life and has caused me much distress." Richard gestured for the bishop to continue. "Please, without further delay, enlighten me."

"The details of the story that I told George," the bishop paused and licked his lips, "were the details of a contract of marriage to which I was witness." Richard looked deflated instantly and his teeth clenched as undisguised irritation flashed across his face. "A contract," the bishop continued quickly, spying the displeasure, "between King Edward and Lady Eleanor Butler in the year of our Lord 1461." The Bishop stopped and watched Richard's face move from anger, through growing confusion and into astonished disbelief. "Three years before his marriage to Queen Elizabeth." Stillington added in confirmation. Now, he said no more and awaited the Protector's response. He turned to Anne, who stared at Richard, her jaw involuntarily open. Richard's mouth moved slowly as if trying to give voice to the thought process unravelling into a dark realisation.

"Such a contract is binding both in law and in the eyes of the Lord?" The duke asked for confirmation of what he knew in an unsteady voice.

"It certainly is." The bishop replied.

"And if it occurred before his wedding to Elizabeth Woodville, and if this Eleanor Butler lived," the bishop nodded almost imperceptibly to confirm that this was the case, "then..." Richard found himself unable to conclude the statement. He twisted in his seat and tried to compose himself. "Then his marriage was adulterous and therefore illegal, void in the eyes of Church and state."

"Yes." Stillington said slowly, as if inviting Richard to arrive at the next step of the revelation. He saw Richard searching for his meaning and within only a few moments, a new extreme of shock exploded across his face. He looked quickly at Anne, back to Bishop Stillington and rose slowly from his seat, turning away from the table. Fixing his gaze upon a stone in the wall, he pondered whether he dare give voice to the conclusion at which he had arrived. Eventually, he could not escape it any longer.

"If Edward's marriage was illegal," Richard spoke to the wall, "then the children of that marriage are illegitimate and cannot inherit the throne of England."

"Correct!" Stillington called jubilantly from behind. Richard spun on his heels and fixed the elderly man with an angry, blazing stare. The bishop realised that his tone had been wholly inappropriate.

"Why is it that you have kept this a secret for so long?" Richard snapped, leaning his hands on the back of his chair, his eyes narrowing accusingly.

"Well," the old man squirmed in his chair, clearly rattled, "I had little choice. This drove George almost mad and ended up costing him his life. His threat to reveal this news and stake his own claim to the throne saw us both passing time in the Tower. I only escaped the executioner," Stillington continued, pre-empting the duke's next thoughts, "by promising to keep the secret. I made oaths then that I do not break lightly even today. The queen was not going to allow news of this to escape and ruin everything that she had built, man of the cloth or no."

"The queen?" Richard exclaimed as he had another moment of realisation and his mind leapt back to the long moments that he had stood on the Tower steps waiting for the sound of Elizabeth's footsteps to pass. Had he felt so on edge at the prospect of being discovered there because something deep within his soul was warning him of the danger that would surely have resulted from becoming a party to this secret at that time. He almost smiled at the soothing notion that the Holy Spirit was watching over him. This sensation was eased aside by the surfacing of an uncomfortable, knowing thought. His brother had died because of the queen's desire to protect herself. He had been executed because of her.

"There is more." Stillington ventured cautiously.

"More?" Richard sounded truly amazed, astonished by the idea that the unreal revelation that he had heard was not all that there was. Rounding his chair, he took the weight from his legs as he began to fear that they may buckle beneath him. "What you have already told me has turned my world upside down, inside out and left it spinning." Richard confessed to his own surprise. "It already means..." He stopped and looked at Anne.

"It means that you would be the legitimate, rightful king," Anne said steadily, relieving her husband of the discomfort of voicing this fact himself, "if it were true." She held Richard's eyes.

"My lady," the Bishop sounded wounded, "I shall swear its truth in any place you would have me do so."

"Yet you sit here now breaking such oaths." Anne turned to him slowly as she spoke, still concerned by the lost look on her husband's face. The bishop dropped his head, filled with shame and burning with embarrassment at the rebuke.

"You can prove what you say?" Richard asked. "Can you produce this Lady Butler?"

"Alas, I cannot produce her person, for she died some fifteen years ago. I can, though, provide documentation as evidence of what I say."

"Very well." Richard accepted that this would need to be resolved later. "What more do you have?" By now, Richard almost dreaded the answer as his mind spun. If all of this was proven, he would indeed be the lawful king.

"I cannot vouch for this information, my lord, and will therefore understand if you wish not to hear it."

"We shall hear it, Bishop Stillington, and make our own judgement." Richard replied flatly, fighting a desperate internal battle to regain himself.

"Then forgive me." The bishop clasped his hands tightly so that Richard was left unsure whether it was his forgiveness the man requested or that of the Lord God. "George told me of another reason for his dissent that he had learned from the Earl of Warwick."

"Another reason?" Richard's eyes narrowed and he spoke absently, unable to believe what he was hearing.

"One that I am loathe to tell you, my lord." Stillington squeezed his own hands more tightly and his face twisted in a pained sort of smile. "It regards certain rumours with little supporting evidence." He stalled.

"Continue." Richard instructed as the bishop's pause persisted.

"The matter in question is that of your brother Edward's own legitimacy." Stillington blurted it out before fear took the words from him. He bit his bottom lip as he endured the silence that followed. Eventually, the Protector rose slowly and, once upright, he pounded both of his fists onto the table. Both the bishop and Anne jumped, startled from their seats.

"You go too far!" Richard roared, his cheeks burned red and the words burst from him like fire.

"My lord," the bishop pleaded, raising his hands defensively, "I shall say no more if that is your wish. I did not mean to insult you." Richard stood still a moment, as if petrified by an internal conflict. Glancing at Anne, who looked unnerved, he exhaled a slow, controlled breath and lowered himself back into his seat.

"Then go on," Richard encouraged, his tone a little more even, "and I shall measure the insult for myself." Richard met Anne's eyes and offered a gentle smile of reassurance, a silent apology. She returned his gesture softly.

"The tale as it was told to me runs thus, my lord." The bishop went back to wringing his hands as he prepared to tell his story. "Your brother Edward was born some eleven months after your father left on campaign in France. If the timing itself were not enough, consider the fact that, unlike yourself, George or Edmund, he had a small, discreet christening in a side chapel with little ceremony. Would this not be odd for the firstborn son of the mighty Duke of York?"

"There is evidence of this?" Richard asked, interested.

"Church records can substantiate the bones of what I have told you. The rest is rumour. I understand that King Louis always referred to your brother as Edward Bleybourne in secret, a taunt about an archer named Bleybourne, a giant of a man whose stature matched Edward's and who many claimed in hushed corners was his true father."

Richard propped his elbows on the table and buried his face in his hands. His mind was spinning, trying to absorb and make sense of what he was hearing. If true, it changed not only his view of his own past but also of the very real present in which he was sitting. As if that present were not complicated enough already.

"Bishop Stillington," Richard said, looking up from his hands and smiling, "I thank you for bringing this news and understand the burden that it must have been to you. I am sure that you will appreciate that we will require a little time to consider what you have brought to us."

"Of course, my lord."

"You will not take this information elsewhere." Richard was not asking.

"No other knows it, my lord, and no other shall discover it from me without you desiring it."

"Very well. If there is anything that you have need of, please let me know. I shall require you here, with all of your evidence, at nine o'clock in the morning."

"My lord." The bishop rose, bent uncomfortably in a shallow bow and shifted quickly to the door as if keen to escape the room. He had been gone for several minutes before Anne broke the silence that filled the room.

"Do you believe him?" she asked softly, almost in a whisper.

"I am unsure," Richard replied, unable to meet her eyes, "but we can see his evidence. I see no immediate reason to disbelieve him. You?"

"I agree." Anne reached across and placed her hand on top of Richard's clasped hands on the table. "Are you alright?"

"Hmmph!" Richard exhaled noisily to show that he was not.

"Even if it is true," she said softly, "you must see this in context, neither your brother nor your mother..." She was interrupted by Richard pulling his hands away and standing sharply.

"My brother lied to me," he raged, "my mother lied to me and your father knew all of this and said nothing. He left me to this as much as they did."

"How dare you blame my father for all of this." Anne stood and spoke quietly but with unmistakeable anger in her voice.

"Oh, I dare, my lady." Richard moved around the table and Anne stepped back nervously.

"Richard?" She found herself for the first time recoiling in fear of her husband. "What are you doing?" The duke stopped at the side of the table and looked at her, his face flushed and his eyes flashing.

"There is only one party to this still alive to tell me the truth. Both my brothers and your father are dead and took their treachery to the grave." He strode to the door, ignoring the pearl of a tear falling from his wife's eye, her lip quivering. He flung the door open and stormed from the room. Anne gathered her dress and ran after him as she felt uncontrollable grief filling her stomach.

"Mother!" Richard was marching along the corridor crashing doors open and bellowing wildly. "Mother! Where are you! Mother!" Eventually, having thundered up the stairs, his mother stood at the doorway of her chamber. She said nothing as her son approached, his cheeks filled with boiling blood and his chest heaving.

"Is it true, mother?" Richard spat, his face burning barely an inch from his mother's. Cecily stepped back into her room and calmly walked to the broad stone hearth. Anne arrived in the doorway as Richard stalked in after his mother. She watched her husband as he stood before his mother again, either side of the fireplace, his hands planted on his hips.

"Is it true, mother?" he repeated through clenched teeth.

"Is what true, Richard?" Cecily asked calmly.

"That you are a whore and my brother a bastard." Richard said venomously. Anne's mouth opened in shock at the tone and the words her husband used to the mother to whom he had always shown such respect. She watched the two face each other. Cecily, who was an inch or two taller than Richard, stood upright and motionless, her face not betraying signs of her encroaching age, nor of any reaction to her son's words. She had been a rare beauty in her younger years and the passing of time had done little to rob her of her attractiveness.

Suddenly, with a frightening swiftness, Cecily's right hand swung in a short, sharp arc that met Richard's left cheek with a painful cracking sound. For his part, Richard barely flinched at the strike, though the palm and finger marks stood out immediately, proud and bright on his already ruddy face, visible even over his burning anger.

After a moment more of silent, frozen staring, Cecily reached down, took her son's right hand and gently kissed the back of it. Replacing it at his side, she lowered her gaze to the hearth. Richard understood. Not least, he understood that the matter was now firmly closed.

Dropping his own head, he turned and marched from the room, pushing past Anne at the doorway, who looked after him down the corridor. She saw as he passed her a tear track running over the hand print marking his face and she decided that it might be best to leave him alone for a while.

Chapter 26

13th June 1483 – Come Out Fighting

Sitting at the head of the long, broad oak table, Richard drummed his fingers on the bare wood before him. A spinning tumult of thoughts and emotions filled his mind. Five days had passed since Bishop Stillington's revelations and matters were beginning to move apace. The day after the visit, Richard had hauled the unwilling bishop before the House of Lords to present his evidence. The elderly man had seemed so small and frail before the gathered magnates and Church hierarchy as he bumbled and fumbled through the tale he had related to Richard, who watched in embarrassed dismay, covering his eyes several times as the struggling bishop nervously rummaged through and repeatedly dropped official documents on the chamber floor. Many of the Lords Temporal found great amusement in the sight, with the Lords Spiritual gazing on with uncomfortable disapproval. Somewhere between the two reactions, Richard feared that the message would be lost and found himself strangely glad, and more than a little relieved, at the occasional gasp and outbreak of murmuring as the bishop finally spoke. The sensations were closely followed by a cold stab of guilt. This was hardly good news for anyone. Stillington delivered only the news concerning the Butler pre-contract and illegitimacy of his nephews. At this stage, he wished to judge reaction to this disclosure and had little desire to bring his mother's reputation before these men for open gossip.

By the end of Stillington's muddled and disjointed presentation, the Lords appeared to have absorbed his meaning and were immediately arguing as to whether the young Edward should be allowed to assume the throne. The Lords Spiritual took the firm stance that he could not and began to reach the conclusion that Richard himself was the legitimate, rightful heir. Almost as one, the Lords Temporal were far more cautious, urging a deeper investigation and more discussion on the matter. Doubtless, Richard mused cynically, they wanted more time to weigh the political implications for themselves. Still, the ball was now rolling.

That same day, news had reached Richard of a meeting that had taken place the previous day. He had, since his arrival in London, had a handful of key people closely followed. His military experience had taught him the value of information, of knowing your enemy's movements and intentions. He had applied the same logic to his foray into the politics of Court. The intelligence that he had received had disturbed him greatly and his confusion had only been swelled by a visit to his mother's residence by a delegation of Archbishops who had impressed upon Richard in no uncertain terms his obligation to assume the throne, that he could not legally nor morally allow his illegitimate nephew to be king. Richard had spoken little, taking care though to assure the delegation that he would pray upon the matter. He had undoubtedly been flattered, and this left him a little unnerved, disappointed in himself. All of these conflicting sensations had added to his confusion.

On 10th June, he had written to the City of York asking for their help. He requested that they send a force of men to his aid as he feared that plots against his person were afoot. He had considered whether or not to send the letter. It seemed something of an over-reaction, yet his fear was growing that the Woodvilles, those meeting to plot against him or some other adherent to his brother yet to be revealed would manage to organise an armed uprising, or worse, that two or more of these factions would join forces against a common enemy. Any support for Richard was several days march north of London and to await a revolt would leave him with no chance of reinforcement, nor of victory. At least if a force were mobilised soon and its march to London was underway it had some hope of reaching him in time to be of aid. Besides, if he ended up having no need of the men, he would lose nothing by having them close at hand, and they may act to deter any planned opposition.

Drumming on the table with growing agitation, he reflected that he had, in the past few days, been distant in his dealings with Anne. She did not deserve the treatment that he had meted out to her, though he had not given it deliberately. He had found himself confiding more and more in Buckingham and the two had spent much time discussing, exploring and revisiting Richard's options. He felt a little guilty at Anne's exclusion from these deliberations, for she had long been at the heart of all of Richard decision making. Henry consoled him by assuring him that, if anything, it was prove of his love for Anne. His reasoning was that Richard simply did not want Anne to see him uncertain on his course because it would upset and unsettle her. Perhaps it was true. Perhaps Richard knew it was too close to watching her father all of those years ago, but he still felt a gnawing in his mind that tried to convince him that he was wrong to remove Anne from the core of such a decisive moment in both of their lives.

It was true, though, that Richard remained confused as to what he should do. Having spent all of the past twelve years fighting, almost continuously, to keep his brother on the throne and to secure the future of both of his nephews as king and prince and that of his own son as chief subject, he now found all that he knew torn to pieces. Having believed that he was doing his duty all this time, he was now being told on many quarters that his duty was actually to deny his own nephew the succession. Yet more factions advised caution in the matter, and indeed he found the notion of abandoning those years of loyalty to his brother more than difficult. So entrenched was his sense of duty to Edward that it almost outweighed the evidence before him. What weighed most heavily upon his conscience was still the assertion of the Archbishops that under canon law he was required to take the throne. That God's law insisted that it be so. He lurched painfully between anger for his brother's lies and lack of faith in him and a staunch loyalty born of love and long service. He gritted his teeth as the conflict gripped him once more.

As it approached 9 o'clock, the appointed time, the door to the room where Richard sat opened and five men entered. Lord Stanley passed through the doorway first, striding to a chair at the opposite end of the table to Richard. Rotherham and Morton followed close behind, passing each side of Stanley and sitting, Rotherham to his left and Morton upon his right. Neither looked at Richard's staring, blank face as they took their seats. Finally, Lord Hastings entered with Buckingham behind. Hastings smiled at Richard as he sat on his right hand. The Protector did not return the greeting and noted the hint of nervous tension that tugged slightly at Hastings' smile. Buckingham was the last to take his seat in the silence.

Suddenly, as if snapping from a light sleep, Richard straightened in his chair, placed his palms flat on the tabletop and smiled as though a passing thought had amused him momentarily.

"Good morning, gentlemen." Richard's voice was as clear as the morning air.

"My lord." Hastings replied. The others muttered similar salutary responses.

"Thank you for attending this extraordinary Council meeting." Richard glanced at Buckingham, who sat staring at his own hands clasped tightly together on the table. His whitening knuckles gave away his attempts to suppress a smirk.

"I understand that a separate meeting is taking place as we speak at Westminster." Bishop Morton said with a frown. "Why should this be so, my lord?"

"Well," Richard smiled, drawing out the word as he reclined a little, "I have left them with some trivial matters to resolve, for we have some real meat to chew over this morning." He was pleased to see all of their eyes dart around the table at each other. "This group has very particular matters to discuss." He allowed the comment to hang in the air unexplained.

"What do you want of us, my lord?" Stanley's broad frame shifted in the chair, a forced, simpering smile barely veiling his disinterest.

"I find myself in need of the counsel of men such as yourselves on a matter of the utmost importance." Richard said ponderously.

"Then we are at your service." Lord Hastings croaked, his throat drying as his stomach began to churn. He looked around, but the other men did not seem at all unnerved by the situation, nor by Richard's words.

"Ah!" Richard said slowly. "I appear to have forgotten some papers to which I shall need to refer. Please, gentlemen, excuse me a short while." All of those gathered rose courteously as Richard stood. Straightening his crimson doublet, the Protector nodded at the men and swept purposefully from the room, the door closing with a heavy thud behind him. Buckingham now reclined in his seat, wrapping his fingers together across his rotund stomach. The other men sat in silence and Henry revelled in the fact that it was only his presence that held their tongues.

Richard descended the spiral staircase from the meeting room with a satisfied smile on his thin face. The men would surely be writhing within the chamber, but would be restrained by Buckingham's continued attendance. His planned absenting was supposed to last only a few minutes, long enough to reach his man John at the foot of the stairs. As the light crept wider, signalling that he was approaching the bottom, he jumped the final three steps and slid with a stony grating to a halt before the open doorway where John stood waiting. Another idea had just come to him.

"My lord." John swept low, his accent as broad as ever.

"My good man," Richard smiled, "what news from Westminster?"

"There is no opposition my lord." John's tone was steady and perfunctory.

"Good." Richard said, wrapping an arm around John and walking him away from the building. "Now," he began, "may I ask you to go to Lady Anne and request her presence in the gardens? There are things that I should say." He added the final sentence unnecessarily, and immediately wondered why. Perhaps the proximity of one he felt sure that he could trust had become a liberating rarity already.

"Of course, my lord." John replied, his face still straight and strong, unaltered by Richard's strange confidence. He jogged away along the gravel immediately. As the crunching of his footsteps faded, Richard meandered toward the gardens and leaned against a broad ash tree, staring at the branches, heavy with deep green leaves swaying in the breeze. The sun flickered through the moving shield creating a white haze in his eyes that seemed to penetrate to his mind. He could not guess how much time had passed before a familiar voice pulled him from his daydream.

"You sent for me?" Anne asked, and the wistful smile sank from Richard's lips as his gaze fell upon her sullen, unsmiling face. He jumped to attention.

"What have I done to you Anne?" he asked, full of concern.

"Does your question require an answer?" Anne retorted firmly, having no intention of providing him with one.

"No." Richard said, lowering his head and staring doe-eyed from behind his forehead at her. It was a look that always worked to soothe her. Well, so far, at least.

"Do not, Richard." She snapped.

"I have not been myself these last few days."

"I would not know, having barely seen you."

"Ouch!" Richard clasped his left hand to his heart as though wounded, grasping Anne's fingers with his right. He sank to one knee, feigning failing strength at the injury.

"Forgive me?" he asked plaintively. "I have need of your wisdom and level counsel."

"So you want me now and I am to jump as instructed?" She put the question to him with a raising tone that showed she was not yet placated.

"No, no." Richard quickly offered. "I am in the middle of a Council meeting but would apologise to you before I conclude matters there." Anne's face remained straight, as hard as granite. Richard suddenly realised the hurt that he must have caused her. He swept up her other hand as he stood upright again, the gesture of kneeling now seeming utterly inappropriate. He pressed both of her hands to his chest. "Anne, I am so sorry." At that word, Richard watched a broad smile spread over Anne's face.

"You had better be." She said softly.

"I am." Richard assured her, with no small feeling of relief.

"Richard," she said, pulling his hands to her chest now and holding his gaze tightly in her deep blue eyes. "I know that these last weeks have been difficult and the past few days impossible for you." She caught his eyes as he began to look down, as he always did, and forced him to maintain their eye contact. "You should not exclude me for my sake, my love. I am *always* here for you." She raised her right hand and slowly ran her fingers down Richard's pale, hollow cheek with a gentle softness that robbed Richard of any sense but the sight, scent and touch of his wife. "I have missed you." She said cocking her head slightly and using the smile that Richard knew hid the threat of a tear. He gently lifted her hand from his cheek and pressed her palm to his lips in a lingering kiss.

"I am in trouble, Anne." Richard said quietly as he drew her hands away. "I find myself unsure how to proceed."

"Tell me what the matter is." Anne said with a solidity that Richard found comforting. Little ever seemed to fluster her.

"The Church wants me to take the throne, the nobility are nervous of it, there are four men upstairs who have been meeting to plot against me and I do not know what I should do." He looked at her uneasily, an odd, uneven smile twisting his lips.

"That does not sound like you."

"Nor do I like the feeling." Richard confessed, sensing that uncomfortable twinge that he always experienced when telling Anne the things he would not tell another living soul outside of confession. She remained the only person he could ever expose his darkest doubts about himself to, but the rending open of his own weakness was still an awkward sensation he struggled to master even with Anne.

"Then an end must be put to it now." Sliding her arm through the space between Richard's arm and side, she tugged gently, encouraging him to walk with her. They began a slow, steady sidle along the path. "What," Anne asked thoughtfully, "do *you* want?"

"To do my duty." Richard answered without pause. "Yet for the first time I am unable to fathom what that is. Loyalty binds me is my chosen motto, but I no longer know where my loyalty lies to be bound by it"

"The voices around you are but noise and distraction." Anne said wistfully. "You must master them if you are to rule, as Protector, or as King. The men of the Church would have you as their king for your strength and pious devotion, a contrast to your brother's wayward tendencies. Perhaps they think this would grant them some measure of control over the Crown. Men of politics rarely display such conviction. They see a strong leader or a boy, a threat or a puppet, security or dangerous weakness, Plantagenet or Woodville, each with benefit, each with peril and they will always be reluctant to declare openly for one faction or the other. Such is the nature of politics." Anne looked across at Richard, who frowned a little as he took in her succinct summary. "You will find no answers in such quarters."

"You are, of course, correct." Richard mused, the corners of his mouth turning down as he realised it. "Then where are answers to be found?"

"I can offer you two thoughts." Anne stopped and stepped in front of Richard so that their eyes locked together again. "What is the highest authority to which you must answer?" Her tone was suddenly serious, full of meaning.

"The Lord God." Richard answered without delay. Anne nodded.

"Then be led by your conscience, for it is the voice of the Holy Spirit that speaks softly to each us. All we must do is quieten the noise of the world to hear it. If you were stood before God on the day of judgement what would He say that you should have done? What does His law require?"

"God's law is clear. I should be king." Richard replied flatly.

"Then that must be your answer." Anne smiled, holding her husband's eyes. "All other considerations should hold no sway in the end." There was a long silence and Anne watched Richard's face twist through the notion. She knew familial loyalty would be a difficult thing for Richard to bypass. Finally, his face settled into an expression of acceptance.

"You make a good point, my dear," he said eventually. "It would seem that I have over thought matters, where you see them so clearly."

"It is the place of a wife to guide her husband to the correct decision." Anne told him playfully. "I have simply allowed you to know that I was doing it this time." Richard laughed, but then frowned suddenly.

"You spoke of two thoughts. Will the second lead to the same answer or am I to be confused once more?" The duke smiled through his look of mock bewilderment.

"The second is more conclusive still." Anne informed him, her tone steady, calm yet firm. "Your decision was made the moment that you placed Bishop Stillington before Parliament. Had you not believed that you should take the throne, you would not have made public evidence that would make you the only legitimate heir." There was a long pause as the two stared at each other. Anne's bright eyes pushed her point home and she watched as a fleeting moment of objection crossed her husband's face before he bit the corner of his bottom lip and lowered his eyes. Anne knew the expression well. Richard looked like a naughty child caught at mischief.

"You think I acted too swiftly." Richard stated as though expecting to be chastised.

"No." Anne answered immediately. "Our first conclusion proves that the decision was the right one. Dealing with such matters quickly and decisively was your commitment before we arrived here and it is serving you well."

"Well," Richard's chest heaved with a weighty sigh, "I have use of it again now." He looked up to the Tower where five men awaited his return. This could prove to be another defining decision.

"Is your mind set?" Anne asked.

"I know what I should like to do." A wicked smile curled his lips and his eyes flashed with mischief again. "I am sure though that it should be tempered." His look unmistakably asked Anne's advice. She nodded, prompting him to continue.

"Hastings, Stanley, Morton and Rotherham plot against me. Or, at least, they plot and I fear that it is against me." Richard told her, a sombre tone driving out any notion of playfulness.

"What is it that you would like to do?" Anne asked.

"Have them all executed for treason." Richard spat and he felt a burning sensation rising in his chest.

"Why do you feel that you must temper such justice?" The question surprised Richard a little.

"In the case of Morton and Rotherham I should need papal dispensation which would take time and appear desperate." Richard gnawed at his bottom lip again.

"What of Stanley and Hastings?" Anne asked, leading her husband's thoughts. Richard pondered the question a moment.

"Stanley," he began thoughtfully, "is a man at the head of a mighty family. There is history between us in the north and I have no love for the man." He tilted his head, weighing his own argument. "His retinue is largely a fair distance from London," his head lolled the other way, "but if it descended in anger it would prove awkward. The Stanleys would make for bad enemies."

"And Hastings?" Anne asked, moving him along toward his conclusion.

"Hastings is a self made man." Richard eyed Anne darkly. "He has neither root nor branch to be concerned with. There is a small force of men loyal to him, but they are contained within London and should be easily dispersed."

"Is your decision made?" Anne asked him with a solid, matter of fact tone.

"If any must be punished, it must be Hastings," he replied, but the heat of his anger had cooled quickly and he wondered whether he needed to be so drastic. Anne's face was as though carved in stone. "Tell me what you think," he pleaded.

"You must set an example, Richard." Anne told him firmly. "If you are to be king, you cannot tolerate dissent at this stage. If you do, it shall surely be viewed by all as weakness and taken by rebels and falterers alike as encouragement. If Hastings is the easiest to make an example of, then he must be your primary conspirator and must take the brunt of your fury." Her voice rose as she spoke on. "Play it well and this moment will serve you for years to come. Unleash your vengeful wrath upon them."

Richard clenched his teeth hard. She was, of course, entirely correct in her unnervingly frank and ruthless analysis of the situation and now the Protector allowed his rage to boil within him, stoked by the vision of the four laughing faces around a table mocking him and plotting his downfall. How dare they?

Charged by his wife's incitement and stung by his erupting temper, Richard held his jaw so tightly shut that it began to ache, gave a sharp nod of farewell to Anne, for he dare not speak now lest it dampen his hot resolve. He span on his heels and marched like a well drilled soldier across the battlefield to meet an enemy.

Anne watched him leave, his lifted shoulders betraying his tension. She held her breath, hoping that she had counselled him correctly, that Richard would do right, that this moment would define rather than destroy her husband, and their life. 'You thought that you could do a better job than your brother.' Anne thought after him. 'I believe in you too. Now prove it to everyone else.' She looked at the ground, hoping that this course was the right one, before she slowly strolled back toward Baynards.

"What is happening?" Stanley demanded of the air angrily, slapping his palm on the table. Only Buckingham also remained seated, his arms folded, the look on his face convincing Stanley that he knew more than they did. It was an uncomfortable feeling, but he grew more concerned that this discomfort was the very intention. The other three men all stood, Hastings and Rotherham pacing different flagstones anxiously whilst Bishop Morton simply gazed out of the high, narrow window at the wispy clouds drifting through the pale blue summer sky. He seemed lost in some waking dream, or else was immersed in a silent prayer. Stanley's gruff voice and the resounding slap of his hand broke nearly half an hour of silence.

All of the men had wondered the same, including Buckingham as the minutes passed. The Protector had left the room nearly an hour ago. Polite chat had not lasted long and a mixture of irritation and growing concern nibbled at four of the men present.

"I dare say that some matter of great importance keeps him." Buckingham told them without looking at anyone in particular. His own concern was growing. Richard was only meant to have left for a moment to check on news from the other meeting. That he had not returned yet led the duke to fear that all was not well. Had Richard been forced to personally visit the meeting to push things through? Still, he would not allow the conspirators to see his unease and retained his expression of knowledgeable confidence.

"He shall have to learn," Morton began with the tone of a sympathetic teacher, "what is truly important quickly now." He turned his gaze from the window to Buckingham. "Where he should spend his time," the Bishop's face was hard, though his voice remained soft, "and where he cannot afford to squander it." Slowly, he returned his eyes to the window. The duke's brow crumpled without his willing it at the cryptic words. Had Richard allowed the astute Bishop the time to work out what was happening? There was another long moment of silence before a whining creak drew all eyes to the doorway.

Richard's chest heaved and he felt each prolonged, thudding beat of his heart. He was unsure whether the pace of his climb up the tower or the swirling storm of his fury caused it, but he inhaled deeply, pulling the feeling into his core to fuel the fire of his anger. He felt a thin smile stretch his lips. It felt a little sinister, but he couldn't help enjoying the thick tension in the atmosphere as he entered the room. All faces pointed toward him with confused, lost expressions. Even Buckingham. Perfect.

Striding across the room to his chair, Richard soaked up the moment. Sitting, he waited for the other men to cautiously resume their seats. He looked slowly around the table at the anticipation, tempered by annoyance, that was plain on each face.

"You seem to have forgotten your papers again, my lord." Bishop Morton observed calmly. Stanley, Hastings and Rotherham looked sharply at the empty table before the duke, where his palms spread out to emphasise the absence of the papers that he had left the room to retrieve.

"I have all that I require now, gentlemen." Richard assured them. He fixed Buckingham's gaze a moment as if sending him a silent message. The faintest nod acknowledged the signal. "The issue before us today is a simple one. What should be done with a group of traitors who plot against my life?"

"They should be executed immediately as an example." Hastings blurted the words out as if releasing waves of built up tension. Indeed, he had been clambering into something of a panic as time had gone by. Perhaps there was no need after all. It appeared that the remainder of the Council met elsewhere because Richard suspected a traitor amongst them. Having been Edward's closest and most trusted advisor at Court, it would make sense for Richard to trust him in this matter. His shoulders lowered as he eased himself back into his chair. "Now is the time for strength and the building of a firm foundation." As his fingertips met in front of his chin, a chilling thought flashed across his mind.

Richard looked around the table once more. Rotherham and Stanley nodded their approval. Buckingham's face unsurprisingly betrayed his desire to smirk. Morton, though, stared directly at Richard, no expression plain on his face, his head almost imperceptibly but unmistakably shaking slowly as the two held each other's stern gaze.

"So be it." Richard muttered darkly. He rose slowly, his eyes burning into Morton's hard, blank face. Bent over the long, dark table, Richard suddenly smashed his tightened fist onto the surface of the wood with an echoing thud that caused all but Morton to jolt in their seats.

"Guards!" Richard bellowed with a gurgling ferocity that seemed impossible from a man of his size. A shocked confusion washed through the room. "Guards!" Richard called again. "Treason. I am betrayed!" Stanley, Hastings and Rotherham leapt to their feet bemused. Buckingham chuckled uncontrollably. Morton remained in his seat, staring sternly at Richard. Before any of the men could protest, the door was flung open and a dozen of the Tower guards thundered and clattered to surround the table and block the doorway.

"My lord?" Hastings exclaimed questioningly.

"Do not presume me a fool without knowledge of the scheming of those surrounding me." Richard spat the words loudly at the protestor.

"You are mistaken, Richard." Hastings whimpered pleadingly.

"I am not!" Richard shrieked angrily, his whitening fist pounding the thick oak once more. "I have all of the evidence that I require." He forced his shrill tone lower as he addressed the silent guards. "Arrest them." He waved a sweeping arm across the room.

"Richard, I," Hastings began, but could not finish. The Protector flushed bright red as rage overtook him.

"How dare you address me in the familiar." He strode around the table, his swelling chest aimed squarely at the retreating, cowering figure of Hastings. "You who were so much a part of my brother's debauchery, who encouraged the wanton vices of his Court." As he closed menacingly on Hastings, the others watched on motionless. Even Buckingham's laughter had ceased. "You shall have your very own choice of justice." Richard growled through clenched teeth, his nose within a hair's breadth of the other's, his hot, panting breath flooding Hasting's face. It took a moment before the realisation crashed into Hastings.

"I, I ...," he stammered, lost in the moment.

"You have no defence?" Richard hissed menacingly.

"My lord, please." Hastings was almost crying, his eyes shimmered, his cheeks burned and his lips trembled uncontrollably as he tried to absorb what was happening to him. Why had Richard taken against him so? He had only ever been a faithful friend to Edward. And plotting against Richard? Slowly, achingly, like the gradual spread of dawn's first light, a thread in his memory was pulled and a picture began to form in his mind of himself and the three others present. They were sat at a different table, laughing, and they were discussing keeping the new Protector in check. Was this what had found its way to Richard's ears? He felt an acid burning in his throat. "No." He shook his head. His voice quivered. "No."

"You are pathetic." Richard hissed into Hastings' ear. "Perhaps I shall have this done with right away." As he leaned back, Richard sneered as the other shook his head solemnly, unable any longer to prevent tears from rolling from his eyes, his breath escaping from him in spluttering bursts.

"Take them away." Richard told the guards with a wave. "Lord Hastings is to be executed." With a final, momentary gaze deep into Hastings' glazed eyes, Richard turned and marched from the room, leaving the rumbling commotion behind him.

Chapter 27

26th June 1483 – Destiny Settled

Baynards Castle was flooded with the pale, reaching rays of the breaking day's light. Each piece of furniture cast a long, densely black shadow against the floor and wall behind it. Richard strode along the open corridor that looked out upon the twinkling water of the River Thames, gazing absently at the ripples lapping the bank. Buckingham, whose joviality and pride had grown in equal measure as events had gathered pace, bounced along just behind Richard. On the very edge of his attention, he heard Buckingham remonstrating with someone that Richard had no time to hear "the bleating of some lamb-less ewe today of all days". He could not help but smile as he heard the duke's sleeve material swishing through the warming air and pictured some absurdly flamboyant arm waving. In essence, though, Henry was correct. Much rested on the outcome of this day's events and Richard had tried to assure himself that he had prepared as carefully as was possible.

It had been almost two weeks since Richard had taken control of his circumstances at the council meeting and since then he had stoked a determination to retain that momentum. Only three days later, on 16th June, he had arranged for Prince Richard to be removed from his mother's possession in sanctuary at Westminster. The fact that his young nephew had been forcibly taken had offended Richard and he had not been keen to violate the Church's sanctuary laws, yet he felt little choice had remained when Queen Elizabeth had refused the Protector's request for her sons to be reunited under his protection. Edward was melancholic and asked repeatedly after his mother, brother and uncle. Richard could hardly afford to send the boy back to Elizabeth to spearhead her attempts to regain power. Rivers was no longer an option either. Edward would surely be cheered by his younger brother's presence and the boy's removal from Elizabeth's grasp would aid in both holding her back from open rebellion and from controlling a potential figurehead should she become desperate enough to shift focus from Edward. Still, the need for it had not lessened Richard's dislike of it. At least, he consoled himself, Edward did seem a little buoyed by the familiar company of his brother.

By 22nd June, events had begun to gather pace. Dr Ralph Shea gave an address at St Paul's Cross to a group of Londoners detailing in plain terms the charges of illegitimacy levelled against the Princes. This exercise had largely served to test the waters, to gauge the public's reaction to Richard's intentions. His brother had been a reasonably popular king and there was a danger that the Protector would be viewed as the evil uncle usurping the throne of a young innocent. That was something Richard wished to avoid at all costs. However, the address had been received better than Richard had dared to hope. The charges had been greeted with shock, but had been quite readily accepted and when Dr Shea proceeded to advance Richard as the only legitimate heir and rightful king, the crowd had cheered and applauded. The news of this had lifted Richard's heart and allayed his fears that he was too unpopular in the south to be embraced as their king. It had given him cause, and momentum, to continue.

Two days later, Buckingham had spoken at the Guildhall before the Lord Mayor and aldermen of the City of London. This address, too, had been well received and offered Richard the support of the more middle class portion of London. The work had been completed the following day when Parliament had gathered. It had been called to recognise Prince Edward as king but instead was presented with the evidence, written and oral, of his illegitimacy. With surprisingly little obstacle, Edward was formally declared illegitimate and Richard was proclaimed the legal heir to the throne of England. In the end, it had all fallen into place so easily.

As he walked the corridor, Richard reflected on the one thing that had caused him some discomfort in the midst of the positive events of the last few days. It had come as something of a surprise. Richard had given orders that Rivers, Grey and Vaughn be executed, following a trial which would find them guilty on charges of treason. This was hardly unexpected, evidently not least by Earl Rivers who had written a new will a few days earlier. In itself, this was no news. However, Rivers had named Richard as the executor of his new will. This step had vexed Richard greatly, in the main because he could not with any certainty fathom the reason behind it. Anne had told him that it was clear that Rivers was able to see beyond the current circumstances to recognise Richard's probity and to trust in his justice. It was true that three months earlier Rivers had submitted a property dispute to Richard's judgment. Although he had been warmed by the notion, Richard sought some deeper purpose. Was Rivers conceding that he had deserved his punishment? Did he believe that Richard would seize all of his property anyway? Despite his searching for some hidden meaning, he had been forced to accept that Rivers simply had faith in Richard's sense of duty and honour. This act had muddled Richard's feelings. Rivers had long been his deeply respected nemesis. Richard hated the fact that they were so alike, yet saw in Rivers all of the things that he would have others see in him. This final act of respect and, Richard was forced to concede, friendship, had caused him a twisting knot of guilt, even regret, though he would not allow this to take away from the need that it be done.

Buckingham tugged Richard from his wisps of thought. They had reached the end of the corridor and Richard turned, noticing that the man to whom Buckingham had been talking was disappearing in the opposite direction at a nervous scurry.

"They are awaiting you." Buckingham told him, smiling expectantly, brimming with the events of the last few days and with the expectation of those to come. "Are you ready?"

"Of course." Richard smiled softly, hoping that he was not betraying the uncomfortable unease that he was feeling. After so much preparation, today was to finally settle matters.

"Then to it, Richard." Henry clapped him on his shoulder. "To your destiny." A lump swelled in Richard's throat. He fought to ignore it as Buckingham pushed the large wooden doors open to reveal the hall of Baynards Castle.

Inside, some fifty or so citizens of the City of London stood in a rough group in the centre of the room. As Richard entered an instant silence fell heavily in the room. All eyes were upon him. With a managed confidence, Richard strode across the hall until he stood before the delegation. Henry stood at his right shoulder, rocking on his heels. Richard's irritable glance at the duke's feet settled him immediately, and he straightened himself. After a moment, a man who appeared to be in his forties, and whose swelling waist suggested some affluence, stepped out of the ranks, proffering a large parchment scroll which he balanced on his pudgy open palms and regarded with a reverential fear, as though he expected it at any moment to erupt into flames. His relief was tangible as Buckingham strode forward to take the document, allowing the man to melt back into the crowd.

Richard took a long, slow, deep breath as Henry broke the seal with a crack, followed by a rustling as he began to unfurl the Rolle. Although fully aware of its contents, he found himself holding his breath without intending to as Buckingham began to read aloud the carefully prepared document. He barely listened to the words of Buckingham's shrill voice as his mind raced again over the events of recent weeks and then gathered pace through today before leaping headlong into the future that spread before him, his wife and his son. Today would open a door. He had to be sure that he wanted to pass through it. After this, it would be too late for regrets.

He shot a brief glance at the gallery above the far end of the hall, behind the gathered citizens and saw Anne, her dark hair tied back, her beauty glowing across the distance like the sun, her ruby red dress adding to the warming feeling that grew in his stomach. He could not help a faint smile from stroking over his lips at the thought of making his love, his queen, *the* queen. She stood perfectly still, her hands resting on each other in front of her stomach. Still she could fill him with the most childlike awe. His eyes met hers briefly and he felt a crackling shiver run the length of his spine. She smiled softly and the shock hit his stomach. Slowly, his eyes drifted to Anne's right, where his mother stood.

Henry had reached the most controversial portion of the Rolle, the part that Richard had found the hardest to include. As Richard's eyes met those of his mother, he heard the words they had used to criticize his own brother's time as king. Henry's voice rang through the room as he proclaimed that "... the order of all politic rule was perverted, and the land ruled by self will and pleasure, fear and dread, all manner of Equity and laws laid apart and despised." Eyes still locked together, Richard could read nothing from his mother's expression. He searched for some sign of displeasure or disapproval, but could discern nothing through her polished dignity. Buckingham continued to read. "The land was governed by those delighting in adulation and flattery and led by sensuality and concupiscence who followed the counsel of persons insolent, vicious and of inordinate avarice." Richard had allowed these accusations to be included only after tempering the original language Buckingham had suggested so that it reflected only his own conviction that the later years of Edward's reign had seen him allow himself to be ruled, even overrun, by self interested sinners.

Then, finally, refusing to withdraw his gaze lest it appeared to be from shame, he saw a gentle, almost imperceptible forward tilt of Lady Cecily's head that was clearly meant for him only. He took it as consent, forced himself to hold her stare a moment longer, and then returned his focus to those gathered before him.

Buckingham had finished reading. There was a pause and then a tall, lean man dressed in black took an almost ridiculously long stride from the crowd, straightened himself and cleared his throat.

"My lord." His voice was deep but betrayed a nervousness drawn out of him by the circumstance in which he found himself. Richard smiled and nodded encouragingly. "The citizens of London and of England petition you to assume your God given position upon the throne as the only correct and legitimate ruler of this land." The man shuffled his feet uncomfortably. "My lord," he stood rigidly straight, arms locked to his sides, "will you take up our plea?"

Silence fell heavily upon the hall. Richard felt the weight of a hundred eyes focussed on him, burrowing into him. All that he could hear was the slow, steady sound of his own breathing. He felt as though his body was rocking to the rhythmical pounding of his heart. This was it. Time to define his life. He would not answer immediately lest it appeared a rushed, ill considered decision, or he should seem improperly keen. That would be most unseemly following the accusations just levelled against his brother, the man he had served loyally for all of his adult life. He knew also that there would be a moment beyond which those gathered would have their anticipation dissolved by an uneasy concern at petitioning one so indecisive to lead the country, particularly when he was renowned for his firm action rather than prolonged ponderings. Suddenly, he felt it.

"I shall do my duty." He spoke slowly, his voice deep and even. "I am deeply honoured that our Lord God should appoint me this office and that the loyal people of England should so desire that I occupy it. As you have shown such strength and loyalty in asking this of me, so shall I show strength in protecting every person in this land from any danger, be it from within these shores or beyond them. I swear now loyalty, to the Lord God, to the office and purpose of the Crown and to every one of you." He paused, sweeping both of his arms out into a wide embrace and casting his eyes across the faces pleasingly transfixed by his words. "I vow to you now that for as long as I have your loyalty, that you shall have mine, complete, devout and resolute as it is."

Almost immediately the room erupted with clapping, cheering and calling that echoed and reverberated around the stone walls so that it felt as though a thousand voices had been raised up. Richard felt his chest swell with pride whilst at the same time the responsibility that he felt so ready for began to tighten the muscles of his stomach. Had he been naive? Now was the time when he would have to deliver all that he believed he was capable of delivering.

Something caught Richard's ear at that moment that hit him like a mace to the chest. He wasn't sure at first, but like fire through dry straw, the words spread until they became a chant, unmistakable, clearly ringing out around the hall. He could not help but smile.

"God save King Richard!"

Chapter 28

6th July 1483 - Coronation

The bright, clear Sunday morning sun draped itself gently over the carriage as it slowed to a halt before Westminster Abbey. Crowds lined the streets of London in all directions, clapping and cheering. Children scurried around the knees of men and women to get a better view, or else to relieve them of an unwisely visible purse. Shouts of support and congratulation rang out alongside the pealing bells of the Abbey that announced the coronation of England's new king.

"The Lord shines upon you today, sire." Anne leaned in gently to her husband and smiled softly at him.

"Indeed he does smile upon *us*." Richard stressed the final word deliberately as his eyes met Anne's. The clattering of hoof and wheel ceased and the two broke their bound gazes as the carriage door was opened for them.

Richard stepped down barefoot, as custom demanded, from their transport and waited for his wife, soon to be his queen, to stand by his side. He felt the warmth of the sun soaking into him. Inhaling deeply, he absorbed the moment, allowing it to penetrate every portion of his being. They stood side by side for a moment, as if frozen, held for eternity in a perfect instant. Richard thought that he would be happy there, in that moment, forever. Had he known it, Anne was beside him thinking exactly the same thing. He wriggled the toes of his bare feet against the cool stone floor.

Together, they stepped slowly, rhythmically toward the Abbey and as they passed through its immense carved oak doors, flung open before them, the formal ceremonial rites began to gather around them in perfect synchronicity. Henry Stafford, Duke of Buckingham, carried Richard's train and also bore the staff of the Lord High Steward with an undisguised pride. John Howard, Duke of Norfolk, had the honour of carrying Richard's crown, perched in shining splendour atop a sumptuous red velvet cushion that enveloped his forearms. The blunt Sword of Mercy rested in the arms of the Earl of Northumberland, Henry Percy and the Constable's mace was carried by Lord Stanley. As a further act of reconciliation Anne had selected Lady Stanley to bear her train. Even Richard's nephews had joined the throng.

As the procession passed along the aisle of the Abbey, Richard looked around at the gathered aristocracy and felt awe at the moment. Not only was all of the nation's nobility gathered here, to witness his coronation and to accept him as their king, but for the first time in his memory, he saw members of the House of York together with those of the House of Lancaster, apparently united behind one figurehead at last. His dream of ending this unhealthy civil warring was moving closer with each barefooted step toward the altar. There would be no more need for strife and rivalry. The corners of his mouth twitched slightly with the hint of a wry smile as he passed a bishop who he recognised as a Woodville relative of Elizabeth's. Even they would be reconciled, willingly or no. He refocused upon the altar, set in the awe inspiring Abbey and its lavish decorations. Excitement mingled with nervous tension and caused a gripping sensation in his stomach.

Cardinal Bourchier smiled as Richard and Anne reached the steps before the altar and knelt. The Abbey fell silent. To each of the oaths asked of him by the Cardinal, Richard gave his well rehearsed response. He would protect his people, his nation, its laws, and he would do so under the gaze of the Lord God and His Holy Roman Church. All of this he swore solemnly and with all of his heart.

With the oaths made, he and Anne were stripped of their gowns and outer garments. Cardinal Bourchier then anointed them both with holy oil and they were redressed in splendid, shimmering cloth of gold. When all of this was completed, the

Cardinal placed the crown upon Richard's head. He closed his eyes and felt its weight settle upon him as Anne's crown was lowered gently onto her head. He opened his eyes again, as King of England, to the booming, echoing tones of the Abbey's great organs resounding in every corner of the building. Richard allowed himself a wandering thought; 'The real work of my life begins now.'

It was several hours later before Richard and Anne sat in the throne room of the Palace of Westminster, alone for the first moment in days at Richard's instruction. They sat upon their mighty seats, imposed upon the empty room, and gazed at each other. It had taken over an hour to extricate themselves from Westminster Abbey amid frantic congratulations from every peer of the realm, each of whom wished to bow to the new king and queen and wish them the longest and most successful reign. Each of whom, Richard also knew, wanted to press some claim, push for some advantage or jostle for position or smooth the settlement of some personal score. He and Anne had struggled under the weight of their crowns and regalia to offer thanks to each of those that wished them well before making the slow journey by carriage to the Palace through a mass of humanity that seemed to have no end. Richard wondered if all of England lined the streets of London. The noise of the cheering threatened to deafen them and caused the horses to snort nervously.

Wearily, Richard allowed his hand to slip onto Anne's beside him in the throne room. It was the sort of movement made of comfortable long use, without the mind having to will it. It was late afternoon and the day was beginning to ebb his energies, but this motion required no effort. Anne smiled softly at his touch and then he saw something flash across her face, gone almost before it was there. Nothing to anyone but him.

"What is it, my queen?" The words felt strangely comfortable, right.

"You know me too well, my king." Anne dropped her gaze and did not see Richard's smile, both at her words and at his new title. He felt his passion stirring against his weary body as she raised her gaze again.

"Tell me your desire, my love." Richard stared deeply into her eyes with an intensity that always made her cheeks flush with warm blood.

"It can wait, Richard." She spoke softly, like a mother tucking in a sleepy child.

"It can, but it will not." Richard replied, more sharply than he had meant. "It is clear," he continued, evening his tone deliberately, "that something is on your mind and that you wish to give it voice." He took a deep breath. "So please," he gestured broadly, opening his arms into the empty chamber, "give it freedom."

"Very well." Anne hesitated at her husband's tone. He was clearly tired and would be in no mood for what she had to ask of him. Yet experience had taught her that Richard's temper was at its worst when caged, pent up. She saw this building in him now, though he was trying to disguise it. When released, his temper burned hot and quickly. A brief loss of himself and then his mind was calmed. This, she had learned, was the best way to deal with him.

"So?" Richard asked a little impatiently.

"I would like you to hear one petition today, your first as king." She waited for his response. He rose from his throne and strode down the broad stone steps to the flagstones of the chamber, his steps echoing in the cavernous emptiness.

"Why?" Richard chewed his lip.

"Because I am asking it of you." Anne replied evenly. She watched Richard pace back and forth, shooting her sharp glances every few steps. "Please, Richard." She smiled and the king felt her words wash over him like a cooling breeze in the heat of summer. He stood still and looked up at Anne.

"How can I refuse?" he smiled. "Who would you have me hear?" He skipped back up the steps, his previous weariness seemingly evaporated, and retook his seat.

"Lady Stanley, who bore my train today, wishes to ask something of you." Anne told the king in a business-like manner. "She became so distressed in the retelling of her tale that I am afraid that I was moved to promise her that I would ask this of you today." Richard glanced at her, frowning. "Yes," Anne's eyes flashed with a mischievous smile, "I know. I shall insert various riotous comments about women, emotions and business." Richard laughed aloud and sighed.

"I was going to say no such thing, my love," he grinned. "Let us hear your Lady Stanley." He was already wary. Lord Stanley's wife.

"Thank you, Richard." Anne rose.

"I have agreed to nothing she asks for yet." Richard replied cautiously.

"I know." Anne answered as she moved down the steps. "I thank you for allowing me to keep my word, and my honour, in spite of your tiredness and my poor timing."

"You are welcome." Richard called after her as she made for the side entrance to the hall. His voice was light again, but his mind was beginning to work.

Anne pushed open the door and beckoned beyond it before turning and striding back toward her husband. A moment later a short woman stepped through the doorway. She was older than Richard and Anne but held herself at her full height and walked with the confident ease of one used to such surroundings and proceedings. Her dark hair was tied tightly back and showed the beginnings of greyness. Her face betrayed a far from carefree life in its many lines. Despite this, Richard noted that she retained her noble bearing. She reminded him in no small measure of his own mother.

Anne stepped up to stand before Richard and, taking his hand, knelt before him.

"Forgive me, Richard." She whispered so quietly that he barely heard the words. He leaned closer to her for she clearly did not wish to be heard by Lady Stanley. "I have been able to do that which my heart tells me is right as a mother by assisting Lady Stanley and also that which my duty as queen requires by bringing the matter before you for your ruling. I fear that you shall not have the same luxury as both a father and a king." She rose and sat beside Richard again, leaving him somewhat confused and concerned. At that moment, Lady Stanley halted a few paces beyond the bottom step.

"Your majesty." She curtsied low and Richard nodded to acknowledge the respectful greeting. "Thank you for agreeing to hear me, today of all days." Her voice was deep and melodic, not the harsh, shrill voice that Richard had expected.

"You have the queen to thank for that, Lady Stanley," he replied coldly, trying to sound like a king. He squinted at the lady before him. There was something familiar about her that he could not place. Perhaps it was simply the long day taking its toll.

"Of course." Lady Stanley turned to Anne. "Thank you also, your highness." Richard turned to see Anne looking deeply uncomfortable at the situation.

"What would you ask of me, Lady Stanley?" Richard regained the attention in order to spare Anne.

"Sire," Lady Stanley's voice rolled gently around the walls, "you may be aware that my son, Henry, has been living in exile these last many years." She lowered her head. Richard noted that this fact clearly pained her. Or at least she wished Richard to believe that it did. "He has committed no crime and I beg you to allow him to return to me now, so that he may join us all in celebrating the peace that you are bringing." She bowed her head again to signal that she had finished speaking. Richard remained silent for a long moment, until her eyes flicked up to him, as if checking that he had not vanished. He had seen his brother employ this tactic on numerous occasions, telling Richard that it always served to remind people who was in control and to keep them feeling uncomfortable. Richard smiled as it appeared to work for him now.

"If your son committed no crime," Richard raised his hands, palms upturned, "why is he in exile?"

"An accident of birth, your highness, and of association. His family connections were to your late brother's enemies." Her gaze met Richard's and he saw great resolve and determination in her face. There was also that nagging feeling of recognition again.

"Have we met before, Lady Stanley?" he asked her directly as though he had not heard her reply.

"I," she began slowly, clearly a little unsure of the line of questioning, "was at your coronation today, your grace."

"Yes, yes." Richard waved a hand dismissively. "I mean before that. Some time ago, perhaps."

"I have been at court for some years, your majesty, so it is possible that..."

"Ah, I can place you now!" Richard leapt to his feet in glee. "I saw you leaving Edward's office some years ago when I visited him and my sister, did I not."

"You may well have done, your highness." Lady Stanley straightened her back, clearly uncomfortable.

"Do I assume that you petitioned my brother for your son's return also?" Richard sat again, but on the edge of his throne, leaning forward.

"Yes, your majesty." Lady Stanley replied, holding his gaze steadily.

"Do I also assume that your petitions were unsuccessful?"

"Yes, your highness. Your brother never really took this matter very seriously."

"So several petitions failed?" Richard grinned, feeling pleased as he picked at Lady Stanley's request.

"Yes, your highness." Lady Stanley reported stiffly.

"I see." Richard reclined casually. "So if my brother kept your son in exile, and your son never posed a threat to him from that exile, why should I now seek to reverse this policy?"

"In order to assist in healing the old wounds." Lady Stanley had clearly anticipated this line of questioning, or else had heard it before from Edward. "To demonstrate that you are merciful as you are strong, and to distance yourself from one of the policies of the previous administration, an administration that you have been roundly condemning."

"Good points." Richard conceded tapping his finger on his chin in thought. "Although you must also view this from my perspective."

"Your majesty?" Lady Stanley queried.

"Well, you see the healing of old wounds. Perhaps. But perhaps it would prove a maggoty stick prodded into those wounds as yet unhealed and causing them to fester further." Richard sat upright. "You say to demonstrate that I am merciful. I say that it may appear that I am weak and easily swayed." Now, he sat forward in his seat again. His voice began to rise, though he did not shout. "You would have me distance myself from the old regime, but by discarding one of their policies that was an absolute and unmitigated success." Richard rose and descended the steps to stand face to face with Lady Stanley. "If you were in my position," he motioned to the now empty throne, "would you allow a potential threat to return to the fold on the very day of your coronation?"

"I..."

"Would you," Richard interrupted, "allow a viper into your bed before you had slept in it even one night?" The two stared at each other for a long moment. "You have my sympathy for the distance between yourself and your son, my lady, truly you do." Richard spoke quietly now, his face full of sincerity. "But I cannot risk this threat to the security of the realm at this early stage. Perhaps, in time..."

"But your highness, I..." Lady Stanley interrupted, emotion spilling into her tone now.

"Lady Stanley," Richard snapped, waving away her words, "I have made my decision. Now, if you please, it has been a long day and I am tired, so..."

"Your grace," Lady Stanley said shakily, tears bulging in her eyes and threatening to escape, "you have my word that Henry will never pose any threat to you if you allow his return." Anne winced in her seat. This would be an interruption too far for Richard.

"Enough!" Richard boomed, and Anne saw Lady Stanley physically jump at the word. Then Richard spoke, almost at a whisper, his face beside hers so that he was speaking directly into her left ear. "Your word?" Richard hissed. "Your word?" he repeated. "Like soft petals your words fall from your lips, a sweet scent trailing them on the breeze." Richard gritted his teeth, almost snarling now. "Until the wind changes and the petals are scattered and the sweet scent replaced with the stench of betrayal. I have seen it often enough before, madam, and I see it here. Whatever you and your traitorous husband are conspiring ceases now." He pulled away slowly and met her eyes again, speaking slightly louder now. "If you wish to be reunited with your son on English soil then time and patience are your only allies. Is that clear?"

"Perfectly, your majesty." Lady Stanley stood her ground, Richard's breath hot in her face and she managed to regain control of her tone. She found herself wishing that she held a knife in her hand. The smallest of movements and she could bury it in Richard's cold heart. The king withdrew and turned, climbing the steps again with heavy legs.

"Now, please, leave us Lady Stanley." He motioned toward the door without facing her.

"Yes, your highness." Lady Stanley responded. "Thank you for taking the time to see me." Her voice was straining to remain even. Richard waved a vague gesture of acknowledgment. "As you suggest, I shall be patient, and I shall await my time."

The slight change in tone of the final few words caused Richard to pause at the top step, but as he slowly turned and sat, Lady Stanley was already walking toward the door purposefully. There was a resounding thud as it closed behind her.

"I am sorry." Anne eventually said softly.

"I should have preferred not to have dealt with that today." Richard said. "Do you disapprove that I have chosen my duty as king above my father's heart?"

"For what it is worth," Anne placed her hand on his, "I believe that you have done the right thing. I do not believe that you had any choice."

"How often is today's correct decision tomorrow's folly?" Richard asked absently. "No mind. At least today is over."

Chapter 29

Taking a Breath

Sir Thomas More stopped speaking and gazed into the fire as if awaiting a response from the leaping flames. Holbein fancied that his host may be trying to interpret or translate the crackling, spitting voice of the fire. Hans reached for his tankard and took a long draught of the cooling liquid. Although he hadn't spoken a word, his mouth was dry, perhaps from the dry heat of the room, or from the tantalising tale Sir Thomas was weaving for him. He found himself wrapped by the story. Though much of the fact, the chronology, was common knowledge, he was intrigued. He even found that he was liking those personalities traditionally considered to be despicable.

"So," Sir Thomas said slowly, turning to look at Holbein, "Richard is king," he smiled softly. "Here, as always," he raised a finger instructively, "interpretation is everything." Holbein frowned, and Sir Thomas needed no further encouragement to expand upon his meaning. "A man nobly performing his duty?" He raised a hand, and continued as he raised the other. "A victim of circumstance?" With both palms raised, he pulled up his shoulders too. "A fool rushing in where the angels would take care?" Sir Thomas paused, his eyes flashing in the firelight, clearly enjoying tantalising his guest. He sank back into his chair again. "Perhaps a scheming maleficent who saw, and seized, his opportunity for power?"

Holbein's mouth opened and closed like a landed fish as he sought a response.

"We can never know." Sir Thomas interjected. "The truth of this is lost to us. All that we are able to do is to apply our interpretation to the events and, after all, each person's interpretation will be personal to them. Each of us will see light and dark in different degrees in the same situation."

"What would be your interpretation, Sir Thomas?" Holbein enquired with genuine interest.

"My interpretation would be," Sir Thomas straightened in his chair, leaned forward slightly and opened his right palm before him, "meaningless." He saw the deflated anticipation draining from Holbein's face. "I am simply here to tell you a version of my story that will assist you in your task."

"Very well." Holbein said slowly, not even trying to hide his bemusement.

"Forgive me, Master Holbein." Sir Thomas reclined. "I do not mean to tease, but merely hope that all will become as clear as it needs to be by the time that I am finished. When I began to write my history of King Richard, my research uncovered more than I had bargained for." He reached for his goblet and sipped slowly as he decided how to continue.

"Following their coronation," Sir Thomas returned his eyes to the hearth as he sank back into his storytelling, "the king and queen made a royal progress to show themselves to their new subjects. They left London on 20th July for Oxford, moving on through Gloucester, Warwick, Coventry, Leicester, Nottingham and Pontefract. At every point they were well received and conspicuously generous. On more than one occasion a subject offered coin to Richard to praise him and he told them to keep their money, for he would rather have their love. Such stories are well known. It is in York that we shall rejoin our protagonists."

Chapter 30

31st August 1483 – York Triumphal

The castle of Sheriff Hutton was alive with activity. Servants and maids, pages and messengers darted and scurried through the corridors, each with orders to complete or messages from, or to be delivered to, nearby York. The air in the castle was thick with the smell of roasting meat and filled with dozens of voices trying to co-ordinate efforts and to discern who was still available to be instructed amongst the throng that busied about the corridors and passageways.

King Richard sat in the large office that had been created for him, bright, warming light streaming into the room through two tall windows to his right. The fire crackled lazily, contentedly, in the hearth away to his left. Behind him, a large tapestry depicting St Anthony of Egypt and the faithful boar that had protected him hung. The story of St Anthony had first inspired Richard to take the boar as his symbol. Anthony was a hermit living in the wild and the devil instructed a wild boar to attack him. The boar refused, and when the devil sent other wild beasts instead, the boar steadfastly protected Anthony so that none could harm him. The moral that Richard had taken from the story was the importance of resisting the urges of nature inspired by the devil. Moreover, resisting the temptations of the flesh would not suffice. They should be actively, consciously and ferociously fought at all times in order to do that which is right, that which God demanded of him. Richard had sought to model himself to this end under his emblem of the boar and with prayers to St Anthony. He knew that he had not always succeeded. Were, he often wondered, noble intentions enough? He had allowed temptation to plough a thick furrow through his moral plain when gathering power and influence as a younger man, most notably, he winced at the memory, when dealing with Anne's mother in attempting to match George's settlement of her father's estates. Then there were his dealings with another dowager, the Countess of Oxford, whom Richard had relieved of her estates by using thinly veiled threats. At the time he had seen both as a means to an end, and after all he had not actually harmed either of the ladies. He questioned since, in the following years, whether the means could be justified by the ends, by his achievements in establishing himself and securing his son's future. He had told himself that the collective effect of each of these things was the man that he was, and the position that he occupied, today. He also told himself that this was an insufficient blind pulled around the matter. One day, he knew, he was going to find out whether his noble intentions were enough for his final judge. And what of more recent events? He placed his forehead into his right palm, elbow propped on the desk, and absently tapped a gold seal stamp on the desk. What of his treatment of his nephews?

His train of thought was broken suddenly by a soft knocking at the door opposite his desk which seemed to grow from his own unconscious tapping. He sat up in his chair.

"Enter," he called in an even tone. The door swung slowly into the room to reveal Anne, her deep blue dress filling the width of the door at her hips, but pinched tightly to her body at the waist. She stepped into the room and closed the door behind herself, appearing to float across the room to him, her feet unseen below her skirts.

"All seems to be moving apace today." Anne said lightly, a shaft of morning glow falling across her face as she smiled and sat opposite Richard.

"Indeed." Richard said mournfully. "The noise is interminable."

"You asked that your instructions be followed with all haste." Anne frowned, her tone almost chastising.

"I know," Richard drawled, "but I can barely hear myself think."

"Yesterday was a long, and loud, day." She offered as an explanation for his mood.

"It was." Richard accepted and smiled.

"York is truly behind her new king." Anne told him. "There were near riotous scenes in every street when you arrived. Everyone wanted a glimpse of the city's champion now that he is king of all England."

"I am certain that each of them will expect something of me now," he grumbled, but caught himself and smiled again. "It was glorious, though, was it not?"

"Fittingly so." Anne agreed, flattering him to try and lift his ill concealed poor spirits. His lips curled into a real, spontaneous smile now.

"This," Richard lifted his arms into the space around him, "will make a fine place for my household in the north."

"It will." Anne agreed.

"Our nephew, the Earl of Lincoln, should do a fine job of managing affairs here for us, though the Earl of Northumberland will like his appointment little. I fear it will put an end to his hopes of a revival of Percy fortune in the north. I hope Lincoln will prove a good influence on George's son also. Here he is far enough away from plotting and intrigues in the south and I should rather young nobles such as he grew back to loyalty by the nurturing of their noble nature than by breakable promises and unbinding gifts." He looked down at the desk. "Such a situation served me well and will provide the basis for the rehabilitation of tomorrow's nobility."

"You speak," Anne was reluctant to risk turning his mood again, but something was clearly on his mind, "of plotting and intrigue as if it is current."

"When is it not?" Richard mumbled without looking up. There was a heavy silence for a moment before Richard raised his right fist and pounded it on the desk. "What is wrong with the nobility of this land that they cannot be loyal to anyone?" His voice was raised, but fuelled by confusion rather than anger. "If they give their word, why can they not keep it? If they promise something, why can they not do it? I see so little that is noble in the nobility of today."

"There is little new in this, my love." Anne leaned toward him. "This country has been in upheaval for so long that all the nobility know how to do is protect themselves in preparation for the next turning of the tide. They need to learn how to deal with stability. My father..." She reclined again and without willing it her eyes fell to her lap as they always did when she spoke of him. Richard had never determined, and would never ask, whether it was sorrow or shame that caused her to do it. "My father once said that those best suited to power are those who do not desire it, and those who seek power should be restrained from it." She looked at Richard without raising her head.

"He said something similar to me." Richard smiled softly to comfort Anne. They shared the briefest moment of silence, but it meant a great deal to Anne.

"He was never much for practising what he preached either." Anne smiled a little uncomfortably.

"No." Richard acquiesced, a dozen warm memories of his former mentor washing over him. "Then is chivalry truly dead?" Richard sighed sorrowfully.

"Not as long as England has a chivalrous king to lead it into the light." Anne's voice was suddenly as solid as granite, all doubt gone. "What has happened Richard?" she frowned. "What vexes you so?"

Richard eyed her for a moment, clearly trying to decide what, if anything, to tell her. This Anne found deeply unnerving.

"I," he finally began, but was instantly cut off by a loud knocking at the door that seemed to evaporate the growing tension within the room. "Enter." Richard called, his eyes flashing to Anne's. She was certain that within them she discerned relief at the interruption. The door opened and the tall, broad frame of Sir Robert Brackenbury strode purposefully into the room. Sir Robert was amongst Richard's closest and most trusted friends and his face betrayed concern that the news he bore was not good news. He snapped to a halt before the desk.

"Your majesty." He bowed to Richard, his gruff northern accent gravelly and serious. "My lady." He turned to Anne and bowed again.

"Sir Robert." She acknowledged him with a smile.

"What news, Sir Robert?" Richard asked, a concerned frown on his brow.

"Sire, I have had the Duke of Buckingham under close watch as you instructed." Sir Robert stopped short as he saw Richard's eyes dart to Anne.

"You know how," Richard searched for a word, "fragile Henry can be."

"Of course." Anne agreed, inviting further explanation.

"When he joined us at Gloucester he said much that concerned me. More than my usual concern where he is involved. He," Richard paused, again apparently seeking the correct way to say that which he wished to say. "Well, he made such suggestions as you would not believe regarding the securing of my position. We argued and he stormed out, intimating in his enigmatic way that he had already set into motion certain things which he believed, or at least claimed, that he did for my benefit." Richard took a long, slow breath in. "I know not sometimes what is fact and what is idle rhetoric with him, and so I have been watching him closely." Anne nodded a laboured motion of understanding. Richard returned his gaze to Sir Robert, who took the cue to continue.

"After he left, he travelled, with but a few stops, to his castle at Brecknock." This appeared to mean something to both men as Anne looked from one face to the other.

"Richard?" she queried when no explanation was offered.

"Bishop Morton." Richard snarled through gritted teeth without looking at her. Anne looked up to Sir Robert.

"Bishop Morton has been held by the duke at Brecknock since his conspiracy was uncovered, my lady." Sir Robert's tone was softer now, though his accent was still thick.

"My error." Richard offered unbidden as if to the space within the room as much as Anne or Brackenbury. Anne frowned again.

"Amongst his many failing," Sir Robert continued, "lies one particular talent for persuasion."

"I am aware of Bishop Morton's reputation." Anne told them both. "If the king regrets placing him in Buckingham's care then I am more concerned as to what this may mean about Henry than the Bishop." There was an uncomfortable silence. "Are you concerned that he may fall under the influence of the Bishop, or that he already has and is reporting back?"

"When I first contacted Henry," Richard sighed, "I knew that it was a risk. It appeared to have been a well judged one, for his support has been undoubtedly invaluable. Perhaps that is what caused me to entrust the care of the most dissimulating of my enemies to the most vain and unstable of my allies."

"Yet you now have some reason for your concern?" Anne asked, unwilling to mention their earlier near conversation regarding the duke's visit to Gloucester.

"Indeed I do." Richard replied firmly.

"It would appear that your fears are well founded, sire." Sir Robert interjected. "I have received word that the Duke of Buckingham has written to Henry Tudor in exile urging him to bring an invading force in order to liberate the sons of Edward your brother." There was silence. Anne and Richard gazed at each other with open mouths. Richard tried to form words that would not come. Eventually he was able to find his voice.

"What game is this?" he breathed, blood filling his cheeks. His fists were clenched tightly on the desk in front of him.

Anne watched him trying to fight back the searing heat of his temper. He failed, both of his fists thudding into the oak desktop and his arms then sending paperwork skidding across the room toward the fire. "How dare he!" Richard shrieked in rage. "After all that I have done for him, all that I have made him. A regent in Wales, Constable of England for life," he bellowed, throwing a silver tankard at the carved stone of the fireplace, "Lord Chamberlain, his Bohun estates." Richard rose, his chair grinding against the floor as it slid away behind him, echoing his own swelling rage. "Is this not enough for him?" Richard turned to Anne. "Do you see now what I meant?"

"I do, Richard." She said, her tone even against his anger in an effort to soothe him. He heaved to draw breath but managed to control it as he held Anne's deep, calm eyes.

"I understand," Sir Robert continued as though the king had not just leapt into a rage at all, "that the issue of the Bohun settlement is a portion of the problem."

"What?" Richard said quietly, with genuine disbelief that wrenched his eyes from those of his wife. "Have I not settled those estates he believes were taken from his family upon him?"

"With respect, your highness," Sir Robert said, clearly unafraid of Richard's outburst nor of the worsening tidings he delivered, "you made the completion of the matter subject to the approval of Parliament."

"A formality." Richard replied blankly.

"One that is being used against you nonetheless to suggest to the duke that you do not intend to fulfil your promises once you no longer need to rely upon him."

Richard's fists met the desk again with a crushing thud. Sir Robert did not flinch. He had seen Richard's temper enough over their many years of friendship not to be afraid of it. It was generally well directed and those loyal to him had nothing to fear from it but ringing ears.

A third knock upon the door interrupted whatever may have followed. Richard did not speak as his chest heaved to drag air into his aching lungs. There was another, tentative rap. Richard slowed his breathing.

"Enter," he called as coolly as he could manage, his arms and legs trembling slightly as the anger began to dissipate. William Catesby entered the room cautiously. As he surveyed the scene that greeted him it became clear that Richard had been ranting. He too knew from experience both the signs of his lord's wrath, and not to fear it.

"Sire." He bowed. "My lady." Bowing again to Anne. "Sir Robert." The two nodded at one another and exchanged the briefest, faintest of smiles of knowing at their friend's latest loss of humour.

"William." Richard retook his seat, sliding it beneath himself as he sat at his desk again, forcing a smile back onto his lips. He looked at Anne as he always did to apologise without words for his outburst. Her smile accepted his look immediately.

"Sire, messages flow from the continent today with news of great importance." Catesby, another of Richard's long standing, common born, close friends always attempted to sound what he believed was statesman-like when divulging such information. Richard struggled to restrain a laugh as he saw Brackenbury's shoulders shaking at the southerner's delivery. Catesby clearly knew what was going on. He relaxed a little and spoke in his more familiar manner. "There are two missives of which you need to be aware immediately." Catesby continued quickly. "Firstly," he fixed Richard's gaze with a look approaching excitement, "King Louis is dead." All of the four in the room looked from one to another and back again, trying to digest the news in a shared silence.

"So," Richard said softly, "the old enemy is dead." He looked directly at Catesby. "Long live the old enemy."

"Indeed." Sir William smiled. "King Charles assumes the throne of France, but in his minority, his sister Anne of Beaujeau is to act as regent."

"Interesting." Richard mused upon his own recent situation. "We must keep close eye upon developments. They may work in our favour, or against it."

"There is no doubt," Brackenbury offered, "that an unsettled French court is desirable. It keeps their attention focussed firmly upon themselves."

"Ay," Richard flashed him a smile, "just the way the French like it." The three men laughed and Anne smiled amusedly.

"There is further news, sire." Catesby resumed as the laughter settled.

"Then do tell, my dear William." Richard's tone was light, lifted by his amusement.

"Duke Francis of Brittany has requested a detachment of four thousand archers to assist against the threat of French invasion." Catesby delivered the news coolly but watched Richard straighten in his chair, his face instantly serious.

"Four thousand?" Richard repeated, holding Catesby's eyes.

"Yes, sire," Sir William confirmed, "with a further four thousand available in reserve." Catesby was a lawyer by training and always delivered such news dispassionately. That was not to say, Richard knew, that he was disinterested or without well formed opinions. As a member of Richard's close knit inner circle, he was trusted completely and valued beyond measure. Richard's mind flashed back to all of those years earlier when Edward had denied their sister similar assistance. At the time Richard had been prepared to go to her assistance himself but Edward had refused any aid.

"We should offer him whatever he requires. He is our ally" Richard said flatly. Sir Robert nodded.

"If I may, your grace." Catesby said slowly. The king knew all too well that the counter argument was about to be made. He gestured for Sir William to continue. "Perhaps this would not be the best moment for you to divest yourself of eight thousand highly trained men at arms."

"Explain." Richard insisted in a tone he often used with Catesby to reflect the other's business like demeanour. He did not like his resolve on such matters being clouded by political reality.

"We are uncertain of the full situation in France, as Duke Francis himself must be. He is simply panicking and we can hardly afford to send large forces of archers every time a foreign ally has a nervous moment."

"There is also Burgundy to consider should Brittany fall. There lies an issue of family." Richard countered staunchly.

"With respect, Richard," Catesby's tone dropped as he used the familiar name, "so is almost anyone in England or Europe in enough power to fear losing it." Sir Robert stifled a chuckle. Richard and Anne exchanged glances and then Richard too smirked. It was true that much of the English nobility were closely related, most being their own cousins several times over due to the small circle of suitably high ranking options for marriage. When matches made abroad were considered too, it became more a question of degrees of relationship than family ties alone. This did, however, also offer the option to choose a side based on interests other than just family, since questions of blood loyalty could almost be removed.

"There is also the issue of Buckingham." Sir Robert offered. "Perhaps William is correct, since we do not yet know the extent of his intentions."

"This is true." Richard saw the look of unease on Sir William's face. Clearly he was not yet aware of this news, and that pleased Richard. He could at least be sure that he was hearing such important tidings first without matters being discussed before reaching him. There was nothing to hide amongst friends, though. "It appears that the duke is plotting something, William, perhaps with this Henry Tudor." The shock on Catesby's face was completely undisguised, but

Richard saw the unmistakable signs of the lawyer's mind processing the information.

"Sire," he said slowly as the thoughts formed, "Henry Tudor is held by Duke Francis."

"Then am I being blackmailed?" Richard asked astutely.

"Perhaps." Sir William said. "Duke Francis has never offered to hand Tudor over, even to your brother, but it should be pointed out that he has probably never been asked to do so. If King Edward felt it was sufficient to keep Tudor at arm's length in the care of an ally, then Duke Francis has played his part."

"So perhaps we should assist him?" Richard asked. "Not least in an effort to secure Tudor." Richard was already growing frustrated with the circular argument.

"I doubt," Sir Robert offered, "that Duke Francis would be keen to lose control of his best bargaining tool so quickly."

"Yes," Catesby agreed, "particularly if France remains an unknown quantity for a time."

The room fell quiet for a long minute. Richard spun his wedding ring on his finger and looked at Anne, who met his gaze, held it a moment and then touched her own wedding band. It was a signal that they had settled upon to show that Anne would trust to his judgement. Richard was more than happy for his wife to speak her mind, particularly between such close friends. He valued her opinion above all others, but she had told him that as king he must stand strong and must not appear to rely upon her. Such weaknesses led to the downfall of Henry VI and she insisted that Richard must not offer anyone such an opportunity to criticise him. The signal that she now gave showed him that she had no firm opinion, or that she saw no clear right or wrong and that she would support whatever decision he made. It helped only to confirm the absence of an easy answer.

"William," Richard's voice was now firm, his mind obviously made up, "send for Francis, Richard and James if you would."

"Sire." Catesby bowed and swept from the room.

"Sir Robert," Richard turned to Brackenbury, "please find Sir James Tyrell and have him join us also."

"Of course." Sir Robert bobbed his head to Richard, then to Anne, and strode out of the door. As it closed, Richard released a heaving sigh.

"There is much to consider here, Richard." Anne said quietly in response to his lengthy release of breath.

"Is it always to be so?" Richard asked with barely masked melancholy.

"Such is the nature of your position, my love." She told him affectionately.

"I know," Richard replied solemnly, "and I do not mean to complain, but I barely have a moment to think and, though I did not expect it yet, finding no peace is wearing."

Anne frowned. This was most unlike her husband. He was usually full of such drive that he did not seek peace, indeed he avoided it. He had relished every challenge placed before him since they had been married and sought out challenges when none were presented to him. Controlling the lawless Scottish borders and the conflict riddled nobility of the north of England had kept him more than busy, oftentimes busier than these last few months, and he had never baulked at the load, nor at the prospect of its increase. She could only imagine that the sudden change was caused by the momentous tumult of recent events. Perhaps the revelations and decisions had affected him more deeply than she had thought.

"Your peace will come," she told him firmly, "when you have built it." Anne could not imagine that sympathising, allowing her husband to wallow in his ebbing emotions, would help him at present. He needed to focus on the events at hand.

"Well then," Richard rose from his chair sharply and began to pace behind his desk to and fro, "let us earn it." Anne smiled, satisfied. Richard's sprawling thoughts were interrupted by a knock at the door. "Yes!" Anne was pleased by the vigour returned to his voice and the flash in his eyes as he smiled at her.

Catesby re-entered the room, followed closely by Francis Lovell, Richard Ratcliffe and James Harrington. The four men swept their arms and bowed low in unison.

"Gentlemen!" Richard called to them, beaming. "Friends." He threw his arms open in greeting.

"Sire." Lord Lovell acknowledged, striding across the room to clasp his right forearm over the desk. Sir Richard Ratcliffe and then Sir James Harrington followed suit. Richard held on to Sir James's arm, pulling him a little closer.

"How are you, James?" he asked.

"Well, sire." Sir James replied, his accent betraying his north western roots.

"You sound wearied, James." Richard frowned. "Rest assured, my friend, that matters pertaining to Hornby Castle and your various other outstanding grievances shall be resolved."

"I know it, my lord." Sir James smiled a tired but sincerely friendly smile.

"Your loyalty shall be properly rewarded now and Stanley's treachery shall avail him no more." Richard was still speaking quietly but with great earnest.

"We all look forward to the day that that spider's web-weaving is untangled." The two nodded and exchanged smiles again before Richard released Sir James's arm.

"Gentlemen." Richard repeated to all of them. "There is a great deal that we must discuss and resolve." His eyes scanned the faces before him. These men were just about his closest and most trusted allies and friends. Men he had known for years and with whom he had forged bonds stronger than steel during his time in the north. He trusted to their unwavering loyalty and they had nothing but faith in his good lordship. Both parts had been earned and proven over many years. The Harrington family had long been loyal to the Yorkist cause and had served Richard in the north west and his brother as king in general in outstanding fashion. Both of their ancestors had fought side by side for King Henry V at Agincourt, that chivalric legend of victory and honour. Yet it had been the Stanleys' political manoeuvring in their own self interest that had paid dividends in the region. They had switched allegiances as it suited them and reaped the rewards of seeming to turn tides. Hornby was the Harrington's possession but stood in the way of Stanley's expansion and so Lord Stanley had fought to seize it, eventually winning a legal decision and the support of King Edward in the matter. Such things had been political reality to Edward but had always offended Richard's notions of loyalty and chivalry.

"We are just awaiting..." His words were interrupted by a loud pounding at the door. "Ah, enter." Richard called and the opening door revealed Sir Robert Brackenbury, closely followed by the broad frame of Sir James Tyrell. He was tall also and his ruddy skin was testament to so many more years spent out of doors, on the road, than the others in the room. He was well travelled, a trusted messenger par excellence and a man who seemed happy to accept any commission and able to perform it completely and without fuss. He was a lord's, and now a king's, dream.

Tyrell bowed low to Richard and then to Anne. He stood beside the other men and Richard nodded without willing it, an involuntary demonstration of approval of and satisfaction with the group arranged before him.

"My friends," Richard began, his chest puffing out, "much is occurring with which we few shall deal decisively. King Louis is dead and France has a minority government. This may leave them weakened and distracted but much will depend upon the regent." He looked around at the men. "Linked to this is Duke Francis of Brittany's request for eight thousand archers against the threat of French invasion." The men looked at one another, obviously surprised by the figure requested. "Indeed." Richard answered their unspoken alarm. "I intend not to send these troops without openly refusing Duke Francis's request." He paused, inviting opinion.

"You have always been on good terms with Brittany in the past, sire." Lord Lovell stated questioningly. "Should you not seek to preserve such an alliance?"

"A fair point, Francis." Richard smiled. "I do not intend to endanger our ties with Brittany, but we cannot be sure of the situation in France. Brittany may be under no threat at all and there are matters at home that must be resolved before any aggressive continental posturing may be contemplated." He felt a flutter in his stomach as he spoke. He, and those gathered, had long dreamed of restoring English honour on French soil and to now baulk at an opportunity seemed painfully disappointing. "We may yet have need of those troops on English soil soon." Again, the men looked one to the other. Brackenbury and Catesby knew what Richard referred to, but the others clearly did not.

"As you are all aware," Richard began again, "Lord Stanley is travelling with us." There were echoed tuts and much shaking of heads at the mention of the name. "This is in order that he may be closely watched." Richard explained in response to the general derision. "Yet this does not appear to have prevented his wife from colluding with the Woodvilles to forward a claim for his step son, one Henry Tudor, to be acknowledged as a viable heir to the House of Lancaster." There was obvious bemusement amongst those who had been unaware of the news. "Furthermore," Richard continued, settling the men, "it would appear that this," he waved his arm dismissively, "uprising, has been joined by none other than our cousin the Duke of Buckingham."

Harrington, Tyrell and Lovell burst into rounds of curses and a commotion grew in the room as each man suggested a course of action, complete with their desired fate for Henry Stafford, Duke of Buckingham. Richard allowed the men to rail for a while in order that their anger and sense of betrayal might fuel their commitment to him and galvanise them against the rebels.

"What is to be done?" Lord Lovell eventually addressed Richard.

"We must crush any such notions of opposition," Sir James Harrington shouted above the subsiding voices, "before the rebels adopt a viable rival to royal authority."

"Viable?" Catesby queried. "There is no viable rival to our king's authority." His cool tone was met by a heated glance from Harrington who clearly felt chided.

"Enough." Richard said softly, almost absently, yet all of those gathered fell instantly silent. He paused a moment, holding their attention, looking deep into Anne's eyes. "Sir William," he turned to meet Catesby's keen, eager eyes, "I would know all that may be known of this Tudor pretender. His parentage, how it is that he dares to challenge my throne and how much support he may expect to gain."

"Yes, sire." Catesby smiled with relish at the task and nodded.

"Sir Richard," the king continued, turning to Ratcliffe, "ensure that Buckingham remains closely watched. I would know his every move. He is, I know, intelligent, eloquent and ambitious. To date these qualities have served us well and I fear them being put to use against us. Henry is far from the fool that he would have everyone believe him to be."

"Sire." Ratcliffe's tone was less assured than Catesby's, as though he was expecting some other instruction.

"Sir James, I leave to you the watch of Lord Stanley." Richard smiled at Harrington mischievously.

"With pleasure." Harrington grinned back.

"Watch, mind." Richard matched his grin. Harrington tilted his head in mock disappointment. "Francis," the king now turned his attention to Lord Lovell, "begin preparations for a general levy of troops against this possible uprising."

"With respect, sire," Ratcliffe cut across Lovell's acknowledgment, "should we not take more direct action to cut off this rising at its root?"

"Perhaps." Richard mused, turning his eyes to his wife again. She nodded imperceptibly to him. "But I shall use this opportunity of distance to give heart to my enemies. My absence from London and distance within the north should serve to draw out those willing to oppose me." Richard moved his gaze over the faces before him. "I shall allow them to declare, clearly and irrefutably, their opposition before acting so that none may later plead that they were not truly in rebellion against their king. Then, being prepared, we will crush each and every one of them." There were general nods and murmurs of approval at the planned entrapment, with one exception.

"Richard," Lord Lovell stepped forward, using the familiar name of their long friendship to underline the personal nature of the point that he wished to make, "it may prove more prudent to negate this plotting before it becomes public knowledge. Rebellion is like the plague." The parallel cut deep. The country had only recently begun to fully recover from the apocalyptic curse of the Black Death. "Once it is broken out it may spread with lightening speed. That which has never erupted may not infect others." There was a long silence.

"I hear you Francis." Richard's tone was serious and heavy with sincerity. "Your point is true and well made, and I acknowledge it. Indeed, it is the reverse of the coin that I have been turning over since hearing this news." Richard rose from his seat. "However, I am determined to root out those nobles and gentry who would dishonour their oaths to me." He clenched his right fist before himself as he spoke. "There can be no place for such men in our new England. For too long this nation has been shaken to its foundations by civil unrest and quarrelling nobility. If honour and chivalry are to be restored to our England, then blood infected with self-serving disloyalty must be let, and I should prefer to only need to do it once."

"So be it." Lovell conceded, accepting that his piece had been said, though overruled. The two men held each other's stare for a moment before breaking with the faintest smile at each other.

"Sir Robert," Richard turned to Brackenbury now, "take word to the Duke of Norfolk to be prepared at the first sign of any uprising to move in force upon London and secure the capital in my name. Then, return to the Tower and be watchful, my friend."

"Yes, sire." Sir Robert returned.

"Very well, gentlemen." Richard surveyed them with satisfaction. "We may have turbulent times ahead but if our resolve remains strong and our course true," he flashed a glance at Harrington, "and if the weight of Stanley's forces can be kept restrained," Sir James smiled broadly, "then we may end the troubles as quickly as they begin and concentrate upon the real business of reforming our realm for the common weal."

A rumbling of agreement rolled around the room and the men began to move out of the office to perform their respective tasks.

"Sir James Tyrell," Richard called at the last moment. Tyrell turned, a frown shadowing his handsome face. "I have neglected to give you instruction. Please, return."

"Of course, your majesty." Sir James' deep voice filled the room and he strode back to the desk, his spurs clicking and chinking with each step. He halted and stood to attention with a final, resounding clack of his heels.

"James." Richard shot an uncomfortable glance at Anne, who furrowed her brow at the obviously uneasy expression on his face.

"Sire." Sir James' voice snapped Anne from her wondering.

"James." Richard stood and moved around the desk to the other man, coming so close that he was forced to look upward at the taller man. "There are some items that I require from the Royal Wardrobe for our son's investiture as Prince of Wales." The king reached over to his desk, lifted a folded parchment and paused to stare at it for an instant as though unsure how, or whether, to continue. In the following instant, his mind was clearly settled. "Please ensure that these are retrieved."

"Yes sire." Sir James responded evenly.

"You are aware," Richard continued, fixing Sir James with a firm gaze and narrowing his eyes slightly as he tried to push home his words, "of the rest of your purpose in London?"

"I am aware of it sire, but..."

"Then it is settled." Richard interrupted. "To London, Sir James, and see that your tasks are completed in time for the investiture."

"Very well, sire." Tyrell swept a low bow and marched from the room.

"Do not look at me so, Anne." Richard said wearily whilst still looking at the door that had just closed behind Tyrell.

"I do understand your reasoning, Richard." She said tenderly.

"And I," he replied, turning to face her, a tear spilling from his eye, "understand that this is far from my greatest moment." He drew in a long breath as though he tried to recover the stray tear. Anne rose and stood before him.

"Time will tell," she said as she placed her palm upon his cheek and stroked the lone tear away with her thumb, "the wisdom of your decision, for time and the Lord God are the only judges you need worry about." Richard moved his hand up to hers on his cheek and pressed, smiling silent thanks to her.

Chapter 31

31st October 1483 – Rumours, Rebellions and Requests

It was cold. Or perhaps exhaustion was sucking the warmth from his marrow. Richard inhaled deeply, opened his eyes and blinked at the shimmering gold arrayed upon the altar of Salisbury Cathedral. It glowed with the same burnished orange as the autumn sun that sank slowly toward its evening rest. The flagstones beneath Richard's knees were chill and hard. He pulled his heavy fur cloak closer around him, shifted on his knees in search of a moment's comfort, closed his eyes again and forced his mind to focus upon his prayers. The freezing rain outside seemed to tap at the beautiful stained glass and thump on the vast roof so that the space above the king's bent head echoed with a cacophony of baying distractions. His lips moved silently as he fought to concentrate upon his words. He knew them well but they suddenly felt like a distant, elusive memory, as though he was trying to recall a song from his childhood that danced just beyond recollection. His mind wandered unbidden to that which had dominated the last fortnight. Submitting, he shifted his prayers to these matters, for there was indeed a great deal to be thankful for amongst the turmoil.

At that moment, the rhythmical clicking of riding boots on the stone floor behind him grew above the raging of the storm outside. His shoulders lowered a little in resignation and he opened his eyes again, fixing them on the jewelled cross upon the altar as he crossed himself. With an almost imperceptible groan he straightened his stiffening knees as the steps halted behind him.

"Are you getting too old for kneeling on stone floors, or has the crown softened you so much already?" The voice was instantly recognisable as it reverberated around the space.

"If only we were not in church, I should have a choice suggestion for the positioning of your lips." Richard could not help the smile that peeled across his face as he turned. He faltered a little as his left knee protested against the stiffness, causing Francis, Viscount Lovell to roar with laughter.

"Come, sit down, my king." Francis gestured to a pew as he regained control of his voice.

"Church or no, I'll make that suggestion, Francis." Richard smirked as he fell into the wooden seat which was every bit as hard as the stone floor. Lovell sat beside him.

"I did not mean to interrupt." Francis apologised, suddenly serious.

"You did not." Richard looked upward into the cavern of the ceiling. "This evening seems to conspire against prayer." He listened to the pounding rain a moment and was sure that he heard the distant roll of thunder. He turned his head to Francis, who had clearly shed his riding cloak but whose dark hair was soaked flat to his head. His boots were darkened by damp to his ankles but his smile did not falter.

"If I know you, Richard," Lovell's green eyes flashed to match his smile, "the storm outside is less of a distraction than the one inside."

"I sometimes think," Richard said thoughtfully, "that it is dangerous to surround myself with people who know me quite so well." He rolled his gaze to the other's face and was pleased to see that his grin had slipped a little into concern. "But the rest of the time," Richard smiled warmly, "I am glad of it. It does not become the king to be seen in such turmoil."

"But it does become the man," Francis told him, "to feel the turmoil. It is the mark of the man that he settles the turmoil and the mark of the king that he draws order from the chaos." There was a long pause.

"Where did you get that from?" Richard eventually exclaimed.

"I must have heard it somewhere." Francis shrugged and the two laughed again.

"Then I must draw some order from this." Richard concluded purposefully.

"Richard," Francis turned in the pew to face his friend, "I believe that you have dealt with these events perfectly and that order will be yours as a result. Tudor has failed, the Stanley's have failed and Henry Stafford has failed. You have succeeded."

"I have?" Richard's eyes burned into Lovell with his question, drawing a frown of undisguised confusion.

"Richard," Lovell felt suddenly defensive, "I admit that I was wrong in York. You have been proven right in allowing your enemies to show their hand clearly to all and then crushing them so decisively."

"Yes," the king slumped into the bench as though suddenly overcome with exhaustion, "but that I have had to is my failure." He looked up at the altar again. "The Stanley's involvement is hardly unexpected. Lord Stanley is Tudor's step father and loyalty is not a family trait at the best of times, yet even keeping him here is no protection. Must I shackle myself to the whole Stanley clan in order to prevent their mischief?" Francis could not be sure whether the question was addressed to him or to the cross at which he stared. "Then there is this Henry Tudor himself. A man in exile for over a decade with little more than a drop of royal blood, and none of that English. What was it Catesby discovered?" Richard shifted up in his seat as if re-energised by his anger. "Great grandson of the Bishop of Bangor's butler?" Richard spluttered with contempt. "His father the result of an affair with Henry V's French widow and his mother spawned from a line of bastards of the second son of Edward III, a family explicitly disbarred from succession by Henry IV." Richard looked across at Lovell, who sat looking into his own lap. "Am I ranting again?"

"Oh," Francis shrugged, "no more than I am used to." He smiled gently.

"But," Richard continued, waving a finger, "when Stanley meets Beaufort, ambition allied with ambition, I think I should do well to be cautious."

"Indeed."

"I also suspect that there is some truth in Catesby's theory that France may seek to support Tudor's designs on my throne. The only royal blood he really possesses is French. Better for them, then, that he remains focussed on and hopeful of the English throne whilst they have their own problematical minority to negotiate."

"Yet," Francis took a brief moment to choose his words, "it must be Buckingham's betrayal that cuts the deepest." Richard shot him a fiery glance.

"Yes," he contemplated, "and no. I trusted him and he betrayed me, this much is true, and painful. Yet this seems to be the way of power hungry nobles. I saw his ambition and sought to harness it, only to find that I had underestimated it." There was a long pause as Richard again stared at the altar, his face betraying his internal grappling with his own thoughts. "However, he proved as impotent as he is shallow. We burned a few bridges over the Severn, the Lord sent raging storms to swell the river, and his men deserted him before he even left Wales. He did little harm, exposed himself as a base traitor and has now lost everything that I gave him." These last words emerged through gritted teeth. Francis did not doubt that Richard was making light of his true feelings on the matter. There was silence again, broken only by the sounds of the rain above and that beyond the windows.

"I am afraid," Lovell began hesitantly when the quiet became strained, "that I bring news from London that will do nothing to lift your mood."

"Oh Francis," Richard's voice was surprisingly light again, "your kindness knows no bounds." He flashed a smile at his friend, but it was not returned this time.

"Richard, it is about your nephews." The two men held each other's gaze a moment, the smile sunken from Richard's lips.

About a mile from Salisbury Cathedral, outside the king's lodgings, two dozen horses emerged from the sheet of rain and deepening evening. As they were reined in the door was opened and a guard tentatively called for the riders to identify themselves. The horses were sodden and steaming from the exertion of their ride, the men hidden, even at close quarter, by dripping riding cloaks. The steeds snorted loudly, thudding their hooves into the mud as the lead rider threw back his hood. The guard squinted into the dusk, aided by the faint glow of the fire lit room behind him.

"Is the king within?" demanded the deep voice of Sir James Tyrell.

"No, sir, he is not." The guard replied. "I believe that Lord Lovell is seeking him at the Cathedral."

"A shame." Sir James replied darkly. "I have something that I think he wants."

The guard peered around Sir James' broad form to see a horse behind him now clearly discernable as being boxed in by the other riders. As the guard frowned, the rider to the figure's left reached over and pulled the hood back from the man's face. Flinching as the cold rain began to strike his pale, rotund face, the figure smiled, mustering all of his composure. The guard's jaw fell open.

"Perhaps, my good man, we could continue the introductions inside?" Henry Stafford quipped. Sir James dismounted, the Duke of Buckingham flinching at the motion as if expecting a cuff. The two men on either side of the duke also climbed down from their saddles.

"See to the horses, then get yourselves fed and warmed." Tyrell instructed the remaining mounted men. "Bring him in," he said to the other two. Buckingham was roughly hauled from his saddle amid squeaks of protest. He landed awkwardly on his feet, stumbling in the mud. The guard saw his cloak fall open to reveal his bound wrists, doubtless the cause of his instability. The remaining riders caught up their reins and those of the empty horses and rode in the direction of the stables.

"A small misunderstanding," Henry explained as he noticed the guard's eyes upon his restraints, "soon to be rectified." He smiled jovially, only to be pushed toward the doorway.

"It will be rectified," Sir James growled as he passed over the threshold, "when your head is separated from your neck."

"Such confidence is admirable," Henry's voice was still light, though his face twisted maliciously, "but we shall see what my cousin the king has to say." Buckingham stumbled over the threshold with the aid of a further shove.

"Hardly your most graceful entrance," Sir Richard Ratcliffe called from before the fireplace, "my lord," he added with a deliberate sneer.

"Enough." Henry Stafford, Duke of Buckingham, stamped his foot on the floor petulantly. A flurry of raindrops erupted from him like a dog shaking itself dry and he skidded a little on his muddy boot as it met the rushes beneath it. The dozen or so men at arms gathered in the room roared with laughter at the sight. Henry's face burned red at such insolence and he straightened himself. "Fetch me to my king this instant," he demanded shrilly.

"Sir James." Richard Ratcliffe offered a large tankard of ale to Tyrell as he strode toward the fireplace.

"Thank you, Sir Richard." James took a long draught of the warming liquid before shrugging off his heavy cloak. "The king is not here?"

"Indeed not." Ratcliffe replied, eyeing the duke. "Though perhaps that is no bad thing. He may need to prepare himself before giving an audience to this silver tongued snake." The men spoke quietly, yet Buckingham stared at them as though he heard every word.

"True." Sir James conceded. "I shall find him and warn him before he returns."

"My friend, you are soaked to the marrow." Ratcliffe smiled. "Take a moment to tell me how the snake was cornered and I shall go and find the king."

"You are too kind, Sir Richard." James held out his tankard for the offered refill and shivered as the heat of the fire began to penetrate him.

"Walk with me." There had been a long silence before Richard stood sharply and spoke to Lovell again.

"Sire?" Francis queried, but when the king crossed himself, turned from the altar and strode back along the aisle, he was left with little option but to follow. After crossing himself, he caught up with Richard. "There is disturbing news from London."

"There always is." Richard replied glibly as he turned sharply left into the south transept.

"Rumours abound regarding your nephews and they do you no good, Richard." Lovell's tone was pleading with his friend to listen. Richard halted, studied Lovell's face for a moment and then walked on through the transept door and into the cloisters.

"Do you know what is kept here, Francis?" Richard asked over his shoulder as he strode along the eastern side of the cloisters, the open central garth revealing the ferocious rain.

"Of course, but..." Lovell's exasperated words was cut off as Richard reached a doorway half way along the wall and turned into it. Following, Francis entered the Chapter House and saw what Richard spoke of. In the centre of the octagonal room, in a glazed wooden framed display case held at waist height by four thick legs of dark wood was the Magna Carta.

He watched as Richard circled the table, his hand brushing lightly around the sides as he passed, watching Francis with a smile growing across his face.

"We, as a nation," Richard began with obvious fervour, "have held this document in awe for over two hundred and fifty years." He stopped moving at the far side of the table from Francis. "Why is that?" He spread his arms enquiringly.

"Because," Francis began to walk slowly to the display case, knowing that there would be little point in attempting to return the king's mind to business, "it symbolises the rule of law in England. It protects every man's rights and tells us that no man is above the law, not even the king." Lovell arrived opposite the king with these words and a meaningful glare.

"Then it is a failure." Richard said flatly with a nonchalant shrug.

"It is a cornerstone of English law." Francis argued in dismay.

"Then the law is failing." Richard retorted. Lovell looked surprised. "This was a document forced upon a weak king by mighty barons. It has at its core the finest principles but they failed in their application. We live in a world today in which mighty lords seek to equate themselves with a king, or place themselves above him, not because he is a bad king or for the greater good of the common man, but for their own vain glory. My father fought against this until he lost his way, and his life. My brother suffered at the hands of the Earl of Warwick who would have been the maker and controller of kings. This country has been at war with itself for decades."

"Richard, I don't know..." Lovell began.

"Do you know the very core clause of this document?" Richard again interrupted him, as though he had not heard Lovell speak. Without awaiting a reply, he continued. "No free man shall be seized or imprisoned, or stripped of his rights or possessions, or outlawed or exiled. Nor will we proceed with force against him except by the lawful judgement of his equals or by the law of the land. To no one will we sell, to no one deny or delay right or justice." Richard stared at the document as he spoke, his voice full of poignant awe.

"Worthy indeed." Francis concurred, for lack of anything else to say.

"But does this sound like the England in which you and I live, Francis?" Richard fixed his gaze on his friend. "Have you not heard of men being denied justice to suit a lord? Have I myself, may God forgive me, not done that which this document supposes to prevent?"

"You have always been the noblest of men, Richard. None may deny that."

"Yet not noble enough."

"More than any other you have supported the common man's rights, even against those lords that seek to breach them."

"'Even against' you say, Francis, 'even against'. You, then, hold the rights of a lord above those of the common man in law?" Richard turned away and paced to the far end of the room before turning back.

"I did not mean that, sire, but there is a way to the world. A lord has more to protect than a common man and is responsible for many men too." Francis shrugged as he spoke.

"Just because it is so," Richard strode back, "does not make it right." Richard broke into a half smile. "I do not mean to rail at you, my friend; rather at the world. I would seek to correct this wrong, to see this sentiment," he tapped on the glass above the parchment, "hold real force in England."

"We are all with you in this, Richard." Lovell told him sincerely.

"I know, my friend." Richard moved around and clapped Francis on the back. "I will be remembered as the king who completed what Magna Carta began. A strong, just monarch, supported by loyal, well rewarded nobles and beloved of a safe, secure populace, all overseen by the rule of law." There was silence. The rain pattered on the roof as Lovell sought for something to say. He was saved the trouble by a broad, northern voice from the doorway.

"Noble sentiment, sire." Sir Richard Ratcliffe bowed as he entered the room. Richard nodded his greeting. "Though I dare say every king would claim to want the same. The real world has an unerring knack of getting in the way."

"Northerners." Richard shook his head to Lovell. "No tact."

"Thank you, sire." Sir Richard replied with a low bow. The king smiled broadly and Lovell's face lifted a little.

"You have news for me too, Sir Richard?"

"Indeed, sire." Ratcliffe replied cheerily.

"You are yet to hear my news." Francis insisted.

"I thought that you may have taken the hint, Lord Lovell." Richard eyed him wearily.

"There are some things that you need to hear." Lovell told him.

"Very well." Richard motioned for him to continue with resignation.

"Rumour is abroad in London," Lord Lovell's voice was low and full of concern, "regarding the condition of your brother's sons and it spreads like wild fire in the drought of real information."

"No doubt the flames are well fanned." Richard eyed Lovell, measuring the other's unease.

"You accuse the king of creating this 'drought'?" Ratcliffe enquired without a hint of malice.

"Yes." Lovell replied flatly, smiling a little at Sir Richard. "It is within his power to drown out the growing clamour."

"Is it?" Richard asked absently. Both men looked at him with a surprised concern darkening their faces.

"Richard," Lord Lovell spoke to the king but shot a frowning glance at Ratcliffe, who met and then mirrored it, "this rebellion began with the stated aim of placing your nephew Edward on the throne, yet switched to follow Tudor with unerring speed and conviction."

"Indeed." The king concurred, unconcerned.

"This was because of the rumour that your nephews are dead." Lovell spoke plainly, trying to draw a reaction from the uncharacteristically impassive king. None came. "And that you have had them killed." Lovell added, forcing the issue, pushing Richard in the hope that he would push back. Instead, Richard turned slowly and stared into the display cabinet again. Lovell looked to Ratcliffe once more and saw his own mystification reflected on Sir Richard's face. "Richard," Lovell said sharply, "you must produce your nephews and dispel these ugly rumours."

"I must?" Richard asked jadedly, keeping his back to the other men. Ratcliffe drew a breath but did not have time to speak. "What if I cannot?" There was a long silence. Looks of confusion melted into undisguised horror.

"What?" roared Lovell. His voice echoed around the room like a boom of rolling thunder above the storm outside.

"Even you, Francis," Richard's voice was tired and cracked a little with emotion, "and you, Richard," he guessed at the other man's expression and grimaced, "are so quick to judge and to condemn."

"Then explain your meaning to us." Ratcliffe implored his king.

"Consider the possibilities, and the probabilities." Richard told them straightening himself and turning to look at them, his face grave despite the forced beginnings of a smile. "Perhaps I have had my nephews murdered." He said the words in so matter of fact a manner that Lord Lovell felt a sickening knot tighten in his stomach. "A new king can bear no rival. This is not new. My brother found himself in a similar situation with King Henry VI and I am sure that neither of you need a lesson in the strife and instability caused by rival claimants to the throne, nor in the innumerable examples of their removal." It was true, both men were forced to silently acknowledge, that dealing ruthlessly with rivals was a matter of necessity and that the period during which King Henry and King Edward both claimed to rule and fought unendingly for superiority had left a ragged scar across the nation, which only began to heal when Henry was dead. "If, then, I have had it done, I have done what was necessary, however distasteful it may be."

"But they are children, sire." Ratcliffe retreated to formality as shock bloomed into disgust within him.

"'If', Richard," Lovell spoke to the king with his keen eyes boring into his friend's, "you say 'if' you had it done."

"Indeed." Richard smiled briefly, pleased that Francis had picked up on this. "Consider the traitor Buckingham." Richard offered, spreading his palms to the ceiling. Ratcliffe caught himself. He had forgotten the reason for his own presence. "He has had the means to do such a deed."

"He stayed in London after we left." Lovell recalled.

"Access would not have presented a problem to him, either." Ratcliffe agreed, hatred of the duke rekindled within him.

"But why would he do it?" Lovell asked. "What did he have to gain?"

"My favour?" the king returned instantly. "Could I have used him to do the work for me? Could he have believed he did something for which I would thank him? Possibly. Could it have been the opening gambit of his own rebellion? Did he seek to clear the path to the throne for Tudor, or more likely for himself?"

"You believe that Buckingham wanted the throne?" Ratcliffe asked, the notion not seeming out of place.

"What else would be the ultimate goal for a man whose ambition knows no bounds?" Richard replied. "Once his plans were realised, he could even blame me for the murders to swell sympathy for himself."

"Sire," Ratcliffe began, "I..." Sir Richard was losing sight of what his king was trying to tell them. Little did he know that this was precisely what his friend was trying to do.

"Consider still," Richard raised a finger to halt Ratcliffe, "Margaret Beaufort, Lady Stanley."

"Tudor's mother." Lovell acknowledged another suspect. "The queen has become quite close to Lady Stanley and has been generous to her. She could gain access to the Tower."

"Her motive too would be obvious." Ratcliffe concurred. Richard smiled as the two men realised the complexity of the possibilities.

"Furthermore," Richard continued quickly, building momentum, "young Edward was unwell and under his physician. Could not nature have overtaken the brothers, one or both?"

"Very well." Ratcliffe said. "Whatever the reason or method, why not release the story of their deaths?"

"Because to do so would stir sympathy for the poor, innocent children, betrayed and murdered by their ruthless uncle. Such sympathy may do them no good, but could be harnessed by my enemies and would at least do me some small harm."

"Then blame Buckingham, have him executed, mourn your nephews and be done with it." Ratcliffe pleaded, exacerbated.

"And admit that I have so little control over those around me that I cannot protect two children under my care? How then could I claim to be able to protect this entire nation?" Richard asked, flinging his arms open.

"Natural causes?" Lovell asked, suspecting that Richard had considered this matter in great detail already, meaning that he knew of, or had anticipated, this issue. He did not like to consider what that may mean.

"It would be cruel of nature to take one young boy, well cared for as he was." Richard smiled darkly. "Yet it would appear convenient if nature were to remove two threats in one fell swoop." Lovell had to agree. Given that rumour was already growing, this would be an unsatisfactory explanation and would serve only to fuel the talk of conspiracy and cover up. "All of this," Richard's smile grew, "presumes that my nephews are, in fact, dead, by my hand or by my negligence."

"Then they are alive?" Sir Richard asked excitedly his head spinning.

"Though none could deny the benefit of their 'disappearance'." Lovell interjected, sure that Richard was not yet showing his hand. Richard met his gaze with a steely stare that confirmed this.

"If they are alive," Ratcliffe was jubilant, "simply produce them!" He looked from Lovell to the king with glee.

"Why?" asked Richard. Ratcliffe's face sank and then contorted as he sought for the king's meaning. Lord Lovell laughed.

"Well," Ratcliffe floundered, "I..."

"Am I," Richard saved him, "to produce these boys upon demand whenever my enemies choose to speculate upon their fate? How weak do you believe that this would make me?" He paused to watch Ratcliffe's mouth moving like a landed fish. He glanced at Lovell's smiling face and grinned.

"Not to mention," Francis offered, "that such repeated parading of the boys would keep them, and perhaps their cause, at the front of the minds of the populace rather than allowing it to fade into the deepest recesses of the public consciousness. All of this and it offers them a status that they should not hold." Lovell and the king gazed at Ratcliffe.

"So I am the fool who does not grasp the matter?" Sir Richard asked defensively.

"Hardly." Richard consoled his friend. "I am merely seeking to demonstrate that this matter is fraught with problems. There is no right or easy answer."

"Then what are we to do?" asked Lovell.

"My mother," Sir Richard volunteered, "used to say 'If you have nothing nice to say,'."

"Say nothing." Richard completed his friend's advice. "That is much the conclusion that I have reached for the moment."

"Leave all of the doors open." Lovell reflected.

"I may have need of one of them." Richard told him. "Closing them all now may prove unwise later."

"Are you going to tell us the truth of the matter?" Lovell suspected that he knew the answer.

"This is not the moment." Richard told him, smiling to acknowledge his friends' indulgence. "Now, Sir Richard," he continued lightly, "you have news also?"

"Indeed I do." Ratcliffe smiled. "Henry Stafford is captured." The king shot an exited glance at him. "He is at your lodgings in the city," he said in answer to the look.

"Where was he?" Lovell asked, resigned that he would get no further with his news tonight.

"Apparently the reward placed upon his head proved too tempting for one Ralph Banaster, a man with known Lancastrian sympathies who had concealed the duke in his home." Sir Richard beamed as he retold the tale. "Banaster turned Buckingham over to the Sheriff of Shropshire and Sir James Tyrell, and it is Sir James who has arrived here tonight, thoroughly soaked, with his prisoner in tow."

"So the betrayer was betrayed." Lovell mused.

"What of his son?" Richard asked, narrowing his eyes.

"There was no sign, sire." Sir Richard told him. "Sir James was able to glean from brief enquiries that the duke may have had the infant hidden by the child's nursemaid. One source told how the babe was disguised as a girl and taken far away to certain safety."

"He must be sought out." Richard told the pair earnestly. "I would have him placed in my rehabilitation program in the north and brought back into the fold." Both men nodded their agreement.

"Buckingham's wife is not hidden, though." Lovell reminded Richard. "What of her and the other captured rebels?"

"Henry remains the only noble to enter into open rebellion." Richard reflected. "I take comfort in that but I have given much thought to the handling of the aftermath." In fact, it had been Anne who had urged him to consider this matter. Richard was so focussed on dealing swiftly with the breaking threat that it had not crossed his mind. It was Anne who had advised him that, assuming his victory, the most important matter was balancing his reaction to it. He must, she believed, see justice done to those who oppose him, but too harsh a response may only serve to alienate those on the fringes of rebellion and push them further into the arms of his enemies. There should be reconciliation where possible and appropriate, applied as thoroughly as his justice.

"We hold a number of the rebellion's key activists." Sir Richard reminded the king. "It is true that none are nobles, simply minor gentry with Lancastrian ties and a few men of your brother's former household."

"These men must be executed." Richard said evenly after a brief moment. "They will provide the demonstration of my justice and act as an example to those who would oppose my authority. Their treason is clear." The king's teeth clenched for a moment before a gently malicious smile spread over his face. "The duke's wife will lead the exhibition of my determination to reconcile those at the very edge of loyalty. She is a sister of my brother's wife, a Woodville." Richard turned up his nose in a deliberately exaggerated gesture of feigned disgust. "I will grant her a generous pension, pay the duke's not insubstantial debts so that they will not haunt her and she will be sent to join her sister in sanctuary. Perhaps she will convince Elizabeth of my mercy and reconsider the return of Henry's son." Richard looked from Lovell to Ratcliffe and back again. Their faces betrayed their surprise at the rather generous package proposed for the Woodville wife of a treasonous traitor. "Ha!" Richard pointed at the men's expressions. "I hope to shock my enemies in such a way also. Perhaps then they will consider that I may not be that which they believe I am."

"No doubt," Francis agreed, "they will be caught unawares if she is not dispatched to a nunnery in poverty and disgrace."

"Surely, though," Sir Richard narrowed his eyes, examining the king, "you cannot be so lenient with Tudor's mother?"

"Therein lay my greatest dilemma." Richard began to pace across the room. "She is dangerous, of that I have no doubt. Of her involvement in this plot there can be no doubt. Perhaps I should have allowed her son to return when she requested it, under a public oath of loyalty." He stopped and met the two men's gazes as though judging their reaction to the suggestion, but neither offered any insight. "Yet if it was a mistake, it is made and cannot be unmade. I must live with it now." He resumed his thoughtful striding. "There is no chance of his return now that he has declared his intentions." He passed the central display case around which the other men still stood. "Still," he tilted his head to one side, "I must handle Lord Stanley with care. Cornering him would surely force his wealth and vast reserves of men at arms into his stepson's arms. Whatever drives his wife, he did not join this rebellion."

"Only because he is here, with you." Sir Richard sneered.

"Perhaps." Richard mused standing still again. "Perhaps he was convinced enough of the rebellion's failure not to show his hand yet. But I cannot," he gestured to Sir Richard with pinched finger and thumb, "condemn him for that which we suspect he may have considered trying to do had he perceived enough personal gain. Neither can I afford to drive him into opposition. As distasteful as I find it, I need him on my side. Or," he corrected himself, "at least not openly against me." He returned to the centre of the room to face the others. "Lady Stanley will be attainted for treason." He noted the grin immediately gracing Sir Richard's face. "Her lands will be forfeit." He paused a moment. "But," he continued sharply, "her lands will be given to Lord Stanley and she will be released into his custody." The words hung between them for a long moment while the storm raged outside.

"Harrington will not be pleased." Sir Richard said emphatically. Lovell nodded.

"Sir James Harrington," Richard replied softly, "knows what is to be done. He has my word that his cause is in hand and that justice shall finally be his." He eyed the two men sternly. "That is enough for him." The words sounded like a challenge.

"Richard," Lovell accepted the test, "you should take care that you do not begin to play Stanley's games Stanley's way."

"And you, my friend," Richard told him gently, whilst managing to lace the words with the faintest hint of malice, "should take care in what you say to me."

"Sire," Lovell straightened his back, "I cannot stand by and watch you become that which you, and all who love you, despise." He saw Richard stiffen. "I see the benefit in appeasing Stanley and not driving him into rebellion but he cannot be trusted."

"That is what I am counting on and preparing against." Richard said darkly. "He has given me no reason to act against him yet and will know that I shall be just unless he forces my hand, when I shall relish the opportunity to repay his fickle, self serving, ambitious version of loyalty. He can no longer hide behind his wife's skirts." Richard's face darkened. "If his wife continues plotting whilst in his custody, he will be responsible. If any of her assets are used to support Tudor, then Stanley shall be responsible for it. He must now play my game or else expose himself." As he finished speaking, Richard smiled at the other men. Francis lowered his head in a long nod to show his approval. Sir Richard was also rocking his head slowly. The king moved away from the Magna Carta, his left palm lingering on the case, and started toward the door.

"Sire," Sir Richard's thickly accented voice rolled around the room, "Buckingham is asking for an audience with you." Richard halted and his gaze fell to his own feet. When he raised his head, he was looking at the door, the back of his head shielding his face from the men.

"I shall not see him." Richard tried to keep his swelling emotion from his voice and hoped that he had succeeded. "He will not use his sharp knife upon me again. I have been duped by his honeyed words already. He will stand trial and be executed as a traitor." As he finished, the king felt his voice cracking. He shot a glance at his friends who did not display any sign of noting the wobble.

"Tyrell tells me," Sir Richard offered against his own judgement, "that the duke claims to have been working from within the rebellion to ensure its failure and expose your enemies." He had known that Richard had sought to end what was obviously a painful discussion, and he had no desire to offer a means of escape to Henry Stafford. "Apparently he keeps insisting that he was acting in your best interests." There was unconcealed loathing in his voice. The king flinched, as though wounded by the words, and turned his face from them again. Sir Richard looked to Lord Lovell, who turned his head to face Ratcliffe, his eyes narrowed. Clearly, they were both reminded of their previous discussion regarding the king's nephews.

"I shall not see him." Richard repeated, his teeth gritted and his fists clenched into tight, white balls. "He will be executed as the traitor that he is."

"Yes, sire." Lord Lovell offered quickly. He bowed sharply. Sir Richard followed suit, though the king could not see them, and the two men strode past him and out of the room. The king turned and wearily walked back to the display case. He leaned over it, suddenly exhausted, and tried to allow the sound of the storm outside to drown out that of his swimming mind.

Chapter 32

20th April 1484 – The Castle of My Care

"All of life should be this way." Anne said carelessly as her hand brushed over a lavender bush, the warm spring air absorbing the gentle aroma hungrily. The gardens of Nottingham Castle, perched high above the city, were filling with colour and scent as the sun looked down on the king and queen.

"It should." Richard agreed, his absent tone caused by the sight of his wife so wrapped in bliss. "Cambridge was pleasant." It was almost a question, inviting her to tell him again how much she had enjoyed her time there.

"Oh, Richard," Anne threw up her arms like an excited child, "'pleasant' does it no justice at all." Her face was alight with a smile brighter than the promise of the summer to come that made the splendid gardens seem to Richard drab and dull. He could not help but grin. "The gifts to the University," her arms glided through the air as though in a dance of their own, "the glorious reception, the time in their libraries." She suddenly looked at Richard, chastened, as though caught in a moment of inappropriate joy.

"I am glad to see you enjoying being queen." Richard smiled at her warmly.

"Enjoying," Anne corrected him, taking his hand as they strolled, "being your wife, as I always have." She gazed at him as though searching for something. "We have come so far, Richard." Her voice was more serious now. "Farther than we ever imagined." She saw a flicker of something darting over his face. She knew that it was guilt, for she knew that he had dared to imagine this. "Fate has dealt us this hand," she consoled him, "we have but to use it to the best of our ability." She fixed his eyes again. "You are a great king,

Richard. There is no other on earth with whom I would be but you." They smiled at one another in a perfect moment of distraction.

"If I were so great a king," Richard's shoulders sank, "we should not need to be here."

"Greatness," Anne countered firmly, "attracts those jealous of it, those who covet it."

"So this present threat," Richard frowned, but smiled playfully at the same time, "is a measure of my greatness?"

"Hardly." Anne returned. "A thousand worthy rivals may provide a measure of your greatness. One Welsh pup is an insult." Though her tone was soft her voice was as hard as steel.

"Then I shall have satisfaction." Richard felt the strength of her gaze coursing through him. "My council should be awaiting us." He had been reluctant to hurry her from their strolling, but was overdue at the meeting. Arm in arm, they meandered back toward the castle buildings.

In the Great Hall, an enormous table, lined on either side with broad, high backed chairs, was dwarfed in the centre of the room. Lavish tapestries hung over the cold stone walls, erected for the visit of the king and queen, to add colour and warmth to the room. The enormous fireplace, framed by a mantel of beautifully carved oak, sat quiet. A fire had been laid but the morning had been warm enough that it had not been lit. Sir Richard Ratcliffe, Viscount Lovell, Sir James Harrington and Sir William Catesby sat around the table making jovial small talk. The Sheriff of Nottingham Castle, Sir Richard Edwards, paced to and fro before one of the tall, slim windows that overlooked the gardens. The rhythmic footfalls suddenly stopped, there was a long, low creak as he tilted himself expectantly toward the window before spinning around and scurrying to the table.

"They are coming." The sheriff trilled excitedly. His short, slightly plump frame flapped around the table rearranging chairs, jugs and goblets until each individual item met with his approval.

"Have the king's seat and goblet been correctly warmed?" Ratcliffe enquired of the sheriff gravely as the man's face relaxed. Instantly, his face flooded with colour and he was gripped by panic.

"Bah, uh...," he spluttered. As he looked at the chair, full of fear, Ratcliffe jabbed his elbow into James Harrington, who was struggling, quite unsuccessfully, to stifle a snigger. Harrington jumped in his seat and grabbed at his own tankard to cover his mouth.

"The king will not stand for a cold seat, nor a chilled cup." Ratcliffe's face remained as straight as an arrow, his tone sombre.

"But, but... What?" the new sheriff stammered, clearly floundering.

"Warm them man!" Ratcliffe instructed him helpfully.

"And be quick about it." Harrington insisted when he had composed himself enough to lower his drink. Lovell and Catesby shook their heads at each other, both happy to remain above the game, but both enjoying the display nonetheless.

"Warm them!" Ratcliffe forced, pointing as the man fell further into panic. The sheriff threw himself into the king's chair at the head of the table and began frantically rubbing his backside into the seat. No one had warned or instructed him about this. He grabbed the goblet set out for the king and rolled it between his hands, rubbing the sides and holding it close to him, all of the time slipping and sliding on the chair. How was he to have known? But would the king accept feeble excuses? He was oblivious to the door that silently opened to his right, directly in front of Ratcliffe and Harrington, who both instantly sat perfectly still, faces of graven stone.

King Richard stood in the doorway, with Queen Anne on his right arm, in silence for several long seconds. He eyed the two men before him, who stared at the table in front of them, the very images of impassive innocence. His gaze then moved to the frenetically writhing figure of the sheriff, who seemed to sense the eyes falling upon him and slowed, then halted and slowly, painfully slowly, turned his head to his right. At the sight of the king, his jaw dropped and he leapt from the chair as if stung. He stood, frozen to the spot, beside the table, slack jawed, staring at the king. For an aching moment, he feared that he was going to have to initiate an awkward explanation. Looking down, he suddenly realised that he was still hugging the goblet. Lurching it back onto the table he took a deep, quivering breath, still searching for a word with which to begin.

"My good sheriff," the king said sternly, seeing the man flustered, "perhaps you could take," he glanced at his chair, then back to the man, "your own seat?" He and Anne strolled to the table.

"Yes, sire." The sheriff's voice cracked as he spoke. He scampered down the far side of the table and dragged a chair back noisily, throwing himself into it. The instant that he sat, the four men rose to their feet and, Lovell and Catesby turning, all bowed to their king and queen. The sheriff shot out of his seat so sharply that it rocked back. His own low bow was enough to ensure that it crashed backward. He looked on in horror as the king winced at the noise, returned a polite nod to all five bows, moved back the chair at the right of the head of the table, beside Lovell, and allowed Anne to be seated. Next, the king took his seat and the other four gentlemen retook their positions. The sheriff tried to calm himself and right his chair, eventually sitting, red faced with a sheen of sweat covering his forehead and top lip. He was utterly convinced that his short time in office was ended.

"How long have you been Sheriff of Nottingham, Sir Richard?" The king's face was severe, his tone dry.

"Two months, sire." The sheriff tried to compose himself but his voice betrayed the fear that he would not make it to three. He offered a pained, apologetic smile.

"Then I am willing," Richard said louder, "to allow this to pass."

"Oh, sire..." Sir Richard Edwards began, relief flooding his voice.

"But," Richard cut in, raising a finger, "there is to be no repeat of this display. Is that clear?" The sheriff took a deep breath to acknowledge the chastisement with no small measure of relief, but his words never left him.

"Yes, sire." Two voices spoke in sarcastically apologetic unison. The sheriff looked around, jaw gaping, as Ratcliffe and Harrington hung their heads like naughty children caught at mischief, both with shoulders shaking in suppressed laughter until Sir Richard Ratcliffe finally cracked and sputtered into uncontrollable, booming laughter. In an instant, the other three joined him, roaring with delight. After almost as full minute of laughter, during which the sheriff had managed to close his mouth and was smiling, clearly amused but painfully self conscious, the mirth subsided.

"My dear sheriff," the king began smiling softly, "I must apologise for these 'gentlemen'." He waved a hand around the table. "They have a will to make fun at every opportunity. You really should ignore, or at least distrust, everything that they tell you, particularly about me."

"Yes, sire." The sheriff smiled, abashed.

"To business." Richard was instantly stern, all trace of the prank gone. "How go the works upon the castle?"

"The beautification progresses well, sire." The sheriff spoke stiffly.

"Good, good." Richard acknowledged thoughtfully. "I do like this place." He looked at Anne with a wistful smile.

"Nottingham is honoured." The sheriff straightened in his seat proudly.

"It has benefits other than its pretty aspect." Ratcliffe said flatly.

"A perfect base of operations from which to access every corner of the kingdom quickly." Sir James Harrington elaborated in his thick north-western accent, his blond hair framing a ruddy but handsome face.

"A good point too," Lord Lovell looked at the king and gave a knowing smile, "from which to visit Middleham, and the Prince of Wales."

"Indeed," Richard reached below the table for Anne's hand. "It seems so long since we have seen him and he is growing up so quickly."

"That bodes well for your dynasty." Catesby cut in. There were general nods of agreement.

"Speaking of which," Richard released Anne's hand with a gentle squeeze, "the main reason that we are here must be addressed."

"Campaigning season fast approaches, Richard." Ratcliffe shook his head sombrely.

"Would that we were planning our own campaign into the very heart of France." Excitement flashed over Richard's face. His stomach lurched at the thought of a glorious army, with himself and his company of knights at its head, sweeping through France to glory eternal.

"You will have your Agincourt." Sir James said with a fiery passion.

"We," Richard corrected, slowly and deliberately moving his gaze over each face, "we shall have our Agincourt."

"For now," Lord Lovell interrupted the silent reverie, "we must worry about our own shores, not foreign ones."

"True." The king conceded dejectedly. "Is there any word?" he directed the question to Catesby.

"Your spies work tirelessly," Sir William replied, "but have no word as yet of Tudor's plans, though we do know that he has not moved from Brittany."

"Good." Richard mused.

"Perhaps." Catesby said slowly. All eyes moved toward him.

"Go on." The king eyed him, knowing that the lawyer's mind was again at work.

"When you did not supply Duke Francis of Brittany with the archers that he requested," Catesby explained, "he in turn aided Tudor's abortive invasion last year."

"Is this a history lesson, William?" Ratcliffe grinned. Sir William shot him a withering glance.

"You," Catesby returned his focus to the king slowly, "then sanctioned naval operations against Breton ships." He leaned forward. "As you are aware, this action soon escalated to include Scottish and French shipping."

"Yes, yes." Richard said irritably.

"My concern," Sir William took the hint that he should move forward apace, "is that such aggression against these three states will give them a common cause."

"Mmm." Richard nodded pensively. He looked around the table to see the other men glancing at each other and nodding also. Even Anne looked concerned.

"If they were to unite," Lovell began.

"They would have a ready and willing alternative." Harrington completed the thought.

"A comparatively appealing one, too." Ratcliffe looked at his king.

"Tudor." Richard growled. After a moment he thumped the table, resigned to the ill tidings.

"I think," Catesby began coolly, "that the time is right to pursue peace with these enemies in order to keep them from our other enemy."

"This makes sense." Richard conceded morosely.

"Unfortunately." Ratcliffe grumbled his agreement to sympathetic chuckles around the table.

"I would suggest that we sue for peace with the Scottish." Catesby told the men.

"Very well." Richard said after a moment of searching for an alternative. "If you can find someone inoffensive to the Scots." Richard grinned. The northern men around the table each had a long history with the Scottish over years of border skirmishes and all had taken part in Richard's victorious march on Edinburgh.

"France," Catesby continued after noting the instruction, "still has internal problems. The Duke of Orleans is trying to organise a challenge to the regency government. The word is that Anne of Beaujeau is seriously concerned."

"Good." Lovell said. "That should keep them busy enough."

"Indeed." Catesby agreed. "I have received communication from the Duke of Orleans seeking your support, sire."

"Hhmmphh!" Richard snorted.

"Richard," Catesby persevered, "it would keep France from interest in Tudor's cause."

"Or push them closer to it should the duke fail. I will not," Richard continued vehemently, "assist, and thereby endorse, any other claimant to a throne that is mine by right."

"Perhaps tacit assistance in prolonging the disharmony?" Catesby suggested.

"No." Richard said flatly in a tone that all present knew was not to be argued with.

"Very well." Catesby acquiesced.

"What of Brittany?" Harrington's voice rolled across the table.

"We could," Richard thought aloud, "offer Duke Francis the archers that he requested last year on the condition that he hand Tudor over to us." He looked around the table at the general nods of agreement.

"There is," Catesby interjected to groans from Ratcliffe and Harrington, "news from this quarter also."

"Go on." Richard rolled his eyes at the endless twists.

"Duke Francis is unwell." Catesby continued curtly. "His Chancellor, Pierre Landlais, rules on his behalf at present."

"I see." Richard frowned with interest.

"He is deeply unpopular in Brittany and has a well known mistrust for France and French intensions. He also has a love of gold."

"An interesting concoction of a man." Lovell commented.

"So we bribe Landlais, just to be sure." Richard suggested.

"Precisely what I was going to recommend." Catesby smiled.

"Send Sir James Tyrell to Brittany." Richard said quickly, the notion leaping into his mind and out of his mouth. "This requires someone with tact whom we can trust." Richard shifted in his seat as one more matter occurred to him. "What news from Wales?" he asked a little uncertainly.

"Ah." Catesby sifted through his papers for a salient sheet. "Following his refusal to join Buckingham's rising in Wales, Rhys ap Thomas has, as per your instructions, been promoted to Principal Lieutenant in south west Wales, complete with an annuity of 40 marks for life."

"Good." Richard replied thoughtfully. "Hopefully promoting from within the old Welsh nobility will play well with the province.

"It should do you well." Ratcliffe nodded approvingly.

"Thomas has forwarded the following oath." Catesby lifted the page before him to read. "He vows; 'Whoever ill-affected to the state, shall dare to land in these parts of Wales where I have employment under your majesty, must resolve with himself to make his entrance and irruption over my belly'."

"Well," Harrington mused, "that is quite eloquent for a Welshman."

"The question, though," Richard responded without the amusement that rippled through the rest of the room at the comment, "is whether or not he can be held to his word."

"Well," Catesby weighed the king's query, "Thomas is well respected in his lands and renowned for his honour."

"Did he send his son here as I requested as surety against his oath?" Richard asked.

"He, er," Catesby moved to another sheet of paper, "he sent a request that he be excused from separation from his son Gruffydd. He assures your grace that nothing, not even the threat to his son, could bind him to his duty more strongly than his conscience." There was a long silence.

"Do you believe that he can be trusted?" Richard asked again.

"If his reputation is to be believed, then I would say so." Catesby offered.

"Very well." Richard acquiesced. "Perhaps a little compromise will assist in building bridges."

"Perfect." Catesby agreed. "I shall set these things into motion immediately." Richard nodded his assent to Catesby's departure and the other rose, bowed and swept from the room.

"Now," Richard returned his attention to the sheriff, "you must tell me how January's Parliament has been received in the midlands." He leaned forward expectantly.

"Sire," the sheriff smiled, "it has been welcomed joyously in all quarters." He felt all of the eyes around the table upon him, but he had prepared himself for this line of enquiry. "The common man hails your actions to free juries from tampering and intimidation. Your new system of bail is likewise applauded as protecting and increasing your subjects' access to justice irrespective of rank."

"Excellent news!" Richard clapped his hands together and beamed at the other men around the table. "Go on, go on," he urged the sheriff excitedly.

"Your moves to protect buyers of land from undisclosed defects of title have been met well by the gentry and merchants," the sheriff's voice was steady and deliberate now, "the latter being especially pleased by the outlawing of deceitful conduct in wool manufacture, something of particular importance within our region."

"Benevolences?" Richard asked, struggling to contain his swelling excitement.

"The growing merchant class is pleased to be protected from having to make forced gifts of money to the Crown, sire." He smiled at the king. "Not only do they feel more secure to invest their wealth in increasing trade, but they view it as a clear statement of your intended financial assurance in the management of Crown affairs."

"I am unsure that I am able to deal with all of this good news, sheriff!" Richard's voice echoed his delight around the room. "All is as it was meant to be."

"For how long, though?" Lord Lovell's cool voice cut through the heat of Richard's excitement.

"Francis," Richard drawled, slumping back in his chair, "why must you always dampen my triumph?"

"Because a true friend will when required to do so." Lovell smiled genially. "Though much of what your Parliament has done pleases the common man, the gentry," his eyes flicked around to his friends at the table whom he included in this group, "and the merchants, what you give to them is, in equal measure, taken from others."

"If I give them security and justice," Richard leaned toward Lord Lovell, "I do not remove it from anyone. Rather, I give it to all men, instead of just a few."

"Such matters are traditionally entrusted to regional magnates. It is their position that you are eroding and they will fight to maintain what they consider to be their rights."

"If they were not abusing, or allowing flagrant abuse of, justice then such measures would not be required." Richard fixed Lovell with a challenging stare as his face began to fill with colour.

"All that I am saying," Francis continued, ignoring the gaze, "is that you should take a little care in handling such ingrained traditions."

"And I say," Richard roared, the red heat of rage now filling his cheeks, "that it is they who should take care. It is over two hundred and fifty years since the barons forced Magna Carta upon John to protect their positions from an abusive Crown.

The time is coming when the common man will assert his right to freedom from the abuses of the barons in exactly the same way. The Crown must decide whether to fight against this or mediate the change peaceably."

"Everyone is aware of your care for all of your subjects, Richard." Francis again paid no attention to the king's tone. "I am urging only caution, not a change of policy. The nobles will not like it," he said flatly, now returning the challenge.

"John did not like Magna Carta. He tried to oppose the barons, to go back on his word after the signing and it eventually cost him his crown and his life." Richard was growing angry. Although he knew that Francis had a valid point and did not really mind that he had made it, the subject matter itself irritated Richard to his very core.

"I am not sure," Francis narrowed his eyes with concern, "that threats will help."

"Is your noble nose feeling pushed out?" Sir Richard Ratcliffe interjected, smirking.

"You know very well," Francis flashed a jovial smile at Ratcliffe but his green eyes were severe, "that my nose is the least noble nose amongst noble noses." The king laughed a little. Lovell returned his focus there, still smiling. "I share your dreams, Richard, we all do, but there is danger here in charging in." There was a tense silence.

"Publishing the laws of your Parliament," the sheriff offered, uncomfortable at the confrontation that these men braved with their king, "in English has also proven popular in Nottingham, sire," he smiled uncertainly.

"Also dangerous." Lovell said to the man in a tone so calm that it unsettled him. "This also removes something from the hands of those who have traditionally managed it."

"That is the very point." Richard said, as though surprised that Lovell would not understand.

"I know," Francis responded, "that many nobles are outraged by this."

"Good." Richard said flatly. "Tell Lord Lovell why it is a popular move, sheriff." Sir Richard Edwards gulped. He had no wish to offend Viscount Lovell, but less of a mind still to argue with King Richard.

"Sire," the sheriff began slowly, trying to avoid Lord Lovell's intense stare, "although many people cannot themselves read, the very fact that laws are published in their language makes them feel that these are their laws." The king was nodding. Encouraged, the sheriff expanded. "The law has always been the preserve of the Church and the nobility. To the common man, the law was what they were told it was by these educated institutions. In order to find out what the law was, they would have to ask it of one of them. The people were judged by something distant and distinct from them and their lives. If the law is in the language of the people, it can belong to the people. It can be the law of the people." He dared a glance at Lord Lovell whose gaze was fixed upon him, though thankfully he showed no outward sign of disgruntlement. "This allows every man, whatever his rank or status, to feel that the law is his, for his benefit, protection and preservation." He looked around the faces at the table, each apparently wrapped by his words. He swelled with pride and continued. "This is a move that makes every man of England feel like England belongs to him and that he belongs to England, that we are all one and equal." There was a long silence during which the sheriff's unease crept back in. Slowly, those around the table began to look at one another. Sir Richard Edwards swallowed. In that instant the quiet was broken by an echoing crack. The king began clapping his hands loudly. Smiles erupted around the table.

"Well said, Sir Richard!" the king boomed. "Well said indeed." He beamed a broad, satisfied grin. "Perhaps this would be a good moment to take some refreshment."

"Yes, sire." The sheriff rose sharply, lifted by his own relief at the king's reaction. He bowed and positively strutted to the door.

Richard rose from his seat and stretched. He reached a hand out to Anne, who took it lightly and rose, smiling gently. As she rose, the other men stood politely. Acknowledging them, the queen moved with the king to one of the windows overlooking the gardens, their conversation lost to those still around the table, who had already begun their own, louder tale-telling. Sir Richard Ratcliffe and Sir James Harrington were beginning to howl with raucous laughter as they shared the memory of a hunt during which a particularly keen young squire had been so desperate to recover the quarry that he had leapt from the bushes as the shot was fired and had intercepted the arrow with the meat of his buttock. The door opened and a parade of food and drink was deposited upon the table and the fire in the huge grate was set ablaze against the weak spring sun.

Ratcliffe and Harrington filled their platters urgently, seeming not to have eaten for a week, and took their food to stand before the now roaring flames. Francis remained seated at the table, absently picking from the dishes of meat as he watched Richard and Anne in the window. He was concerned by the changes that he perceived in his friend. Once so open, he seemed now to be shutting himself up from them. Doubtless he was under significantly more strain than ever before but a part of his strength and attraction to men like Lovell, Ratcliffe and Harrington, had always been the fierce loyalty that he inspired in others by his willingness to trust in them and to reward the treasuring of that trust. Now, he needed that kind of passionate attachment from more than just a few friends and followers. He needed it from a whole nation, including those who currently may call themselves his enemies, and Francis saw him neglecting rather than using this unrivalled ability.

Anne was laughing at something that Richard had said to her when the king's eye was caught by Lovell's grave face watching them. His smile slipped a little and a frown creased his forehead. It was a moment before Lovell's mind caught up with him and he realised that Richard was gazing at him, smiling but clearly concerned. The king cocked his head sideways questioningly, pushing his smile wide and raising his goblet as if in toast to Lovell. The Viscount hesitated. He considered not responding to draw Richard's attention, or even taking the gesture as an invitation and using the platform to challenge Richard. But to challenge what exactly? Before he really knew it, the moment was gone and he smiled courteously back, as one woken from a distant day dream. The king's frown melted. His broad smile returned to his eyes and his attention moved back to Anne. Lovell rose, picked up a goblet of wine, raised it to his lips and turned toward Ratcliffe and Harrington at the fireplace. As he walked the few paces, though, he could not shake off the feeling that the king's eyes were at his back.

"Francis." Ratcliffe's deep voice greeted him almost at a whisper. "Francis, we have been wondering, along with most of the country," he looked at James Harrington for approval, which he received, "about the Woodville's return to court."

"Wondering what, my dear Richard?" Lovell asked blankly, though he knew what they wondered, and he knew that the rest of the nation whispered too.

"Come on, Francis." Sir James intervened, flashing a glance at the king to ensure that he could not hear them. "If anyone knows what happened it is you."

"Then nobody knows." Lovell answered with a shrug.

"You know Richard best of all of us." Ratcliffe conceded. "Has he really not told you how and why the former queen and all of her daughters have suddenly left sanctuary after all of this time and returned to court?"

"No." Lovell replied, smiling softly.

"Then it becomes more curious still." Harrington frowned.

"Something," Ratcliffe pondered, "has led them to give up their sanctuary after a year in its safety."

"Richard must have promised her something." Sir James said confidently.

"It is common knowledge what he has promised her." Francis's tone held a hint of chastisement at the men's speculation, but if pushed, he would have had to admit to similar concerns.

"Yes." Ratcliffe waved away Lovell's guarded responses irritably. "We know that he has guaranteed their safety and promised suitable marriages for her daughters. The question is why, and why now?"

"The why, for both parties," Lovell contemplated aloud, "is not difficult to fathom." He looked from the fire to the faces either side of it and saw their bemused expressions. "For Elizabeth Woodville, life in sanctuary must be a trial after the opulence of her former surroundings. She must have feared for her future, so a guarantee of safety would be a great relief. Whatever else they may think of each other, we know that the Woodvilles trust in Richard's sense of honour and justice." Lovell shrugged a little as he continued. "A guarantee of good matches for her daughters is more than she could have hoped for too."

"But why would Richard concede all of this?" Ratcliffe asked. "He had the Woodvilles safely tucked away."

"Perhaps." Lovell mused. "I do not know for certain, but there are many possible reasons. It may be that enough time has passed for the passions of betrayal to fade and if Richard is to reign for all of the years that we hope for, then issues such as this must be resolved. It cannot be Elizabeth Woodville's fault that Edward could not legitimately marry her. Most in her former position would seek to strengthen the standing of their family and would in turn do all that was necessary to prevent their world from collapsing around them."

"Hhmmpphh!" Harrington snorted. "Sympathy for the Woodvilles. Well I never." The three men smiled.

"Sympathy," Lovell challenged, "or the reality that must be addressed?"

"What of the other reasons?" Ratcliffe asked intrigued. "I can see that one less enemy at a time like this would be appealing."

"Precisely." Lovell agreed. "Let us not forget that Elizabeth Woodville's son the Marquis of Dorset, is currently a part of Henry Tudor's faux court in Brittany."

"So Richard hopes to destabilise Tudor by reconciliation with the Woodvilles?" Harrington eagerly continued the notion.

"Why, though," Ratcliffe said slowly, as though organising his thoughts as he spoke, "would Richard reinstitute what he disliked so much before, and the cause of so much unrest, by allowing the Woodvilles strong matches in the marriage market?"

"Ah," Lovell raised a finger, "Richard only promised fitting marriages to gentlemen. That is very different to the best matches in noble circles and should reflect the family's lesser standing whilst simultaneously offering more than they could have hoped for."

"I should think also," Harrington offered, "that giving Elizabeth Woodville something to lose could prove useful." There was silence. He looked nervously at the other two men, who glanced at each other.

"Bloody hell, James." Sir Richard shook with laughter. "Do you need a sit down?"

"Sod off!" Harrington retorted, his face bright red with embarrassment but his shoulders shaking as he tried not to laugh.

"A good point, though." Lovell smiled. "Richard would leave himself with an unknown quantity if he kept Elizabeth Woodville as an enemy who had nothing left to lose. Who knows what she may be capable of then?"

"Yet she has more to gain if Tudor were to succeed and follow through on his vow to marry Elizabeth's eldest daughter. Her blood would again be upon the throne."

Harrington looked at the men again but the mocking was clearly over.

"I would imagine," Ratcliffe considered, "that the bird in her hand would have to be worth more to her than two in a French bush."

"Well said." Lovell smiled. "I would hope that it reflects also on Tudor's lack of prospects."

"Francis," Harrington said enquiringly, "you mentioned that the 'whys' in all of this were the easy part. So what is the hard?"

"Thinking and remembering in one day." Ratcliffe chuckled. "I think I need a sit down now." He saw James's face flush again and watched him draw a deep breath, no doubt to give wind to endless curses. "James," he reached a hand out to the other's shoulder, "I am teasing and I am sorry, my friend." Harrington nodded, willing to forget as he returned his attention to Lovell.

"Indeed," the Viscount sighed, "the why is easy. There are many benefits to both parties." He looked at both men with a stare so stern that both of their faces became serious and they leaned toward him a little. "The hard part to understand is the how." Ratcliffe and Harrington's frowns deepened. Lovell took a deep breath. "Rumours abound as to the fate of Richard's nephews. Rumours which he will neither confirm nor contradict. Therefore we must conclude that Elizabeth Woodville would have strong reason to believe that Richard has murdered her sons by his brother." He looked at the horror struck expressions of the other two men.

"Do you think...," Ratcliffe began.

"What I think," Lovell interrupted him, "is irrelevant. We are discussing what Elizabeth Woodville believes from her secluded sanctuary has befallen her two young sons in their uncle's care. If she suspects Richard, how could she return to court? How could she hand over her remaining children to the man that she believes has murdered her beloved boys?"

"She could not." Harrington concluded flatly, concern at the conclusion etched on his face.

"Unless that is the reason for so public a promise of their safety." Ratcliffe offered. "If she fears him, she would at least know that he would not wish to dishonour himself by breaking such a vow and she would foresee a public outrage if ever he did."

"I had not considered that." Lovell conceded, a little deflated. "Still," he gathered himself again, "if she believes him capable of the first deed to take the throne, why not the second to secure it?"

"Aacchh!" Harrington exclaimed. "This is all so damned complicated. At least with the French or the Scots we know who the enemy is."

"True." Ratcliffe chuckled. "War is easy. This is politics. War is open confrontation. Politics is subtle distraction. But both are those who have power trying to keep it from those who want power and are trying to take it."

"So we are no closer to the how?" Harrington asked Lovell.

"I told you, James, this is all supposition." Lovell shrugged.

"You have a theory, though?" Ratcliffe narrowed his eyes at his shrewd friend.

"Only the obvious one." Lovell sipped slowly from his goblet, staring into the fire. There was a pause.

"Which is?" hissed Ratcliffe in a demanding whisper.

"Which is that Richard must have given Elizabeth Woodville some firm, believable and irrefutable proof regarding the fate of her sons." There was a longer pause. The fire crackled.

"Then," Ratcliffe said slowly, uncertainly, "they are still alive? He must have shown them to Elizabeth."

"Perhaps." Lovell sighed. "But it is also possible that he told her how they met their deaths and convinced her that it was neither at his hand nor instruction."

"Buckingham?" Harrington asked. "The rebellion last year switched quickly from the boys' to Tudor's name."

"True." Lovell agreed. "Buckingham was not really the prime mover in the rebellion though." The other two looked at him expectantly. He fixed his eyes firmly on Harrington, who frowned and then opened his mouth in realisation.

"Stanley," he spat the name of his old adversary.

"Lady Stanley." Lovell corrected.

"You think that Lady Stanley killed the boys?" Ratcliffe whispered.

"How many times must I tell you?" Francis's frustration was evident even at a whisper. "I do not know. I am merely trying to piece this together but can find a dozen answers to each question. Certainly she had motive. They stood as figureheads for a rebellion by which she wanted to place her son on the throne. She had opportunity. Access to the Tower of London would have been within her compass, particularly as she made sure to ingratiate herself with the new queen. Lady Stanley may well even have sent word to the Woodvilles in sanctuary that Richard had done the deed in order to garner support for her son. In fact, she may have passed such information without any knowledge whatsoever of their fate in order to convince the otherwise cut off Woodvilles to support Tudor."

After a moment, Harrington and Ratcliffe both blew out their cheeks as the words sank in. They were clearly struggling to digest all of the permutations. Was their friend a murderer, or at best a politic realist of the most extreme kind? Or was he the victim of a series of plots to undermine him? Both shot a glance at their king, still lost in pleasant conversation at the window seats with his queen.

"Why does Richard not put an end to this and tell everyone what he knows?" Harrington eventually asked.

"I think," Lovell replied, "that he would ask why he should. Do we not know and trust him? Should he need to prove himself to us again?"

"No, he should not." Harrington hung his head a little.

"Yet here we are." Ratcliffe opened his arms. "Doubting him." He was manifestly irritated with himself.

"There is one more key point, upon which we touched earlier." Lovell appeared to want to mention this in spite of himself.

"Which is?" Ratcliffe was clearly upset.

"Tudor's promise to marry the eldest daughter of King Edward, the young Elizabeth."

"As we said," Ratcliffe waved the issue away, "a ploy to buy the support of the Woodvilles."

"And probably," Harrington ventured, "that of Edward's other disaffected adherents."

"Indeed." Lovell replied in a tone that caused Sir Richard Ratcliffe to narrow his eyes. "Yet there is something deeply sinister that bubbles just below the surface of this vow." Ratcliffe's eyes remained pinched and fixed on Lovell, clearly trying to decipher his meaning. Harrington frowned and cocked his head.

"Well?" Sir James finally conceded with a sigh.

"Assume, may God forbid it," Lovell looked up meaningfully, "that Tudor were to succeed and look to make good on his promise." He saw the unconscious snarl on Ratcliffe's face and smiled soothingly. "What now is the only bar?"

"You mean," Ratcliffe spat, "apart from my sword up his..."

"Yes, Richard." Lovell chuckled. "Apart from that." Ratcliffe and Harrington both grinned.

"Ah!" Harrington pointed at Lovell. He smiled, clearly pleased with himself. "She has been declared illegitimate by Parliament."

"Precisely." Lovell said darkly.

"Tudor would be in a position to reverse this though." Harrington said, frowning again.

"Indeed he would." Francis replied.

"But," Ratcliffe picked up Lovell's lead, "in order to do so he would also have to legitimise her brothers."

"Creating for himself," Lovell continued, "a rival with a far stronger claim to the throne, probably more public support and sympathy, certainly the support of the Woodvilles and his father's faction upon both of whom Tudor is seeking to rely by making the gesture in the first instance." There was a stunned silence. Ratcliffe shot another glance at the king.

"Richard will know this." Ratcliffe stated.

"I do not doubt it." Lovell agreed.

"Surely," Harrington ventured hesitantly, "this means that Tudor cannot really intend to go through with his proposal. He is lying and Richard has told the Woodvilles this."

"I would that it were so simple, James." Lovell said solemnly.

"If," Ratcliffe began to explain, as much to himself as Harrington, "he can so confidently make such a vow, and assuming that he does intend to honour it," he looked at Lovell, "then he must know that doing so would not create for himself the rival that he could not tolerate."

"Ergo," Lovell completed the thought, "he must know something definite of the fate of the two boys."

"Which would point the finger back towards..." Ratcliffe began.

"Lady Stanley." Harrington concluded. "That witch must have had the boys done away with."

"Possibly." Lovell cautioned them. "Possibly he is a liar, possibly an ill advised imbecile who has failed to think the matter through before making his grand gesture. Possibly he knows that they are no longer an issue."

"Well," Harrington said, "he cannot know that it was done by another since no one else seems to know as much."

"I truly do not know what to believe." Lovell conceded.

"But you suspect that Richard does?" Ratcliffe asked bluntly.

"I do." Francis was almost apologetic. He felt disloyal, dirtied, talking like this behind Richard's back.

"Then ask him." Ratcliffe snapped as though reading his mind. Lovell had already decided in the instant before. He drained the remaining wine from his goblet, set it on the mantle, wiped his sleeve across his lips and took a wide, determined stride toward the king.

Lovell's second step faltered mid pace as the door to his left flew open with an unceremonious thud. He watched, an amused frown rippling his forehead, as Sir William Catesby, his face bright red and his expression like thunder, positively dragged a young man into the room. To see Catesby, usually such a model of composure and always so measured, in such a flap was new. Sir William wordlessly hauled the other toward the king. Puzzlement replaced the amusement as Lovell noted that the man was dusty and muddy and still wearing riding gear. Clearly he was a messenger. Just as clearly, he did not want to deliver his news.

"Tudor has landed?" Sir Richard's hot voice came quietly over Lovell's right shoulder. He considered the idea for a moment but saw in it no reason either for the rush, or for the reluctance. He felt Ratcliffe move by his side and toward the king, clearly keen for the fight. Lovell threw out his arm to bar Sir Richard's way as Catesby reached the king.

"I do not think..." Lovell was too lost in the scene to complete the sentence.

The king stood to meet the noisy interruption, clearly as puzzled as Lovell was. Catesby reached him with, if anything, an even deeper shade of red darkening his face, and the messenger still wriggling in his wake. As soon as they halted, the man stood bolt upright and bowed. Clearly his instinct to behave correctly had not deserted him. Catesby nodded curtly to the king, his lawyer's face suddenly softening. He spoke a few words quietly to Richard that caused the queen to also rise. Francis sensed Ratcliffe and Harrington straining behind him to hear what was being said. The king was clearly urging Catesby to deliver the message. Sir William drew himself up and spoke calmly, still too quietly to reach the desperate ears on the other side of the room. Then, the silence was shattered by a soul rending scream from the queen who wavered, throwing a hand out to her husband's shoulder.

Richard then grabbed the messenger by his tunic and shook him. Although Lovell could still not make out the words, his voice was raised and he clearly demanded some confirmation from the man of Catesby's words. The messenger shot a look of desperate appeal at the three men by the fireplace before he was shaken again. An instant later, Richard had slapped the man across the cheek. He looked as though he would have fallen under the weight of the strike but for the king's other hand holding him upright. Lovell looked back to Ratcliffe and Harrington, his own bewilderment at their friend's actions mirrored on their faces. As he looked back, the man gave the affirmation Richard sought. The king released his grip and the man stepped unsteadily backward. Richard himself seemed to stagger and then his legs gave out beneath him and he fell, as if slowed, into the window seat behind him. The queen, one hand gripping her stomach as though a knife had been buried there, the other clasped over her mouth, ran from the hall. The messenger took the opportunity to slink further back. Catesby leaned forward to the king who seemed stunned like a fish bashed upon a rock. Sir William turned an appealing look to the other three men, who began immediately to hasten across the room, but before they could reach the window Richard had regained himself, risen unsteadily and pushed Catesby's protests aside. He sprinted awkwardly from the hall after his wife. For the first time, Lovell heard his voice clearly.

"Anne!" It was unmistakeably cracked with raw emotion.

Viscount Lovell, Sir Richard Ratcliffe and Sir James Harrington arrived at the side of Sir William Catesby, all four looking at the spot where the king had left the room.

"What is it, William?" Ratcliffe demanded.

"It... I..." Catesby was still flushed and clearly unable to articulate the news again.

"Do I have to slap it out of you too?" Sir Richard's tone was menacing and there was a strange squeak from the messenger. Catesby stood up straight again, took in a long, slow, steadying breath and fixed his gaze very deliberately on Lord Lovell.

"The Prince of Wales has died." His words fell on a dumb silence. Each man looked to the other as if begging one amongst them to wake from whoever's nightmare this was. "He died suddenly a few days ago after a short illness." Catesby's voice was faltering.

"May the Lord have mercy upon his poor little soul." Harrington's voice was steady but, as all four men crossed themselves, a tear tracked his left cheek.

"Poor Edward." Ratcliffe seconded.

"Richard, Anne!" Lovell exclaimed and moved to follow them.

"Francis!" Catesby caught his shoulder, turning him. "This will have repercussions that must be dealt with straight away." He saw Lovell's jaw drop. "Francis," Catesby insisted "the Prince is dead and we are threatened with invasion. The weakening..." He stopped speaking. Lovell's mouth was closed again and his jaw clenched. His bright green eyes burned into Catesby.

"Do not presume," Lovell said quietly but with the ferocity of a wild animal backed into a corner, "to lay hands on me as though I am some common messenger to be dragged to your will." He slowly looked down at Catesby's hand, still upon his shoulder. The other man withdrew it sharply. The granite hard gaze crushed Catesby a moment more, then Lord Lovell span on his heels and sprinted from the room. Ratcliffe and Harrington followed.

"I only meant..." Catesby called after them apologetically.

"We know what you meant, William," Ratcliffe stopped in the doorway and looked back, "but your timing is unforgivable." Then they too were gone. Catesby sank into the window seat abandoned by Richard and stared vacantly out of the window.

A few days later, Richard sat in the chapel of Sheriff Hutton Castle in Ryedale, North Yorkshire. The past days had been some of the longest of his life. Anne was distraught. He had been barely able to speak to her and she had taken to locking herself in her room. Matters of state had been left to others. Indeed, Richard's only cause to be grateful had been his friends' determination to keep all of the business that needed attending to from him. As for himself, he was not sure how he felt. He was not even sure that he could feel anything. More to the point, he knew that he did not want to feel anything, did not want to connect with the pain that must swim somewhere inside him seeking the surface. All that he had built lay shattered before him, hidden inside a small casket. A fresh tear spilled from his reddened eyes. He looked from the small coffin to the altar. Rage began to mix with his aching grief.

"Why?" he hissed in a cracked whisper to the altar. "What have I done to deserve this? What could he have done?" His eyes fell to the silent coffin. A thick, heavy tear spattered onto his hands, clasped together in his lap, but his gaze did not move from the wooden box that contained his son and kept him from reach. He rose and walked on numb legs to the coffin that lay on a table before the altar, prepared for tomorrow's funeral service. He stretched out a trembling hand but withdrew it, unable to bring himself to touch the casket. Looking to the altar again, he clenched his fists at his sides.

"What could he have done?" Richard roared, his voice filling the chapel and booming around the walls as though a hundred other voices demanded the same answers. He stood in the silence that followed for a protracted moment, as if expecting some reply. "You will tell me what he has done to deserve this!" His voice rang out again but trailed away as emotion gripped at his throat.

"I am not sure that is the way it works, sire." The soft voice caused Richard to jump. He turned, ready to release a tirade of abuse upon the man who dared to interrupt him, but as his mouth opened, his anger evaporated.

"John." His shoulders sagged as he relaxed a little. He tried to compose himself. "It has been too long, old friend."

"There has been much to keep us all busy this past year, sire." John smiled gently. "I am truly sorry for your loss, your grace." John spoke with a sincerity that raised the corners of Richard's mouth a little in appreciation.

"Thank you." Richard replied. There was an uneasy silence.

"Your lunch is ready, sire." John eventually filled the empty space. "Will you take it in the hall?" The tone was hopeful but not expectant.

"In my room, please John." Richard said quietly.

"Very well, sire." John bowed and turned.

"What did you mean, John?" Richard asked.

"Sire?" The man turned, his pleasant smile still in place.

"When you said that it is not the way it works." Richard fixed his eyes on the older man. "What did you mean?"

"Just that, sire." John replied softly with a gentle shrug. "I do not think that people die young because they have done some wrong before God, much less that someone else has." His dark eyes met Richard's own meaningfully. "Such judgements are not made on earth, they are for the Lord God to make in his Heaven. Our only concern is the life with which we meet Him. That is our case and evidence for a place in His Kingdom." Richard turned back to face the altar and bit his lip to stave off more weeping.

"I do not find such wisdom in the Bishops and Archbishops who spend their lives studying philosophy." The king tried to sound light hearted.

"You tease me, sire." John was clearly abashed.

"No, John." Richard said firmly. "No I do not." He looked down again at the coffin. "If only life were as vigilant as death." Richard felt a fresh wave of intense sorrow lapping at his throat. "We all meet our death. There is no avoiding that." He took a deep breath. "But not all enjoy a life first." He held off the tears. "I swore to him, John." Richard spoke without meaning to. "I swore to him on the day that he was born that I would protect him." He was barely holding himself in check now as emotion ripped through him. Grief, guilt, sorrow and anger all fought for supremacy. "I swore that he would never know the uncertainty and insecurity of my life." He barely forced the words out before his throat tightened.

"Then with respect, sire," John's tone was even, "you have done as you promised for your son."

"Have I?" Richard turned to face him, his voice shrill as it tried to escape him.

"Indeed." John replied calmly. "Prince Edward grew up in security, in the boundless love of his mother and father, watching them rise and go from strength to strength. The only moment of uncertainty, when you brother passed away, probably passed him by. Even if it did not, there was the briefest moment of potential insecurity until his father seized the reins and steadied matters. His stability was not threatened." John held the king's gaze. "Excuse my saying so, my king, but can you say that your father did the same for you?" There was a long, intense silence. Richard's eyes shimmered in the candle light but John's remained steadfastly kind.

"Do you know what my first memory is?" Richard asked, knowing that the man could not possibly know the answer. He had only ever shared it with Anne before.

"No, sire." John replied.

"I was standing in the market square outside Ludlow Castle with my mother, George and my sisters." He hung his head. "My father had been defeated by King Henry's army and had fled with all of his allies, including my two older brothers. My mother and we children were left to the mercy of the victorious army. I tried so hard to stand straight but I was only a young boy, just turned seven, and all that I wanted to do was hide behind my mother's skirts. To this day I believe that it was only the strength of her presence that kept us alive. Perhaps I can see now that my father had his reasons for leaving us there and fleeing, but all that child felt was abandoned."

"Well, sire." John told him. "I think that you have answered my question."

"So many believe that wisdom is the reserve of the rich and educated." Richard smiled softly. "They miss so much, my friend." John shuffled uncomfortable, looking at his own feet. Seeing his unease, Richard took a deep breath. "I shall eat in my room, please John."

"Very well." John replied courteously, as though nothing of note had just passed between him and the king. He bowed low and backed through the door, pushing it quietly shut.

Richard closed his eyes, heaved in a deep breath and turned around. When he opened his eyes again and looked down, he saw his hands, fingers spread out, upon the top of the coffin. The dark wood of the casket felt cold and solid under his palms, like a barrier keeping him from his son. Heavy tears splashed freely around his fingers as a fresh tidal wave of grief washed over him. His shoulders shook sharply. Time seemed to mean nothing and when he finally gathered himself, Richard could not tell whether seconds, minutes or even hours had passed by. He ached all over and his eyes stung. Now, he found himself unable to take his hands away, his fingers clawing slowly at the wood, trying to grip the smooth surface. He told himself that he must let go, but his hands would not obey. He pictured his beautiful son, lying still within, and imagined that he was only asleep. He leaned over the coffin, his face so close that he could smell the wood.

"I have to go, my son." He inhaled the aroma deeply. "Be at peace. I am sorry that I shall not see you grow into the man that I know you would have been." He drew in another quivering breath and continued at a whisper. "I am sorry, Edward, my beautiful Edward." Tears rolled to the end of his nose and had hardly to fall at all to reach the hard surface below. Moving still closer, Richard kissed the wood, a long, slow kiss lasting several uneven breaths. "That," he whispered as his lips parted only slightly from his son, "is to keep you safe until I see you again."

Drawing himself up, Richard removed his hands, crossed himself before the altar, gave a final smile to his son and turned, leaving the chapel without looking back. He had felt foolish for wanting to re-enact that little custom, but now that it was done, he found some small measure of comfort, and strength, in it.

Chapter 33

31st October 1484 – Like Sand Through Our Fingers

Hallowmas had long been a favoured festival of Richard's. This, All Hallows Eve, would be followed by All Saints Day and All Souls Day. He recalled one of his tutors telling him of the Celtic root of the festival, the ancient notion of Samhain. The Celts would celebrate the end of summer and beginning of winter, believing that on this night the spirits of the year's dead would roam the earth. The thought sent a shiver down his spine. It was tradition that on All Hallows Eve people would pray for the souls of the departed loved ones of friends and family and in return, cakes were given in appreciation of the prayers. This had particular resonance for him this year. The king had ordered cakes sent to his closest friends along with a request for their prayers for his son. He had received many offerings himself at Westminster and had ordered that the Abbey's monks pray for all lost English souls.

The dimness of the evening seeped over London early but was, this evening, being warded off by the eruption of dozens of bonfires, some small, some enormous. Richard smiled as he recalled being taught that this was to ward off the spirits of the dead that roamed, lost. He had been terrified by the notion as a boy and always complained that he was cold on this night so that a fire was set in his bedchamber, piled high to burn all night. Now, as he and a small bodyguard rode through the streets of London from the Abbey to the Palace of Westminster, costumed figures were beginning to move in and out of shadows and ally-ways to gather in the main streets. There was music, but it was harsh drums and pipes designed, like the costumes, to confuse and drive away spirits that may wander into the area. Smiling, Richard knew that the ale would soon flow into the proceedings and the raucous, macabre parades would become unsettling in themselves if taken as anything more than boisterous, drunken revelry.

He felt tired, but urgent news had led him to summon a council meeting this evening. John Howard, the faithful Duke of Norfolk, would be there. Although now in his sixties, his support and loyalty had been invaluable to Richard. Catesby, Ratcliffe and Lovell would also attend, as would Sir Robert Brackenbury. Catesby had sent word of worrying news from spies on the Continent and Richard knew that this could only mean one thing.

As he dismounted and climbed the steps into the Palace his mind raced ahead. It was too late in the year for an invasion fleet to try a crossing of the Channel now, yet Catesby's message had been pressingly forceful. He grew more tense as he approached the office where the other men should by now be gathered awaiting his arrival. As he reached a hand out toward the door, he stopped. As it so often did these days, an image of his son's angelic face flashed through his mind. He clenched his outstretched hand into a fist so tightly that it shook and a pained expression gripped his face. He pushed the vision from his mind by a sheer force of will and, before he could dwell on it further, relaxed his hand and opened the door.

He entered the room to see all of the faces that he had expected. Voices immediately ceased their casual chat and all of the men rose. The stone walled room fell eerily silent. The men were seated around a large rectangular table, the seat at its head left empty in anticipation of his arrival. A bright fire blazed in the hearth, causing shadows to dance lightly around the walls. A shiver ran the length of Richard's spine. The scene was unnerving, on this of all nights. Suddenly, Richard noticed that one figure was still seated at the table. He had missed the extra person when he entered and the others stood. In the usual place, on the right of his chair, Anne sat with her back to him. He frowned at her presence as he moved toward his seat.

"Good evening, sire." Ratcliffe boomed into the silence, a warm grin on his face.

"Your grace." Followed Lovell and Catesby. John Howard and Sir Robert Brackenbury nodded their respectful greetings.

"Gentlemen," Richard addressed them with a distracted smile, "please be seated." As they resumed their positions, he sat, his eyes fixed on Anne's face. She was ashen and her eyes dark, lacking their usual keen sparkle, yet this was how she had been for the past six months. After their son's death, Richard had been required to return to his duties and this had, to some extent, distracted him from his own grief. Anne, however, had neither found nor sought any diversion or solace. It had become clear that the shock of the loss had scarred her deeply and, Richard feared, permanently. Still, this would be her first return to state business and there was no denying that Richard was as pleased to see her as he was surprised.

"Anne," he whispered softly as he sat, placing his hand on hers on her knee, out of view. She flinched a little, though did not withdraw her hands, and turned her head toward him, her eyes lowered. Richard's stomach knotted to see her so melancholy. Before he could think further, he was jolted by Ratcliffe's thundering northern tones again.

"Let us hear it then, Catesby," he bellowed, folding his arms. "There is praying that should be done this evening."

"I doubt," Catesby countered instantly, "that all of London's taverns shall run out of 'prayer' before we are done, Sir Richard." Brackenbury and the Duke of Norfolk chuckled before Ratcliffe released his own roaring laugh. Richard and Anne remained silent, the former transfixed by the latter, a fact that did not escape the attention of Lord Lovell.

"Sir William," the king gathered himself, dragging his gaze away from his wife, "please, share your news." He offered a crooked smile.

"There are several issues to address, sire." Catesby told him.

"Then please begin." Richard replied distractedly.

"Very well." Catesby was slightly flustered by the king's tone and sifted through a pile of papers on the table before him. Finally, apparently deciding where to begin, he cleared his throat. "Perhaps most vital," he spoke slowly with all of his lawyer's measured composure, "is the news that Henry Tudor has escaped Brittany." There was a moment of silence, which Catesby knew to be the calm before the storm. He also knew that this was set to be a most stormy evening.

Richard's fists met the table with a sickening thud that caused the other men at the table to wince in sympathetic pain, though the king displayed only rage. He stood, throwing his chair behind him as he turned and paced heatedly from the table. The other men looked from one to the other. It was, to a man, a look of knowing, for Richard's rage was hardly a surprise, yet all shared as little dismay that it had surfaced quite so quickly. Anne was unmoved.

"Incompetent," he hissed, "useless...," he roared, but seemed unable to find any more words. He stood still, facing the rear wall with his right palm across his forehead, his shoulders rising and falling to a slowing rhythm. "Go on." His voice was softer but he did not turn to face them.

"My sources tell me that he feigned a visit to a friend, left the road at some point, apparently swapped clothes with a servant and fled across the French border." Silence hung heavy once more.

"Why now?" Richard eventually asked, his arm returning to his side, though he still stared at the wall. Catesby looked at the other faces around the table as if imploring someone else to answer, but no one else could, even if they had wanted to.

"It seems that the old thorn Bishop Morton is working his way into our side again." He saw Richard's frame tense at the name. "Even in exile he remains remarkably well informed and seems to have got word to Tudor of your plan to have him handed over."

"At least you had yet to divest yourself of..." Ratcliffe clearly tried to inject a little humour. Before he could finish, Richard span around and marched back to his place at the head of the table.

"Why," he bellowed, "am I so constantly surrounded and plagued by incompetents and traitors?" He scowled at each of the men in turn but no answer came. "I try to return fairness and justice to this nation and yet I must be faced with dishonourable snakes who are determined to work against me. Why can no one rid me of them?" He slapped his palms onto the table but still no answer was forthcoming. "Can I trust no one?" The table rattled again under the weight of another blow. Even as his fists met the surface, the sound was answered by a thud from along the table and Richard shot a glance at its source. Lord Lovell was on his feet, his face a picture of barely contained outrage. His eyes burned into the king. Richard was clearly taken aback by the response.

"How dare you question the loyalty of the people within this room." His tone was as even as ever but his green eyes flashed. "Above all others the men here," he passed a sweeping arm around the table, "have risked all that they have for you and your vision and you would still accuse us of these things? You dishonour me, sir." The two men locked eyes for a long moment in the stunned, deathly silence.

"I think," John Howard offered eventually, "that although Lord Lovell may have lost his restraint for a moment,"

"I," Lovell tried to retort but was cut off as the duke continued over him softly.

"He makes a reasonable point." Richard seemed to have to wrench his gaze from Francis as he turned to look at Howard on the other side of the table. The older man's face was creased into a kindly smile that belied his quick mind and disguised his experience and expertise on a field of battle. Even into his sixties, he was a force to be reckoned with, but at the present moment adopted the persona of a benevolent old sage. "Each of us owes a great deal to you, Richard. I alone owe to you my Dukedom of Norfolk, but each of us has also risked a great deal to follow you to this point and you should not allow the treachery of the few to cloud your view of the many. That way lies tyranny. A scared king is a dangerous thing." Howard knew that this last comment would touch a nerve with Richard. The king drew in a long breath, as though filling his lungs with air to give voice to his judgment, but then his shoulders slumped as he sank lower over the table. As though sensing the sentiment within the room, Ratcliffe intervened.

"Well," he told them all, his arms folded before him, "this will get us nowhere." He glowered at the other men. Richard turned silently to retrieve his chair and sat down again. He shot a concerned glance at Anne, who had remained silent and still throughout the discussions. She lowered her head and slowly turned her ashen face away from him. He frowned at her as he returned his attention to Catesby.

"Continue, Sir William," he said absently.

"I am hardly sure that I dare." Catesby replied with a thin smile. Richard shot him a look that told him very clearly that it would be considerably less favourable for him if the king had to ask again. He was obviously in no mood for frivolity still. "There is further news that exacerbates Tudor's flight."

"Do not make me wait any longer, William." The king's tone was dark and laced with the type of menace that he usually reserved for his enemies.

"Yes, sire." Sir William frowned at the malice in his friend's voice. "An old enemy of your house and a most formidable threat has been able to join Tudor in France." Catesby paused as long as he dared and swallowed hard. "John de Vere, the Earl of Oxford, has escaped his prison at Calais with some of his followers." There were gasps from all but Richard and Anne as Catesby relayed the news.

"Well this," the Duke of Norfolk reflected, "places the wolf among the lambs."

"In more ways than one," Ratcliffe agreed, "for now the Welsh lamb has a pet wolf at his side."

"Indeed." Lovell was clearly shocked. "Oxford is our deadliest enemy. For all of his opposition it is impossible not to concede that he is the most experienced English military leader currently living." He looked at Richard, who was biting his thumb nail. "This news adds a new dimension to Tudor's threat."

"How was he able to escape?" Richard moved in his seat, looking at no one in particular.

"James Blount," Catesby explained, "the Captain of Hammes Castle at Calais, along with his lieutenant, one John Fortescue, defected to Tudor's cause, releasing Oxford and taking much of the Calais garrison with them."

"But that garrison," Ratcliffe said in disbelief, "is the closest thing that the king has to a standing army."

"And," Lovell added, "they are some of the most experienced professional soldiers in England."

"Must I always suffer these threats and betrayals?" Richard buried his face in his palms as he repeated his earlier sentiment.

"Of course you must." All eyes but Anne's turned to the Duke of Norfolk who seemed suddenly surprised by the attention. He fixed Richard with a steely gaze, his kind old face masking the strength that the king perceived in his eyes. "Well," the duke continued, "it is a universal truth that whenever there is a job for one man, there will always be more than one man ready to take up the job." Lovell, Catesby, Ratcliffe and Brackenbury all chuckled. Even Richard raised a smile.

"Ah, Jack," the king said quietly, "you are correct. I have suffered one rebellion and my brother lost his throne for a while to name but two examples."

"Precisely." The duke smiled. "All that is to be decided is how we will go about ridding ourselves of this present trouble."

"Very well." Richard thought for a moment and then seemed to recover himself. Sitting straight, he was renewed. "Offer pardons to the garrison for all those men who return to their duties immediately. If they were seduced into deserting it will not take too long before they yearn for the security of their wage and position serving the Crown." The men around the table nodded and mumbled approval. "We shall send Sir James Tyrell to take control of Calais and restore order there."

"Very good, sire." Catesby noted the decisions.

"We must keep a close eye upon our enemies." Richard said. "The recruitment of the Earl of Oxford will doubtless encourage Tudor's cause. He now has that which he previously lacked, and if the French add their support, then an invasion is inevitable."

"As is its failure." Ratcliffe scoffed. There were determined mumbles of agreement.

"Good." Richard smiled. "Is there any other business for us this evening?" He addressed the question primarily to Catesby.

"Errm." There was a long, ponderous, contemplative noise from Sir William. "No," he said at length. "Nothing pressing, sire." He began to gather up his papers.

"William?" Richard asked through narrowing eyes. "What is it? Let us clear the decks whilst we are all here." He smiled enquiringly.

"Well." Catesby weighed his words. Richard's mood had improved but could switch instantly again if he did not wish to discuss the matter. However, he would definitely be angered if Catesby failed to respond. "There is still the matter of your heir to be addressed."

A tense silence descended on the room at once, adding to each man's unease. The king shifted in his chair suddenly, realising that for the first time since his arrival in the room, Anne was looking directly at him. He frowned, puzzled. His wife was suddenly focussed intently on him and for the first time he could clearly see how the last few months had aged her. Anne's eyes were dark and sunken. Her skin was pale. With his mouth ajar, a tear began to swell in Richard's eye and his throat tightened. She had shut herself away for a long time and barely saw anyone since their son died. Richard was fighting his own rising emotion as he digested its effect upon his wife. There was no warmth in her face any longer and the bright spark was nowhere to be found in her deep pool like eyes.

"As I said, sire," Catesby broke the silence somewhat unwillingly, "the matter does not require resolution just yet."

There was a pause again. Richard looked down at his left hand and realised that he was spinning his wedding ring. With a gentle smile he looked back to Anne. She remained motionless, offering no response to his subconscious request for advice. He stared at her a moment longer, a desperate frown folding his brow, before he returned his attention unwillingly to the room.

"We shall conclude this now." Richard stated, working to keep his voice steady. "Uncertainty about the succession will only provide fuel for our enemies."

"Very well." Catesby said quietly. "There remain the two primary candidates. Your nephew Edward, Earl of Warwick, the Duke of Clarence's son is perhaps the obvious choice in terms of primogeniture succession. The other candidate is your sister's son, John de la Pole, Earl of Lincoln." Catesby looked at Richard, who was transfixed by Anne, and then he flashed his eyes around the other men, inviting their input. The quiet persisted until Lord Lovell drew a long, deep breath.

"I would suggest that Lincoln is the preferable choice at present." Francis offered.

"Well," John Howard countered, "the son of Clarence has a better claim to the throne and is Richard's natural heir now."

"That much I concede," Lovell replied slowly, "but young Warwick is barely ten years of age, in need of a minority government should he come to the throne for some years yet, a fact that would be a destabilising cause for unease amongst our allies and would offer encouragement to our enemies." There were murmurs of agreement. "Lincoln is a grown man. Not only that, but he is already playing an active part in politics with the Council of the North." Lovell looked at Richard. "Following in your very footsteps." The king started and met Lovell's gaze, his face still betraying preoccupation. Francis smiled softly.

"Yes." Richard said absently. "A fair point." He turned to Anne, again touching his wedding ring. Again, she turned her face slowly, deliberately, from his. His lips parted as a fresh wave of desperate grief gripped his stomach. Then, a moment later, he caught himself and was aware that his distance may seem to his closest friends and allies to be uncertainty or weakness.

"The Earl of Lincoln shall be my heir." Richard announced looking around at the others. "I acknowledge that the Earl of Warwick's claim may be stronger but for the present, his age is too much of a barrier."

"Very well sire." Catesby beamed, seemingly pleased with the return of the more decisive Richard. The king nodded, looked at Lovell and smiled slightly. The motion was mirrored and the two friends knew that their earlier argument was forgotten.

"Now gentlemen," Richard stood and strode to the door as he spoke, "if you would all be kind enough to leave me alone with the queen for a while." He opened the door as the men rose and bowed to their queen. They left the room, filing past Richard, paying their respects as they exited. Lord Lovell ensured that he was the last left in the room. As he reached the king, he leaned in close, placing a hand on his friend's shoulder.

"Richard," he whispered, gripping the shoulder more tightly, "be gentle with her. The most precious things are often the most fragile." He moved away a little to look into Richard's eyes. "I see there something so very precious to you. Take care." Lovell smiled. Richard nodded, slightly abashed and embarrassed that Francis clearly saw through the barrier he presented to cover his emotions. Lord Lovell squeezed Richard's shoulder once more before leaving the room. Closing the door gently, Richard left his palm on the hard, cold wood for a moment and then leaned forward until his forehead met the solid surface too. He inhaled deeply through his nose and turned to face back into the room.

"Anne," Richard spoke softly, "my love." His wife made no movement and offered no response. Richard moved around the table and crouched beside Anne's chair so that his face was level with hers. He took her hand with both of his and kissed it. Still she remained impassive. "Anne, please talk to me." Slowly, she turned her face to meet his gaze.

"What would you have me say, sire?" she asked slowly without a hint of emotion.

"I would have you tell me what I may do to make you feel better." His voice betrayed an uncomfortable mixture of annoyance and desperate confusion.

"You cannot give me back my son." She fixed her eyes on his and they flashed with venom, the first light on her face in such a long time. "And so there is nothing that you can do for me." She pulled her hand free of his and returned her gaze to the table. A wave of nausea crashed over Richard.

"I would wish for nothing else, Anne, every bit as much for myself as for you." A tear rolled unseen down his cheek. Anne snorted a resentful laugh.

"You seem to be getting on well enough with the business of being king." She bit her lip.

"Oh, Anne." Richard's voice shook. "I have my duty to do but that does not mean that I feel the loss any less than you."

"I," Anne hissed through gritted teeth, turning to look at Richard again, "can barely breathe the foul air of this rotting world, yet you go on as though nothing has happened."

"I do not!" Richard insisted vehemently. "Just because I do not deal with this in the same way that you do, do not belittle my suffering. You," he was raising his voice, "do not have more right to suffer than I do, and you do not suffer more than I."

"Yet on you go." Anne's voice was growing louder also as she threw out her arm to reinforce her point. "On with business, on with your plans to preserve your throne, on with replacing our son with a new heir." Her voice was like molten steel pouring over Richard, searing him to his core as her eyes cut through to his very soul. Suddenly exposed, he began to weep uncontrollably. Huge, heavy tears, held in tightly for so long, rolled down his cheeks, splashing onto the table and he fought to steady his breathing as his shoulders shook.

Anne felt a gentle flutter in her stomach as her husband broke down. She had never seen him so openly upset in all of their years together. For a brief moment she pitied him as much as she did herself and involuntarily she moved her left hand toward Richard to comfort him. But her overflowing rage had been building for so long, fed by grief and resentment until it was unbearable. Her fleeting softening toward Richard was gone almost before it began and the weakness galvanised her further.

"Anne." Richard's voice was pleading as he drew himself up into the seat behind him and wiped his eyes on his sleeve. He had seen none of Anne's moment of doubt through the cloud of his own tears.

"It is over, Richard." Anne shouted over his plea in a shrill voice that was louder than she intended it to be. "Everything that we built was for our son." She stared at him. "Now it is all for nothing." She allowed the words to hang between them as Richard gazed at her open mouthed.

"I." Richard was staggered at Anne's words. In all of their years together he had never known his wife to be so aggressive nor so fatalistic. He felt as though all of the breath left his body. It occurred to him now that the vein of indomitable strength she had always possessed could easily turn to a threatening rage, but he had never before witnessed it. Furthermore, it was always she who saw the positive in any situation, she who countered his own pessimistic tendencies. He tried desperately to think what she would say to him if the positions were reversed. He took a deep breath to steady his voice and spoke as evenly as he could manage. "Anne," he looked deep into her eyes but felt as if he was being pushed back, "we can rebuild our future together." He forced what he hoped was a comforting smile onto his face. "We are still young and we can..."

"Have more children?" Anne interrupted him, her voice chillingly calm. "Is that what you were going to say, Richard?"

"I, I," he stammered. It was what he was about to say and it was clearly the wrong thing to have been about to say.

"I am not so young as you would like to believe." Anne coughed a rasping, chesty cough as she shouted at her husband again. He reached out to her in concern but she knocked his hand away. Catching her breath she straightened herself. "Give me your prayer book." She opened her hand before Richard. He frowned. "Give me the book." Anne coughed again, standing as her breath drew short. Richard stood and moved to place a hand on her back. She shrugged him off. "The book!" she spluttered.

Richard's hand went directly to his doublet pocket where he always kept his book of prayers. These were a collection of important scripture, psalms and prayers, some personal to Richard. The pages were well thumbed and many contained hand written notes that Richard had added. He took it everywhere with him, so Anne had no need to ask if it was present. Slowly, uncertainly, he drew out the little book that he had commissioned all of those years ago and that had been his constant companion since. He placed it reluctantly into his wife's hand, hesitating to release it. She flicked through the pages and then turned the book to face Richard, showing him the beautifully illuminated page that he knew all too well. It was the prayer of St Antony.

"Your reign," Anne said, her unnerving calm regained, "our life, is like this book." For the first time, Richard thought that he glimpsed some sign of softening in his wife's face. "It was written to your specification and you worked so hard to make it everything we wanted it to be. It was perfect," a tear spilled from her eye, "but without our little Edward," her voice shook as more tears rolled down her cheek and her face seemed to plead with Richard like one committing a reluctant suicide, "it is no longer perfect." With these words, she tore the page containing the prayer of St Antony from Richard's precious book and screwed it up tightly. With her husband watching dumbstruck, Anne held out both of her hands, one palm covered by the closed book and the other containing the tight ball of vellum. Wide tracks of tears were clear down her cheeks now.

"Do you see, Richard?" Anne's voice was suddenly filled by the emotion that overflowed from her face, her resolve evaporated. "From the outside, it looks intact. No one would even know." She placed the book onto the table, her hands trembling as her whole body shook with renewed sobbing, but her voice carried through the turmoil. "This," she raised the palm containing the ball of paper, "you may have this stitched back into place." She began to open out the page until its crumpled form sat, curling upward, on the flat of her palm. For an instant, Richard mistook this gesture for an apology. "You may try to repair it." A measure of venomous rigidity was returning as she spoke, her voice growing steadier. "But it is like us, Richard." She whispered, holding her palm outstretched toward him. "Our marriage, our love, your reign." Anne hissed as Richard glimpsed something like hatred dancing across her face. "You may try to repair it, and it may fool some for a while, but you and I, Richard, you and I will both always know that it can never be perfect again."

Richard's mind swam as if he were in a dream, watching some nightmare scene unfold, unable to act to save his wife or himself. Their love was over, she was telling him, and they could never repair the damage that had been done. Then there was his book. She had destroyed something so precious to him in order to make a point that, in reality, he already knew to be true. To him, the book had always represented a connection to God, through prayer, that he was able to carry with him everywhere, to offer succour and comfort anywhere and at any time. Now, even that was being taken away from him one piece at a time. He clenched his teeth and refocused his eyes on his wife. Wide tracks of damp tears streaked her face, which glowed red at the cheeks. Her chest and shoulders heaved as she drew rattling breaths and puffed them out. Her soft lips that he had kissed a million times were pinched cruelly. And her eyes. In those eyes he had seen such strength, determination, gentle kindness, such love and such passion. He had seen there his own reflection magnified and made perfect by her love. Now, he saw red-rimmed burning balls of hatred. A fresh, bulging tear rolled from his eye as he wondered where his beloved wife had gone. A mixture of indistinguishable emotions constricted his throat to deprive him of words as he pitied her, pitied himself, missed her so completely and despised what the world had turned her into. As though still watching a dream, he felt his right hand rising. He clenched his teeth tighter still and knotted his brow as a red mist of rage obscured his vision. His right arm swung with the devastating force of many years of martial training and battlefield experience and his open palm connected with Anne's left cheek. The familiar jolt that ran through his body from the contact instantly jarred him from his dream-like state. His palm throbbed as he looked at it. Horrified at the power that he must have used, he forced himself to look at Anne. She was twisted and bent over the table, her left hand covering her cheek. As she straightened to look at him, she withdrew her hand and looked into her own palm. Richard knew that she expected to see blood. There was none there but her cheek glowed a more fierce red than it had before, a large area of it beginning to rise and swell at the point where he had struck her. Struck her. Struck Anne. Richard reeled back a step and desperately searched his shocked mind for a way to begin to apologise. His eyes met Anne's again. In that instant he saw the young, frightened girl that he had rescued all of those years ago, returned after a decade's absence and he faltered another step back. As quickly as she was there, timid and uncertain, the girl was gone, replaced by the forged steel of Anne's resolve. She fixed him with a stare that caused his very soul to shiver, straightened herself until she stood proud and upright, released the tight bun that held her dark hair so that it fell about her neck and cheeks like deepest midnight covering the scarred landscape of a battlefield. Her composure broken only momentarily by a cough, and without a further glance at her husband, Anne moved to the door and was gone from the room like a shadow.

Richard had wanted to call her as she left. He had wanted to throw himself down onto his knees before that frightened girl and beg for forgiveness. Above all, he wanted not to have struck her. But none of that was possible now. His legs trembled and threatened to cease supporting him. He stumbled back a few more paces and met the stone of the wall. So cold and solid was it at his back that even this seemed disapproving and unforgiving. His shaking legs gave way beneath him and he slowly sank against the wall until he sat in a crumpled heap on the icy floor. He looked back at the table where his book lay with its damaged page beside it. So beautiful, so precious and with so much of his life invested in it. Ruined now. Ruined, though to what extent he could not yet tell. Ruined because of a book. He had undone in one blow over a decade of careful, devoted work, not just on their relationship and position. That seemed to matter so little now. He had saved a frightened young girl from an uncertain fate and delivered her to an equally unsure one. He had dedicated time and his every effort to convincing Anne of her security and of her right to it, whether she was his wife or not, and for years he had revelled in watching her grow and flourish as a woman, a wife and a mother. She had been cruelly deprived of one of these already and he could not fight off the feeling that he had just robbed her of another. He had seen that terrified, lost girl again tonight and above all of the other reasons for regret, this one, as he sat on the cold stone floor sobbing uncontrollably in the empty room, broke the king's heart.

Chapter 34

25th December 1484 – Christmas Presence

The Christmas celebrations of the royal court at Westminster Palace were in full flow. The Great Hall was filled to overflowing with music from the lute, the pipe and drum and the mummers that had been invited in danced vigorously for the entertainment of England's great and good at the court of King Richard. Food covered every part of every table and was replenished every bit as quickly as it could be consumed. Wine and ale seemed to flow endlessly from bottomless pitchers into insatiable mouths. There was the rumbling undercurrent of a hundred voices, pierced by frequent eruptions of shrieking laughter, joyful screaming and the clattering of plates, platters, jugs and goblets.

From his perch at the raised top table, the king surveyed the scene, contented by the feast that he had provided for the most influential of his subjects and resenting every moment of the happiness that surrounded him. As much as he detested the excesses apparently traditional at court all the year round, it was right and proper to celebrate the birth of Christ. Richard stifled a yawn. It was apparently around seven o'clock and the evening outside was already gripped by a black chill. Inside the Great Hall though, Richard felt the cumbersome warmth. Midnight Mass had been a long time ago now, but was an occasion that Richard had observed gladly and solemnly all of his life. His stomach was full, his head light with the strong French wine. The problems of the past year and the threats of the coming one all seemed pleasantly distant for a moment. His gaze drifted across the room and he allowed himself the smallest smile at the merriment. Instinctively, he turned to his right to share the moment with his wife. The smile evaporated slowly from his face like a disappearing morning mist. It had been nearly two months since they had argued. It had been the first time that Richard could remember them having exchanged cross words. Certainly it was the only time that he had ever struck her and he had never regretted anything more in his life. For her part, Anne had made no fuss over the incident, remaining out of public view for some days as the angry swelling bruised and coloured. This had not raised eyebrows, since she had been so rarely seen out of her chamber since Edward's death. She had refused Richard's requests to see her but none of her ladies in waiting had cast him a glance that had caused him to doubt that she had not divulged the cause of her unsightly injury. She had dutifully played her part on occasions of state, or when her absence may have caused tongues to wag, but had removed herself at the earliest opportunity without exchanging pleasantries with her husband.

It had also occurred to Richard that it was on that very evening that he had first noticed Anne's cough. This had, apparently, worsened in the ensuing weeks, only adding to Richard's swelling sense of guilt. When it had been reported to him that she had collapsed in a fit of coughing in her chamber he had sent the royal physician to her immediately. She still refused to see her husband and the doctors had advised against upsetting her. Having sent them from his presence, he had cried at the doctors' news. They believed that Anne was afflicted by the same disease that had killed her sister Isabella, wife of Richard's brother George. Consumption was an evil blight for which the physicians knew of no cure.

As he stared, Anne looked back at him and smiled softly before raising the folded cloth that was her constant companion to her mouth to muffle a cough. As she lowered the handkerchief she folded it over again, but not before Richard saw the specks of red on its pure white surface. He looked back at her face and she smiled softly. He frowned enquiringly but she nodded to tell him that she was fine. He doubted that this was the case. Over the last few weeks Anne had softened to him slightly. They had begun to speak, uneasily at first with Richard trying to apologise and Anne denying the need for it, but some of their familiar comfort had begun to return. To Richard's dismay, though, she still refused to allow him to see her whenever the illness gripped her, and these moments were becoming increasingly frequent and prolonged. She had moved permanently to her own chambers not only because of the risk of infection but because her coughing fits, fevers and night sweats would make sharing a bed impractical. These periods of separation stung Richard, however necessary they may be. He placed his hand on hers and gently squeezed. She looked at him and he smiled again. Her dark hair had begun to show silvery strands, evidence of her suffering, both physical and emotional. Her face had altered too. The disease was beginning to eat away at her body and she was visibly losing weight. Her cheeks were sunken and her face grew lined. Her arms, too, looked almost skeletal. Richard doubted that the changes were enough for most to notice, or at least be concerned by, but concealing her illness was growing more difficult as it took hold and tightened its grip. She was dressed tonight in a beautiful dress of velvet and silk, made for this feast in a cornflower blue, deliberately light in colour so that it did not exaggerate her pallor. Above and beyond all of these things, Richard could now look into his wife's sapphire eyes and see returned there the woman that he loved. Changed, perhaps, but restored, in his eyes at least. He prayed every day for a miracle. He prayed that the Lord would heal Anne in spite of the physicians. He prayed that he be saved the loss of his wife. In his moments of quiet contemplation, he had come to realise, and was struggling to accept, that what Anne had demonstrated in that room using his prayer book was correct.

The king was hauled from his musing by an eruption of noise and giggling in front of his table. He looked down to see three of his nieces, Elizabeth, Mary and Cecily, holding hands and skipping faster and faster in a ring to the crescendo of the music. Their mother, Elizabeth Woodville, stood to the side watching her daughters with a disapproving amusement. The eldest, eighteen year old Elizabeth, tall, slim, with long blond hair that fell in curls about her shoulders, wore a dress of the same material as Anne's. It had been a gift from the queen, who had become close to their niece since her family's return to court. The two had spent time together sewing and walking the gardens and had developed a friendship that blurred the decade difference in their ages. The companionship had lifted Anne no end too. The dress was a token of affection from Anne, but for Richard it also served as an obvious statement of family unity to all in attendance.

He laughed as the music ended and the three spinning figures fought to stop themselves without staggering and falling over each other. The three ladies suddenly realised that they were at the steps below the king's table. They hurriedly gathered into a line and curtsied in unison. Cecily and Mary flushed bright red and giggled, but Elizabeth smiled, nodded gently to the king and queen, who each tilted their head in return, and then looked across to her mother. The elder Elizabeth began to shepherd her daughters up the steps. At the summit, all four curtsied again to the king.

"Sire," his sister-in-law began, "please forgive my daughters their exuberance." The troubles of the last eighteen months had taken their toll on the former queen, but her dignity was unshaken and she remained an attractive woman. Richard often wondered how long it would be before she remarried and if she were to, that would bring with it its own set of perils. Still, she showed no intentions in that direction yet.

"Please, Elizabeth," Richard replied, smiling, "you need make no excuse for the light that your daughters bring to the room." The young ladies giggled again.

"Thank you, sire." Elizabeth smiled an almost imperceptibly awkward smile. "I hope that the queen is keeping well." She turned to Anne with a genuine concern.

"As well as may be expected, thank you." Anne replied.

"Be assured that you are in all of our prayers, your majesty." She bowed her head before returning her focus to the king. "Sire," she began.

"Elizabeth." Richard interrupted. She started. "Can we not dispense with such formality? We are, after all, amongst family." He smiled what he hoped was a friendly smile. Elizabeth nodded.

"Richard," she began again, "I have something to ask of you."

"If it is mine to grant, then it is yours." Richard replied.

"I would ask for your approval for a match for my daughter, Cecily." Elizabeth motioned for the girl to step forward. Cecily flushed, took a step forward and curtsied low.

"Lady Cecily." Richard bent his head toward her. "To whom do you wish to be married?" The girl shot an uncertain glance at her mother, who smiled and nodded reassuringly. Richard had promised suitable matches for his brother's daughters and had sworn to treat them as befits members of his family. He had not actively sought to marry them off to be rid of them. If nothing else, they provided a focus for his sister-in-law that should keep her somewhat compliant. Aside from this, though, they were his nieces, his brother's children, and that meant a great deal to him as his family continued to shrink. He hoped to see them happy if at all possible, but he dreaded their deposed, formerly Lancastrian mother seeking matches for them amongst his enemies. He caught himself spinning his wedding ring without meaning it. He often seemed to do this recently when Anne was on his mind or when he was worried about something. Realising what he was doing, he flashed a look at Anne. She frowned, a motion imperceptible to anyone else, and placed her hand on his right thigh gently. Instantly, his tension evaporated. He released his ring and returned his focus to his niece.

"Uncle," she began uncertainly, "I request your permission to wed Ralph Scrope." She dropped her gaze and bit her bottom lip.

"The younger brother of Thomas, Lord Scrope?" Richard queried, knowing of no other Ralph Scrope.

"The very same, uncle." Cecily looked up at him and smiled coyly.

"Do I sense, child," Richard smiled at her, "more than a hint of love in this match?"

"You tease me, uncle." Cecily's cheeks flooded with colour again.

"I do not mean to." Richard chuckled with a mixture of playful delight and relief. Thomas, Lord Scrope was a member of Richard's household and his family were loyal supporters. This match was perfect.

"Ralph and I have known each other for some time, uncle, and it is true that we have fallen in love." She looked away embarrassedly. Richard beamed at her, and then at her mother, who returned his smile with a little more reserve.

"Well then," Richard grinned excitedly, "who am I to stand in the path of true love? You have my blessing and I shall await my invitation."

"Thank you, uncle." Cecily shrieked and turned to leave. Then, she caught herself, faced the king again, curtsied low and bowed her head.

"Go." Richard told her. "Go and find your betrothed. I shall have a dance played in your honour," he called after her as she skipped down the steps.

"Thank you, Richard." Elizabeth tilted her head. "You have made her very happy."

"I am glad to have been able to." Richard replied as he stood. He called a young man from behind him who appeared from the shadows instantly. The king whispered in his ear and the lad scuttled around the outside of the hall toward the musicians. "Now," Richard said to his sister-in-law, "would you do me the pleasure of taking this dance with me?"

"How am I to refuse such an honour, Richard?" Motioning to her other two daughters, who curtsied and ran down the steps after their sister, Elizabeth waited for the king, who strode along the back of the table, around its end and toward Elizabeth, reaching his hand out to her. As the music began, slower than before, she placed her hand on top of his and the pair moved toward the space in the centre of the room. Others were gathering as the drum began to beat out a slow rhythm and a lone pipe peeped a joyful tune. Richard and Elizabeth strode deliberately toward Ralph Scrope and Cecily who had taken their place already. The young couple bowed and curtsied low. Richard tilted his head in appreciation.

"Congratulations to you both." Richard called above the music, then, turning to Elizabeth, he bowed, awaited her curtsy and they began to dance. As they did, other couples also began to join in the dance, until the space was filled.

"You must be very proud." Richard spoke just above the music but only loud enough to allow Elizabeth alone to hear.

"Of course, Richard." She fixed him with a stoical gaze.

"Is all well since your return to court?" Richard asked, matching her stare.

"We are well provided for by your grace and generosity." Elizabeth replied a little flatly.

"You have enjoyed," Richard moved closer to her, "your travels?" She paused mid step and her eyes flicked around those figures moving about them.

"Of course." She eventually replied, barely allowing her mouth to open.

"Good," he smiled, pleased to have so disarmed her.

"I understand that John of Gloucester and his sister are to move to Calais." Elizabeth stated gathering herself, hoping to unbalance Richard equally.

"Indeed." Richard replied lightly. "My bastards are to spend some time in Calais." As the two moved closer with the dance, Richard lowered his tone. "They bring me no shame. They are of a time before I was married and I acknowledge them proudly as mine." He fixed his eyes on hers sternly. "Bastards they may be, but they are mine." The dance continued around the floor and for a while the king and his sister-in-law continued in silence.

After a minute or so, Richard caught sight of Lord Stanley and his wife dancing together, seemingly moving closer to his position. He smiled darkly and began to move toward them.

"Richard," Elizabeth began hesitantly, "I have another favour to ask of you."

"Then ask." Richard replied lightly.

"My son," Elizabeth said quietly, "the Marquis of Dorset." She hastily added as Richard flashed her a concerned, confused glance.

"Ah, yes." Richard acknowledged ponderously. "Is he still with Tudor in France?" he snarled.

"That is what I wish to talk to you about." Elizabeth was clearly on the defensive. "I understand that you are preparing to issue a statement listing Tudor and his allies as traitors and condemning them."

"I am indeed." Richard replied, pleased that Elizabeth was on the back foot.

"Is my son on that list?" she asked as they danced past each other.

"He is with Tudor." Richard stated.

"Richard, please," Elizabeth seemed flustered, "please give me the chance to try and bring him back. Tudor has used my son's fear of your wrath to seduce him. Thomas wants to return."

"He wants to return," Richard countered, "or you want his return?"

"I am asking for some space to bring him home." Elizabeth pleaded. "He feared you Richard, and not without cause, but I can convince him that you are treating us well and that he can return in safety and security."

"It would make you happy to see him return?" Richard asked pensively.

"Naturally it would," Elizabeth smiled at him, but her face was soon stern again, "and it would serve as quite a victory for you to bring one of Tudor's noble allies back into the fold." They danced a moment in silence as Richard thought over the proposition.

"He rose with Buckingham against me." Richard told Elizabeth.

"He made a mistake, Richard. Allow him to now make amends." Elizabeth pleaded.

"Do you know how rare the second chance that you request is in circumstances of treason?"

"Of course," Elizabeth's eyes dropped, "but I have to ask it of you." There was another silence as they danced.

"Very well." Richard replied. "If Thomas returns, I will pardon him, but I will also hold you responsible for his future behaviour."

"Thank you Richard." Elizabeth smiled brightly, an expression that Richard rarely saw on her face, but which suited her. Suddenly she looked so much like her young daughter Elizabeth. "I will ensure that you do not regret your clemency." There was a spring in her steps now.

"Young Elizabeth looks radiant tonight." Richard eventually said to the girl's mother.

"Indeed." The elder Elizabeth replied. "She adores the gown that the queen kindly favoured her with."

"Anne has taken a shine to her." Richard faltered a moment. "For her part, she lifts my wife's humour no end in the time that they spend together." He caught sight of the Stanleys again, edging toward them. "Does she show no sign of selecting a match for herself yet?"

"She does not." Elizabeth replied.

"You are aware," Richard again hushed his voice further, "that the Tudor whelp has vowed to marry her and seize my throne."

"Of course I am aware of it." Elizabeth replied a little coldly.

"Do you intend to allow the union?" Richard asked, smiling at passing couples.

"No more than you intend to allow him to take your throne. Have I not just asked for my son's return from his grasp? Why then would I send my daughter in his place?"

"A fair reply." Richard said absently as he sought the Stanleys out, for he had not expected any other response. They were close now.

"Perhaps," Richard raised his voice slightly, "I should have young Elizabeth married and be done with the threat." He shot a glance at the Stanleys and was pleased to see Lady Stanley's face twisting, though she did not notice his brief look at her. When he returned his gaze to Elizabeth, her eyes had followed his and she frowned as she looked back to him.

"I do not send her to him in France, Richard." Elizabeth spoke quietly. "I have too much to lose. But I would not wish her forced to marry in order to meet even your convenience."

"Very well." Richard smiled as the music ended. He bowed to Elizabeth and she curtsied in response. Taking her hand, Richard courteously placed a gentle kiss upon it, but she prevented him from releasing her hand as he stood upright. Leaning forward, she whispered softly, her head lowered.

"I do not appreciate myself or my daughters being used by anyone, Richard." She saw a genuine look of apology in his face as she looked into his eyes and released his hand. Elizabeth watched from where she stood as the king returned to his seat and spoke to Anne. Her loss, and her fall, had been complete, but there was no doubt in her mind that she could trust Richard. Whatever else he may have done, his sense of chivalric honour bound him to his word. He would find suitable matches for her daughters and allow her to live freely. Yet in the unlikely event that Tudor succeeded, her offspring would, one way or another, sit upon the throne of England.

"My lady." Elizabeth's train of thought was interrupted by Lady Stanley's greeting.

"Lady Stanley." She returned. "My lord." She offered to the portly Lord Stanley.

"I trust that you and your daughters are keeping well." Lady Stanley asked with exaggerated concern.

"We are." Elizabeth smiled.

"The king treats you all well?" Lady Stanley asked the question as though she knew something that Elizabeth did not.

"As was his oath, he treats us as befits members of his family."

"A terrifying thought indeed." Lady Stanley frowned.

"Margaret." Elizabeth's tone contained more than a hint of warning, but she was not allowed to continue.

"You do know," Lady Stanley interrupted, her tone mysterious, "that certain quarters hold that the king is poisoning his wife to clear the way for a more fruitful belly."

"Mind your tongue, Margaret." Hissed Elizabeth, looking about them as though expecting to be overheard.

"I do not say that it is so." Lady Stanley feigned shocked offense. "My only concern is that he is not preparing your oldest daughter to be that new belly." She looked to the top table where the young Elizabeth laughed with Anne, who held her handkerchief over her mouth. "They are even dressed alike." She sneered. Elizabeth followed her gaze and felt a knot in her stomach at Lady Stanley's words.

"I know," Elizabeth whispered, "that you would simply have me and my daughters be your puppets rather than his to court favour for your son." The two women locked eyes in a fiery stare. "What you do not appreciate is that Richard asks no such thing of me."

"How do you defend him?" Lady Stanley asked in bewilderment.

"Because," Elizabeth snapped, but she halted. Richard was looking at them with undisguised concern. Immediately, she turned away and marched from the hall. After watching her leave, Lady Stanley looked to the king's table. He was scowling at her. Carefully placing a sickeningly pleasant smile on her face, Lady Stanley curtsied low, took Lord Stanley's arm, drawing him away from his distracted chatter and strolled to mingle in the crowded room, pleased with her evening's work.

Chapter 35

16th March 1485 – Death and Denial

Spring had well and truly taken hold of England. Lush grass and colourful daffodils and bluebells dotted the countryside. New life was springing up all around and even within the urban confines of London the air bore a slightly fresher note. People seemed brighter and friendlier on the streets as the days grew longer and warmer and winter's grip began to slip from memory. As Richard gazed from a window high in Westminster Palace, he wished for the time to dwell on such things.

"Richard," Catesby's voice drifted into his consciousness, "something must be done."

"Why?" Richard asked absently, irritably and without looking back into the room. Catesby and Ratcliffe had requested a private audience at evening meal and Richard had distractedly agreed. He regretted it now as time grew short.

"Have you not heard what I have said?" Catesby enquired with a definite edge of annoyance in his voice.

"Yes." Richard replied, redoubling any inflection in the lawyer's tone. "To hear it does not explain why it requires an answer from the king."

"Not to answer it not only suggests at its truth but allows it to grow and will encourage future use of such rumour against you." Catesby explained, his voice calmed and returned to its impassive, oily tone.

Richard strode from the window to his desk. His chamber seemed dark even compared to the fading light outside and his eyes took a moment to adjust. A fire blazed on the wall to his right, for the gentle warmth of spring had not yet driven the chill from the palace's stone. Above the fire hung a large tapestry bearing Richard's coat of arms, the white boar. The wall before him was also decorated in tapestry hangings, four in total depicting religious scenes from the life of Christ. Two hung on either side of the large, carved oak door. To his left was a wall all but obscured by Richard's private collection of books, the only break provided by an identical door that led to his private bed chamber. In the centre of the room stood two of his best and oldest friends and most trusted advisors. He was, however, finding it difficult to accept their counsel on this occasion.

"I will not," the king began firmly, "be forced into such embarrassment by the whispers of intangible ghosts." He pushed his right palm up his forehead. "Do my people truly believe such things of me?" There was just a hint of despair lacing his words.

"The people continue to love you for your generosity, equity and chivalric values." Catesby told him. "This much is not at issue, but it is not the people who will determine the level of your support should Tudor invade." Ratcliffe looked at the lawyer with undisguised admiration of his bravery.

"I rule for the people," Richard began.

"In the name of all that is holy!" Catesby shouted over the king, who stopped talking and stared at the man, mouth open. Ratcliffe took a side step away as though he expected a thunderbolt to strike instantly. "The reality of the land that you rule is simple. The people owe allegiance to their lord. He decides whether they sleep in a bed or in the mud, he decides whether they eat or starve. He decides whether they live or die. It is on that basis that they exist from day to day and when their lord calls upon them for service, they provide it in order to ensure that they keep a bed, a meal and their lives, for themselves and their families. To withhold service when it is demanded is not within their grasp and it cannot sway them whether the service is for the Crown or against it. Your role is to control those lords who control the people. Your great, great grandfather Edward III was so prolific in his reproduction and so ambitious for each of his offspring that most of the nobility of the land can claim royal descent and therefore some measure of royal blood. This has caused several depositions and years of civil war as those with a grievance press their claim and differing degrees of title and right are scrutinised. What has really happened is that the remaining, old noble families have been able to play with the Crown to suit their desires. Why tolerate an unpopular king when there is a more popular alternative who will, of course, be grateful for his throne? Why allow a weak king to be controlled by your enemies or put your lands, or the kingdom, at risk when there is a stronger candidate who still must be grateful and has so many offices to fill? The most successful king since Edward III has been Henry V who managed to distract the nobility from their squabbling with the promise of foreign treasure and glory eternal." Catesby's breathing was heavy after his animated speech. But he had not yet completed what he wished to say. "You, Richard." His shoulders fell and his tone was suddenly subdued. "You are the last of that male line in adulthood and the chance is yours to end this abuse of the Crown and its people by those in between. Accomplish this and you will move into legend to rival King Arthur." He paused a brief moment, his pleading eyes fixed on the king. "To accomplish this, you must focus on and gain control over the nobility."

The silence in the room was complete and palpable. Even the fire seemed to have subsided in nervous anticipation of the king's response. Ratcliffe eyed Catesby with a dumbstruck awe as though a mute had just recited a beautiful sonnet. Richard stood completely still, transfixed by his friend. For his part, Catesby heaved his breath in and out and looked from Richard to Ratcliffe and back again, suddenly reconsidering the wisdom of his tirade.

"Well," Richard pulled out his seat and sat down after a painfully long pause, "thank you William for the history lesson."

"Sire, I." Catesby leapt to his own defence but ceased when the king's raised palm warned him to go no further.

"William," Richard said wearily, "I think perhaps, for the most part, you have it right." Catesby visibly shuddered with relief and Ratcliffe slid back to his side, clapping him firmly on the back, his own relief tangible. "I maintain that this system cannot endure and that one day there will be no barrier between the people and their government. In the meantime, you are correct. We must deal with the structure that we have until it can be changed. So, what do you suggest?"

"You must deny these rumours." Sir Richard Ratcliffe told him.

"I should publically deny false rumours of my own misdeeds?" Richard asked with disbelief.

"Yes." Ratcliffe answered bluntly.

"To do so would appear weak." Richard told them both, narrowing his eyes but inviting opinion.

"Not to do so would hint at some truth in it." Catesby retorted.

"I will not," Richard gently bounced his clenched right fist on the surface of his desk, "be dictated to by Lady Stanley and her games."

"Her games are powerful ones, though, Richard." Catesby warned. "You issue public decrees regarding your title and intentions. She uses rumour and whisper to slowly dissolve the foundations of your support. Such propaganda is silent but devastatingly effective."

"Such tactics are despicable," Richard retorted, "the work of deceitful cowards and I will have no truck with them."

"Yet deal with them you must." Ratcliffe pleaded. "Gossip has a way of spreading, and in spreading, becoming accepted fact. It is within your power to end this now." The king looked beyond the pair at the door in the far wall thoughtfully. He was expecting a knock at any moment.

"Very well." Richard conceded. "What do you advice?"

"Well," Catesby began, "the rumour started that you were poisoning the queen." He watched Richard tense at his words. "I see the hand of our old enemy Morton in this, using Bishop Rotherham, Lady Stanley and no doubt others to spread his lies. I believe that the addition of your motive as your intention to marry your niece was the work of Lady Stanley herself. It certainly appears to have sprung up around her over the past few months." The king shifted in his seat.

"The rumour regarding Anne is the most damaging." Ratcliffe considered. "And I know that it is the most hurtful to you, Richard."

"More than you can imagine." The king replied with a solemn smile.

"Will she still not see you?" Ratcliffe asked with a wince.

"She will not," he replied closing his eyes. "She tells the physicians and priests that she does not want to distract me from important business." He opened his eyes to look at the two men and a tear escaped him. "She has so little time left and I am robbed even of that."

"Queen Anne is a queen indeed." Ratcliffe offered, admiring her determination to allow Richard to perform his duty in spite of her own rapidly failing health. He and Catesby knew that the rumours used this fact to fuel the notion that Richard was spurning his wife and eagerly awaiting her death. They suspected that the king himself was aware of this too and that it caused him immense hurt.

"Her family's power base in the north is the concern, though?" Richard asked.

"Yes." Catesby confirmed. "You are loved in the north, Richard, but Anne's family are respected of old and if they and their faction were to believe these lies then all could be lost."

"My brother suffered sufficiently at the hands of the Neville family's power and influence." Richard agreed. "Yet a public denial that I am killing her may both seem desperate and prove pointless. After all, I would deny it, would I not? And my denial would change nothing." He lowered his eyes as he said this and found his left hand stroking the wedding ring on his right.

"I see your thinking." Catesby agreed, his lawyer's brain firing into action. "Better to offer a positive statement that can be evidenced."

"Exactly." Richard looked at the door. The knock should have come by now.

"You could deny your intention to marry your niece. The evidence lies in you never doing so and it would simultaneously serve to remove motive from the rumour regarding the queen." Catesby was growing excited. "You can destroy both rumours without giving any credence to the notion that you would harm the queen."

"So be it." Richard conceded. "See that it is done, Sir William, though it remains against my better judgement."

"Very good, sire." Sir William bowed. He and Ratcliffe turned to leave following the latter's bow.

"Ah, William." Richard called after them.

"Yes, sire?" Catesby asked, facing the king again with a smile.

"Do you still have the draft of the document outlawing Tudor and his allies as traitors?"

"I do, sire." Catesby informed him. "The list of names is all but complete and it should be ready soon."

"And the Duke of Orleans's rebellion?" Richard asked thoughtfully.

"He, er," Catesby frowned at the line of questioning, "he seems to be losing support. I suspect that his campaign will collapse in the coming weeks.

"Very well." Richard tapped his chin. "Have the proclamation prepared but see to it that the name of the Marquis of Dorset is omitted." He saw the confused look between Catesby and Ratcliffe. "I have my reasons." He fixed them both with a stern glare.

"Of course." Ratcliffe said with a note of uncertainty.

"It shall be done." Catesby assured him as the two men swept from the room. As the heavy door swung shut, Richard mused again on his missing knock, but before the latch could click home, a hand appeared through the final crack in the door and pushed it back open. A young man dressed in a tunic and hose puffed in the doorway.

"It is about time." Richard stood. "You will knock in future." He moved around the desk.

"Sire." The man panted.

"Never mind. I will allow it to pass this time as you are late."

"Sire, the queen." The voice was breathless and nervous.

"What is it?" Richard demanded urgently.

"The Bishop was preparing for the queen's evening service when the physician visited to inform him that," the man paused, "that..." He froze.

"Tell me what is wrong!" Richard roared. The man gulped.

"The queen has called for the last rites." The messenger shrank in the doorway as he delivered his news.

"No." Richard whispered as he stood on quivering legs. He suddenly felt as though the walls drew away from him and he stood, scared and alone in the vast, cold darkness of a future without Anne.

The stabbing pain was unbearable and blood filled her mouth with each cough. Anne leaned over the side of the bed and spat the warm, acidic contents of her mouth into the pot set there for the purpose. She spluttered and panted as a maid, her nose and mouth covered against the infection, helped her lie back down and began to mop her brow with a damp cloth. The disease was tightening its grip by the hour. She could feel it and she barely had the strength to clear her chest anymore. She had not seen her reflection in days for fear of what would glare back at her. Her weight loss had accelerated so that she was almost skeletal now. Her hair was matted with sweat in spite of her ladies' best efforts and it was streaked now with thick tracks of grey. Her eyes were sunken and dark and her breath rattled.

"Your majesty." Her physician had entered unseen and was looking, his hand over his mouth, at the contents of the pot.

"The Bishop." She panted, her voice cracked and dry.

"He is on his way." The doctor replied solemnly. "Your highness, the king..."

"No." Anne interrupted hoarsely with a splutter. "I have not let him see me before I reached my worst." She painfully drew several short breaths. "I will not let him see me now." She hacked weakly. "I would have him remember me as I was."

The doctor looked to the doorway and shook his head slowly. There was some commotion outside and Anne's head pounded in protest at the noise. A moment later the Bishop of Westminster glided through the doorway in his deep scarlet robes followed, as he always was, by five monks in long, black habits, hoods obscuring their faces. The lead man swung an incense burner and the other four's hands were lost in their sleeves, pressed together in prayer as all five chanted.

"More," Anne forced herself to smile, "than your usual prayers tonight, your grace."

"You are ready?" he smiled gently down to her. She coughed a terrible, rattling hack as she tried to reply and nodded urgently instead. As he took out his prayer book, the chanting of the monks reached a crescendo and the Bishop began to deliver the last rites. Anne struggled to retain any focus on the proceedings. The Bishop leaned over her. "Do you have any final confession, my lady?" Anne shook her head. The Bishop then began her final Holy Communion, offering her a tiny piece of bread and gently lifting her to sip of the blood of Christ. She stifled a cough as he lowered her back down. The doctor crossed himself. Now, Anne was forced over the side of the bed by a hoarse, rattling cough that brought with it a hot gout of blood. The bishop took a clean cloth from a lady in waiting who stood beside him in floods of silent tears. He gently wiped the queen's mouth. Her breathing was shallow. She fought with all of her failing strength to draw in another breath.

"Richard," her dry voice cracked.

"Your majesty?" the bishop frowned at the queen and looked around at the doctor and the line of chanting monks as though seeking some aid.

"Richard." The effort of the word was inscribed all over her face.

"You instructed..." The bishop offered weakly.

"I...want...Richard." Anne forced out the words breathlessly, a tear spilling from her eye.

"But..." The bishop looked from the doctor, who shrugged, to the ladies in waiting who sobbed, to the monks who continued chanting.

"Richard!" The hoarse croak was as close to a plaintiff call as Anne could manage. She collapsed onto the bed, her eyes heavy and her chest burning as it begged for air. The room blurred around her and she heard muffled voices but could discern no words. Her vision swam as she made out the bishop and doctor moving backward from her bed. She felt that she was slipping away, alone. Suddenly, from the grey haze of the line of monks something moved and then a word cut through the fog like a warm spring morning driving out the night's dark chill.

"Anne!" The voice called and she forced her eyes to focus. The grey figure had stepped forward and thrown off the habit. She could not see clearly but had heard the voice well enough.

"Richard." She whispered, the faintest trace of a smile on her pale lips.

"Leave us." The voice demanded and Anne saw shapes move into the mist. One shape, though, moved closer and became clearer. As the form sat on her bed and pushed damp hair from her forehead, she saw her husband's concerned smile.

"You are here." She stated, wincing at the pain of the effort.

"I am always here, my love." He forced his smile wider.

"Do not look." Anne tried to hold a hand over her face between them but Richard caught it and held it to his chest.

"Anne," he said softly, "I have seen you every evening for weeks when you say your prayers. I beg your forgiveness, but I could not leave you." His voice was pinched and a shiny glaze covered his eyes. Anne sucked in a breath. "Hush." Richard soothed. "All that I see is my beautiful wife, my queen, my Anne. My tower of strength with her gentle eyes. All I see is my love."

The queen's darkened eyes ran freely with tears and her body shook as she fought for breath.

"How," she spluttered, "did we end this way?" She coughed and gurgled as her mouth filled. Richard eased her over the side of the bed and she allowed the blood to fall from her mouth. The king reached for a clean cloth and gently dabbed her crimson lips.

As he lifted her back, he sat on the bed beside her, his arm behind her neck so that her head rested on his chest and he kissed the top of her head. He had often pondered over her question recently himself. He did not see a sickly woman in his arms, though, only his radiant wife. No fading light, but a bright beacon, a constant throughout his life.

"Think not of endings." He smiled out of Anne's view as much to prevent his tears from falling as to cause his voice to sound light. "Think of beginnings. A wise man once told me that this life is all that we have with which to meet God. This is our beginning. Meet Him as Queen of his England, as mother of the Prince of His Wales. That is our beginning. Think not of endings. Think of our love that grew daily and shall continue to grow. Think of our son." He could prevent the flow of tears no longer but tried to maintain his even tone for Anne's sake.

He felt her body tense and winced as he tried to deny its meaning. With immense effort, she lifted her right arm and threw it across his body, a shaky finger pointing to her payer book on the table at the bedside. Richard reached his left hand around and passed the book into Anne's quavering hand. With almost no control left over her fingers, Anne pushed the front cover open. From within, an envelope slid into Richard's lap. He fell silent at the sight as he lifted the paper.

"Promise." Anne croaked. "Bury it with me." She pressed the envelope into Richard's palm. He was struck silent as fresh tears blurred his vision, but he knew the letter instantly. It was the very one that he had written to Anne and left with her after he had rescued her all of those years ago. He had given no thought to it since, but Anne had apparently kept it safe all this time.

"I promise." Richard's voice was strangled by emotion. Anne coughed in his arms again. He kissed the top of her head firmly as tears rolled from his eyes. "That," he whispered softly, "is to keep you safe until we are together again." He felt Anne try to hug him weakly. He kissed her again. "Give this to Edward from me when you see him." Richard wept freely out of Anne's view now. She coughed again and wheezed, her body shuddering. "Do you remember," Richard fought to control himself a while longer, "at Middleham when Edward was four years old?" He felt Anne's body relax a little. "He so wanted to come hunting with me that he somehow lashed a cushion to one of my hounds as a saddle," he smiled at the memory, "and rode across the courtyard with a poker for a lance and his nurse falling over her skirts to try and catch him," he chuckled, but then fell silent. Anne felt heavy against him and her rattling breathing was quietened. He held his own breath for a long moment, listening desperately, but no sound or movement came. Eventually, he pressed his lips to the top of her head and his whole body shook as his restrained sobbing finally erupted from him. His eyes poured thick tears onto Anne's damp hair. Catching his breath, he whispered to her softly. "I hope to see you both again soon, my love." With that, he gave himself over to sorrow and had no idea how long he sat there, crying and holding his wife and her precious letter in his arms for the final time.

Chapter 36

Finale

Sir Thomas More exhaled a melancholy sigh. He lifted his gaze slowly from the subdued flames of the fire and looked across to his guest. Holbein's eyes shimmered in the flickering light from the hearth and he dabbed them with his sleeve as he realised that Sir Thomas was gazing at him with a soft smile creasing his face.

"He lost so much so quickly." Holbein said aloud without meaning to.

"Indeed he did." More reflected. "After all of the years he had taken to meticulously build his reputation, his position, the security of his family, it was ripped from him within a matter of months. He found few that he could have faith in outside of his very tight circle of friends. He was loved by his people but mistrusted by those who really mattered in a political sense. The king saw plots and betrayal all around him and had lost his very reason to retain his grip on all that he had built."

"The plots that he feared were very real though." Holbein told Sir Thomas.

"The Tudor love of propaganda and propagandists began with Henry VII's mother Margaret and Bishop Morton. Their whispering campaign and rumour war played upon the fears and desires of those in the country that did not hold loyalty to the king above their own interests. Unfortunately for Richard, that was most of the influential nobility of the country. And so Morton and Lady Stanley continued their insidious operation, a form of warfare so foreign to Richard that he struggled to deal with it. For a man used to facing his enemy directly across the field of battle and measuring them in one on one combat, such tactics were incomprehensible."

"And with nothing left to fight for..." Hans pondered, but was cut short.

"Oh, no." Sir Thomas straightened in his chair and wagged a finger at Holbein. "I do not believe that King Richard would agree with you. He was the last of the Plantagenet male line in adulthood. His family had ruled England for over three hundred years and he had taken a huge gamble to preserve that precious blood royal on the throne by removing his own brother's son. There was a natural heir in his nephew the Earl of Warwick who would maintain the Plantagenet grip on power given time. I believe that Richard would have felt duty bound, whatever his personal tragedy, to maintain the throne and to hold it in trust for his nephew. It may not have been what he originally intended, but it was no less his responsibility. I also believe that he would be committed to handing to his nephew a secure throne, free from threat at home and abroad and a reformed one, no longer gripped in the chokehold he perceived the nobility to have on government. The only question is whether his solid sense of duty and loyalty could override his aching losses."

"I see." Holbein nodded at the rebuke.

"As it was, though, Henry Tudor had no choice if he wished to press a serious claim to the throne than to mount an invasion. His mother's tactics could loosen Richard's grasp but it would still have to be wrested from him by her son in person. Less than six months after Queen Anne's death, Henry Tudor landed at Milford Haven in Wales with a ragtag band of French soldiers and continental mercenaries and set about discovering what crop could be harvested from his mother's seeds. It was here that the betrayal so offensive to King Richard's chivalric honour began too. Do you remember the Welsh lord promoted by Richard who swore that any army hostile to Richard would only pass through Wales over his belly?"

"Yes." Holbein raised a finger as he sought for the alien name. "Rhys ap Thomas." He was pleased that he could recall it.

"Thomas should have engaged Henry's army the moment that it landed, for it was within his sphere of authority, yet he very quickly joined Henry Tudor's army and began to recruit for him throughout Wales." More informed his guest.

"After he had made such a vow?" Holbein asked with unmasked disapproval.

"He was not without some sense of honour." More moderated. "In order to absolve him of his oath, it was suggested that he allow Henry Tudor to stride over him as he lay on the ground, thus fulfilling the caveat of his pledge. Thomas could not allow himself to be so humiliated in front of his men, so agreed instead to stand below Mullock Bridge at Dale while Henry Tudor walked over the bridge. Accordingly, Henry Tudor marched through Wales over the body of Rhys ap Thomas. And on he marched to Bosworth."

"This was where the king decided to meet him?" Holbein enquired.

"Not precisely." More answered. "The king insisted that his army kept to the roads as it marched. Henry Tudor did not." Sir Thomas saw the confusion on the artist's face. "Richard was adamant that his troops not destroy any crops on their march, since that would deprive his subjects of a harvest. Henry had no such concerns, and indeed subsequently had to pay reparations to areas that suffered from his passing. And so it was that they encountered each other at Market Bosworth."

Chapter 37

22nd August 1485 - Revelation

Richard awoke sharply in a cold sweat, lurching up from his bed. His eyes darted around his tent as though he expected to see some shadowy phantom poised to spring upon him. There was no one there. He wiped the icy damp from his brow. A confused furrow appeared across his forehead. After a painful moment, the dreams from which he had awoken began to swirl in his mind like a spinning whirlpool in a muddy pond. Fighting to push through the murk in his mind, Richard began to remember disparate details but could not piece them together into anything coherent. Suddenly, in a painful flash, he recalled seeing face after face of dead friends, family and enemies. Anne, their son Edward, his brothers Edward and George, Hastings and others that he could not remember. Each had approached him in turn, arms wide open and a welcoming smile across their faces. To each, Richard had stretched out a hand in greeting but as soon as he had touched them they had been altered. Their skin had flared away to leave rotted flesh and exposed bone and the hand with which Richard had touched them had turned icy cold. He winced at the memory. Frozen in fear, he had watched as most, including Edward and Hastings had raised long, thin daggers above their fierce, terrible faces and swung them down at Richard, the decayed body vanishing just before the blade struck his chest as he stood immobilised. Clarence had laughed at him, a haunting cackle that sucked out Richard's breath so that he screamed in silence. Clarence only vanished when Richard felt he was about to suffocate. Anne and little Edward had been the worst. Both had acted as the others, but he had not quite managed to touch them as he reached desperately before they had changed so hideously and then begun to slide back from Richard into the blackness. The harder he tried to run after them, the more he felt restrained, and the faster they glided away from him again. He had felt an excruciating pain as he watched their faces slip away. As Anne had changed he had been hit, as though with a metal gauntlet, by an overpowering sense of sorrow, reflected on Anne's face as tears poured silently down her cheeks, washing blue black flesh away with them. In Edward's case, the emotion that pounded at him was fear, but not fear of the terrible sight of his son, it was the fear that Edward was feeling lost, alone and was reaching for his father, but he too was drawn away by some unseen force and absorbed into the darkness. That was when Richard had awoken, still filled by a small boy's fear and loneliness. He rubbed his eyes as he fought back uncertain tears and the choking knot in his throat.

Climbing heavily from his bed, Richard moved to the bowl that lay on a table in the centre of the tent and filled it from the pitcher at its side with cool water. He splashed his face over and over again, hoping to wash away the memories that haunted his mind, but they flashed before him in turn each time he closed his eyes. To combat this, he tried urgently to wrap his mind around what today would bring. Pulling on his shirt, he pushed aside the opening of his tent to allow the early morning light to pierce the darkness. As he looked back, he was pleased to see most of the shadow gone from the gloomy tent, though his own stark outline sat heavily on the ground, made taller than him by a trick of the early morning sun. For a shuddering moment, he wondered whether his own twisted face was going to lunge up at him. He shook away the thought, only to replace it with another. He found himself wondering whether his nightmare reflected his own feelings of betrayal and loss, or whether the souls of the dead haunted him with their own message for him. He did not know, nor did he wish to think on it any longer. He looked down at his feet, where they met his shadow, and forced his emotions and his questions to the back of his mind as he spun and marched away from the tent, shivering in the cool morning dew.

Across the king's camp, John Howard emerged from his own tent stretching away the stiffness of the chill night. He surveyed the preparations underway. Men scurried about collecting armour and weapons and the large guns were being hauled into position. He looked around for his squire. He had not worn his full armour for many years and did not want to hurry his preparations. His old bones were no longer as eager for the battle field as they once were. As he cast his gaze around the fields of canvas something caught his eye flapping in the breeze on his tent. With a frown, he stepped closer to it and squinted to bring it into focus. It was a note, pinned to the fabric of his tent. He read it and his frown deepened. He reread it and then snatched it down, looking around in part to see if anyone else had noticed the paper, and in part to search out anyone who may have placed it there. He saw nothing out of place in the milling soldiery about him. Looking down he read the words again.

'Jack of Norfolk, be not too bold,
For Dickon thy master, is bought and sold.'

With a final look around, he shrank back into his tent to prepare for the trial ahead.

The 22nd August had arrived swiftly and the king's army had positioned itself squarely between the invaders and the capitol. Richard had chosen the top of Ambion Hill, just outside Market Bosworth, to intercept Tudor. The field at the foot of the hill provided an ideal place to engage, whilst the hill would offer a perfect view of the battle for Richard. The north side was steep, so protected from attack and to the right, the south was guarded by marshy land that would prove as good as impassable. It was two hours until the time Richard had appointed for the men to muster and only one hour until the final strategy meeting. Having spent much of the previous day debating tactics, both with his captains and alone with his prayer book, the king had pushed such things from his mind before taking to his bed. Now, he welcomed it back as a distraction from his haunting dream. Strolling aimlessly through the forest of thick material tents that seemed hunched under the weight of the damp morning, much as Richard himself did, he sucked in a long, slow lung full of the chill air in an effort to blow the swirling mist of fear and uncertainty from his thoughts. He had never felt this way preparing for a battle before. As the swelling noises of the rousing camp surrounded him, the king decided to return to his tent to prepare himself.

As Richard finally entered the council meeting, he was greeted by Norfolk, Northumberland, Ratcliffe, Harrington and Lovell, who rose in respectful greeting. He frowned as he rounded the long table and took the centre seat of the long back edge. The others sat as he did. Lord Strange also retook his seat at the far end of the table and Richard eyed him accusingly.

"Lord Stanley is late." Richard stated to the room without taking his eyes from the young man to his left.

"He was summoned my lord," Norfolk spoke in a slow, deep tone, "but sent word that he suffers from the sweating sickness and must decline your invitation."

"It was not an invitation." A flash of red rashed his cheeks to contrast against his pale complexion at Stanley's disobedience. He was sure that he saw a smile flick Lord Strange's lips momentarily. "What," Richard enquired, lightening his tone, but keeping his eyes upon Strange, "of my message that his failure to declare decisively for me this morning would result in his son's execution?" He was pleased at the worried glance that Lord Strange shot at the tent entrance. However, the question went unanswered. He eyed each of the others in turn as they shifted uncomfortably, clearly not wishing to impart that which they all knew. His eyes came to rest on Lovell and he raised his eyebrows enquiringly whilst trying to push down his growing frustration.

"Stanley sent an answer, Richard." Francis spoke quietly and his hesitance sent a surge of anger through Richard like a scalding pot of oil poured over him.

"What was his answer?" Richard demanded, slamming his hands onto the table, his body shaking in rage.

"He said," Lovell paused, and then realised that to do so would be a very bad idea. This was unlike his friend. "He said that he has other sons, Richard." All of those gathered seemed to hold their collective breath awaiting the king's response. Richard looked slowly to Lord Strange, who tried to disguise his unease behind a smug smile.

"Well, Lord Strange." Richard matched the man's self satisfied look. "You have already told me of the conspiracy that you and your uncle Sir William have undertaken with Tudor. You have provided the evidence that has seen your uncle declared traitor." The young man's grin faltered. "I do not doubt that your father is involved, albeit at arm's length. Presumably he will not commit to either side openly for fear of selecting the wrong side. This is his way." The other looked down at the table. "It would seem that loyalty within your family does not even manifest itself between father and son." Lord Strange was now clearly deeply uncomfortable. Richard smiled. "Your father," the king roared, causing the young man to jump in his seat, "will not even declare for me to save your life. Let us see what he will do to save his own." Richard pounded his fists onto the table. "Leave!" he bellowed. Strange grasped the opportunity and strode quickly from the tent, his bravado evaporated. Richard stood, his teeth and fists clenched tightly. With a roar like a wounded bear, Richard lifted his thick limbed chair and launched it at the place where Lord Strange had just exited. It met the fabric with a soft thump and crashed to the rug below.

"Now," Richard began again with an instant calmness as though nothing out of the ordinary had occurred, "to the arrangements of the day." He slid a chair over from further along the table and sat back down, enjoying the grins on the faces of Ratcliffe and Harrington. "Norfolk," he smiled softly at the duke, "you shall lead the vanguard with your son the Earl of Surrey and your men."

"It will be my honour, sire." John Howard nodded, his voice deep and full of burgeoning aggression. He was a man changed from the gentle elder statesmen that they all knew when it came time for battle.

"May I suggest," Northumberland ventured a little nervously, "that I hold the ground to your rear, sire, lest Stanley should attack from the flank, or your lines be breached," he smiled uneasily. Richard was silent, but aware of the mutterings of Ratcliffe and Harrington, as his eyes bored into those of the Earl, a thin man with pointed features. He was a little older than Richard but with a smoother complexion that betrayed the luxury in which he now lived. His family's sympathy's were previously Lancastrian, but Richard's brother Edward had brought the ancient and mighty Percy family back in from the cold in order to assist in the taming of the north in which Richard himself had been so instrumental. He was not one of Richard's favourites.

"Very well," he eventually chirped. "The rearguard is yours."

"Yes, sire." Percy sounded relieved.

"In less than one hour, your men must be ready to destroy this impudent invader." Richard told them all.

"Yes, sire." Norfolk boomed excitedly.

"Your grace." Northumberland concurred and the two men, along with Ratcliffe and Harrington, rose to leave the tent. Watching them make their exit, Lovell folded his arms and spoke to Richard without looking at him.

"You do know that Stanley will not intervene until the outcome is decided, or until he is able to decide the outcome, whatever you may threaten?" There was no answer. "Richard?" Lovell tried to get his attention, but still there was no reply. "Richard!"

"Not today, Francis." Richard replied wearily. "I know what you would say, but I have things that I must say to you."

"I would say my piece anyway." Lovell challenged.

"No," Richard snapped, "you shall not."

"Forgive me, Richard," Lovell rose to his feet and suddenly his tone became firm, "but I shall." He moved around the table until he stood squarely before his friend, planted his palms wide on the table and leaned forward toward Richard. The king looked up at his friend's chiselled features purposefully, his eyes ablaze. "This is not you, Richard." Lovell frowned deeply as he spoke. "We have known each other for twenty years or more and I barely recognise the man before me now. The Richard that I know and love would not allow another to lead out his army onto the field of possibly the most important battle of his life."

"Norfolk is a capable man." Richard said absently. His mind churned over his dreams again, the plans for today, Stanley's evasiveness, his reign, his losses. He could concentrate on nothing that twisted within his mind.

"That is not the point," Lovell shouted, trying to snap Richard out of his melancholy, "and you know it." He paused a moment. "There would be no harm in moving back toward London if more time will help."

"Never." Richard's eyes sparked.

"You are still in there then?" Lovell smiled at the flash of his old friend.

"I am so tired, Francis." Richard allowed the words to escape him. "Anne was the first and she will be the last person to define who I am, to define the way that I feel. My thoughts were once a ship on a steady course but I realise now that Anne was my mast. With her gone, I have only broken splinters working their way into my mind. Without her, I am struggling, my friend. How is it that our deepest scars, the ones that touch our souls, are the very ones that cannot be seen?"

"I see them, Richard." Lovell placed a hand on his friend's shoulder and gently squeezed. "We all know how you suffer, just as we know that you will do your duty today."

"I think," Richard said, as if suddenly returning to the room, "that much is being made clear to me today that I have not wanted to see."

"Stanley has always been fickle." Lovell guessed at his meaning. "It is the secret of his family's success."

"No," Richard chuckled casually, "nothing so simple."

"What is it Richard?"

"You shall know as soon as I do."

"I am worried about you."

"And I thank you for it." Richard rose and placed a hand on Lovell's shoulder. "You are a true friend, Francis. It is for this reason that I must ask this of you, that I would ask of no other left in this world."

"I have but to know what it is and it is done." Francis frowned, his concern growing.

"You will be with Northumberland in the rearguard and you will not join battle even if the rear does."

"What?" Lovell floundered for words.

"You will remain in the rear and you shall not engage. Is that clear?" Richard reiterated. There was a moment of silence.

"It is clear." Francis conceded sadly.

"I have a letter here." Richard reached inside his tunic and pulled out an envelope secured with his own wax seal. "If this day goes ill, this letter contains instructions for the most important of tasks. Open it and do as it asks." Richard saw the dismayed confusion on Lovell's face. "Please, my friend."

"Of course." Lovell replied flatly. "And if the day goes well?" he asked with a smile.

"Then I shall have the letter returned, the seal unbroken." Richard returned the smile.

"Very well. I look forward to handing it back to you by this afternoon." Francis clasped Richard's forearm and felt the king place a tight grip on his own. They stood for a moment, requiring no words.

"Away." The king eventually released his grip. After lingering a moment in puzzled concern, Lovell turned and left the tent.

Richard slid back into his chair and began to chew on the fingernails of his right hand. After checking that he was definitely alone, he surrendered to his swelling sadness and a single tear rolled down his cheek. He sat alone until a nervous squire tugged aside the tent flap to ask whether he was ready to put on his armour. Composing himself, the king nodded and several men clattered in with various parts of his fine plate mail, before a familiar tone softly rolled through the tent.

"Leave us." John's voice was strangely welcome. Richard smiled and moved to the centre of the tent where he stood in silence as John buckled each piece to him with care. Finally, he lifted the king's belt and buckled that before gently sliding Richard's sword into its scabbard and his mace into the loop at his waist. He stepped back and handed the king his helm. He bowed low and Richard smiled softly at him. He felt more relaxed now. His thoughts cleared under the familiar weight.

"Thank you, John."

"Sire." The man bowed again and turned to leave.

"One more thing, John." Richard suddenly called after him.

"Yes, sire." The man replied.

"Go to my tent and fetch the contents of the chest at the end of my bed, if you please."

"Of course, sire." John lowered his head, a little puzzled.

"Thank you." Richard said softly. John left the king standing in his full splendour, ready to take the field of battle.

Chapter 38

The Battle of Bosworth Field

The sun pierced the thinning clouds above as Richard mounted his steed at the head of his retinue. A shadow still lingered over Ambion Hill but the flat of the fields below was now bathed in bright light that enhanced the vivid green of the lush grass that wavered in the breeze, shaking off the last of the morning moisture. The air was growing warm but it moved refreshingly. Ranks of men stood before the king and to his rear as the lines made final preparations for the battle. Opposite, across the open fields, blocks of dark figures were discernible. The enemy was clearly lining up and making ready for what was to come. Richard glanced to his right and, as if sensing his movement, Lovell turned to meet his eyes. A smile pushed the corners of the king's lips, but was met by a look of concern on Lovell's face.

"What do the scouts report?" Richard asked, ignoring the anxious gaze.

"Tudor has fielded around five thousand men." Lovell reported.

"Stanley?" Richard eyed Lord Stanley's position to his right, some half a mile away.

"He and his brother command around four thousand." Lovell sneered as he looked over to Lord Stanley's force.

"Our force is around ten thousand?" Richard asked for confirmation.

"Indeed." Lovell replied.

"If we can ensure that Stanley remains neutral, then the odds favour us." Richard pondered.

"Richard," Lovell began, leaning in his saddle toward his friend so that he could quiet his voice, "is all well? You seem," he thought for a moment, "preoccupied."

"I think," Richard replied, turning his eyes to the distant shape of Tudor's army, "that it is time to address the troops." Allowing no time for further discussions, the king wrapped his reins around his left hand and spurred his horse to the left to ride around the massed ranks of Norfolk's men. Lovell's eyes followed him with a growing, knowing concern.

As he rode, Richard's mind strayed back to his dreams and he wondered whether the scenes that haunted him reflected his own feelings, his state of mind, or whether they were a warning. An omen that this day was doomed. Rounding the front ranks, he shook such things from his head. This was not the time for doubt. Norfolk's mount stepped out of the lines and the duke deftly turned the horse to face his king, bowing low in his saddle. Acknowledging the gesture, Richard pulled his own horse up before the duke and stood in the stirrups, turning his body to face the men. The early sun flared in his eyes as they tried to adjust. Finally, he saw a positive side to today. The enemy would be fighting into this low glare. Allowing the tension of the moment to build, Richard passed his eyes slowly over the rows of faces before him.

"Englishmen!" the king roared at the top of his voice so that all of those spread over Ambion Hill could hear the word rolling clearly through the morning air. In an almost instant response, the Hill erupted into a cacophony of cheers and roars, mixed with the ringing of steel blades clanking on shields. "My Englishmen," Richard continued, his voice loaded with emotion, drawn out by a sudden rush of adrenaline, "some Welsh milksop of a mother's boy," he paused as approving laughter broke over the Hill, "has brought the contents of France's prisons," again he paused, this time to allow the ripples of disapproving booing to subside, "to our England because he," Richard swung an accusing finger toward the far side of the field, "believes that he would make a better king than I." Now, roars of 'No!', 'Never!' and 'God save King Richard!' filled the air, each man before the king growing more excited as the atmosphere became charged at the thought of foreign invaders on English soil.

"They have come," Richard continued, reaching to the satchel at the right of his saddle, "for this!" He pulled out the bright circlet of gold and jewels and raised it above his head. There were audible gasps of awe from all parts of the Hill as the Royal Crown glinted in the sun above the king's helm. After a moment Richard reached up with his other hand. "If they want it," he bellowed as he slowly, deliberately lowered the crown to sit atop his helmet, "they will have to come and take it from me. Now," Richard roared, tugging his horse's reigns so that the steed reared up, "who is with me?"

The noise that followed this question was deafening as Richard kept his mount balancing high on its hind legs. Sliding the mace from his waist, he circled it in the air as all of the men in the ranks before him chanted his name in unison.

"Richard! Richard!" A shiver ran down his spine as the excitement began to grip his body. As the shouts began to ebb, he pushed his mace higher into the air.

"England!" he roared as he galloped along the front line and back to his position. The call was echoed in his wake like thunder rolling over the hill.

To the north, unseen by the king, Lord Stanley picked at his teeth, turned up his nose and strode back into his tent. He plucked up a letter on his small desk and read through its contents again, pondering his options.

"Very nice." Lovell nodded as Richard returned.

"It seemed to do the job." Richard smiled without looking as though he meant it.

"Do you think that," Lovell nodded at the crown atop the king's helm, "is a good idea?"

"It did no harm at Agincourt." Richard replied.

"You have marked yourself out to every archer and soldier over there."

"Good." Richard snapped. "Let them all try. I am still the King of England and if there is a man out there able to take this crown from my head, then I deserve it no longer." There was a long silence as Lovell's eyes bored into Richard, who sat watching Norfolk prepare to move forward. "You should take your position, Francis."

"If I must." Lovell replied obstinately.

"Do you have the letter?" Richard ignored the tone.

"I do." Francis kept his eyes locked on the king. "I shall return it to you before this sun sinks."

"Good." Richard replied, finally turning to meet Lovell's eyes. "I hold you very dear, Francis." Richard smiled uneasily.

"You frighten me, sire." Lovell confessed, no longer able to restrain his concern.

"I am frightened too, old friend." There was a hint of a laugh in the king's voice.

"You are never afraid, Richard." Lovell shifted in his saddle. "What is it that has you so troubled?"

"That I have not yet concluded." Richard said darkly. "One thing that I have resolved is that whilst kings need men like me, men like me make poor kings." He did not allow Francis to draw breath to counter him. "My vision of empowering people is naive, I see that now. The many do not rule this land and the few who do have too much to lose to allow the status quo to change, and so they will not let me change it." He looked up to Stanley's position. "Perhaps one day it will have to change." He looked at the ranks of men before him and bit his lip. "I miss my wife and son so much." The king looked down at his gauntlet under which he felt his wedding band. He reached a hand out to Lovell. "God be with you this day, Francis, and may it always be so."

"Richard," Lovell clasped the king's forearm filled suddenly with dread, but he was unable to give voice to his trepidation as a loud trumpet blast pierced the air. Lovell turned his horse, still looking at his friend, and, as ordered, rode to join Northumberland's rearguard.

Richard drew his sword and raised it high, circling the air silently. A few hundred yards in front, Norfolk mirrored the motion in acknowledgement and a slow, rhythmical thud marked each step as the front section of Richard's army began to move forward. In the distance, the entirety of Tudor's army was mobilised. Apparently not using the traditional three guards, the whole force moved forward behind the unmistakable banner of the Earl of Oxford.

As Richard began issuing orders to runners around him, a hail of arrows flew from his archers, a cloudlike shadow drifting over Norfolk's men before diving into the midst of the advancing French force. A few fell, more stumbled, lamed, and only seconds later a volley was returned. Canon fire thundered intermittently from both sides causing wild carnage. The arrow and canon ceased as the two blocks of men neared each other. Ringing metallic clanking filled the air, punctuated by the roars of adrenalin fuelled frenzy and the screams of men whose flesh was sliced from their bone. For twenty minutes the conflict raged below Richard and all of the time he felt out of place not being at the front of the melee. He was almost overwhelmed by the urge to spur his horse forward and take his men into the fray. The battle seemed evenly poised when he decided to test the waters of loyalty.

"Order Lord Stanley into the fray. From his position on the flank he could end this in moments." A runner moved to the array of flags and banners and began waving the appropriate signal. All went calm around him in anticipation. The banner was waved again, a little more frantically. There was no movement.

"The evil old…" Ratcliffe bellowed at Richard's right side.

"Did we ever doubt it?" Harrington asked at the king's left hand.

"When this is done, he will pay for his betrayal." Ratcliffe growled through clenched teeth.

Before any more could be said, Richard's eye was caught by the main combat again. Norfolk's banner was nearing that of Oxford. Shifting in his saddle, he knew that this could prove a decisive moment. Squinting, he picked out the duke in his armour atop his steed. A moment later, the old man fell from his horse and was lost for a moment in the raging melee. Seconds later, he seemed to erupt from the press around him, his great sword swirling skilfully and crashing into target after target. Richard swore that he could hear the old man's roar above all the clamour as a wider arc emptied around him. Then, there was a gasp of shock from the men around Richard. The thick shaft of an ash arrow thudded into the duke's face and ruptured the back of his helm, dripping shining red blood. The old man staggered, fell to his knees and then vanished from sight as the hole that he had opened up swallowed him.

"Signal Northumberland," Richard called down to a lad immediately, "to wheel around to the left and attack the flank." The young man disappeared to carry out his instruction. "Without John, his men will crumble." Richard felt a lump in his throat but pushed it down. "Northumberland can press their flank and the marsh will force them toward Stanley," he told Ratcliffe who nodded fervently. "It will present Stanley the ideal opportunity to finish them from their rear and if he wishes to betray me, he will be behind the rest of Oxford's men."

"Excellent, sire." Ratcliffe was clearly excited as his own adrenaline coursed through him.

The signal was given, but there was no movement from the rear guard. The flag waved once more. Nothing moved.

"Damn you." Richard mumbled darkly at the earl's failure to assist. He looked back to the fight and saw Oxford's banner pushing on hard. He could no longer see Norfolk's standard and though the battle raged and the tumult showed no sign of subsiding, Richard knew that the lines would fail soon. He looked up to Stanley's position. "Damn you both." His muttering was cut short as a curious sight caught his eye. As his gaze fell down the hill and he weighed the point at which he would throw the middle into the battle to personally reinforce the vanguard, he saw a group of some twenty riders and as many infantry, a banner flying above them, riding hard toward Lord Stanley. It was Tudor and his retinue. Clearly he too was uncertain of Stanley's loyalty and, Richard supposed, he was intending a personal plea to bring the weight of his step father's force into play. The riders were skirting around the battle, giving it a wide berth, but there was open space between the melee and the foot of Stanley's hill. There was a small space remaining too between the marshy ground at the foot of the Hill to the king's right and the remainder of Norfolk's force, but it was slipping away as they were pushed back. The decision was made.

He turned his horse to face his men, arrayed behind him. Surveying them, he was suddenly hit by a guilty pride that they were all willing to sacrifice their lives to preserve his throne.

"Each and every one of you," he called with all of the authority he could muster, "has my thanks and my blessing, this day and always." He surveyed the confused faces and smiled softly. Wheeling his horse around, he called down to a squire. "My lance." The man scurried to the wooden stand against which were propped two dozen lances of dazzling red and white bands while the king slipped his shield over his left arm. As the squire passed the fierce weapon to him, Richard's eyes drifted upward in silent prayer. His eyes focussed on the flapping banner above him. His white boar rippled furiously toward the enemy as though straining to be released onto the field. Richard burned with the same desire.

"I think I see it now," he said to no one in particular.

"See what?" Ratcliffe's face was contorted with uncertainty at Richard's call for his lance and his words.

"That wave." Richard said with an eerie calm.

"Richard," Ratcliffe warned, "this is no time for some brave gesture."

"It is only brave," Richard smiled with a tranquil malevolence, "if you are afraid." He reared his horse. "It is an honour to take the field with you, gentlemen." He offered a softer grin to Ratcliffe, Harrington and the other dozen knights of the body around him as he pushed down his visor. "I do not ask any man to follow me."

"That is why we will all follow you, your majesty." Ratcliffe replied gruffly, a dark smile on his own face as he pulled down his visor. "Lance!" His call was echoed by all of the other knights.

The king reared up his charger high and long, his crown glinting in the bright sun, and then dug his spurs into the horse's flanks. In a moment, each of the knights around him held a lance and barely a second after the king, they all charged down the hill to intercept Tudor. The ground shook beneath the weight of the giant steeds as they thundered down the hill, riders tilting their lances. All seemed to slow around Richard. Through the narrow slit in his visor he saw the shocked faces of the rear rank of old Norfolk's force as they turned to see the cause of the thunderous roar. Shouts of 'God save King Richard!' and wild cheers sprung from the rear lines and they moved forward in a wave crashing against Oxford's press. Richard pounded on, digging his heels hard into his horse to meet Tudor before he could make the base of the hill upon which Lord Stanley surveyed his two suitors coldly.

The king was pleased to see Tudor's retinue notice the charge and alert the pretender. Their horses lurched into a gallop and Richard spurred his own mount on harder still. He felt the other knights right behind him, pressing every bit as hard. A dozen riders peeled away from Tudor and rode toward the king's charge, drawing swords as they did so. He picked his target at the front of Tudor's group and levelled his lance. With a thud that jarred his right shoulder the lance slammed into the man's chest plate, piercing it and holding him in midair as his horse rode on from below him before the wooden shaft snapped with a crack half way along its length and the body slammed into the ground. Other riders passed either side of him and there was the sound of crashing and thudding, though he could not see what was happening from behind his visor. He pushed on toward the small group still around Tudor. Another rider blocked his way and Richard swung the shattered lance at the rider's chest, crashing into him and throwing him from his saddle. Behind him, Ratcliffe unseated a second rider, Harrington, bearing Richard's standard, struggled to match the king's pace. Five other riders broke out of the press with them. The remainder were absorbed into a small battle of their own, some unseated and fighting hand to hand.

Realising that they could not evade the oncoming charge, Tudor's group turned to face the oncoming riders. Half a dozen mounted men clustered around Tudor as the infantry formed into four lines of five men in front. Richard grinned beneath his visor as he saw the soldiers' nervous faces as he and the seven behind him bore down upon them. He threw the splintered lance to his right and pulled his mace from its holster in front of his right knee. His head was filled with the pumping of his own blood and his limbs trembled with a nervous excitement that he had not felt in years. Richard circled his heavy mace menacingly in the air and as his horse slammed into the front rank of men, he brought it down with a sickening crack, splitting the leather helmet of the man below and spraying thick gobs of blood into the air. He swung the shaft and its flanged head across his body to crush the arm of a soldier pushing his sword toward the king. There was a scream of agony before Richard saw a sword slide through the man's torso. He looked across to see Ratcliffe hauling the sword out and hacking at the man's neck. To his right also, riders crashed into the small band of men. The first line was decimated in seconds but the unwieldy mounted knights lost their advantage quickly in the small space and the second rank began to hack at the legs of the mounts. Three horses fell in a bloody heap of desperate neighing and their riders wrestled to free themselves, but swordsmen were upon them before they could stand in their heavy plate. A couple of Tudor's men fell before the three knights were overwhelmed. Richard, Ratcliffe, Harrington and two others pressed on, slashing and crushing the foot soldiers. Now, three more horses fell including Harrington's. On his way to the ground, James hacked at his attacker and severed his arm. He was on his feet incredibly quickly and pushed his sword through the man who fell with a scream. The two other knights did not fare so well.

Seeing that the advantage of his mounted position was lost, Richard reared his horse, the hooves crashing wickedly into the two men before him. The soldiers stumbled back and Richard took the opportunity to deftly swing himself from the saddle and land on his feet, wincing under the weight of the armour that pulled him down hard. He stood with his horse between himself and the swords that sought him and a moment later the beast was felled. Ratcliffe too had dismounted and moved to Richard's side. Harrington was catching his breath just behind. James pulled the king's standard from his fallen horse and raised it high in the air with a blood curdling roar. He slammed the pole into the earth and raised his sword.

The fear on the faces of the remaining soldiers, less than a dozen now, caused Richard to grin. He strode forward and swung the mace, smashing it into the shoulder of the man in front of him who crumpled under the force of the strike. He was forced to push the mace down to deflect a thrust from his right and saw Ratcliffe fell another man with a savage slash of his sword. Harrington rushed forward to Richard's right and skewered another with the point of his sword. The earth underfoot was becoming boggy as thick blood soaked the soil and the fighting churned the earth. A shock ran up Richard's left arm as a blow thumped his shield. The surprise shook it from his grip and it clanged onto the floor. He brought his mace across his body and it crushed another skull. Ratcliffe and Harrington roared and they slashed further into the men.

Suddenly, there was a clang at Richard's right and he looked across to see Harrington's sword, held in both of his hands, holding back a sword that had been falling onto the king's shoulder. Richard jabbed the end of his mace into the man's midriff and he bent double, winded. Harrington whirled his sword up, and with a mighty downward swing separated the man's head from his shoulders.

"Thank you." Richard looked up to Harrington's face but saw that his helm was gone and his face was contorted. Looking down again, Richard saw a blade buried in Sir James's side. He fell to his knees. "No!" Richard roared and swung his mace over Harrington's head and into the chest of his attacker, sending him flying back. Sir James struggled to get to his feet, pulling the lodged blade from his flank. His legs buckled beneath him and he fell back to his knees.

"God save King Richard." Harrington gurgled quietly as his mouth filled with his own warm, bitter blood. He coughed and fell onto his side, his eyes open and staring emptily.

"No!" Richard bellowed again and lunged at the last man he could see standing before him, who crashed to the ground under a fierce blow. He looked across to Ratcliffe who stood beside him heaving for breath. Richard's own chest burned as it ached for air. The two men looked at the remaining group before them. Richard shot a glance behind and saw the rest of his knights fallen. A small band from Oxford's flank had broken off and helped to crush them. The half a dozen knights and Tudor looked to be weighing whether they should ride for Stanley or try to finish off the two remaining men and thus end the battle. Four men dismounted and drew swords, squaring up ten yards in front of the king and Ratcliffe.

"Richard!" The slow roar caught the king unawares and Ratcliffe's body flew into view from the right edge of his visor. He saw the body rock and then it began to fall back toward Richard. He caught Ratcliffe and lowered him to the ground. He saw the long shaft of an arrow poking out from Ratcliffe's chest. It had pierced his chest plate and was close to his heart. He fought to suck in a breath and pushed back his visor.

"Richard." The king's voice cracked with emotion as he pulled off his own helm. A tear mingled with the sweat pouring from his brow. "What have you done?" As he discarded his helmet, he failed to notice the crown rolling away from it.

"That," Sir Richard choked out the words, "is no way for King Richard to fall." He smiled. "A truly chivalric charge of the cavalry, my king." Ratcliffe grasped at the king's shoulder as the pain overwhelmed him. "Go," he spluttered, "go and make for yourself a death that will be remembered for all time."

Richard's head fell but he felt his blood burning and refuelling his aching muscles. As he looked up, all seemed to fall silent around him. He saw the blue coats of Sir William Stanley's men rushing toward the body of the battle as his own middle guard pushed to join the fighting. The odds had swung against him and his only remaining hope lay in the destruction of Tudor himself. Laying Ratcliffe gently onto the ground, he pushed himself up on his mace and looked across. He saw a giant figure hauling a man from his horse beside Tudor and punching him viciously in the face. Then, he turned to face Richard, holding his arm in front of the other three, and strode several paces forward.

"You have my apologies, sir." The deep voice rolled out. "There was no honour in such an attack."

"Sir John Cheney." Richard panted a respectful greeting as he stood up slowly under the weight of his armour. "I am glad that there is one amongst this coward's army of foreign invaders who holds a notion of honour." Sir John Cheney was a famed soldier, a veteran of at least as many battles as Richard. He stood every bit as tall as King Edward had and, if anything, was broader of chest. A lesser, or perhaps wiser, man than Richard would have fled at the mere sight of his huge frame, an immense war hammer that most men would struggle to lift held like a wooden training sword in his left hand. "You have selected a fine day to die, Sir John." Richard smiled softly and he tried to slow his breathing. He could not decide whether to remove the armour that restricted his movement and slowed him, knowing that doing so would expose him. Since speed was not his opponent's forte, Richard thought it better to retain some protection from a heavy blow.

"We shall see, sir." Sir John drew up his muscular form in preparation. He took a long stride toward the king, more than aware of his opponent's reputation and fierce ability, but knowing that if he were the man to kill Richard, the new king would surely be eager to reward him. As his foot met the ground with a heavy thud, Richard passed his mace to his left hand, drew his sword with his right, lowered his frame and ran headlong at the other man using the weight of his armour to carry him dangerously out of control.

Cheney raised his hammer in both hands and swung it down. Richard ducked under the blow and swung his sword up Sir John's right side as they met, grazing and sparking along the chain mail under his breastplate but causing no damage. Cheney lifted the hammer with deceptive speed and the head of the mighty weapon struck the back of Richard's right shoulder. Pain shot through his body. There were cheers from behind Cheney as Richard staggered back. Cheney advanced, but as he did his breastplate fell away where Richard had sliced through the leather straps. He glanced down, shocked, and then looked back to Richard, who raised his sword in explanation. Sir John ripped the plate from his chest and threw it to the ground. He swung the hammer in a circle around his head and strode toward Richard again. The king stood perfectly still. As Cheney swung down his right arm, Richard stepped forward so that Sir John's elbow crashed onto his left shoulder. Both men howled. Cheney dropped the hammer and Richard crumpled to one knee, but in the same instant, he swung the mace in his left hand into the side of the giant's knee and pushed the sword in his right up under the waist of Cheney's chain shirt and the man fell forward further onto the blade as his knee gave way. Sir John wavered, placed a hand on Richard's right shoulder, causing him to wince as the injury there seared, and fell to his knees. The two men knelt before each other for a long moment.

"Sire." Sir John bobbed his head.

"Sir John." Richard replied gravely. Cheney fell slowly backward to reveal the three men and one rider now between him and Tudor. A glance to his left told him that the field was all but lost. A group of Stanley's blue coats and a small band of Welsh warriors had broken away and were moving toward Richard. Time was short. He withdrew his sword from Cheney's gut with a wet squelching sound and staggered to his feet.

"Sire!" A call came from his right that caused him to jump. He turned to face it, a heavy frown and stern expression on his face. John leapt from a horse beside him and landed at a run beside Richard. "Sire, take my horse and fall back," John implored him in his thick northern accent, "that you may fight another day."

"Get back into the saddle, John." Richard growled. He immediately softened at the look on the other man's face. "Good John, seek out Lord Lovell and offer him your assistance. He will have need of true men such as you."

"But sire," John begged, "I will not leave you to this fate."

"It is my fate." Richard told him forcefully. "I swore to myself a long time ago that I would never run and hide again, surviving at the whim of others whilst it suits them. That life is not for me. I shall leave this field as the undisputed King of England, or I shall not leave it at all." John's face contorted pleadingly. "I would not be the king that you want nor that you deserve if I were to run now. That is not the man that I am." Richard looked around as men closed from the left and those in front prepared to advance. "After all of these years, John, will you ignore my final instruction?"

"No, sire." John's head fell. "I will not."

"Into your saddle, then, my friend." Richard smiled softly as the man hauled himself heavily into his saddle.

"My lord," John said, his voice loaded with sorrow, "it has been an honour."

"It has, John." Richard smiled. "It truly has." With that, he slapped the flat of his sword on the steed's haunches and it bolted back toward Ambion Hill. John did not look back. He could not.

Now, Richard returned his attention to his front. The blue tunics were fanning out to his left and moving around his rear, clearly seeking to encircle him. He clenched his jaw tightly, his hollow, pale face flushing. His dark hair blew in the breeze as he pushed his sword into the earth before him. Flexing his right arm, the crushed plate rubbed painfully on the bruised bone below where Cheney's hammer had caught him. He slid his dagger from his hip, eying the men moving around him on all sides now, forming a circle some twenty yards from him. As he had done to Cheney, he slit the leather straps at each side of his own breastplate and threw it to the ground, bearing his chain shirt. Next he cut away the straps of his greaves to release his legs. Slowly, he turned his head to the left, then back to centre and to his right, making contact with each set of eyes that he passed. Throwing the dagger into the earth he moved fluidly to lift his sword. He rolled his neck and shoulders to loosen them, widened his stance and bent his knees slightly.

"Stanley!" Richard roared into the weighty silence. There was no reply, but Richard had not expected one. "Damn your treachery!" Gripping his weapons tightly, Richard felt his muscles tighten, each sinew of his being ready to react to his command. "Tudor!" Richard roared and felt himself burn with rage. "Face me now or face my ghost for the rest of your days!" Again, there was no reply. Some of the men surrounding him shifted uneasily, clearly shaken by the king's immense personal presence even as he stood alone and surrounded. There was a long silence during which Richard stood, his frame heaving with excited anticipation. One of the dismounted riders stepped forward from the ring.

The two men stared at each other as the tension became tangible. The soldier took broad, confident steps toward Richard, increasing in speed as he neared his static target. As he closed in, the man raised his sword above his right shoulder and let out a roar. Richard did not move a muscle but stared coldly at the oncoming figure. Suddenly, as the attacker's sword descended, Richard stepped to his left to avoid the blade and heaved his right arm up, cleaving the man's arm halfway between shoulder and elbow. At the height of the sword swing, he twisted his hips and pulled his right arm back down to add momentum to the arc of the mace in his left hand, which crashed into the back of the soldiers head as he staggered. There was a sickening crack of shattering bone and the man was propelled several paces behind Richard collapsing in a crumpled heap. Silence descended again. It was the king who broke it.

"Come on then!" he called to all of those around him, resuming his defiant stance. A moment later, several men broke from the ring on all sides and charged Richard. There was a flurry of movement, ringing of steel on steel as the lone warrior deftly blocked blow after blow and dispatched six men swiftly with little visible effort. The king roared as the final body dropped to its knees before him and he whipped his mace heavily into the side of the man's head. Richard's chest heaved from the exertion and his arms began to burn as his muscles tired. Tracks of blood splattered the king's legs and arms and ran down his chain mail shirt. He sucked in a long, steadying breath.

"Take him!" The cry came from somewhere toward Tudor's position but there was no movement toward Richard in the uneasy quiet. "Take him now!" The call was louder and more desperate. A few began to cautiously advance and then the entire circle began to draw in and constrict about Richard, who remained still. The men edged forward, swords outstretched. When they were a few paces away, Richard sprang to his left, circling his sword and mace like a barrier before him. Three men fell with crushing thuds and screams. A blade fell towards him but Richard swept it aside with his mace and thrust his sword into the ribs of Sir William Brandon, Tudor's standard bearer. Tugging the blade out, Richard pushed it behind him into the stomach of a soldier about to swing at him. At the same time he brought his mace down on the thigh of a man to his left, flooring him. An instant later, Richard felt a hot pain across the middle of his back and knew instantly that he had been struck. He spun around, fighting the desire to stop and pushed his sword into the attacker's stomach, crashing his mace across his face. He winced as he tried to straighten, hot blood seeping through a slice in his mail shirt. He cut down another man but as he did his thigh was pierced with a stinging slice. Richard flailed wildly with his sword and mace and both hit home again before the back of the same thigh burned where it was cut open again. He collapsed to one knee, raising his sword to block a blow and swinging his mace across the attacker's kneecaps, but he could feel his strength draining from him as blood poured from his back and leg.

He struggled back to his feet, pushing a blow aside with the shaft of his mace. In the press around him, someone shoved Richard and he toppled to his knees. A dull blow struck the back of his head. He wavered as a sharp pain shot through his skull and a white light flashed before his eyes. He pushed his sword upward but it was parried and a leather glove thudded into his right cheek. His lip split and blood sprayed from his mouth. Closing his eyes, the white light flashed again. Richard tried to stand but a blade sliced the backs of his knees and he could not suppress a scream as the pain seared every nerve of his being again. There was cruel laughter around him now. He fell and something solid slammed across the back of his shoulders. His eyes closed and the whiteness returned, less bright now. A punch shook his jaw. The whiteness flared again and suddenly there was no one around him. As he opened his eyes the hoard returned. He swung his mace weakly but it was kicked from his hand. He looked up at a sneering face as its owner punched him on the temple. His eyes closed. He was alone in the field. His eyes opened and a blow stung the base of his spine, another crashed into his left arm. Eyes closed. He was alone again, but dark figures stood on the other edge of the field. Eyes open and his jaw jarred under another blow. Blood splattered from his nose. Eyes closed. Two figures were moving toward him. He fought to open his eyes and tried desperately to stand, but was pushed back down and kicked in the stomach. Doubled over, a muddy boot thudded into his jaw. Eyes closed. The two figures were close. He looked at them in shock. Eyes open. A blow across his side and a loud crack as his ribs broke. Eyes closed. He looked directly at them. Anne and his son stood just a few paces away. He reached for them. Another kick to the ribs shook him and his eyes opened to the mud soaked ground. The hoard around him fought for the chance to land a blow. He closed his eyes tight. Anne was whispering to Edward, who stepped forward. Richard stretched out his hand to them but his eyes were forced open again by more kicks to his sides and a blade pushing through his thigh. No. He wanted to close his eyes now. He forced them shut to see Edward only a few paces from him. He stretched his arm out, but opened his eyes as someone kicked his head and another blade pinned his right arm to the ground. He could barely feel the pain now and his eyes felt heavy. He glimpsed the crown that had rolled from his helm in the forest of legs and it disappeared again from view. A sensation spread across the back of his head that must have been pain. He closed his eyes slowly and the legs vanished. Looking up, he saw his young son's beautiful face smiling down at him, his hand outstretched. Richard reached up to it and grasped it gently. Instantly, a warm sensation of peace flowed through him and he was lifted to his feet as though he was as light as air. Looking into his son's eyes, emotion overwhelmed him. He looked to Anne. She smiled softly and beckoned the two of them to her. Holding his son's hand tightly, Richard surrendered to it and followed, smiling.

On the field, the crowd kicked, punched and stabbed at the limp corpse. A group of horses pushed through the crowd to the centre. The men stopped as the nobles reached the middle. Henry Tudor looked down on the defeated king and covered his mouth. The once proud form lay twisted, beaten, cut and swollen in a pool of blood and dirt. Lord Stanley was alongside him. He dismounted at Tudor's left and pushed some of the men aside. A glinting had caught his eye.

"Long live King Henry!" A call went up, and was echoed and grew. Stanley emerged, a bright gold circle resting on his palms. He stood before Henry and offered up the crown. Henry took it and slowly, deliberately raised it above his head, held it still a moment, and then lowered it to the delight of the crowd.

"What of the body?" Tudor asked Stanley in a hushed, uncertain tone. Lord Stanley thought a moment.

"Tie it to a horse." Stanley shouted, pointing at the limp body. "We shall drag the dog behind us to London for all to see." A roar of appreciation went up and men jostled to tie rope around the dead king's legs, pulling the remaining mail and the tattered, bloody cloth beneath from him until he was naked but for the drying gore and mud.

"We should leave for London immediately." Henry told Stanley. "There is much to be done. We should secure the Tower."

"Yes, sire." Stanley replied. "Though I am sure that your mother will have it all in hand."

"Yes." Henry pondered. "She usually has."

Chapter 39

Acta Est Fabula

Sir Thomas More stared, lost, as the embers of the fire began to fade. He hadn't spoken for several minutes, as though soaking up the tale that he had dispensed. Holbein sat, equally mesmerised, as he tried to absorb the finale of More's story. Transfixed by the unravelling of the events, he wondered how much of what Sir Thomas told him could be true, since it varied so dramatically from what was well known both in England and across the Continent. The artist's mind darted around.

"Sir Thomas," Hans ventured hesitantly, "how is it that you tell me a version of events that no one else seems to be aware of?"

"A version," Sir Thomas raised a finger in correction, "that no one else tells. There is a difference." He smiled like one dangling a tantalising secret before another who ached to know it. "The story that I have told you," he continued quietly, "is known to a few, a diminishing few, and its preservation is the reason that I have added you to that few." Sir Thomas seemed pleased with his own cryptic words.

"I do not see how you wish this to affect your family portrait, Sir Thomas."

"It is only the background to the secret that you must hide for all to see."

"I fear," Holbein frowned, "that I do not understand you."

"The reputation of King Richard is not the issue at stake." More paused a moment. "There is someone that I would like you to meet." Sir Thomas clapped his hands loudly, making Holbein jump in his seat. The painter followed his host's gaze to the door. There was a lengthy silence. Holbein glanced at Sir Thomas, then back to the door. An instant later, the door began to slowly open. Holbein felt a rising anticipation as a hand wrapped around the door and a tall, slender man stepped uncertainly into the room. Greying dark hair fell down to his shoulders and a round, good looking face showed strong features, weathered by time rather than hardship. "Please," Sir Thomas addressed the new arrival politely, gesturing to a chair, "please take a seat." The man strode across the room to the empty third chair and sat, eyeing Holbein a little nervously. For his part, Hans examined the man closely and looked to Sir Thomas sharply, enquiringly. Sir Thomas smiled.

"Hans Holbein, meet Dr John Clement." Sir Thomas watched the painter closely. He looked confused at another layer to this puzzle, but offered a respectful nod. "Now," the host continued, "Hans Holbein, meet John Plantagenet, son of Richard, Duke of York." Shock was instantly evident on Holbein's face as his eyes shot to More, then back to the other man. His jaw opened as he looked again at Sir Thomas, who nodded slowly. "The son of the second son of King Edward, who was presumed killed in the Tower of London."

Holbein did not know where to place himself, nor how he should behave before a man More was claiming to be royalty, a man who would technically have a stronger claim to the throne than its current incumbent. Could King Henry know of this? Surely his father could not have, since in removing his queen's illegitimacy, he would have necessarily gifted the throne to this man, or to his father, and more particularly to his uncle if he too had survived. Yet the concealing of such a thing would be no easy task. How had he come to be in the household of Sir Thomas More, who now sought to preserve a secret that would restore the reputation of a man vilified by the current regime? Questions flew around his mind so that he did not know where to begin.

"How..?" the word fell from his mouth. "What...?" No more words would come.

"Calm yourself, Master Holbein." Sir Thomas was clearly amused by his guest's dismay. "Perhaps now you will begin to understand the reasons for my insistence upon secrecy."

"I certainly do." Holbein said flatly. "But how is it that such a person is secreted within your household?"

"We have little time for another lengthy tale now." Sir Thomas dismissed the question with a gesture. "Perhaps another time."

"What of Edward's other son?" Holbein could not resist another enquiry. "If he were still alive, he...," he glanced quickly between the two men, "well, he..."

"Yes." Sir Thomas confirmed the silent notion. Holbein's mouth moved, but no words came forth. More gestured to Dr Clement, who shifted in his seat.

"My father," Clement paused and looked a little sorrowful at the word, "was taken to Colchester early in 1485 as campaigning season approached and entrusted to the care of Abbot Walter Stansted." He took a breath before continuing but was interrupted.

"Colchester Abbey," Sir Thomas put in helpfully, "was considered a safe haven by Yorkist dissidents well into the reign of King Henry VII and Abbot Stansted was well trusted, having been in office there already for some twenty years." He looked to Dr Clement and motioned him to continue.

"I believe," Clement continued solemnly, "that Francis Lovell, along with Humphrey and Thomas Stafford, arrived at Colchester a few days after the Battle of Bosworth and claimed sanctuary. They brought with them King Richard's final instructions."

"Instructions for your father and your uncle?" Holbein could not resist asking. More shot him a disapproving look.

"I do not know whether my uncle was there also." Clement replied. "He may have been, or perhaps they had already been separated." Clement looked away. "I also know that he was closely treated by his physician all of his life and would suspect some congenital condition that may have been enough to rob him of life in his youth." The doctor looked back at the painter. "This, I am afraid, I do not know."

"Indeed." More rumbled approvingly. "Please, continue your tale John."

"Of course." Clement acquiesced. "It is known that Lord Lovell and the Stafford brothers remained at Colchester for some six months. This goes beyond the forty days allowed for men in sanctuary to decide between exile and," he looked at his lap again, "royal justice. Yet the new King Henry made no effort to seize them, these last of his enemy's most loyal friends. Instead, he opened discussion with them to try and bring them into his new fold. Unusual, particularly considering that the only other remaining member of Richard's close household, Sir William Catesby, was executed only three days after the battle." More shot a chastising glance at Clement that Holbein noted. Clearly this detail was not part of what the man was intended to recount. "I merely say this," the doctor was talking to More now, "to point out that there must surely have been a reason for them to go there, to stay there and to be allowed to stay safely, even being courted by the new regime."

"But..." Holbein began in confusion.

"Enough." More said genially but with a forceful edge in his lawyer's voice. "Please, Dr Clement." The other nodded, chastised.

"In 1490," Clement continued, "at the age of seventeen, my father met my mother, a young Colchester girl. They fell in love and were married in secret, since my father was under the care of the Abbey and such a union would not have been allowed. I was the result of the brief time that they stole together." Dr Clement looked longingly into the dying fire. "They were discovered and there was a great deal of trouble. My mother, Eleanor Kitchen, for she had never been able to take my father's name openly, was taken into custody until I was born in secret. Afterward, in February 1491, she was issued a royal pardon for her 'crimes', although these were apparently unspecified, and forced to live as a widow in the care of her parents, committed to never marry again and to remain in the custody of her family for the rest of her life."

"This is so sad." Holbein sighed sincerely.

"I do not believe that they ever saw each other again." Clement's voice was heavy with sorrow. "I have never met either of them, for I was removed from Colchester as a baby and raised away from them until I, and my secret, were entrusted to Sir Thomas." The lawyer nodded at Holbein's glance. "King Henry and his father both knew of my existence and identity. The king's father even gave me my name. John, to remind me of the last and only king with that name lest I seek to press some claim."

"Why not Richard, if the last king was to be vilified so?" Holbein asked.

"He could not know at that stage if he would succeed in creating a monster from his predecessor. Plots and rebellions surrounded him still and Henry Percy, the Earl of Northumberland, had not so long before been lynched in York. Supposedly the crowd took him and his own guards did not protect him in protest at his failure to fight for King Richard, the beloved son of that city, at Bosworth." Clement appeared to smile a little at the tale. "No, he could not know how Richard would be remembered. It was also," he added, "my father's name. The connection would have been dangerous. But no one would want another King John, would they?" Clement looked at the painter.

"I suppose not," he conceded.

"Even my surname, Clement," the doctor continued with a dark smile, "was designed to remind me of the new king's kindness. I lived only because of his clemency." There was a pause and a new, fresher smile passed over the doctor's face. "Aside from this, though, I have been allowed to live my life in peace and comfort for as long as I remain true to my vow to never seek out my mother or my father or the throne. No doubt the trap works well, with my father remaining anonymous to protect his lost love and his son and my mother likewise. I imagine that we are all held at the points of the triangle by the same vows, and by the threats levied upon its other points should we stray."

There was a long and weighty silence in the stuffy room. Holbein thought over what he had discovered today and his excitement grew, yet he was filled with pity for this man and for his parents, the lovers kept distant by their son's very existence.

"Is that all?" The doctor asked Sir Thomas wearily.

"That is all, thank you John." Sir Thomas replied like a father to a son of whom he is very proud.

"Then I think I shall retire for the evening."

"Sleep well, Doctor Clement." Sir Thomas spoke softly. "Soon, you will be immortalised." Clement smiled uncomfortably, rose from his chair and left the room. Thomas More eyed the distracted painter with amusement.

"I have had the honour of seeing the letters with which Lord Lovell arrived at Colchester." Sir Thomas told Holbein unbidden. "King Richard asked not for forgiveness but for understanding of what he had done. He wrote that he was offering an opportunity denied to most of his family. He wished to provide a long and happy future in anonymity and begged that the power that destroyed the rest of his family and ripped the country that he loved apart at its seams was left alone." More looked a little distant, as though reminiscing. "I do not know what may have happened had he been victorious at Bosworth, but I suspect that he would have ensured that they were well cared for and perhaps even restored to some degree in time."

"You speak of both nephews, Sir Thomas." Holbein stated excitedly. Sir Thomas seemed to snap out of his daydream.

"That is for another time." More rose suddenly from his seat. He ran his hands over his stomach and stretched stiffly. "Now, Master Holbein," he said loudly, "I am sure that you have enough now to understand what I require. The son of

Richard, Duke of York, is to be hidden for all of time in plain view within my family portrait. A secret caged safely so that in some more enlightened time, should anyone care to look closely enough, they shall be able to decipher the identity of Doctor John Clement and even to speak of the consequences of his existence there. I have tried to construct such a cage myself but my writing feels clumsy. How does one cover up a truth without expressly denying it? I suspect that such a feat lies within your scope, though I have struggled with it."

"Very well." Holbein said quickly, excitement still burning in him.

"For now, King Richard will be branded a monster, and I fear that it must get worse before it will get better. And yet," More looked to the ceiling with Holbein following his gaze, "I dare to say that he looks down upon us and would say that if being that monster is what is needed, then he will do his duty."

A surge of emotion rushed through Holbein at Sir Thomas's words, a new respect for Richard filling him as he felt he now knew a man very different from the beast he had known. Taking his leave, Holbein's mind overflowed with ideas, symbols and hidden messages that he could use to convey what he had heard. He tried to commit some of them to memory as they spilled from him. Out in the street, it was dark and a chill bit at his neck. Pulling his cloak tight against it, he hurried along the deserted roads back to his studio. Did he know, he wondered, one of the greatest secrets this nation would ever hold? Would he ever hear the rest of this tale? He resolved then, in the dark, cold, dim London night that he would ensure that he did.

A few moments later, the door creaked slowly open again. Without looking up from the pyramid made by his own fingers resting on each other, Sir Thomas More spoke quietly to the visitor.

"Close the door." There was a clunk.

"Is there a message, my lord?" The sharp voice was young but hissed secretively.

"There is." Sir Thomas thought for a moment. "Tell the king." He paused again, smiling to himself in his chair. "Tell the king; acta est fabula." There was a pause. Sir Thomas guessed that the man considered questioning the message, not understanding the Latin, but thought better of it and left, pulling the door gently shut behind him. "Worry not," Sir Thomas said to himself, "the king will know my meaning. I have done my duty and a man who redeems his enemy to protect his father surely does his. This is far from over"

Author's Notes

Revised March 2013

The discovery in Leicester in October 2012 of bones identified in February 2013 as those of King Richard III have brought back into the spotlight a king who ruled England for only just over 2 years but is remembered within our national consciousness as a hunchbacked monster who killed, amongst many others, his young nephews to clear the path to the throne.

I first became interested in King Richard whilst studying the Wars of the Roses for A-Level History. All of the references to him before 1483 were so at odds with the king we remember him as that I was intrigued. There began a passion that resulted in this novel. The more of the evidence that is examined, the harder it becomes to believe that he was what Shakespeare and More wrote.

Within this novel I have tried to keep to the known facts as closely as possible. That is not to say that it is all completely correct. For example, as King Edward sealed the Treaty of Picquiney with France, Richard had already left for home in a move that clearly demonstrated his disapproval and which would, by the manners of the day, have been taken by the French king as an insult, as though Richard had thrown the money back in his face. I have presented this episode in more dramatic terms but in essence it is what happened.

Similarly, much of the conversation and thought process must be conjecture. I picture Richard as a man who suffered an uncertain childhood, no doubt leaving him with insecurities that he carried into his adult life. His mother's proud stand outside Ludlow Castle after his father had fled is real and although Cecily is remembered for her brave nobility, Richard was a boy just past his seventh birthday standing in the market place, on the losing side of a fight he probably did not understand and watching as the king's army ransacked Ludlow, raping and pillaging until they were spent. Following this, Cecily and her children were placed into the care of Humphrey Stafford, Duke of Buckingham. A pillar of honour, he cared for them meticulously. This may well be the reason that in his hour of need, Richard turned to this family, to Humphrey's grandson Henry Stafford for assistance. As he tried to build a secure future for his family, things always got in the way. He spent time in exile with his brother rather than join the rebellion against him and served King Edward faultlessly in the north of the country. The restriction of his title by King Edward is accurate and almost inexplicable, but went further still to deny him security.

The details of Richard's relationship with Anne is also largely unknown. Anne Neville, daughter of the Earl of Warwick, remembered by history as the Kingmaker, was an heiress to the vast wealth of her father and mother along with her sister, Isabel. When Isabel married George, Duke of Clarence, they effectively imprisoned Anne to prevent her marrying and them having to share the inheritance. She had already been married to Henry VI's son as part of Warwick's efforts to unseat King Edward IV and widowed after the Prince of Wales's death at the Battle of Tewkesbury on King Edward's triumphal re-adaption. Richard's motive for marrying her could have been financial and political, since she brought with her not only wealth but power and influence in the north where the ancient Neville family was deeply respected and powerful. They may have known each other when Richard, along with Francis, Lord Lovell spent time in Warwick's household for their knightly training. What glimpses we get of their relationship in the historical record seem to suggest that they cared deeply for each other. It is a pleasant thought amongst all of the warring of that period that a childhood love could blossom and that the two could emerge from their unsteady youth together and strong.

In 1483, for whatever reason, I believe that he was presented with evidence that made him the only lawful heir to the throne. In his book Eleanor the Secret Queen, John Ashdown-Hill makes a compelling case for the existence of a precontract between King Edward and Eleanor Butler, and evidence of the timing of Edward's birth against his father's departure on campaign and his humble christening were examined by Tony Robinson at Rouen Cathedral in his documentary about King Richard III. If all of this were true, as it now appears to be, Richard would have felt duty bound to deprive his nephew of the crown. That is not to say, of course, that he may not have relished the opportunity that it brought. The acts of King Richard III's only Parliament in 1484 include those described in the book, improving access to justice for the common man. He also introduced a system equivalent to legal aid to provide funding for those without means to access justice. He released much of the restrictions placed on books and the printing press also which improved the ability of this innovation to grow. He could hardly have known the exceptional use the Tudors would later make of easily printable materials. After these events, though, his personal life began to fall apart in the most awful ways which cannot have failed to leave their mark upon the man. He had only one legitimate child who passed away in 1484, followed by Anne in 1485.

William Shakespeare is responsible for much of the image of Richard that has endured, though he clearly drew upon accepted earlier depictions of him, including Sir Thomas More's account, perhaps the first famous vilification of him. John Rous wrote during Henry VII's reign, even earlier than More, that Richard was born after two years in his mother's womb with shoulder length hair, a full set of teeth and a crook back. He also accused Richard of poisoning Anne. Interestingly, Rous was a Neville chronicler who, during Richard's reign described him as a 'good lord', punishing the 'oppressors of the commons'. Unable to retrieve his glowing endorsement of the old king, Rous rewrote it for the new king's benefit, dedicating his Historia Regum Angliae to King Henry VII. He appears keen to distance himself from the old regime and this may explain the beginnings of the willingness to believe such evil of the man. Shakespeare's King Richard III then drew heavily upon these images of evil, but it is important to put the play into context. It was, first of all, a play. It was a depiction of evil for the benefit of an audience and had to be dramatic. There was little entertainment in a man who did his duty and was then killed. Shakespeare also wrote during the reign of the granddaughter of the victor at Bosworth Field, so if ever history was written by the winners, it is in King Richard III's case. He could hardly hold up the deposed last Plantagenet king as anything other than evil without offending Queen Elizabeth I. At the time that Shakespeare wrote this play, England was heading for turmoil. Religious division was an open wound and the aging queen was refusing to name an heir. Elizabeth had a deeply unpopular advisor, Sir Robert Cecil, son of Sir William Cecil, himself a close advisor for all of her reign. It is interesting that Sir Robert Cecil was, in fact, a hunchback and it is possible to surmise that the true meaning of the play was to warn the queen about what happened the last time that the succession was not secured smoothly, though he could hardly talk in such terms of King Edward VI and Queen Mary. King Richard III offered a perfect example of the problems that would resurface to plague the country. It is also entirely possible that a Tudor audience were meant to, and did, recognise the evil hunchback as the unpopular Sir Robert Cecil, dragging the nation into turmoil with his scheming. A Tudor audience may have thought little of the play as it applied to King Richard III but been highly amused with the fun it poked at Sir Robert.

It is no longer possible to avoid the question that everyone would like to know the answer to: Did King Richard III kill his nephews, the Princes in the Tower? It is impossible to know. He may have, in a darker moment, ordered their removal as his brother had done to Henry VI, as Edward III (or his mother) may have done to Edward II and as Henry IV had done to Richard II. Yet they were children and as brutal as the medieval period may have been, there is evidence that they were of a similar opinion to us when it comes to the notion of killing children. That does not mean that Richard did not order it, but it seems, like all else, so far out of his character as to appear unlikely. There are other suspects, including Lord and Lady Stanley who stood to place their step-son and son respectively upon the throne. The Duke of Buckingham may have believed that he did Richard a favour and when it emerged that he had upset the king, it could have led to him joining the rebellion in late 1483. Sir James Tyrell is often blamed for the murder. He was arrested at Calais in 1501 for aiding Edmund de la Pole, Duke of Suffolk, the nephew of King Richard and King Edward by their sister Elizabeth and leading Yorkist claimant challenging King Henry VII. Sir Thomas More alleged that Tyrell confessed under questioning to arranging the murder. He could not say where the bodies were because they had been moved, More said. There is no record of Tyrell actually confessing to any such thing. King Henry is believed to have sounded out one ambassador about blaming Tyrell for having done it at Richard's instruction, but it never went further than that.

King Edward V was known to be under his doctor John Argentine, though the reason is unclear. It is possible that he was serious ill and did not survive the traumatic events of 1483 due to the condition that ailed him, though the fate of his brother would not be explained by this. Had they survived until Henry VII's victory at Bosworth, he would have been faced with the dilemma of what to do with them. As discussed in the novel, he promised to marry their sister but had to re-legitimise all of King Edward IV's children to do so, making Edward V the rightful king again. Had he found them alive when he took power, he may have been faced with the thought that killing them was his only way forward.

It is also possible that the boys both survived into the Tudor period, their identity and therefore their threat, hidden. David Baldwin's book The Lost Prince: The Survival of Richard of York is a fascinating read examining this possibility for the younger boy and evidence alluding to his continued existence. For me, the most compelling evidence for Richard not being responsible for the murder of the Princes is the negative evidence. After his defeat at Bosworth, Elizabeth Woodville was mother to the new queen consort and safe from Richard, if he had killed her sons. Had she emerged from sanctuary and submitted her remaining children to his care through fear, she was now free of that fear. Yet at no point during the rest of her life did she accuse Richard or anyone else of killing her sons. There was no search made for bodies in the Tower and no funeral held. Even King Henry VII, who perhaps had plenty to gain from spreading the word, never blamed Richard for the disappearance of the Princes in public. Sir Thomas More couched his account in terms of 'people say' and 'it is rumoured'. He could not state categorically that it was the case. Only by Shakespeare's time does it appear to have been accepted that Richard had killed his nephews.

There is an urn within Westminster Cathedral which contains two skeletons discovered during building work in the Tower of London in 1674 at the foot of an old staircase. The bones were interred by order of King Charles II as those of the Princes. Medical examination was carried out on the bones in the 1920's which established that their ages were within a range consistent with those of the Princes but gender was not tested and at that time it could not be established how old the bones were nor whether they were related to each other. It is therefore possible that these were two children from anywhere in the previous 600 year history of the Tower if not before. The presence of the bones in that position would also contradict More's account of Tyrell claiming they had been buried at the foot of a staircase in the Tower and then moved to a secret location. Modern techniques could establish whether they were related to each other, to King Richard III or King Edward IV, whose final resting place is known, but the Queen would need to give her permission for such an examination.

The involvement of Hans Holbein in this story is based upon a theory researched by Jack Leslau, an amateur art historian who pointed to Holbein's use of symbols to hide messages and found many hidden symbols within Sir Thomas More's family portrait that pointed to a royal secret identity for John Clement.

Dr John Clement was a doctor and member of Sir Thomas More's household. He married More's adopted daughter, Margaret Giggs, and they had six children. Nothing is known of his early years. There are several entries for this (in continental terms) unusual name, all stating that he had not sworn the customary oath. One entry, in January 1551, reads;

'Dominus Joannes Clemens, medecine doctor, anglus, nobilis (non juravit ex rationabili quadam et occulta causa), sed tamen promisit se servaturm juramenta consueta.'

A possible translation of this is;

'The Lord John Clement, doctor of medicine, English, of noble birth (has not sworn the oath for a reasonable hidden cause), but has nevertheless promised to keep the customary oaths.'

Although described as noble, there was no noble Clement family in England. One explanation for never having to swear the oath is that John Clement was an assumed identity, and the University were aware of this fact. Although not illegal in itself this would mean that swearing the oath would be an act of perjury, placing both John Clement and the University at risk of prosecution. The bracketed explanation is unique amongst almost 50,000 entries from the period.

Dr John Clement was also President of the Royal College of Physicians in 1544. This position was in the grant of the king. Dr Clement was appointed President with no record of his family credentials or place of birth. In the history of the

College, dating from 1518, there are copies or records of the signature of every President to the present day except for one. Dr John Clement.

Dr Clement died in Flanders in 1572 having spent his later years there with his family in exile (perhaps voluntary) since he remained true to the Catholic faith, much as Sir Thomas More had. Dr Clement was specifically excluded from a general pardon issued by King Edward VI for those who resisted the move to Protestantism. He was buried beside the high altar of St. Rombaut's Cathedral, Mechelen, a position reserved at the time for highest ranking members of the House of Burgundy, the family of King Edward IV and King Richard III's sister, Margaret of Burgundy, whose court had been at Mechelen.

On 5th February 1491, a Royal Pardon was issued to Eleanor Kitchen of Colchester, though there is no record of her offense. The conditions attached to her pardon were remarkable. The pardon states;

"General pardon to Eleanor Kechyn, alias Kechen, alias Kechyne, late of Colchester, co. Essex, widow, alias 'huswyf', for offences before 18 December last, provided that she find security not to go at large during the rest of her life, but remain in the custody of her parents or nearest kinfolks."

Eleanor was to remain in the custody of family for the rest of her life, even after her parents' death. One can only wonder what offence may illicit such a royal pardon with such conditions attached to it.

In essence, we may never know the truth of matters lost to us, but they are all the more fascinating for it.

Printed in Poland
by Amazon Fulfillment
Poland Sp. z o.o., Wrocław